DIFFICULT MIRRORS

BENJAMIN X. WRETLIND

Difficult Mirrors

Copyright © 2013, 2021
by Benjamin X. Wretlind

Printed in the United States of America

This is a work of fiction. All the characters, locations and events portrayed in this novel are either fictitious or are used fictitiously.

No part of this book may be reproduced or transmitted in any form or by any means, electronic or mechanical, including photocopying, recording or by any information storage and retrieval system without permission in writing from the author.

ISBN-13: 979-8808486584

DIFFICULT MIRRORS

For Troy: this story started in his classroom many, many decades ago...

PART I: INTO THE VOID

All you have experienced falls in an
unsubstantial heap
if you do not trust this void.
Perhaps you will find there what you thought
lost:
the flowering of youth, the rightful sinking of
age.
Your life is what you gave:
this void is what you gave:
the blank page.
    – George Seferis, *Summer Solstice*

CHAPTER ONE

The headlights of the car illuminated a naked man standing in a puddle of water. He raised his arms up in the glare of the lights then collapsed. The blue Honda swerved as Marie Evans jerked the steering wheel to the right and stomped on the brake pedal. Gravel flew, and the car came to a rest with a soft jolt. The engine let out a sigh of relief, a sputter of agony, and finally fell silent.

Marie gripped the steering wheel of the car, too terrified to move. Shaking, she peered through the windshield. One of her hands left the wheel and mechanically pushed away a tangle of blond hair to wipe away the drool running from the corner of her open mouth.

As she stared, swirling thoughts in her mind coalesced into some form that made no sense whatsoever. Had she hit him? Was he dead? She could barely see the man in front of her, just a dark shape curled in a fetal position.

Breathe.

Okay.

Dark, gravel road, trees, and a naked man in a puddle of water.

Breathe. That's better. I see the trees.

Naked man.

Crazy people.

Did I hit him?

Pretty trees.

Marie pushed back another strand of hair and tucked it behind her ear. She bit her lip. Naked men lying in puddles in the middle of nowhere may not be friendly naked men.

Breathe.

This sounds like a movie: The Naked Man.
What to do? What to do? What to...

The Naked Man moved. He lifted his head up from the puddle and looked at Marie. His eyes squinted at the light blazing from the front of the car. He pushed himself up on his hands, appeared to give up trying to stand as his arms buckled, then rolled over onto his back. From where Marie sat, the man looked pale—almost as pale as the knuckles on her hands, which now crushed the steering wheel. She thought she saw a small trail of blood mixed with rainwater trickle down his face.

The Naked Man looked like he just woke from a long nap. He brought his hands up and rubbed his eyes. A tiny ring on his right little finger caught the headlights for a moment.

Marie relaxed her grip on the steering wheel and sighed. Her mind struggled to find a safe, sound solution to get her out of this situation, but between the trees and the Naked Man, she kept drawing blanks as to what should be done.

Breathe.

The Naked Man sat up and screamed, his face contorted in pain.

Marie jumped in her seat and let loose a squeal of her own. Quickly, she covered her mouth to prevent additional outbursts from startling the Naked Man. She drew a deep breath, afraid to let it out. Her heart pounded faster and faster.

Okay. The Naked Man lying in the puddle is screaming.
Breathe, Marie. Breathe.

Marie let her breath out slowly. She could try to restart the car, turn around, and drive like crazy to get away, but the Naked Man looked injured and might need help. She had taken her share of first-aid classes and was prepared to offer help to injured strangers, but none of them covered how to help Screaming Naked Men in puddles.

I don't know, she thought, but inside something told her to get out of the car, walk over to the Screaming Naked Man and discover the problem. Her mind battled back and forth, until she finally mustered enough courage to step out and face her fears.

Do what you fear. Silly mantra.

The Naked Man stopped screaming as the car door opened. Marie watched him wipe his face and look in her direction.

"Are you okay?" Marie found her voice weak, almost lost in the lump in her throat. She slowly walked closer, size 5 boots crunching the gravel underfoot.

The Naked Man closed his eyes. Aside from the strangeness of it all, he looked like she really had hit him. Blood mixed with muddy water and trickled from wounds unseen. A feeling of guilt rushed through Marie as she edged a little closer.

Another step forward and the Naked Man opened his eyes. Marie found herself within six feet. As she squatted down, he looked up at her.

"Are you okay?" Marie asked again, with the same waver in her voice. Uncertainty hung in the air for a few seconds, and the man stared back at her with bright blue eyes.

The Naked Man opened his mouth to speak, but stopped short. He hung his head, closed his eyes again, and finally mustered enough strength to get his words out. "I think so."

Marie's mind whirled through every scenario which would put her in immediate danger, both by being out of the car and by offering help. She studied him a little closer, looking for any sign of fractures or joints out of place. She saw nothing but the blood trickling down his pale skin.

"I know a little first-aid," she said. "Are you hurt?"

God that sounded stupid. Surely that was the right pick up line you practiced on lifeless manikins in the classroom.

The Naked Man wiped his forehead with a muddy forearm and looked back at Marie. She caught those eyes with her own and found herself locked, as if the man's bright blue could beckon her to a peaceful world away from the nightmare world of her own life. Those eyes spoke to her—paragraphs describing wonders she couldn't understand, words punctuated by vast emotion. In that brief moment as their eyes met, she began to relax and feel comforted by his presence... as if she had known him all her life.

"I need some water," the Naked Man whispered, drawing Marie out of her trance.

A smile crept across Marie's face. "How about a blanket, too? You can't be all that comfortable sitting naked in a puddle in southern Alaska."

The Naked Man nodded, then turned and looked the other way, toward the lights of a city not too far away. "Where did you say I was?"

Marie opened her mouth to answer but paused first. Maybe he was just delirious. Maybe this was a bad idea after all. "Alaska. Just north of Anchorage."

The Naked Man seemed to digest the information. Slowly, he pushed himself up on his knees, placed a foot forward, and tried to stand.

"Are you sure you're okay?" Marie asked. "You look a little beaten."

"Fine."

"I know it may not be my place, but... what happened?"

The Naked Man stood straight and brushed some mud and blood off his arms and chest. He was built, so much so that Marie reveled in that fact. She caught herself, and turned her eyes up, her cheeks warm.

The Naked Man looked at Marie, and cocked his head to the right. He repeated the gesture to the left, like a giant rising from a nap on a tiny couch. "I fell."

Marie's stomach sank as the tone of the man's voice changed. It was now clear and powerful, as if he hadn't been injured at all. She looked into his eyes to find the comfort she thought was there, but the longer she stared, the more the eyes turned dark, then empty. As her heart quickened, the eyes dug deep into Marie and ripped out any feeling of relaxation she might have briefly felt, replacing it with sheer terror.

She took a step back. The car was her only salvation. If she could get inside, she could lock the door and get out of there as quickly as possible.

"I forgot my place for a moment," the Naked Man said, his voice clear and distinct. "I'm sorry. I don't think I've introduced myself." He put his hand out in greeting. "My name is David."

Marie took another step back, mentally counting the distance to the safety of her car. One more step? Two? Ten?

"Correct me if I'm wrong here," David said, inching forward. "Your name is Marie, right?"

Seven steps. Marie turned and ran, thankful the door was still open. Her trembling hands fumbled with the key still in the ignition.

She slammed the door shut and turned the key. "Come on..."

With a sputter of agony, her little car came to life. The Naked Man—now David—took another step forward, directly in front of Marie's getaway.

"You don't know what you're missing," David called out over the rumble of the car.

Instinctively, Marie's foot left the clutch as she stomped on the accelerator. The front tires spun in the loose gravel then finally caught hold.

CHAPTER TWO

"She's seventeen years old, Harlan." Celine Reese reached across the end table and grabbed a pack of Camels. "She's old enough to make her own decisions."

"No she's not." Harlan pursed his lips. Six months after divorce papers had been finalized and there were still battles of will with regard to their two kids. At least Celine was nice enough to let Harlan in the house to argue about things. "What makes you think she's responsible enough to handle herself?"

"What makes you think she's not? She gets good grades, doesn't lie to us—" Celine caught Harlan's quick glance. "Okay, so she doesn't lie *that* often. I still don't see why you're treating her like she's in junior high."

Harlan watched Celine light a cigarette. Over the years, she'd degenerated from a slender and firm, vibrant woman into a slovenly creature, coughing her way through life. Harlan sneered at the smoke and waved his hand in front of his face. "Do you have to do that in here?"

Celine blew smoke in Harlan's direction. "In case you forgot, this is my house."

Harlan sat on a chair in the corner of the room, the same chair he'd slept in for nearly a year before finally moving out. "You give me no credit."

"Credit? Credit for *what*? You keep these kids locked away from the world and don't let them grow up on their own. You get them on the weekend and they do nothing but listen to you complain. What kind of credit do you want? Father of the Year?"

"Don't be sarcastic. I thought we decided to make decisions about the kids together, not alone." Harlan turned away and looked out the back window. The small patch of grass around her pool needed to be cut, but he guessed she hadn't felt like doing any yard work in weeks. Neither had he, for that matter.

"Go to Hell, Harlan. I'll call Myra's parents myself and see what their plans are."

The idea of watching the grass grow longer was oddly appealing to Harlan. Over the fence, he saw a neighbor trim hedges and chat with his wife. Their kids played in the yard, all of them oblivious to the interplay of egos that existed a few hundred feet away. This argument was tame compared to others, though. Nothing had improved over time, and despite the honest efforts he'd made to make the marriage work after he'd turned a blind eye to the family, the failure of just one single moment had been the catalyst his life needed to spin out of control.

Kind of like the grass.

"Don't bother," he finally said. "She's not going."

Tommy appeared at the bottom of the stairs and smacked a piece of gum. "Where is it?"

Celine pushed her cigarette out in an ashtray and sat on the edge of the couch. "What do you want?"

"My mitt."

"How the hell should I know where it is?"

With an obvious sigh, Harlan stood. "You usually throw it under your bed." He glared at Celine, trying ever so hard to wish she saw how much he despised her. "Get your hat, too, and meet me in the car."

Harlan grabbed the door handle as Tommy plodded up the steps two at a time. "Why do you use language like that in front of a seven-year-old?" he said.

"Why do you care?"

"Because I'm his father and I don't want him to grow up seeing so much hate from you. You already screwed with Jennifer's head so much, she doesn't know who to trust."

"You'd rather him see so much apathy out of you? You

abandoned them. I wasn't the one who fucked up."

Harlan tried his best to let that comment slide. Yes, that's exactly what he showed his kids—apathy—but he was at least willing to *try* to make life a little more pleasant, unlike Celine. It appeared to him, more and more, that she had not only fallen down a hole, she liked it there.

"I'll pick up Jennifer in the morning." Without another word, Harlan stepped outside to wait by his car. In a moment, Tommy followed.

"Are you done yelling at Mom?" the boy asked, the question laced with other questions unasked.

"I wasn't yelling at her, Tommy. Your sister's upset because I won't let her go to the Rim with her friends tomorrow, and your mother doesn't see things the same way. That's it. Now, get in the car."

"Okay." Tommy punched his mitt and smacked his gum. "But it sounded like yelling to me."

THE BLEACHERS were packed with parents—cheerleaders, coaches and the people the children would come to when things became too difficult to handle. While the adults always said they wanted their children to play because they saw the need for weaving teamwork and leadership into their lives, the truth was less noble: they wanted to live vicariously through their offspring. This was the American Pastime, though, and what better way to teach children to work as a team than to subject them to five or six innings chasing after a ball in the outfield or staring down the cocked pipe of a pitching machine.

"*What are you doing?*" A large man in a Cincinnati Reds cap yelled out to the field through cupped hands. "Use *both* hands!" He stood near the top of the bleachers, beer belly hanging out over a pair of shorts too tight for any man.

Off in right field, a young, portly child of about seven looked over at the voice. Harlan wondered if the kid was more embarrassed by his father than by the ball he'd dropped.

Harlan sat with his knees to his chest, smiling at his son on third base. Tommy walked around in a circle waiting for the next pitch and a chance to be a hero. The bases were loaded with two outs and the game was coming to a close. It had been a bloodbath from the beginning, with 21 runs scored between the two teams in the first inning. Now the score was 25 to 23, and Tommy—or anyone else, for that matter—had the chance to stop the inning by getting just one out.

Harlan clenched his fists as the pitching machine wound up and released a ball at fifty miles per hour to a kid at home plate. With a metallic twang, the ball flew toward third base, rising above the ground by inches. Tommy dove for the ball before it passed by on the way to left field.

Too late. In a cloud of dust and scrambling children, Tommy's failed efforts yielded two runs before the left fielder could get the ball into second base.

Harlan sighed and relaxed a bit. Next to him, a scraggly-looking man in a torn windbreaker yelled to someone in left field. "Good job, Michael!" He turned to Harlan and put a hand on the distraught father. "Sorry about that. He'll get it next time, Harlan."

"I know he will, Brian," Harlan wished aloud.

THE SUN slipped past the horizon. Dusk came during the second game, and the children looked haggard. The parents immersed themselves in conversations that remained strangely within ancient gender boundaries. Men talked about how great they had been in sports in their younger years and how positive they were that they had passed on the champion genes to their offspring. The women talked of hair and nails and baking, all of them equally positive they had passed on the common sense genes to their offspring.

Harlan looked down at his watch as the lights to the field came on with a thud.

"I really don't know what's going on, Brian," Harlan said as he looked out toward the field and perhaps beyond it to something he couldn't quite see. "Have you ever felt like nothing works? Something's missing?"

Brian let loose a chuckle that may have been sympathetic. "You just went through a divorce, Harlan. You think this is easy? Sounds to me like you need to stop thinking about how much you hate Celine and move on."

"Move on? I take the kids everywhere because she won't do anything but smoke and plot her sweet revenge." Harlan sighed. "It's so much easier when I have custody on the weekends."

"Is it? You don't get out and do anything."

"I'm a Sunday father, Brian. What do you want me to do?"

"It's Friday, moron. And I think you know what to do. When was the last time you came over and played poker with the boys? When was the last time you went to a game at the ballpark and stayed out with the rest of us afterward? You're not married, anymore. You're not chained down. Once you get that through your head, you'll feel a lot better."

The crack of a bat ricocheted through the evening air and the spectators erupted in cheers and jeers, every parent suddenly on their feet. A heavy hitter for Tommy's team had belted a ball to left field, past an outfielder who had probably been busy with the strings of his glove. The hitter rounded first base, potbelly bouncing in time to his footsteps. The members of the opposing team all ran to be the first to catch the ball if the outfielder ever made it to the fence in time. Out of the dugout, the coach could be heard yelling directions at his team and commanding them to stay in their positions. The batter rounded second, tripping on the base and falling face first in the dirt.

Harlan sat back down with Brian. Tommy was in the batter's box watching his teammate struggle to make third base before the ball came back.

The noise from the bleachers settled back down to murmurs of both pride and displeasure.

"Do you ever have dreams?" Harlan asked, his eyes locked on the field.

"Wet or dry?"

"Seriously. I've been having dreams for the past few months that have put me on edge. I don't know what it all means, but it's the same thing over and over."

The ball rolled into the infield and the catcher — standing

in for the third baseman—picked it up and held it, forcing the rotund batter to stand still.

"What are the dreams about? Are you falling? Do you fly? Is there a theme?"

"No, not a theme, but it's always the same. There's a man watching me. I just think something's not right."

Brian nodded, sat quiet for a moment then turned his face away from the field. Harlan thought he saw a smirk. "Heard from Marie lately?"

Harlan blinked and felt a strange fluttering in his chest. "She's in Alaska recovering," he said.

"Getting her feet back on solid ground?"

"Something like that. I really can't..." Harlan's words drifted off into thought as he looked down between his legs at a piece of gum stuck to aluminum bleacher. With a forced effort, Harlan turned his attention back to the game. "Life deals you crap, Brian."

"Make fertilizer, Harlan."

Tommy stepped up to the plate, and Harlan let his life snap forward to the present. *"Hit it to left! They've got a weak spot, Tommy!"* Tommy knocked the dirt off of his cleats with the bat. Inwardly, Harlan prided himself not so much on his son's baseball ability, but that the boy still kept his ego out in front like so many great players of the past. Teaching them to hit a ball is one thing; teaching them to act like they belong is something else entirely.

One runner on third, one run down, two outs.

Don't mess it up, kid.

The pitching machine whirred to life and sent the first ball directly at Tommy's knees. He jumped back and let it go by.

"Good eyes, Tommy!" Harlan yelled. The batter on third clapped his hands in agreement as sweat dripped from his underarms. The pitching machine whirred back to life.

In the artificial light and backlit by the fading reds of a desert sunset, the ball glowed as it flew toward the plate. Tommy brought the bat back as Harlan prayed his son would remember to keep his eye on the target.

With a sickening crack, the ball bounced off Tommy's rib

cage, sending the seven-year-old future All-Star to the dirt. Harlan jumped up and took a step down the bleachers to comfort his son. He suddenly stopped and turned to Brian.

"Why did you have to bring her name up?" he asked.

CHAPTER THREE

The sun dropped from the sky at a snail's pace, creeping past a few wispy cirrus clouds, past a small hill, a saguaro cactus arm and on and on. In time, the sky changed from a brilliant blue to a deep, blood red with spats of yellow and orange. The day's heat remained, as it typically did in the rainy season of the Southwestern United States. It wasn't quite official yet, but the seasonal shift of wind was only a few short weeks off and the humidity had already shown its ugly face. Off in the distance, a thunderstorm grew taller, its anvil transforming from bright white to orange to red as the sun finally disappeared without fanfare. Lightning flashed in chaotic patterns, stabbed at the desolate landscape and illuminated a torrential rainfall that flooded the land below.

Another thunderstorm moved closer, fed by the unequal heating and cooling of the mountains to the north and the valley to the south. Soon it would be overhead, and in the downpour, Stephen Casey would have a hard time examining the body of a young woman whose head had been crushed by a rock.

Yellow tape, strung between the giant cacti, lent surrealism to the otherwise mundane crime scene. A gentle wind blew the tape back and forth, making the cordon look fragile. On the inside of the taped perimeter, in an area roughly the size of a small house, officers dressed in khaki mixed with the blue uniforms of unneeded paramedics. The body lay in the center of the scene, as yet untouched, and bathed in the final light of the day.

She had been a young woman, about twenty, slender and medium in height. Her clothes were bargain brand, and her shoes looked a few sizes too big. She had no discerning features other than long fingers which ended in chewed-off nails. Her head had been crushed, not by a single blow, but by what appeared to be a methodic erasure of her identity. Matted blonde hair covered with blood and mixed with the dirt of the environment surrounded the remains of her skull like a sick halo.

As Casey knelt down, he covered his mouth with a handkerchief to mask the smell of the bloody corpse that had been sitting in the hot sun for a least a day. He examined the woman from the remains of her head to her feet, looking for a clue, looking for a reason or a method to the madness. His eyes wandered past the skullcap lying in several pieces mixed with brain matter, past what appeared to be eye sockets picked clean by birds, past a nose caved in about an inch. A small spider crawled from the remains of a nostril, zigzagged past a tooth, and left the scene via the remains of a crushed ear. Three earrings lay near the right ear, one of them torn off by the trauma. On the other ear, a single diamond stud remained intact.

Across her neck lay a gold-colored necklace, probably purchased from a street-corner vendor. Attached to it, caked in blood, was a small pendant that might have held some meaning, at least to the woman. The material was stone, like onyx, and possessed a white glow that shone even in the fading light of dusk. It was carved in the shape of two 'R's, linked together with a sword or staff through the middle. It seemed ugly, odd, and out of place. Casey scrunched up his nose in thought, grabbed his pen and made a quick sketch of the symbol.

A light flashed above his head. The crime scene photographer moved quickly, shooting pictures of the body, probable belongings and anything that didn't seem like it was a natural part of the landscape. Casey looked up, pointed to the pendant, and asked for a close-up. Quickly, the camera rose, the picture taken, and the photographer moved away.

Casey continued his cursory examination. Writing rapidly, he noted the meticulous manner in which the victim had been placed—legs together, feet pointing up, arms crossed over her chest. In her right hand, the victim held a tiny yellow flower, dotted with blood. This wasn't a haphazard murder, brought on by rage and carried out with carelessness. The body had been positioned, the flower planted and then—and only then—the head crushed beyond recognition.

"Peaceful looking, ain't she?" The voice came from behind Casey, raspy and full of phlegm.

"From the neck down." Casey stood. He turned to the voice, grabbed a cigarette from his breast pocket and lit it. "Weird, though. What do you think?"

A small man—thin in the neck and face, with wire-rimmed glasses dangling on a pointed nose—cleared his throat, snorted once then spit out a wad of green phlegm as far from the body as he could. "Looks like the perp wanted a piece of ass, got pissed off when he didn't get it, knocked her in the head once, got scared, then crushed her skull so no one would recognize her." He looked down at the body.

"Lover? Pimp? Plumber?" Casey took a long drag of his cigarette. "Take a look at the clothes, Byron. Not from around here."

"No, not from around *there*." Byron pointed over a ridge to the brightening glow of million-dollar homes and upscale golf courses in the distance. "She's from the city. Just look at the shirt."

Casey looked down at the woman's shirt, just below the crossed arms. A cheesy slogan from a local gift shop, black words mixed with stains of blood: "I survived 123 degrees... but it was a dry heat!"

Casey chuckled to himself. *I have that shirt, too.*

The photographer stepped up to Casey. "I'm all done here," he said without looking at anything or anyone in particular. He turned and walked away.

Thunder vibrated the desert floor, muffled only by the humid air and the distance. To the west, the thunderstorm had grown in size and threatened to drown the crime scene. The sun had set far enough that the reds and oranges had faded to deep indigos and grays. Around the perimeter of the cordon, halogen lights illuminated the scene, and a crew of younger officers was busy unfolding a makeshift tarp over the victim's remains.

Casey looked off in the distance toward the expensive homes and sheltered life of planned subdivisions. Just under the lights and on top of a small hill, he thought he saw a man observing the scene. Casey squinted and wished for a moment he hadn't left his glasses in his car. He never wanted to believe his eyesight was failing him, but there were times he chastised himself for not listening to what others had to say.

Byron tapped Casey on the shoulder. "See something of interest?"

Casey thought for a moment of all the times he'd been at a scene and felt the stares of onlookers. He'd been told once to look at all the faces in the crowd; murder is an act, but evasion is a sport. So often, the demons would be there mingling with the anonymous, hoping to gain some insight into what others might find.

In this case, though, the murder was remote. Why would there be onlookers?

"Nothing, Byron. Just thought I saw something."

"Kind of hard to do that without your glasses, isn't it?"

Casey frowned and turned back to the scene. He walked slowly around the body, looking for something different in the artificial light, a tiny detail that might give him an advantage in this game of evasion. Watching where he stepped and avoiding the yellow evidence flags, he moved toward the woman's feet. Once more, he looked at the placement of the legs, the arms, the flower, and the shirt.

He scrunched his nose. Something was wrong. From his vantage point at the woman's feet, he saw just under the area where her arms crossed. Sure there was plenty of blood, but it almost looked...

"Byron," Casey called while still staring at the chest. "Come here and look at this."

Byron walked over. "What is it? More brains?"

"No. Take a look at the chest below the arms, and then the neck. Notice anything?"

Byron looked down at the victim and adjusted his glasses. He made a small noise of interest. "Move the arms out of the way."

Casey walked around the other side of the woman, knelt down, and pulled a pair of latex gloves out of his pocket, snapping them over his fingers. Reaching over the body, he lifted the arms.

His eyebrows stood as his stomach sank. "Where's her heart?"

With a flash of lightning and a clap of thunder, the rain fell. Instinctively, Casey turned back to see if there really had been someone on the hill.

CHAPTER FOUR

There is nothing worse than waiting for the inevitable, whether that be a shot in the arm, a broken leg while falling down a hill, or the death of a loved one. Marie knew this, and as she sat at her dining room table, she cried for the tenth time this month. It was only a dream, but like many dreams, there was more truth than fiction.

Susan stood next to her. Her four-year-old eyes burrowed holes in Marie's heart. "Mommy? Don't you want pizza, too?"

Marie stood from the table and turned away. There are moments in life you can mark as the point between then and now, between what was and what will be. For some, those moments are illuminated revelations, lights shining in the sky that say "Your life has just changed." For others, those moments are quiet, marked by a simple turn of the dial, taking a road unknown or the words that fall innocently from the lips of a four-year-old child.

"I can't," Marie whispered. She wanted to take the words back. If she had said yes, put away her life for a moment and let the souls of those around her come inside, then maybe — just maybe — she would still have a family.

Peter appeared in front of Marie. She looked at her husband through tears while trying to form the right words to say she was sorry.

"I'll take Susan out for pizza so you can study," he said.

Marie nodded, folded her arms around her chest and accepted the end. It was the same end no matter how many times she dreamed it. There was no way she could say yes to

Susan. No way she could take it all back. They were both dead, and she was to blame for it.

She closed her eyes and let the cold envelop her. It was like so many other dreams: when she opened her eyes again, they would be gone, the house would be empty and the moment that marked her life would be shining in front of her like a neon sign, burning its image deeper into her eyes.

"Are you sure they would still be here?"

Marie opened her eyes to the new voice. It wasn't Peter or Susan or anyone else she thought she might recognize. The room was dark and no longer cold.

"Who's there?" she asked.

"Are you sure they would still be alive if you went with them?"

Marie turned and looked for the source of the voice. It was close, but not close enough. Why was everything so dark?

"There are reasons," the voice said. "We all have choices to make, but sometimes those choices are made *for* us."

"Who are you?"

"A friend."

"Jacob? I can't see you. Harlan?"

Wind whipped Marie from the right and pushed her down. She collapsed on what felt like sand. She covered her head with her arms as something small and sharp bit into her skin. Voices—thousands of them, it seemed—screamed at her with high and low pitches and angry and sad words. She tried to listen to them, to sort out the meaning of this dream.

The screams suddenly died along with the wind. Marie slowly opened her eyes and tried to sit up. Sand shifted under her weight as she realized she was sitting on top of a sand dune.

In the distance, fainter than the beat of her heart, she heard a small voice.

"Mommy?"

THE PARK was busy enough for a Saturday. Marie sat on a bench and stared at a statue in the middle of the park. Rust covered it, drawing patterns for her to sort out. She saw so much in them, but knew everything that appeared before her was nothing more than a reflection of her misguided and miserable life.

Why did they have to die?

A woman walked by, dressed in a blue jogging suit and dragging a small dog that looked like it wanted nothing more than a good chomp at her leg. Marie briefly let her eyes drift to the woman before turning away. There was something in her walk, she thought, something that said "Let me live my last days to their fullest."

She frowned at her thoughts. What was she doing? People watching again? Did she really think she was a good judge of those around her?

"Seat taken?"

Marie looked up at an older man, his white beard stained with ketchup or blood or some sort of sauce. He wore baggy clothes and a coat with arms that reached past his gloved hands.

"No," she said, and turned her attention back to the statue of rust. If she left immediately, it might be rude. *But who cares? He's a bum.*

"Bit chilly today, don't you think?" The man coughed and sat forward, his elbows on his knees. "Seems like fall is just around the corner. Ain't seen summer yet."

"Seems like it." Marie hated small talk, but she also hated uncomfortable silences even more.

"How do you feel?"

"Excuse me?" She looked at the old man. A sense of emotion overwhelmed her, but she couldn't tell between the sudden eruption of butterflies in her stomach and the tingling in her fingers, if she was nervous or cautiously excited by the prospect of some stranger asking her how she felt. *What does it matter?*

"Just wondering how you feel. You don't look like you've had much sleep."

Marie shook her head. *Nice compliment*, she thought.

"I mean," the man continued, "take a look at all these people here. You can probably guess how they're feeling the moment you look into their eyes. That woman that just walked by—she's tired of life. She's waiting to die."

"That's a nice thought."

"You saw it, though. Didn't you?"

Marie nodded, more out of politeness than agreement. Then again, she had made that assumption.

"See? It's all in the eyes. All masks have holes for eyes, no matter how much effort is put into a costume."

Marie looked down at the ground and wished the man would go away. Why couldn't she just enjoy the day by herself? Better yet, why couldn't she just wallow in her own self-pity by herself?

"What am I feeling?" Marie whispered.

The man sniffled once and coughed twice. "You're afraid and alone."

Afraid and alone, Marie thought. *Good guess.*

"Just be careful of naked men in puddles."

Marie sat up straight and stared at the man next to her. Her heart raced and the butterflies she felt erupting before suddenly stopped. Her stomach, instead, sank. A gust of wind tossed her hair in front of her face and the old man disappeared like paint splashed with turpentine.

She sat frozen, watching the space the man had once occupied half expecting something else to take his place, and half realizing her semi-sane world had come crashing down around her the moment she'd met a naked man in a puddle of water.

With effort, Marie stood and walked away from the bench. At first, she took it slow, one step at a time with her eyes still focused on where the man had been. Soon, though, her legs pushed her faster until she nearly ran out of the park and jumped into her car.

Was that David?

She started the car, shoved the gear in reverse and backed out of the parking space. In front of her, a few hundred feet away, the same old man stood next to a lamppost. She couldn't be sure, but she thought she saw his face contort into some twisted smile.

CHAPTER FIVE

"She's gone!"

Celine stood in the doorway as Harlan walked from his car. Behind him, Tommy stopped, stunned at his mother's sudden outburst.

"I went in to check on her and found the window cracked." In her hand she clutched the remains of a tissue. "You pushed her too hard, Harlan. She ran away."

For a moment, Harlan didn't know what to say. He'd expected some sort of action from Jennifer—whether in spite or in haste—but he didn't know what or when. "Ran away? Where do you think she went?" he finally asked, then inwardly cursed himself for the pathetic question.

He knew where he'd go.

A WHITE, rust-covered 1973 Chevy Impala sped through the night, the one working headlight illuminating enough of the deserted highway to see where the car was headed. In the driver's seat, a young man of sixteen with a fresh driver's license took a drag of a cigarette and tossed the butt out the window. His long black hair was pulled tight behind him in a ponytail, and a tattered Phoenix Suns cap sat crookedly on his head. He looked in the side mirror, then over at his passenger, hoping she had enough of her skirt pulled up to catch a glimpse of something he was dying to have. He smiled to himself as he reached over to grab a compact disc from the floor of the car on the passenger's side.

His passenger hit him on the shoulder. "Keep your eyes

on the road. What disc do you want?" Frustration was apparent in her voice, but at the same time, there was a playful tone of freedom won.

"The black one. Without a cover." The driver put both hands on the wheel and adjusted his position. He had hoped that if he placed the discs in the right spot, his attempt to lean over and grab one would turn her on. Then the skirt might go up a little higher.

Jonathan Richards was a loner. At fourteen, he saw the last of his friends leave to another school when the district changed its internal boundaries. From that day forward, he stayed in the back of class, talked to only a few people and kept to himself. It wasn't exactly what he wanted, but in the politics of high school, he had to do what he thought was expected of him: keep at a safe distance, no mingling, no socializing with the superstars. And the boundaries had been drawn wrong. Desert View was designed to attract the most elite from the northeast side of Phoenix. In the shuffle, however, one small block in a rundown area of town had been placed inside the bounds making him an outcast. The tight group of friends he'd grown up with through elementary school and Junior High had gone on to a school of more diverse culture, where rich and poor were an equal mix.

His freshman year he found a niche: be the bully. If the rich kids pick on you, kick them hard and walk away. It worked for others in his shoes, so he didn't see any reason to be different. By his sophomore year, he became something of a nuisance; kids parted in the locker bay when he came around for fear his notorious temper might flare up if he heard them talking about anything he didn't have. He liked this angry leper role. He never had to hear anyone talking about his generic clothes or his torn sneakers anymore. He created a zone of comfort that was well worth keeping.

Then she came. The blonde. She sat across from him in Women's Literature—a perfect example of the average woman, and since her father taught at the same high school, she wasn't all that rich. Of course, Jonathan wouldn't stand for any relationship with the people he despised so much, so he spent a good part of the last few months getting to know her better. What was she like inside? Did she care about clothes? Shoes? Would she ever wear a Metallica shirt with ripped up, faded jeans, no makeup, apparently unshowered from waking up late — and still look good?

The latter occurred on a Tuesday.

By Wednesday they'd planned their first date.

TO JENNIFER, school was a bore. The rich kids didn't necessarily care much for her, especially when they learned that her father was — or someday might be — their teacher. She wasn't an ugly girl, and if she really applied herself to the science of makeup and fashion, she would be a prize for any testosterone-laden teenage boy to show off to his friends. That wasn't her style, however, and it certainly wasn't something she thought about night and day.

The world was contained within herself, and pleasure could be found by reading a book, writing poetry, or simply staring at the ceiling while holding her favorite stuffed animal. Tolliloqui, the bear with one eye, had been her friend for life. The bear didn't have a name until she was three when she decided that a bear with no name just wasn't right. Her speech skills slightly behind other three-year-olds, "Tolliloqui" was all she could come up with. It stuck. Now seventeen and free from the burdens of school, parents and annoying little brothers who ask too many questions, Jennifer held tightly to Tolliloqui as she sat in the passenger seat next to her boyfriend.

Jonathan was a fluke. At first, she fell in with his plan, thinking for over a year that he was the bully, the unkempt kid from the wrong side who needed to show off his manhood by getting into fights and causing trouble. She was surprised when he showed up the first day in Women's Literature class, and her mouth nearly dropped when he probed the teacher about one of their required novels of modern feminism. He was definitely different, and his angry leper act was nothing more than a cover. She'd stare at him every now and again. When he began to stare back, her mind wandered. Finally, she confided the secret crush to a friend.

"You've got to be kidding," her friend said over lunch. "He's a bully. He's a loner. He's younger than you." She looked like she was struggling to find more reasons to give Jennifer. "And have you stood close enough to him to catch that *smell*?"

Jennifer rolled her eyes. "Have you?"

"No, but I bet he stinks like... like..."

"He smells like Head & Shoulders, Myra. Now you're making stuff up."

"Fine." Myra picked a hair out from her meal. "He's a wonderful, good-looking, intelligent, motivated individual. But he's poor. How's he ever going to take you out and buy you diamonds, make you feel like a woman?"

Jennifer looked back across the table. "He's got a car."

Myra pushed her tray away from her. "In that case, go for it."

That conversation occurred on a Tuesday.

By Wednesday they'd planned their first date.

Four months later, she was being whisked away to a magical land by the man of her dreams, riding high on love in the passenger seat of a white, slightly rusted 1973 chariot. She kept all thoughts of the family she left behind buried deep inside her. This was her way to prove to them that she could do whatever she pleased, and no amount of lecturing was going to change that.

She'd wanted to tell her father to go to Hell, but this would be enough to get the point across.

THE NIGHT air grew cooler as the Impala navigated the twists and turns of US Highway 87. The desert gave way to chaparral, the chaparral gave way to Ponderosa trees, and just north of Payson in central Arizona, the road began the ascent to the Mogollon Rim. The clouds that rose and fell during the day were all but gone, and the few remaining wisps of vapor screamed through the sky like ghosts, caught in the wind high above. Jennifer looked out the window, clinging tightly to Tolliloqui as the trees passed by and formed words of poetry in her mind. She loved the mountains, and every opportunity she had to see raw nature she would grab a pen and paper and start to write. Paper was something the two lovers had left behind, however, so she wrote on the wrinkles of her memory.

"You've been quiet." Jonathan's words broke the silence. He grabbed a pack of Camels and lit up another cigarette. This was his one trait Jennifer had yet to appreciate or ignore. His habit had turned from one cigarette at lunch, when he could sneak it by hiding in the bathroom, to half a pack in the last two hours. "What are you thinking?"

"I'm thinking that if you smoke that whole pack, you're going to have a nicotine fit by morning and be a cranky jerk." Jennifer held little back, one of the qualities Jonathan honed in on from the start, even if it was directed at him.

"Just enjoying the same freedom you have."

"Where are we going again?" Jennifer knew the answer. She just wanted to hear it. She was overexcited from the first time she'd been asked.

"Under the Tonto Rim. That burnt out section of forest you always camp at has me interested. But I've told you this three times today. What are you really thinking?"

Jennifer sighed. "I don't think my parents bought the Myra story. I'm just nervous, that's all. If she snitches, then I'm a dead girl and I won't be seeing much of anything outside of school. Hell, I bet my mom will send me to live with my dad and I'll be homeschooled the rest of the year."

"Don't worry. Myra is off on a camping trip of her own, just like you said, and no one will know the difference. This is our time." Jonathan looked over. In the glow of the instrument panel, a dim twinkle could be seen in his eyes. He really was handsome and a bit of a gentleman, even if his eyes were drawn to her chest where they rested a moment too long. "We're finally free to do whatever we want."

Jennifer laughed. "*Whoever* you want, right? Somehow I get the feeling you don't want to spend the weekend looking at broken and charred tree branches." She let out another sigh and looked back out the window, a smile pasted to her face. *Neither do I*, she thought.

As the road climbed the side of the monstrously long cliff

that was the Rim, a curve brought the glow of the city they'd just left into dim view. Far off to the south, she knew her mother must have called Myra's parents by now.

The road curved again, and the glow was gone.

"Give me a smoke. I might as well join you."

CHAPTER SIX

Casey stood about five feet from the table and looked at the body of the woman found murdered in the desert. The head was missing for the most part, and a hole in her chest between the breasts was an obvious indication the heart was missing. *Other than that,* Casey thought, *she's got great legs.*

A small woman with a white gown and green gloves stood next to the table. She started a small saw and began cutting through ribs around the hole in the chest. The sound of the blade hit a high pitch as the teeth dug into the woman's breastbone. Casey wondered if this mutilation of the body was really necessary. It was obvious what she died of: crushing a skull into little pieces will kill most anything.

Still, the question of whether she died from the blow to the head first or whether the killer punched through the chest and ripped out her heart before smashing the identity of the victim was one that needed to be answered. There was also the question of drugs—licit or not. He supposed the blow was first, but what would possess someone to continue mutilation past the shoulders if his or her prey lay lifeless on the desert floor? It could have been ritualistic, he supposed. Don't most Hollywood rituals involve hearts removed to pay some sick homage to gods or devils that probably cared less? Then again, the wound was coarse, ragged shards of skin hanging loose inside the cavity. *I could've done better with a butter knife*, Casey thought.

The woman with the saw stood back and shut the tool off. She looked closely inside the wound, picked a flap of skin up here and moved an organ there. Casey watched the medical examiner like he'd done on any number of occasions.

Amanda Harkins, the medical examiner, was short, her auburn hair pulled tight behind her and her face absent of any sort of makeup. Casey found her attractive, with a thin body, and a gentle smile that said: "I'm all yours." She stood upright and took off her gloves, setting them on a table beside her.

"I can't find any obvious evidence inside the cavity as to what ripped through her skin and took out her heart." Amanda regarded the inside of the dead woman again. "Usually in cases like this, there is some indication of a knife or other sharp tool in the skin around the wound. But in this case, nothing."

"So you've seen this before?" Casey undressed Amanda with his eyes.

"Yes. Once in a while a body comes in here with a severe case of a broken heart. The majority are ritualized, but some are just downright messy. There was a man in here a few years ago whose heart and lungs were removed using an X-Acto knife. The killer left it in the spine as a souvenir for us to have."

"I vaguely recall that one." Casey scrunched his nose against the overpowering smell of Vicks VapoRub.

"What about the time frame here?" he asked. "Was she beaten to death first, then... then..." He waved his hand in the general direction of the open chest.

"De-hearted?"

"If that's a word, yes."

Amanda looked over the body once more. "Without taking a harder look and doing a bit of lab work, I'd only be guessing like you. For all we know, she could have been poisoned first then dragged out to the desert. Only toxicology will tell me I'm a liar about the drugs."

Casey walked up to the side of the table and looked inside the chest cavity. He had always been fascinated with the innards of humans, although this was the least desirable part of his present occupation. The lungs were separated in the middle, and Casey could make out what looked like an aorta.

Even after seeing inside several human bodies, he still wasn't sure what anything really was. There was always something in the way.

"How do surgeons see well enough to find what they're looking for?" Casey thought aloud.

The woman looked into the cavity herself. "Ninety-five percent use suction."

"And the other five percent?"

"Miss." She smiled at Casey once again, her small nose wrinkling up under the weight of hazel eyes.

She wants me. He looked back down at the cavity. Amanda looked back also, tilted her head to the side, squinted then grabbed a pair of tweezers. The smell of VapoRub, formaldehyde, rotting flesh and perfume mixed together at once, making Casey's eyes water. He watched Amanda remove a thin object no more than half an inch long from the left lung of the dead woman.

"What the hell is that?" Casey squinted. He really needed to keep those glasses handy.

Amanda turned and grabbed a small bag from the table, then dropped the bloodstained object inside. "That's something you don't see every day."

Casey felt the weight of an unsolved mystery simultaneously lift from his shoulders then slam back down twice as heavy. Here had been a woman, with no identifying marks and no teeth, rotting in the desert night while her killer ran free. Now at least, he supposed he had a way of learning a little more. "How would a fingernail get inside?"

Amanda looked at Casey and shrugged. "The mystery compounds itself." She paused then smiled coyly. "Hey, what are you doing tonight?"

Taking you out for dinner and whatever your mind comes up with, he thought. Casey bit his lip. "Sleeping. I have to work early in the morning."

"On a Sunday?"

"Work never ends."

—

THE DRIVE back to his apartment was lonelier than he wanted. Aside from not having taken Amanda's offer, Casey felt memories sneak out from the closet where he had hidden them for so long. The humid night air and desert heat blew in through the open window of his car as he drove up to a red light. On a corner of the intersection stood a small taco restaurant where his wife left him standing a few months ago. He had no reason to argue about it, though. His career was his life, and the late nights at the office or in the field along with the stress of chasing people who would kill you in an instant if given the chance, wore at his family more than him. They couldn't understand why weeks might go by without Casey taking the night off or why he wouldn't go to the park with them or even eat dinner at the table like any normal American family. To them, Casey was a father and husband who didn't care. To Casey, he was a father and a husband who placed everyone else's safety paramount. He knew his calling was to catch the bad guy and ensure that Justice was served.

His wife never bought that line of clichéd bullshit.

"That's your decision," she said. "I hope that taco tastes good." And she left, taking his son with her.

He did finish his taco, he recalled, and it was good that night, but as he sat at the light and stared at the memorial to the end of his marriage, he wondered if he could have done something to stop the inevitable divorce. Life had handed Casey an emptiness that he couldn't fill, and it wasn't for the first time either. Two romances had gone sour, and with each parting, a piece of his life disappeared.

He began to work even more, stayed out later and later and then took his work back to his apartment so he could have the time he needed in the field. He'd replaced his family with more duty, but now he felt the loneliness heavy on his chest.

Failure in his personal life was all too common to Casey.

As the light turned green, Stephen Casey headed home, a stack of files on the seat next to him and the painful memory of failing twice digging into the pit of his stomach.

—

CASEY SAT back in an oversized black chair, holding onto a bottle of dark beer with sweat running down the side. The television set was still on from the morning when he returned to his apartment, along with the lights in the bathroom, kitchen and living room—about the only places he cared to venture. His lifestyle had degenerated into a routine of two cigarettes and half a pot of coffee for breakfast, in to work by 7 a.m., coffee and a candy bar for lunch, home by 7 or 8 p.m. and a six pack of beer for dinner. Somewhere along the way he managed to scrounge up enough money to buy what passed for a meal at the local greasy burger palace, and then down a few heartburn pills. By the time the local news came on at 10, Casey finally felt relaxed enough to grab a pillow and blanket from the floor and curl up in his chair. It was a lifestyle he didn't like, but at the same time, it kept his energy focused on what was most important in his life: work.

Not that his ex-wife and son were insignificant. Casey missed them horribly, but since they never could come to grips with his self-proclaimed destiny in life, they were better off where they were. He managed to give his wife about three quarters of his paycheck each month, and every other weekend he would take a day to walk with his son through a park, a zoo, a mall, or just sit out on the back patio of his apartment and share stories of the days when he started out as a young cop in the downtown streets of Los Angeles. He valued this time with his son, and there were times he wished he didn't have a work ethic that overshadowed his family life. But the world needed people like Casey. It needed to know that somewhere, underneath a pile of papers and behind the guy on TV, there were people dedicated to the protection of the taxpayer's rights. Of course, this line of bullshit didn't sit well with his ex-wife, either.

Casey finished the beer in his hand and grabbed another from the kitchen. He turned back to the living room and changed the channel from some inane show about families in crisis to the news. The lead story of the day was the same one from last week—the one about a convenience store shooting. Only the names and places were changed to make it sound horribly new. Casey watched as a younger, small man, thin in the neck and face, with wire-rimmed glasses dangling on a pointed nose played to the camera. Byron Jamison fed the reporter some rhetoric about "leads" and "justice served" while simultaneously flashing a big, toothy smile.

Casey sighed. He took another drink and thought about how many times he'd seen Byron on TV. *More than a dozen*, he thought. *More than me.* He sighed again at the thought of not having the fame and luck of this younger detective then realized that if he did, he'd lose time at his desk or in the field. That just wouldn't be right.

The newscaster came back on and looked down at his notes. "In other news around the Valley, a body was found yesterday beaten to death north of Phoenix. Police claim they have little to go on or even know the identity of the victim as questions mount. Detective Stephen Casey, of the Maricopa County Sheriff's Department, told reporters there are few leads and the victim is not from north Phoenix. When asked about the leads, Casey had no comment."

"That's right," Casey told the television. The 25-inch set propped up on two milk crates in the corner flickered back at him.

Casey grabbed the files he had brought home and flipped through them. For the most part, signatures needed to be added to forms, notes jotted down about the day's events, and other miscellaneous tasks. He opened the first file and began to rifle through the papers. The television relegated to the background, Casey tuned out the news of scandal at a local lawyer's office, financial problems for some semiconductor company, and what happened on Wall Street. He was focused on work again, content with the knowledge that he was making a difference. Before long, he set all of the files down on a coffee table and fell asleep, the television still talking to him, the lights in the kitchen and bathroom still on, and a six-pack of beer sucked dry.

IT WAS cloudy and the sun had trouble making any shadows on the landscape stretched out in front of Casey. There were no trees, no bushes, no signs of life. His environment was parched dry, cracked like the safety glass in a car. Chaotic lines stretched out for miles with no recognizable pattern. Off in the distance, a mountain range stood, their jagged edges stabbing toward the sky. It was a scene he had been subjected to before, but he never understood what any of it meant.

If he remembered correctly, he would walk forward for a few miles and turn around. The wind would pick up. The dust would become an entity—breathing, growling, biting. Eventually it would envelope Casey and he would wake up or move on to another dream, oblivious to whatever meaning his brain tried to impart. To Casey, dreams were an avenue of release for the subconscious mind, finally venting frustrations and feelings that were held back during the waking hours by the conscious mind. Unlike most people, however, he remained aware and always tried to sort out some sort of meaning. He was never close to what his mind told him, though, and rather than write it all down, he would try to forget over time.

Casey looked at his surroundings one more time and decided to follow the same path toward the mountains he always took. The ground crunched under his feet. Little sections of dried mud cracked under his weight. Above him, the clouds rolled by, undulating in dark blues and grays. They set a mood he never liked. Not that it mattered much. He would eventually be out of this dream and either walk into another one or just wake up.

Casey took another step forward and stopped. There was something different. He looked down at his feet. Buried partly in the dried mud, he noticed a small pendant in the shape of two "R"s with a sword stuck through them. He picked it up and held it close. A metallic substance, probably silver, formed the first "R". The second "R", upside down and connected to the first by the tail, looked like it was made out of a prism. It changed colors as he moved it around. He regarded it with interest then stuck it in his pocket and moved on. He knew the winds would pick up soon—waited for it with growing anticipation, even. Then he could get out of this dream and maybe have a decent one.

He studied the mountains and tried to judge their distance. Fifty miles? Seventy-five? He couldn't tell. *Of course,* he mused, *it doesn't matter since I won't reach them anyway.*

"Why not?"

The voice came from behind. It wavered in pitch as if it had been delivered through the blades of a fan. Casey turned and saw a thin woman standing about a hundred feet from him, long blonde hair swaying in the gentle breeze. She wasn't looking at him, but off in the distance toward the mountains. Casey walked forward a few steps then stopped. If she wanted to be approached, she would have at least looked at him.

"What makes you think you can't reach the mountains?" she asked. This time the voice resonated through the air like a crystal goblet struck with a spoon.

"I've been down this path before," Casey replied. "The wind will pick up and take me away."

The woman kept her eyes focused on the distant mountains. "Why don't you walk in a different direction?"

Before Casey could answer, the woman melted into the dried mud, a puddle of water forming where she had stood. Casey watched the puddle shrink as it absorbed into the ground. He turned and looked toward the mountains one more time, confused about the direction this dream had taken.

After a moment, he took another step forward and stopped again. The sound of a crying child drifted past his ears then disappeared.

Casey wasn't sure of what he heard or where it came from. He looked around but saw only the vast expanse of the landscape and the mountains. Cautiously, he took another step, listening carefully for any noise out of the ordinary. The wind began to blow a little harder, stirring loose dirt around his feet. What was the woman trying to tell him? The wind was *still* going to blow, the dust was *still* going to surround him, and he would *still* move on or wake up. He walked forward a few more steps before the sound of crying came again.

Casey swung around and looked out over the horizon. This time, the crying didn't come and go, but remained a quiet sort of whimper. The wind began to pull dirt up around his knees, and he suddenly felt time running short. The woman, the child crying? What was so different his mind wanted to tell him? There was nothing out there. Only the dirt, the wind and the mountains. Only the same scenes that wanted to repeat themselves over and over.

Casey sighed and turned back around, content to continue on his fruitless journey toward the horizon.

A small girl pulled at Casey's pants. "Knock, knock," she said, and the world went black.

THE MAN standing on the other side of the doorway looked friendly enough. Of course, so did a million other people with bad intentions, especially when viewed through a peephole. Casey rubbed his eyes and looked over at an alarm clock set above the television. Two thirty-eight. So, not every person who knocked on someone's door at two thirty-eight in the morning was out to do harm, but Casey was leery nonetheless. The man behind the door was tall, about six foot three, with blonde hair. Probably in his early thirties, he could pass for a serial killer if you accepted the idea that most serial killers were male, twenty-five to thirty-four years old, and looked almost normal. Casey pretended he had an eye for the Jeffery Dahmers and Ted Bundys of the world, but the man on the other side of the door didn't quite fit the mold.

Casey opened the door slightly, keeping the chain lock on. "Can I help you?" he asked, wondering at that moment where his gun was sitting.

"I was curious if you could help me," said the man through the door. "I'm looking for a woman."

"You must have the wrong apartment. There's no woman here." Casey began to close the door.

"She wouldn't be here," the man quickly replied. "She was murdered."

Casey's heart skipped. *It's on the counter in the kitchen*, he thought. *The gun is on the counter.*

"I was hoping you could talk to me for a minute," the man continued. Casey slammed the door shut and ran to the kitchen to get his gun. He heard the man still talking. "I won't take but a moment of your time. I'm wondering if she left anything behind."

Magazine in? Good. Casey cocked the pistol, placing a round in the chamber then slowly walked to the door. The man outside had stopped talking, and none of this sat well with Casey. Thoughts streamed through his mind as he walked up to the door. *How does this guy know who I am? Was he at the crime scene?* He remembered the man standing on the hill in the distance. Was it him?

He looked through the peephole again to get a better look at the man he had only minutes before regarded as probably *not* a serial killer.

"Knock, knock." The man outside had his hands in his pockets and rocked back and forth on his feet. "Hello? Is anybody there?"

Casey stood back from the door and yelled. "Look. I don't know who—"

"—I am?" the man interrupted. "Yes, I know that. If I were any dumber, I'd tell you, but I don't have much time, Casey. We need to talk."

"How do you know my name? I've never seen you before."

The man paused for a moment. "Okay, let's understand a little something here, shall we? You have the advantage of a gun, and I am behind this door. Although by looking at it, I could probably punch through the thin veneer and rip your heart out."

Rip my heart out? Casey's mind flashed back to the scene of the woman lying in the desert with a gaping hole in her chest. He put his hand on his chest, felt the pounding of his own heart, and took a step farther from the door.

"I, on the other hand," continued the man, "probably know some things you would like to hear. That gives me an advantage over you, since knowledge is power and right now you haven't the foggiest idea of where to really begin your investigation."

"What do you want?"

"To talk, Casey. Haven't I already said that once?"

Casey lowered the pistol and walked closer to the door. He looked once more through the peephole. The man still rocked back and forth with his hands in his pockets.

"Put your hands up and maybe I'll open the door." Casey felt sweat drip from his forehead.

The man took his hands out of his pockets and waved them at the peephole. "Can we talk, Casey? The distance from here is farther than you think, and I believe you need to know a few things first."

Wiping the sweat from his brow, Casey finally unlatched the door and let the man inside.

CHAPTER SEVEN

Marie looked around.

"Nice place, Jacob."

The man sitting across from her smiled. "Only the best for you."

"You know, you could have picked a place that wasn't between hither and yon." Marie looked down at her coffee cup and watched something swirl in the black liquid. Dishes clanked in the kitchen, cooks mumbled this and that, and waitresses yelled out orders while turning their heads only slightly in the direction intended. Round tables sat empty in the middle of the restaurant while booths against the side—with their orange, torn vinyl benches and soiled tablecloths—were packed with the denizens of the highway.

"Look around you, Marie." Jacob waved his hand slightly. "What do you see?"

Marie brought her gaze up from the coffee. "People. I see people."

A man missing a tooth sipped coffee, his face spotted with uneven whiskers. His eyes, buried beneath a white brow that extended across his forehead, scanned a newspaper in front of him, looking for the next opportunity to jump on, or a job in another rigging company, or a chance to go out on the open sea again. Marie could only guess.

"That man needs a job." Marie found herself inwardly laughing at her words. "You'd think I was psychic."

Jacob smiled. "Something like that."

She frowned as the words of the old man on the park

bench came back to her. *All masks have holes for eyes, no matter how much effort is put into a costume.*

Next to the toothless man in another booth was a big, burly trucker, flannel shirt sticking out of his jeans, black wool cap tightly seated on his head. He sat next to his wife, girlfriend, prostitute or live-in partner, and swapped a guffaw with every joke or a smirk with every mention of whatever it was that would irritate them that night.

Jacob brought his finger up and pointed across the diner. Marie followed his direction and turned slightly.

"Which one?"

"The family of three. The little girl has her eye on you."

Across the diner, a tiny head poked up from behind a bench. She looked around and darted back down next to her mother who sat opposite a man who obviously wasn't listening. His eyes said little as they stared into the emptiness that Marie felt had become his family, missing completely the torrent of words spilling out from the sickly-looking mother. Marie knew; it was the same expression she'd had for so long.

Jacob leaned forward and whispered. "What do you suppose the man is thinking?"

"Kill me."

The girl poked her head up again and looked across the diner toward Marie. She held her gaze as Marie looked back and mindlessly stirred in a chunk of creamer from a little carton.

Thoughts suddenly crossed Marie's mind to a time before Peter, before Susan, before losing everything she had to one drunk idiot. Quickly, she brought her gaze back down and leaned over the coffee. She felt like a foreigner in an Irish Pub, and she the blond-haired misfit off the street. She carefully eyed the rest of the diner, making sure not to look obvious, and quickly shifted her eyes back to her coffee. She took the spoon out, set it on a grimy napkin and looked up at Jacob across from her.

"What made you decide on this?" she asked. A quick smile darted across her face to hide the pain she felt. She wanted to blot out the memories, but the past was too persistent.

Jacob shifted his eyes around, sat up a little straighter, and began to play with the straw sticking out of his glass of carbonated syrup. "Looked like a nice place from the road," he said in an apologetic voice. "I mean, what comes to your mind when you see a sign that reads 'Heaven's Diner'?"

"Probably not the same thing you're thinking, considering the 'n' was out. I thought it read 'Heave's Diner'."

"Sorry. I've seen this place a hundred times driving back and forth to work and just decided to check it out. Pauline said the apple pie was something else. How's your coffee?"

"It could use a few more spoonfuls of sugar, a little more creamer, a new filter, more water, and another brew. Other than that, I'd say it's close to perfect." Marie smiled weakly and took a sip of brown sludge.

An uncomfortable pause descended on the table as Jacob stared at her then shifted his gaze out the window. Marie's eyes followed. The evening sun hung lower in the sky and cast long shadows of cars speeding down the highway. The parking lot spread out from the window to the street, untouched by anything that remotely resembled landscaping. A few wayward Styrofoam cups, flattened by passing cars and trucks, blended in with broken beer bottles, newspapers and cigarette butts.

Jacob turned back to Marie. "You look like hell."

"You're not much for compliments are you? You look like crap."

"Thanks. You didn't sleep last night, did you?"

"No."

"Same thoughts?"

Marie stared at the cars on the highway. "The usual. You'd think I would have grown used to the loneliness by now."

"I don't think that's going to happen anytime soon."

"Lucky me."

"And, I might add, you probably don't *want* it to happen."

Marie chuckled, but not for anything Jacob said that might be humorous. She laughed at the life she'd been living. "You're a psychologist, too, huh?"

"The best in the business. We'd make a team, you and I. The psychic and the shrink."

Marie smiled.

"People would line up for miles."

"What? To see the woman who climbs a mountain of problems every day? To see the wretched beast claw her way through briar patches to places in her mind she never wanted to visit?" She cut herself off and stirred her coffee some more. An audible sigh escaped her lips.

"I didn't mean to bring you down."

Marie felt herself drift away from the diner's environment, the noise relegated to nothing more than a soft murmur. "I miss them," she said. It was enough to turn her stomach.

Jacob reached out and touched Marie's hand. "You know, that's the first time you've said that in a while."

"I—" She stopped. Jacob was right. She'd forced herself to focus on a past that hadn't included her family. It was all that kept the loneliness at bay.

"I miss Harlan, too." She looked sheepishly away. "I sent him an e-mail the other day."

"What good do you think that will do?"

Marie sighed. "I don't know. I don't even know why I did it."

"Because you're tied to him."

"Bound is a better word."

Jacob smiled and sat back against his seat. "So, what's so wonderful about this guy?"

Marie's memory swirled back in time to someplace she often wished she'd never left.

"He taught me things," Marie said, not realizing the irony of her statement.

"Well, considering he was your teacher in high school, I don't doubt that."

"I've never felt closer to anyone, even after I cut off contact with him."

"Why did you do that? I thought you two were in love."

"We were, but he was married and I didn't want to do anything that might spell disaster for his job, his marriage, the chance to be with his daughter."

Marie looked up at the girl across the diner. She bounced up and down in the seat while her father sat motionless and her mother wouldn't stop talking. There were so many times Marie had played the big "What If" scenarios through her mind, but in the end, it was obvious she and Harlan would never be together. It didn't even seem possible after he divorced; she couldn't get over her loss, no matter how hard she tried.

Marie chuckled at her thoughts. "You know, we met in the weirdest of places—an old stable, next to a water tower in some unknown little trailer town, then a desert canyon. You'd think we'd find a motel or something."

Jacob leaned over the table, his head propped on his hands. "Go on."

Marie looked up at Jacob and wondered why he was so interested in her past. Sure, she'd been in love, and then married. Sure, Jacob had listened to her tell a thousand stories, and held the bucket every time she poured her heart out. But why was he so intent on hearing all of this again?

She sipped a little more of the coffee and put the cup down. Outside the window, a man walked by. Marie followed him with her eyes as he passed the next window, the next, the door and finally turned into the parking lot. So many people have so many reasons for doing what they do. What was Jacob's? *Then again*, she thought, *what's yours?*

"There isn't much else to tell, Jacob." Marie brought her gaze back from the window. "I've told you all the gory details a number of times."

"Did you ever tell him the truth?"

"Harlan?" Marie felt a lump grow in her throat. "No, I didn't. I... I told myself that endings don't have to be permanent, you know? I wanted to keep something to myself that maybe I could bring up at a later time. He didn't need to know I was ever pregnant."

Their eyes caught for a moment, and Marie could sense something inside of Jacob. She wasn't sure what it was, but it felt nice, like he really was a psychologist and this session could make a difference. "Do you understand what I mean by that?"

Jacob nodded. "You know I do."

Marie looked down and struggled with her memories. She felt her eyes well up with tears. She needed to change the subject. "I didn't tell you what happened after I left your house the other night."

Jacob adjusted himself. "You stared at the wall?"

"Actually, the door. I almost ran over some guy lying face down in a mud puddle, and I could have sworn he was going to come and get me."

"Really? Sounds like a winner. Drunk? High? Stupid?"

"No, but he *was* naked." Marie paused for a minute then looked up at Jacob. "Scared the crap out of me, really. I was going to help him out, but..."

"But what? Why didn't you?"

"Something didn't feel right about the whole situation."

"Other than the obvious, how so?"

"Well..." Marie struggled to find the words to convey just what she'd felt. At first, the man's eyes beckoned to her, and then turned cold. She felt comforted and then afraid. "I guess I felt something... evil." She replayed the scene. "He told me he fell."

Jacob's eyebrows furled and he turned to the window. Marie looked out the window with him. In the glare of the lights, she saw his face clearly, his nose wrinkled in thought.

"Something I said?" Marie asked. "You look a little pale."

"No."

"So why do you look like that?"

"What?"

"You're doing that eyebrow thing and wrinkling your nose. Either you're deep in thought or you have gas. I haven't been able to tell which it is, yet."

Silence descended between the two for an uncomfortable minute before Jacob spoke again. "Can I tell you something, Marie?" He paused and took a sip from his glass. "You're different. You don't realize that, but you're not like anyone else in this neck of the woods."

"So, I'm a freak. I know that."

Jacob smiled weakly. "There are people in the world who

exist simply to gratify others—they are followers. Then there are others who exist and think of themselves as God's gift to mankind, destined to do wonderful things and get their names inscribed in textbooks—they are doers, leaders."

Marie raised her eyebrows. "Go on."

"Finally, there is the rest of the world, and that number isn't very large. These people go through life, anonymous, but they *feel* things. In that one moment when they understand something, they help without question. They are not followers, but servants. It's those people that are really in a position to do great things, and at the same time, are the most vulnerable."

"Okay. *That* made sense."

Jacob shook his head. "It won't. At least not right now."

Marie felt an inkling of anxiety in her stomach, an acid burn that was more than bad coffee. It was almost like someone was about to tell her something she didn't want to hear, didn't want to know, didn't need to understand. It was a feeling she'd had many times before.

"His name was David, right?"

Marie felt her stomach sink. She nodded slowly. "How do you know his name?"

"How many people do you think saw him lying in the road last night? One? Two? I know it's a gravel road. It's not a freeway, but people still use it more than you'd think. Don't you suppose someone else would have stopped? Don't you think there's a reason behind finding him where he was?"

"I'll ask you again: how did you know his name?"

Marie caught Jacob's gaze. She felt something well up inside of him, boiling at the surface and ready to explode. Life, she suddenly realized, was about to change.

Maybe it already had.

"We all have reasons for doing what we do, Marie."

Silence descended on the two again, and the sounds of clanking dishes and rough men and women laughing at crude jokes dissolved into the air around them. Marie's eyes wandered about the diner, not focusing on any one person in particular, but seeing their souls nonetheless, like glow-in-the-dark bodies in a blackened world.

"Why did you bring me here, Jacob?"

Jacob grabbed his wallet, threw a twenty down on the table and stood.

"Let's go back to your place," he said and took Marie's hand. "I'll tell you a little secret."

THEY DROVE through the streets oblivious to each other. Marie felt weak, thinking at first it may have been the chunk of creamer in her coffee, but accepting finally that she was simply tired of life. And what was she to think?

A man at a bus stop took a drink from a bottle hidden in a paper bag. Through the matted brown beard streaked with gray, Marie swore she saw a smile peek out between parting lips. The smile could have told her a thousand tales, but it would more than likely fall silent following a heartache imaginable to only those in the same position. The man closed his eyes and reared his head back against the back of the bench.

Her fingers tingled.

Jacob broke the silence. "You never told me what brought you to Alaska."

"Sure I did. Several times." Marie kept her reply to Jacob's query short. She didn't feel like having this conversation, but it looked like Jacob was set to pull her into it anyway. She pulled on a strand of hair and twisted it.

"Right," Jacob said. "You wanted to get away from it all. You felt life was missing something, and every time you looked around your neighborhood, you saw nothing but reminders of your family."

The word struck a tone in Marie. Family. They had been so much of her life, to think they didn't exist any longer brought pain through her body in perpetual waves. All it took was one person to drink a little too much, swerve off a center line and plow headfirst into their van at sixty miles per hour.

Marie had sent them off the day they died. She needed to get them out of her hair.

She choked back the feelings that wanted to overpower her and concentrated on making a left hand turn. "You have to bring this up, Jacob?" Her voice was quiet and distant, but terse.

"You once told me you needed a sounding board. All I'm doing is making you talk about things."

Marie sighed. "You want me to talk about what? Talk about that clinic eight years ago? Talk about getting married, having a child I could finally keep? Do you want me to tell you how I felt when I got a phone call that my marriage was ended by someone down on his luck?" She stopped for a minute as the images of that night struck her from deep inside. "What do you want to hear that you haven't heard before?"

"Why are you *here*? In Alaska?"

The aggravation in Marie peaked. She had crossed the border from mildly irritated to just plain angry. "*To escape Hell!*"

Marie looked in the rearview mirror and caught a glimpse of herself. She looked like a woman lost to the world but still in control, confident of herself and her surroundings. Buried beneath those brown eyes, however, was a soul slowly spiraling toward an unknown destination that was neither here nor there. She knew Jacob saw all of this.

"So you said, Marie. But why Alaska? You didn't know anyone. There wasn't any family to support you. The environment is as different as it could be from the desert. You didn't even know where you were going to get a job or much less find a place to live."

Marie pulled up to a stop sign and let her car settle for a minute. She looked to the right, looked to the left, then straight ahead, focusing on the past rather than anything physical in front of her. Tears formed on the inside of her eyelids, waiting for the chance to fall. "I don't know."

"What happened at the airport?"

The airport. She closed her eyes and a tear broke free, falling onto her cheek. The car's engine murmured in the background. She saw herself two months after the funeral, packing. Thoughts of running away streamed through her mind. People kept trying to console her, as if she really needed it after the first month. The more her friends and family tried, the more she remembered and the further she would fall into a pattern of depression that never ended. She ran to the airport, thinking she would simply visit someplace for a while—Bermuda, Florida, California, Higginsville, Missouri. She didn't care where she went, as long as it was away from everyone else.

Marie opened her eyes and looked into the space in front of her car, seeing only the images of the airport. She saw the escalator, the stupid looking model of an angel hung from the ceiling, the rows upon rows of ticketing agents and waiting passengers. The carpet, tan with the occasional stain of coffee or ground-in gum, stretched out for miles. Her memory passed the first airline and headed for the next—the one with no line.

"I asked the ticket agent what flights were leaving in the next few hours."

"What were you told?" Jacob's voice sounded distant and hollow. It was more like a memory than a reality.

"Anchorage, Seattle, Portland, and one going to Albuquerque."

"And you picked Anchorage."

"No," Marie said. Her eyes closed instinctively. Another tear fell onto her cheek. "I asked for a ticket to Seattle."

"The ticket agent—what did she look like?"

"He. Um..." Marie turned to Jacob and tried to focus on her memories. "It's hard to remember. What does that have to do with anything?"

"What did he say to you when you asked for Seattle?"

"He told me... he said... Why can't I remember?"

"Did he tell you that greater joys are found in less populated places?"

Marie turned her focus from memory to the present and looked into the dark eyes of her passenger. A feeling of epiphany rushed in to fill the sickness she'd felt since they left the diner. It was a feeling of knowing someone was trying to lead her in one direction, down a certain path that needed to be traveled, and she was the tourist.

She narrowed her eyes and tried to see deep inside Jacob's, past the mask. "And it's only a few dollars more," she whispered.

"Won't you take the offer?"

"Only if you come."

Jacob smiled. "And here I am."

Marie stared longer, unsure of what to say. She blinked and thought back to Jacob behind the counter in Phoenix. "You looked different."

"I shaved."

A car behind her honked and snapped Marie from her thoughts. She turned left and headed for her house. The two sat silent in the car, much like they were when they left the diner, but this time Marie was more pleasantly confused than she had been.

A few minutes later, she pulled into her driveway and stepped out of the car. Her hands shook as she fumbled for the house key.

She stopped and looked up. "You said people have reasons for doing what they do. So why are you following me?"

"I'm sorry," Jacob said, the words softly falling from his lips. He stood with his hands in his pockets as Marie walked to the front door. "I'm not following you. I'm protecting you."

Marie put the key in the lock and turned around. There was a shy, almost boyish quality to Jacob in the fading light of the day. She chuckled at the absurdity of Jacob's words. "Protecting me from what?" she asked.

Perched on the windowsill on the other side of the living room, David sat with a grin on his face.

CHAPTER EIGHT

Jennifer was excited.

After two hours on the highway, Jonathan pulled the '73 Impala off the pavement onto a small forestry service road lined with Ponderosa trees and ferns. The smell of pine and soil wet from the late afternoon rains rushed into the open window of the car. She was free at last, or as free as she could be for the weekend. Surely no one would think to look for them on this road, assuming they found out that she really wasn't with Myra and the search parties were formed. She imagined her mother crying while sitting in her daughter's room, caressing a stuffed animal that Jennifer really had no feelings toward. Her father would yell at the top of his lungs, no doubt, and threaten to beat her or lock her in a closet until she was eighteen. And Tommy? The little rat of a brother would stand in the hallway dressed in some superhero pajamas looking as clueless as ever. Jennifer smiled at the thought and pulled Tolliloqui close to her chest.

Jonathan's hand rubbed her thigh, and before brushing it off, she began to accept this was okay. Why not? Freedom meant doing things that she had wanted to do for the longest time without the worry of being caught. It was integrity shot to Hell. Freedom meant escape, escape meant growing up, and growing up meant giving herself fully to the man she would someday marry. Jennifer placed her own hand on Jonathan's and guided it up and down her thigh. She enjoyed the sensation of his touch and relished the thought that *this* was rebellion.

Jennifer turned away from the window and leaned over to lay her head on Jonathan's shoulder. She sighed and closed her eyes, imagining just for a moment what it would be like to be married. Of course she couldn't be sure, but if it was anything like her parents, then some things had to be changed. Maybe if she showed a little more love toward Jonathan, then the children—three of them would be nice—could be happier. Maybe if she went out of her way for him, he wouldn't be grumpy. Maybe—

Maybe I don't really know what it's like, she thought.

FOR JONATHAN, rebellion was nothing new; however this rebellion was equal in power to the greatest rush of his short life. The road twisted and turned through the trees, remaining true to the outline of the Rim itself. With a few puddles of mud, a few ruts, and a few bumps, the trip began to seem adventurous. Jonathan guided the car through the curves with one hand, while the other hand was slowly guided up and down Jennifer's thigh. He began to feel flushed and at the same time, tried to keep some semblance of control over the car. He could pull over at any minute, climb over to the passenger side and take Jennifer right then and there, but his romantic side kept telling him to wait until the tent was set up inside the dead forest they drove toward.

He looked over at Jennifer and smiled. He was in love, and no parent or adult could tell him that he didn't know the difference between infatuation and true, storybook-type, mushy love.

The road took a sharp left and Jonathan had to take his hand back to navigate the turn without running off into the forest. He looked ahead and tried to gauge the distance to the dead forest by picturing the map he'd looked at online. He couldn't be sure, but it had to be just around the next bend. Another sharp turn took the road to the right and just at the edge of the Rim. From this point, the early evening lights of the towns below could be seen like diamonds in a grassy field. The moon poked around the remaining clouds and cast shadows far and wide. The whole scene looked surreal.

The road narrowed, pulled slightly north of the Rim and began to wind in between small hills lined with ferns and grasses and dead pine needles. Jonathan sat a little more upright and tried to find the turn off.

A sudden pothole threw Jonathan off guard. The car swerved to the left, hit a rock and blew a tire.

"*No!*" Jonathan cried out. He stared through the windshield as the dust thrown up by his car settled around them.

He weakly smiled at Jennifer while attempting to collect himself and his nerves. She looked at him for a moment then kissed him softly on the cheek.

"I'll wait here."

SHE HAD been in the front seat of the car for a while when Jonathan slammed the trunk of the Impala down. He walked up to Jennifer's window, wiping his hands on a greasy rag. He looked grim.

"Spare's flat."

"What? You mean we're *stuck* out here?" Jennifer's vision of camping in the woods for the weekend with her future husband began to take more of a turn toward *surviving* in the woods with her future husband. "What are we going to do?"

Jonathan looked up at the night sky then back at the trunk of the car. Jennifer knew he was trying to pass off his goofy looks as expressions of deep thought.

"I don't—"

"Trouble with the car?" a man called out. Jennifer looked around in the direction of the voice, but could only make out trees and ferns in the dimness beyond.

"Who's there?" Jonathan called out, the crack in his voice more apparent to Jennifer than he probably anticipated.

"I see your tire's flat, son," the man called out again. He sounded closer. The sound of crushed pine needles and cracking twigs gave away his position.

Jennifer and Jonathan watched as a taller man emerged from between the trees on a slight hill, flannel shirt, blue jeans and beige hiking boots accenting a medium build. As he came closer, Jennifer felt her heart race and grabbed onto Jonathan's shirt.

"I don't like this," she whispered. "I feel something really bad."

Jonathan put his head down to talk to her without taking his eyes off the man coming toward them. "I'll take care of this, Jenn. You sit still."

The man was almost on them. He walked with a limp down the hill, zigzagging between trees and larger bushes. "Can I help you two love-birds?"

"Not really." Jonathan's voice sounded pitifully weak to Jennifer. "Just about to change a flat."

"I thought I heard you say the spare was flat. Correct me if I'm wrong, son." The man stopped in front of Jonathan and lowered his gaze. "That would put you two in a little pickle now, wouldn't it?"

"No, it's just a little flat. We can make it to town on what air is left."

"Really?" The man looked around Jonathan and down at the flat tire. His eye twitched. "I have a compressor back at the cabin. If you want, you and the little miss can come on over and I'll fill up your tire."

"That's nice of you, really, but we can still make it on what we have."

"Got some bacon frying if you're hungry?" The man tilted his head and looked at Jennifer. He smiled, showing every tooth he possibly could.

Jennifer stared into the man's eyes, captivated by a blue which seemed to suddenly beckon, calm her, set her mind awhirl with foggy thoughts. Her heart began to beat slower, her nerves relaxed and for a moment she thought she saw something else in his eyes... something she'd never seen before in anyone else. It was something... powerful.

The punch came quick and Jonathan was thrown into the window. The air rushed out of his lungs with a sickening howl. Jennifer jumped in the seat, letting out a quick, involuntary shriek as Jonathan's back bent farther into the open window, vertebrae cracking with every inch. A spot of blood appeared on the back of his shirt, grew and then exploded. Shards of bone and flesh flew over the inside of the car.

Jennifer screamed and scrambled to the driver's side door, fumbled for the handle and fell out as she pushed the car door open. She turned in time to see Jonathan's heart in the man's hand. The stranger pulled his arm out of Jonathan's chest and let the corpse slump against the door. The boy's head hit the top of the car then fell to the ground.

The man stood opposite Jennifer, still holding the heart of her lover in his hands. He looked at her and smiled again, teeth clenched and face spotted with blood.

"Sure you won't come and have some bacon?" he asked once more. Jennifer choked back another scream and ran up the road, not even once looking back.

"You need to be a little more careful, Jennifer," the man called out. "You just can't tell who's who anymore. You're a part of this whole thing, and there's no way to stop it!"

Jennifer veered into the woods, desperate to get as far away from the man as possible.

Over her shoulder, the stranger called once again. *"Did you hear me, Jennifer? There is no way!"*

THE FOREST is an eerie place. It's eerier when face to face with a real danger. It's nightmarish when you don't know where the danger is at any given moment. The natural twists and crags of branches, the spiny needles sticking out from the ends of twigs, the spiked pinecones scattered about—it all added up to a clichéd background for teenage serial killer movies. Throw in a full moon visible between treetops and drifting clouds and you have the perfect scene for innocence cut to pieces for no apparent reason. It was a stage ripe for the grand old story of evil overcoming love, of mentally ill psychos whose parents beat them, of Halloween mask wearing mute monsters carving up testosterone laden boys and stabbing buxom blondes in the chest with pitch forks and other common farm tools. It was Hollywood at its finest.

It was the last place Jennifer wanted to be.

She had been running for what seemed like hours, but was probably no more than a few minutes. She stopped as her mind screamed at her. The noises she had been making would most certainly lead the bacon-cooking psycho straight to her. She leaned up against a tall Ponderosa and wiped tears from her cheeks. How could this happen? Was this what her parents were worried about? Being hunted? Her future husband lay somewhere out there, a hole in his chest where his heart used to be. She was frightened, and the man who killed Jonathan was coming after her next. He would rape her, cut her throat, and rip out her lungs to keep her from screaming anymore. He would tie her up to a tree and slice each finger off one by one until she fainted from the shock of it all, and then he would drill a hole in her head and let cockroaches eat her fleshy brain.

Of course, she imagined too much. None of this was going to happen — she prayed — and Jennifer was sure she wasn't going to end up a statistic like the six others who were killed two years ago a few miles from where she stood. She sighed and choked back the sensation of crying hysterically. She knew tears wouldn't wash anything away.

Slumping down the tree, she closed her eyes and put her hands to her face. What was she going to do now? She needed to find help, if help even existed in the middle of nowhere in the Tonto Forest of Arizona. Jennifer had no idea where to look or where to run, only where *not* to go.

Her mind replayed the event over and over in vivid detail, focusing on a different aspect each time. She needed to remember the man's features: blond hair, parted in the middle and shoulder length, blue eyes, crooked smile. Next came the visual memory of Jonathan's back exploding, his heart ripped out. There was blood everywhere — on the window, on the seats, on the steering wheel and on Jennifer's clothes. She looked down at her skirt where only a few moments ago, Jonathan had been rubbing his hand. Blood was smeared across the denim, down the material and across her legs.

She closed her eyes and focused again, this time on the psycho's voice. It was almost soothing at first, and Jennifer distinctly recalled being calmed by that tone. She opened her eyes and looked back toward the direction she had just come from.

How did he know my name? She wrinkled her forehead and tried to remember what he said to her as she ran off.

You need to be a little more careful, Jennifer. You just can't tell who's who anymore. You're a part of this whole thing, and there's no way to stop it!

There is no way!

No way...

"Stop what?" Jennifer whispered. She caught herself speaking out loud.

"It's just a game, honey," the man said softly. Jennifer looked up and found herself less than five feet from the psycho who killed Jonathan. The moon shone through the trees and illuminated his whole body as he stood with his arms out. His face was still spotted with blood and his hands a deep, deep red. He smiled at her and cocked his head to the right. "It's friend against foe, like a chess match."

With a pump of adrenaline she didn't know she had in her, Jennifer jumped and ran in the direction she just came. She ran over a fallen tree, around a bush, through a patch of fern in the middle of it all. Her feet pounded the undergrowth, cracking twigs and small, brown needles, carrying her faster than she ever thought she could run.

She jumped over another fallen branch, lost her footing and fell down a small hill, coming to rest next to the bloody remains of Jonathan. She looked at his body, chest covered with blood, ribs sticking out of the flesh. It had been repositioned away from the Impala, and his head had been crushed with a rock, tiny bits of bone smashed into the blood-soaked ground around his neck.

Jennifer screamed as the image of her future husband burned itself into her mind. She scrambled to her feet and ran again.

The forest was more of an obstacle than she expected now, and she stumbled several times. Her chest burned with the exertion placed on her lungs. Tears poured down her cheeks. Forget stopping to rest, however. The last time she did that, the freak caught up with her. She just ran, not caring where she ended up. If she never stopped again, at least she would have escaped. There was no waking up from this nightmare, no turning the page and starting another chapter, no switching the channel to find something more appealing. She was going to die if she didn't keep running, and she knew she needed help.

At long last it looked like help was coming. Stumbling through a large patch of fern, she found herself in front of small cabin with the kitchen light on and the door slightly ajar. Carefully, she looked through the window beside the door. She saw the living room and into the kitchen where the light came from. There was a shadow cast across the living room wall—a tall figure, masked in black, with elongated features and teeth so large they could bite through the torso of a horse. She told herself she was probably imagining the teeth, but shadows have ways of casting themselves with chaotic regard to the shape that created them. She was nervous, but then again, she had no other escape. Behind her was death. In the cabin, there might be salvation.

Jennifer inched the door open with her left hand, clutching the lapel of her shirt in her right. She slowly made her way through the living room, passed some wall that might as well have been the whole hallway, and stepped into the kitchen—shaking with every step. Adrenaline rushed from vein to vein, pulsed inside her head. Her temple throbbed with every heartbeat. Her synapses fired, sending waves of energy through her optic nerves, out to her fingers, through her toes. Screaming electrical impulses of reaction soared throughout her body. She always thought she would be ready for anything...

...but not Jonathan's killer standing over the stove, cooking.

The man stood with a spatula in hand and pushed bacon around in a copper skillet. The light above the stove was on, and in its glow Jennifer could make out two plates, two empty cups and a silverware setting for two on the counter. Why dinner was being prepared for two people was not Jennifer's main thought. She suddenly realized she couldn't move. Try as she might, her legs wouldn't carry her to freedom.

"What do you want with me?" Jennifer's voice cracked, and her hands shook.

The man pushed the bacon around the pan a few more times, letting the sizzle of fat speak for him.

"Why did you kill him?" Jennifer realized the absurdity of the question as soon as the words drifted through the kitchen. "Who are you?"

"Who I am is not important. *You* are Jennifer," the man spoke and turned around, bacon still sizzling in the pan. "Your father is Harlan, your mother is Celine, your brother is Tommy, and your boyfriend is dead. Sorry about the kitchen mess. I'll clean it up when I'm done."

Jennifer tried to force her legs to move, but in the attempt she felt a sharp tingling run from her thighs through her feet. *What the hell?*

"I forgot to mention one thing," the man continued. "Your sister is Justine."

Jennifer blinked.

Sister?

The man slopped the bacon onto a waiting plate and divided the portions equally between the two. He turned off the stove and poured coffee from a percolator into the mugs. "I guess we need napkins, don't we?"

A stream of thoughts ran through Jennifer's mind, combating each other. Each successive one bounced off another and strived for attention. She pulled at her legs again and tried to force herself out of this unwanted paralysis and run outside.

"Never mind," said the man. "I guess we really don't need them." He grabbed the plates and the silverware and headed for a small breakfast nook behind the kitchen. "How do you like the cabin?" he asked from the nook. "I really like the atmosphere, myself."

Jennifer's lips parted, a stream of questions strained in the slips trying to get out. "Nice," she finally said, then stood silent as she wondered where that word came from.

The man walked back into the kitchen and grabbed the coffee cups. He stopped at the counter and turned to Jennifer. "You okay?" he asked, as if this man who Jennifer had never seen in her life until he killed her boyfriend suddenly knew her well enough to know what she looked like when she felt well. "Breakfast is ready." He took the mugs into the nook.

"Who are you?" Jennifer asked again, still trying to move her legs.

"Why don't you relax," the man called out from the other room. "You might as well come in the nook so I can kill you. I already made a mess of the kitchen."

Jennifer felt her heart stop, beat erratically for a moment, then pound again. Her breath quickened in time to the beat and the rush of blood to her neck and shoulders felt unbearably hot. She began to sweat. *Kill you.* The words ricocheted inside Jennifer's skull. *K-I-L-L. I think that's what he just said.*

"Yes, kill you." The man's voice came from behind. "I'm going to rip your heart out and have it for breakfast. Honestly, don't you think breakfast for dinner is a great idea?"

Jennifer's eyes widened. Her mind screamed. Tremors ran through her body. A bead of sweat trickled down her forehead, past her eyebrows, made a right at her nose and fell to her cheek like a tear. Her legs had to start working again!

Rip out your heart...

The words stayed suspended in the air as she suddenly felt the breath of the man on her neck.

Kill you.

Another breath from behind splashed against her skin. The sweat made it seem like a blast of ice. A little closer this time. Jennifer involuntarily relaxed, closed her eyes and willed her legs to move.

It worked.

She shot through the kitchen into the nook. As she passed the table, with its setting for two neatly arranged, she instinctively grabbed a chair and threw it behind her, hoping to trip up the bacon-cooking freak. To her right lay the path her assailant had just taken, and she ran through to the living room hoping to make the front door in time. As her eyes came up to gauge the direction around a couch, she saw the intruder step in front of the door and casually close it.

"You left the door wide open," the man said. "Someone could've walked in and taken this stuff."

Jennifer stopped. Now she realized her only option was down the hall, past the kitchen and into the back of the cabin, where she could either crawl out a window or... or what?

The man took a step forward and Jennifer took off running. The cabin seemed enormously large and the hallway, all of about ten to fifteen feet, seemed to stretch on for miles. This was her only way out, and determination was on her side. This bastard was out to kill — again.

"I hope I don't seem ungracious," the man called out. His voice passed Jennifer's ears in the hallway and echoed against the bedroom door in front of her. "I mean, really. You come into a messy cabin and then I kill you. I suppose that's a little rude."

Rude? Jennifer grabbed the door handle to the bedroom. *Rude? This guy is a nutcase.* She turned the handle and threw her shoulder against the door. Looking back down the hall, she saw the front door was open and the Bacon Man was gone.

Where did he go, now?

Jennifer stepped into the room and looked at the window. Finally, she could get out of the house, away from this nightmare and find help. A sense of relief shot through her veins as she unlocked the window. Outside she saw the trees sway in the wind, the road she was going to run down, and the eyes of the man stare back from the reflection in the glass.

"I'm hurt," he said. "You didn't even *try* the bacon."

Jennifer refused to turn around. In the glass she saw perfectly. The man stood in the doorway with his flannel shirt, hands tucked into his blue jeans. Outside was freedom, and any attempt she made to open the window would be futile. To turn back would be as equally futile.

She was trapped.

To the left, a strange sight crept into Jennifer's peripheral vision: a closet door, wide open. Something seemed wrong.

She turned her eyes to look and found nothing. It wasn't a nothing that made sense, either. Here was a closet where she should at least see some clothes hanging, or for lack of that, she should at least see the *back* of the closet. It was as if her eyes hurt to look at it. A gaping hole would even look different. At least a hole would have edges and blackness in the middle. This looked like the world had been painted on a canvass of nothing and the Master had run out of color at the last minute.

Jennifer blinked. Maybe the stress of the last few minutes created a tunnel vision of sorts that started from the inside and worked its way out. The nothing was still there, and the harder she stared at it, the more her eyes ached.

In the midst of the void, she thought she caught a glimpse of a tree.

"Go ahead and jump in," the man whispered. "Life is full of choices these days, and yours are down to two. Either way, you're still going to die."

"Like hell," Jennifer hissed and jumped into the closet.

The bacon-cooking assailant stood at the doorway of the bedroom and watched his prey jump into the nothingness then disappear.

"Exactly." He turned around and headed for the kitchen.

CHAPTER NINE

Harlan stood at the edge of a great dry lake. The horizon disappeared inside a mirage. Behind him stood a mountain, brown and speckled with chaparral and small trees that looked too young to have seen much of the passage of time. The sky was covered with a gray sheet of clouds. They hung low and barely allowed sunlight to penetrate the curtain. He was alone, and the feelings that gripped him were more real than any dream he'd had before.

This time, Harlan felt, there was something to be said for paying attention.

Harlan looked out toward the lake bed with interest. There were no hidden memories that would have placed him here, no subconscious meaning outside of desolation. He had never actually seen a dry lake before other than the occasional picture on television or in a magazine, and then they were usually much smaller with mountains lining the banks. This was something new.

He took a step forward. The sound of the mud cracking under his weight made him nervous. There was no reason to go forward, but when he looked back at the mountainside behind him, he saw no reason to go back. He considered the option, however, and thought that if he continued on the lake bed, he might fall in. Those were the dreams he hated the most — falling.

Something pulled at him and let him know in no uncertain terms that he needed to cross this vast expanse of nothingness.

Harlan held his breath and cautiously tested the ground ahead of him.

Solid.

He took another step.

Suddenly, the mud collapsed. His right leg was trapped under the soil. He struggled to free himself, but found the harder he fought, the deeper he sank. His left leg bent awkwardly back as his arms pushed himself up on loose dirt. Fearing for his life, he let out a scream and then stopped.

Somehow he knew a man stood just off to his left, watching his every move. He turned his head to look.

The man stood rigidly and looked at Harlan, his black eyes sucking in all light around them.

Quietly, he pointed to the horizon.

Harlan looked in the direction he pointed. A mountain range was faintly visible through the mirage.

"Will it hurt?" Harlan asked. He turned back to the strange man and found him gone.

CHAPTER TEN

The gunmetal gray desk was cluttered: papers were thrown haphazardly in piles; files meant to be closed, stuffed in a desk drawer and cataloged mentally for further perusing, lay open, their contents spilling forth beyond the boundaries of yellowed folders into the ocean of papers. A large desk calendar, marked with notes, small doodles and a few coffee stains, was barely visible through the muck of paperwork. Amidst the hilltops and valleys of reports, forms and scribbled notes stood a small photo frame, its silver border highlighting a family of three. The glass was cracked, and the face of Stephen Casey behind the mother and son was split in two.

Casey stared at the picture frame in front of him, his mind swirling not with thoughts of anything past but of all the information he'd been given the night before by his strange visitor. There was nothing concrete, nothing new that could help him solve the murder of the Jane Doe in the desert, but it intrigued him nonetheless. There were those, the visitor had said, who would aspire to greatness but mean nothing in the grand scheme of things. And there were those who lived life on the edge of anonymity and despair and never knew the magical place they held in the "triad of life, Heaven, and Hell."

Casey thought of the words the man had said: *Ma abad rab*. He questioned the language at first—was it Arabic, some sort of Hebrew, a jumble of nonsense from the mind of a lunatic, or was it something more, something he needed to understand at the core, beyond linguistics?

Whatever those words meant, to Casey it said nothing.

Here was a man who professed to the knowledge of the murdered woman, yet made no further mention of her and offered no solid evidence not already known. The visitor finally left shortly before dawn, leaving Casey's mind a tangled and tired mess. If he wasn't so nagged by the strangeness of it all, he might have even dreamed the whole event

Casey looked down at his desk and pulled an ancient answering machine out from under a pile of papers. Voicemail be damned—the world could still use answering machines. He pressed the play button.

Ma abad rab. The words rolled around Casey's mind as he waited for the first message to start.

Apparently, the course of life, Heaven and Hell was changing and the woman in the desert was a part of it all. But cryptic talk and broad statements in a foreign tongue left little to grab.

The first message was from the M.E. Amanda's voice, heavy and sexually enticing, told a story of negative results to a routine analysis of the fingernail she found in the woman's chest. She'd sent the specimen to the lab for further DNA testing and probably wouldn't hear back for a week or so. Casey frowned at the news then thought to himself about how deserving this woman was for all of her hard work. She needed to be taken to dinner, a movie, and then to bed. He inwardly smiled at the latter thought then frowned at the idea of having to clean his apartment and wash his sheets for such an event.

The answering machine beeped twice, then once more. The romantic images of Amanda faded as Casey's supervisor's voice, in his thick Russian accent, rasped out a "to-do" list through the small speaker and ended curtly with: "Reports have suspense dates, jackass." Casey pressed the "next" button.

The third and fourth messages were hang-ups, a mainstay of the modern world. It seemed that, although people can surf the Internet from anywhere, watch five hundred channels of nonsense on the television, e-mail each other's cell phones, and even receive calls from Hong Kong while trudging through the deserts of central Australia, many people just didn't like to talk to machines. A few would attempt it, sounding mechanical themselves as if the machine cared about voice quality or tone. Most would simply listen to the introductory "I'm not here" blurb then hang up as soon as the machine asked for a response. Casey found it ironic that technology of the mid-twentieth century could be so unsettling to people of the twenty-first. That was one reason he kept the answering machine around.

Probably wasn't important, anyway.

The machine beeped twice, then once more. "This message is for Detective Stephen Casey. Please call Detective Michael Taylor, Coconino County." The voice on the machine spit out a phone number then beeped three times. Casey wrote down the number on the desk calendar before he forgot it. He tapped his pen on the desk three times, looked back at the picture frame in front of him, and took a deep breath. He hoped things were going to start coming together.

Ma abad rab.

A few rings later, a deep thundering voice answered. "Yeah?"

Casey regarded the voice as irritating and decided that his first impression was poor. *This better be important*, he thought. "Detective Taylor? This is Detective Casey, Maricopa County. You called?"

"Yes. About ten minutes ago. You city folk are quick. And on a Sunday, no less. Thanks for getting back to me."

Casey removed all first impressions of the man on the other end of the phone line. Any compliment would do. "No problem. What can I do for you?"

"A body was found up here on the Rim that looks to have the same *modus operandi* as one found north of Phoenix. I talked to your supervisor this morning and he said you were working on it. That correct?"

"Yes, but how did you know it was the same? We never released any detailed information to the press."

"Anonymous tip left last night. Guy walks into the office,

lays a yellow sticky note down on the front desk that said something about a pair of hearts. We figured one was in Phoenix, the other out here."

Casey swallowed.

"Also, there's a search being conducted based on a missing person's report submitted yesterday. Seems the victim was with someone else at the time—a seventeen-year-old female from your neck of the woods."

"You know who the victim is?"

"The head of the victim was beaten to mush, but the killer apparently saw no need to take the kid's wallet. Hold on a minute."

Casey sat listening to the rustle of papers through the phone. His visitor had turned out to be a poor lead, but this was something. Too bad the coroner's office couldn't determine anything tangible.

"Here we go," Taylor said. "Jonathan Richards. Age sixteen. Brown hair, brown eyes. His car was registered to his father, Preston Richards of 4356 East Mariposa, Phoenix. According to a conversation with the father, Jonathan went off to pick up his girlfriend on Friday night. He wasn't heard from since."

"And the girlfriend's name?"

"Well, the father had no idea who his son was dating, but there was a missing persons report submitted yesterday that matched the time and place. A Jennifer Reese ran away from home on Friday with her boyfriend. Apparently she lied to her parents about going off with friends, so the parents automatically suspected she left with her boyfriend. We can't find the girl, just her teddy bear in the front seat of the car. I was wondering if you found anything that might help us."

Casey sat silent for a moment, running the events through his mind. Two dead bodies, same method of execution. If he told Taylor about the visitation he had, it might help matters or confuse them. Of course, this assumed Casey hadn't dreamed any of it. *Plus*, Casey thought, *what information did I really get from the guy?*

Taylor coughed on the phone once. "Are you still there?"

"Yeah. Sorry. We found a fingernail inside the chest of the woman," Casey said. "The coroner's office sent it off for further analysis, but other than that, there isn't much to tell you."

"A fingernail, huh? Well, that makes two."

THE OUTSIDE of the house looked unkempt, disorderly, and almost too shabby for the neighborhood surrounding it. Nonetheless, it was the same design as the others, and from all other outward appearances, this family was normal. There were two cars in the garage and a basketball hoop bolted above the driveway. Inside the house, Casey imagined that chaos reigned like a mirror of the yard. A daughter was missing, a mother was in hysterics, a son was confused and a father was frustrated with all of it. Casey certainly would be.

He knocked on the door and stepped back. He was never one to call distressed parents. He was a father himself. There was a place for the telephone and an equal and sometimes more powerful place for face-to-face contact. But he hadn't dressed for the part when he woke up in the morning, and as he'd sat at his desk getting things together to talk to the father of the missing girl, he thought maybe his typical canvas pants and button-down shirt was too indicative of the stereotypical police detective out for justice. Before he left, he put on a tie. And now, standing at the threshold of Counseling Techniques 101, he felt the knot of the tie tighten against the growing lump in his throat.

Harlan Reese slowly opened the door. He looked tired, and Casey doubted sleep was a luxury he could afford. It looked to him like Harlan's credit card of life was over its limit and he was left with what he had. He was unshaven, his shirt was stained with coffee, and his hair was a tangled mess. Harlan didn't exactly fit the profile of the schoolteacher Casey envisioned in the car.

Casey doubted Harlan had been crying, but the lost father was obviously distressed.

"Yes?" Harlan said. He squinted at the sun shining brightly behind Casey.

"Mr. Reese? I'm Detective Stephen Casey, Maricopa County. Can we talk?"

Harlan looked down at his feet, a hole in one sock revealing his big toe. "I don't have any other leads, detective. I told the police everything I could."

"Yes, sir. I realize that," Casey said. "However, that's a department I don't work in. I'm with homicide."

Harlan looked up at Casey. "Homicide? Is Jennifer... I mean..."

"No, Mr. Reese. She's just missing as far as we know. Can we sit and talk? I have a few questions to ask you about her boyfriend."

Harlan appeared to relax a little as he opened the door to let Casey in. "My w— Jennifer's mother is asleep upstairs. She took some pills this morning to calm her nerves. We can talk in the kitchen."

"You're not married?"

"No. We divorced a few months ago, but I can't leave her like this." He nodded his head toward a recliner. "I'm back to sleeping there."

The kitchen table looked like Casey's desk without the organization. There were dishes piled high with uneaten slices of pizza, a few worn boxes and papers strewn all over. In the middle of it all was a map of Arizona, with roads marked in pink and yellow highlighter, all leading from Phoenix to points north and south, east and west. Casey couldn't tell if there was a rhyme or reason to the roads highlighted.

"Going somewhere, Mr. Reese?" Casey asked, inwardly knowing what the answer would be. He thought for a moment what it would be like if his son was missing. Would he set out on his own, or would he sit idly at home waiting for the phone to ring or a knock at the door?

"I was taking a look at where she might have gone camping this weekend." Harlan sighed. "This is her map, actually. I found it in her backpack last night and I've been trying to piece together everything I know."

"And what *do* you know?"

"Not much. There's this map. She said she wanted to go

camping with friends this weekend up on the Mogollon Rim, but I voted against it. I guess she decided to veto that and set off on her own."

"With friends?"

"No. We called her best friend Myra's parents. She was camping but not with my daughter. She called from a cell phone somewhere near Show Low."

"So, you think she ran off with her boyfriend. Do you think she did this to spite you, or *in* spite of you?"

"*In* spite. I found a note from her boyfriend in her backpack. On it he wrote: 'They won't even know we're gone.'"

"What was his name?"

"Jonathan. Jonathan Richards." Harlan stood and poured himself some coffee. "You want some coffee, detective? I made it last night, so it might need to be heated up."

"No thanks."

"So what does Homicide have to do with my daughter and Jonathan?" Harlan sat back down and looked at Casey. His eyes were heavy and red.

"Well..." Casey tried not to sound abrupt. He looked away from Harlan and instinctively rubbed his chin. "Jonathan was found last night on the Mogollon Rim. The Coconino County Sheriff's Department think your daughter might be nearby and are right now searching the forest."

Harlan's eyes lit up. He looked down at the map on the table and followed his finger on a highlighted road from Phoenix, to the north, up the side of the Mogollon Rim, then west along a forest service road that paralleled the cliff side.

"Damn it! I've looked at this route a number of times. I even thought about driving it last night."

"Why didn't you?"

Harlan nodded toward the stairs. "I don't think Celine can be trusted right now. She's a bit out of it. Tommy—my son—can handle himself, but I don't know about her."

Harlan tapped the map with his finger. "Jennifer said she wanted to camp along the Rim with friends. The only thing that kept me wondering was that call to her friend's parents.

They had gone camping near Show Low, not the Rim like they told their parents. So, if Jennifer *had* run away with Jonathan, I couldn't imagine it would be in the same place she *told* us she was going."

"Kids have strange logic, sometimes."

Harlan looked up and furled his eyebrows. "How come they never called me?"

"I can't speak for other agencies, Mr. Reese, but let me ask you a question. How well did you know Jonathan?"

"Just rumors, really. I never had him as a student." Harlan looked down like he was in thought. "I think he was considered a campus bully, a little too poor for most of the students' tastes." He looked at the map once more. "Where's Jennifer?"

"I don't know. Was there any indication that Jonathan might have enemies?"

"I have no idea. He was the bully, I said. He probably had a hundred people who didn't like him." He pounded his fist on the map, obviously exasperated by all of the questioning. *"Where's my daughter, detective?"*

"Mr. Reese. I assure you the Coconino County Sheriff's Department is doing their best to locate your daughter. She'll be found. It will just take time." Casey winced at his poorly chosen clichés. What would he do? Hell, he would be out there right now, looking for himself, not sitting at a kitchen table listening to some homicide detective ask questions about someone else.

Harlan sat quietly and stared at the map. He traced the route once more with his finger then looked up. "She's just going to have to adjust."

"Sir?"

Harlan sighed. "Detective? What would you do?"

Silence descended on the room, and Casey felt the weight of Harlan's question press down on his shoulders. He knew what he would do, he just didn't know if he wanted to share that with someone else. If he acknowledged he would be out there right now, and Harlan was to end up dead like Jonathan or the Jane Doe, then he would feel responsible for the death of an innocent man at the hands of a maniac. If he cautioned Harlan about going out on his own, and Jennifer was found three days later with her heart removed and her head crushed, Casey felt he wouldn't have done his job correctly and enlisted all of the help that was possible.

Casey's mind drifted back the visitor at his door. What if Harlan were a part of all of this? What about Jennifer? What if Jonathan or the Jane Doe were murdered because they were in the way?

Ma abad rab.

Casey looked at the map in front of him, then up at Harlan. He frowned. "I don't know why you're still here, Mr. Reese. Jonathan's car was found here." He pointed to a spot on the Mogollon Rim. "Now, I don't know how involved the search and rescue teams are going to let you be, so I can't promise anything, but I will tell you this: don't act like an idiot when you get there, and please change your shirt."

Harlan smiled weakly and stood. He reached a hand across the table as a tear fell from his eye.

Casey grabbed his hand and covered it with the other. He looked at Harlan and tried to place himself in his shoes. "What are you waiting for?"

CHAPTER ELEVEN

"And just where do you think you're going?"

Harlan said nothing in response to Celine's query. He stood at the door and stared at her.

Celine sat up in bed. The sun shone through the curtains, and Harlan noticed how tired her face looked. Her hair pulled tight against her scalp didn't help the image she portrayed. He knew she couldn't sleep the past few nights, and who could blame her? Her daughter was missing, and even though he knew she envisioned the worst, he wished her heart would at least hold out for the best. His did.

Harlan didn't tell her of the visit by the Maricopa County Sheriff's Office, or the news that Jonathan's car was found where his body was mutilated. That information didn't need to cross her ears.

Celine grabbed a pack of Camels off the nightstand and lit a cigarette.

Harlan wrinkled his nose in disgust. "Can you handle Tommy?"

"I don't like this, you know," she said, blowing out smoke. "You can't do anything yourself."

Harlan looked down for a moment. The curtains had cast a design on her forehead, making her look even less appealing than she had when she woke up. "You don't know that. And why are you smoking in the house? I thought we talked about that."

Celine chuckled and took another drag. "Are you going to tell me where you're going?"

"I'm going to look for her," he said. "I can't stand waiting around."

"You don't even know where to start."

"Doesn't matter. I have an idea, and that's good enough. If she's with Jonathan camping, I'm going to bring her home."

"How can you be certain where she went?"

"I can't, but I'm not about to sit on my butt and smoke cigarettes, watch TV and wait by the phone for a call I don't want to hear." Harlan hefted a knapsack over his shoulder. "How can you just wait, Celine?"

Celine pushed the remainder of her cigarette around in the ashtray. She set it back on the nightstand, and looked up at Harlan. "What makes you think I can't handle this?"

"Look at you. You haven't showered in two days, you haven't really even gotten out of bed, and you look like crap. I'm missing my daughter, Celine. I'm going to find her."

Celine's face grew red as her temper flared. "How *dare* you say I don't care!"

"I didn't say that."

"You inferred it, and that's enough. I'll have you know that this is tearing me apart, but I'm willing to think she's just out camping and having a good time with Jonathan. I'm holding out that she'll be home tomorrow, probably crying about this or that."

Harlan wished that were true. He thought for a second about telling her Jonathan was dead, but decided against it, pushing the thought out of his mind. If she could remain hopeful, she would be all the better for it. "I'm not that willing."

Harlan turned to leave. Tommy stood at the bedroom door.

"You going out to find her?" he asked, his gaze not really set on either of them.

"That's the plan," Harlan sighed. "Don't worry, Tommy. I'll bring her back home."

"That's not what I'm worried about, Dad." He looked up at his father. "I'm worried that *you* won't come home."

Harlan felt his stomach twist in knots. This was something

he wouldn't wish upon anyone. Sure, Celine had pills to keep her calm, but what did Tommy have? What did a little boy of seven think about at times like this? Harlan tried to imagine what ran through his son's mind, but couldn't grasp onto anything that sounded realistic. He looked at Tommy and forced a weak smile.

"Love you."

Tommy turned toward his room. "Love you, too, Dad."

As Harlan's car sped toward the mountains, the sun shone brightly through the sunroof. He guided the car in and out of traffic, keeping one eye peeled for cops and the other on the road. At seventy-five, the twists and turns of the lower foothills were manageable, but any faster and he wouldn't have enough time to stop should he need to. Bugs struck the windshield and exploded in vibrant yellows and reds, a thorax or wing or antenna holding on for the ride as long as the wind would allow it.

Harlan tried hard not to dwell on the pessimistic, and instead focused on a plan of attack. If the search team would let him, he wanted to become an active member and help out wherever necessary. If they preferred he stay behind in the operation's tent, he imagined he would find a way to search for her himself. Either way, he wanted to do some footwork.

The thought of losing his daughter struck him hard. He felt helpless, tied up in a cage while he watched his oldest child die at the hands of a serial killer or a crazy dairy farmer. His thoughts began to tangent off one another, starting with the image of his family. They had been together a few days ago, and then this. From there came the thought of loss, and bouncing off that, the thought of Marie. He tried to remember the last conversation they had face to face, but came up short. He could, however, remember the way she looked, staring at him with her brown eyes, dark blond hair framing her face. He could remember the blue silk shirt with moons and stars for buttons, and the black skirt that hung just above her knees. She was a paradigm of beauty, a site to behold—intelligent, witty, thoughtful and caring. She was everything that Harlan wanted, and nothing that he had.

His stomach turned sharply as he realized what he was thinking was a far cry from where his mind *should* be focused—his daughter. She was missing, and he might as well be cursed for thinking of anything else.

As if mirroring his darkening thoughts, the sun disappeared behind a curtain of clouds.

YELLOW TAPE marked the end of the trip for Harlan. The forest road Jennifer's map directed him to led to a bend in the road where five uniformed sheriff's deputies stood around smoking cigarettes and talking amongst themselves. With either unsure intentions or no intentions at all, they looked like tall ducks wrapped up in yellow rain slickers, defending their skinny bodies against the onslaught of rain that fell from a darkened sky. Harlan pulled his car to the side of the road about thirty feet from the tape and shut the engine off. Through the windshield—though distorted by the hard rain—he saw Jonathan's car with the driver's side door wide open. One of the tall ducks looked up at the car and walked toward the tape.

Harlan stepped out into a puddle of water a few inches deep. He felt unprepared and cursed at himself silently for neglecting to pack a jacket or umbrella. The rain soaked into the fabric of his hat, shirt and jeans. He wrapped his arms around his body and walked to the yellow line where Deputy Duck waited.

"This is a restricted area, sir," the deputy quacked, raising his voice slightly in response the rain. "You need to turn around and head back to the highway."

Harlan looked past the man and tried to get a better view. The body of Jonathan must have been removed some time ago, but little red evidence flags were stuck in the mud in a few locations. Thankfully, the absence of Jennifer's body made his stomach feel slightly better, but the thought she might end up a victim like Jonathan screamed across his mind and echoed in dark places not visited very often. Shaking the thought off, he brought his gaze back to the deputy.

"My name is Harlan Reese." He wiped rain from his face. "My daughter was supposed to be with the victim. That's his car."

The deputy quickly changed his posture. He raised the yellow tape and motioned for Harlan to come with him. "I think you'll want to talk to the lead."

"Thank you." Harlan ducked under the tape and wrapped his arms around his body a little tighter. The rain had thoroughly soaked through his shirt and hat and was finishing off with his jeans. The deputy led him around the opposite side of the car. As they passed the open door, Harlan looked in and saw Tolliloqui lying on the floor of the passenger side. She was here, and Harlan could only pray she was safe.

A small government issue tent provided a little protection from the rain as long as no one stood too close to the edge. Harlan quickly stepped out from the elements and took his hat off. There was a small card table set up in the center with Geological Survey quadrangle maps laid out, small stickpins poking up like tiny, colorful trees. Aside from the table, there was little else save a radio and a rather rotund man who sat on a metal folding chair and stared out at the forest beyond.

"Sir," the deputy said, tapping the man on the shoulder. "This is Harlan— What did you say your last name was?"

"Reese," Harlan answered while glancing over the map.

"Reese, right. He says he's the father of the person we're looking for."

The rotund man stood quickly and turned around. He was a little older than the others, his face pitted from what might have been the scars of a severe case of childhood acne. Sitting atop his mouth like a sleeping porcupine, a mustache of red, blonde and gray hair breathed in and out on its own. Just above the nose, dangling precipitously, sat a pair of tiny round glasses. He took off his gloves and shook Harlan's hand.

"Taylor," he said, saving the introductory smile for another day. "Sorry you had to come up here, but I think your daughter's going to be alright."

"I take it you haven't found her." Harlan took his hand back and wrapped himself up once more. A slight breeze through the tent made his wet clothes cold and more uncomfortable than if he stood out in the rain with his arms wide open.

"No, but I have a team of capable deputies and some dogs out looking right now. She couldn't have gone far." He looked down at the map. "South of here is the Rim, so we assume she hasn't headed that way. No one on the highway has seen her, either. Are you familiar with this area, Mr. Reese?"

"Very. We used to come camping up here about twice a year. There's a burnt out section of the forest about a mile to the east that kept our interest for a few years. I think that's where they were headed."

"So you knew she was coming up here?"

"No. I mean, she wanted to — with friends of hers — but I told her no. What happened?"

"You know about as much as we do. I can't tell you more than that."

"And Jonathan? What happened to him?"

Taylor looked over at the deputy who stopped just short of pouring a cup of coffee and returned the glance.

"Would you like a jacket, Mr. Reese?" Taylor asked. "You look cold."

"Yes, please. I really didn't expect this rain." Harlan looked down once again at the map and studied the stickpins as Taylor turned to find a jacket. He had some experience reading topographical maps such as this, and he was keenly aware of where he was and what was around him. The forest road at the tent was about a quarter of a mile to the north of the Rim, following a shallow valley. Directly to the south of the road, the elevation changed twice before running into the cliff face. To the north, more shallow valleys ran north-south, indicative of the drainage pattern of streams and creeks in that part of Arizona. To the west, the road curved south again, nearing the edge of the Rim before a sharp hairpin turn back to the north. The dead forest that had become a traditional camping spot was just past the hairpin and over one more hill.

The stickpins that dotted the map were laid out primarily to the north and followed each of the shallow valleys. Only one pin on the south side of the road gave some indication they might have found a clue or followed a dog's trail in that direction. But with the lack of any other pins, it was apparent

Taylor hadn't held out any hope of finding Jennifer there.

Taylor returned with a yellow jacket.

"I don't know what you can do to help, Mr. Reese, but anything you can tell us that might aid the search would be appreciated."

"I'd like to go out searching, if you don't mind," Harlan put the jacket on, acutely aware it was a few sizes too big.

Taylor ran his hand across his face. "That's not exactly an option, sir. I have to tell you, although I appreciate the offer, there are more qualified people doing the job." He quickly glanced up at Jonathan's car. "Plus, you might find something you don't like."

Harlan pulled his eyes from the map and looked at Taylor. "My daughter is a fighter. If she needed to run for some reason..." His words faded off into thought. *What if she was dead? No! Stop thinking about things like that!*

"At least let me look over here." Harlan pointed to an area south of the road, bordered on all four sides by small hills. "I can't just sit around here and do nothing."

Harlan looked at Taylor and tried to see past the eyes and into the soul. He wondered for a moment if he could possibly impart what it was like to wear his shoes for a day. He'd lost a daughter who was last seen with someone who'd been killed, and even though Harlan knew search and rescue operations frequently turned sour, this was different. It was *his* daughter, for crying out loud.

Taylor blinked. "Maybe there is something."

"Anything."

"Alan!" Taylor shouted to a deputy standing not too far outside the tent. "Take Mr. Reese and look over there." He pointed to the south. "I know you've looked it over once, but I guess another set of eyes couldn't hurt."

A tall skinny deputy walked over to the tent and stepped inside. "Where are we looking, sir?"

"To the south. Check out the cabin you found. See if Mr. Reese can find anything you might have missed."

"Not much to miss, sir. Except for some dirty dishes and a pan full of bacon grease, the place is deserted." He looked over at Harlan and smiled. "But maybe you can find something new. Who knows? Maybe you'll find a gateway to Hell in there."

"You're an idiot, Alan." Taylor handed Harlan a flashlight. "Good luck, and don't worry. Your daughter is around here someplace, and we'll find her."

Harlan managed a weak smile and headed off into the rain toward the cabin.

CHAPTER TWELVE

The night air was calm, but a stale vestige of day still lingered and wrapped the city with its moist, unwanted love. The streets, uncomfortably deserted at such an early hour, sat silent. Mirages of heat emanated from the black asphalt, releasing the warmth of the sun's beating heart. In a house on one of those streets, all the lights were on, but not for want of vision, or want of comfort. Perhaps they were on to scare the monsters away, or allow for a good read at bedside. Perhaps they were on for fear of standing in the dark, waiting for the ghosts of the past to descend upon the living. Whatever the reason, virtually every light in the Reese's house burned bright in a Phoenix suburb.

Tommy had long since retired for the night, as much a wreck as the rest of the family. His sister had not been heard from in three days, and now his father was gone, presumably searching. The world crashed down around his head, destroying all hopes of understanding present events. He knew his sister had gone, he knew his father had left the house, and he knew his mother was downstairs, crying incessantly, murmuring to herself over and over, "Not again. Not again." What that meant to Tommy was as mysterious as what was happening to his family.

To Celine, lying on the floor, the meaning was clear; she felt her heart torn into pieces once again, ripped away and left to rot in front of her. Paramount was a second child, the second daughter stolen from her by some god that knew no love or some demon bent on tearing down her walls.

Tantamount to that, however, there was a marriage that had faltered from day one. Each heart knew there were irreconcilable differences, but they had committed to making the family function as effortlessly as possible. In the last few years, however, the effort had become too much. The advent of the teenager and the discovery of Harlan's "innocent" communication with a lover from his past had dug away at the foundation of the very elements she used to fill that void caused by her failures of the past.

He had told her that maybe they simply "ran out of words" to say to each other.

She knew that was a lie if she ever heard one. You don't run out of words, the words run out of meaning. If they had only spoken fifteen words over and over to each other—if the *meaning* never changed—souls would mate each and every time. It was when the meaning ran out—when the silence descended upon their hapless conversation—that the souls became separated and their demise began.

But what was Harlan? Celine thought. She stared at the ceiling fan. It spun slowly with the rhythm of her heart. The tangles of her unwashed hair draped across her cheek, trapped in a tear that had fallen seconds before. *What was Harlan? Was he the answer to my emptiness?* She couldn't remember the reasons she had married him. The memory was blurred by the pain of the moment, but she knew it wasn't for love. Perhaps it was to rebound from the loss of her first daughter and subsequent divorce from the cheating bastard of a husband she originally had. Perhaps she saw in him the answer that any warm-blooded, deeply depressed mammal must see: have another baby, start new.

Perhaps.

Perhaps I should stop finding husbands who are going to cheat on me.

She never told Harlan about Justine, and she liked it that way. Neither he, Jennifer nor Tommy ever needed to know what the pain was like. In truth, she never wanted Harlan to think there was more to her life than him. It hadn't mattered if she wanted to tell him anyway; when she felt it was necessary to bring it up, the words wouldn't come out of their hiding place. It was a chapter that ended nineteen years ago, and there never seemed to be a reason to add it to the family's life. Not yet, anyway.

The night wore on. Celine studied the ceiling fan more and more, intent on trying to meld the relentless spin of the fan blades into some meaning in her misdirected life. It wasn't working.

If only I could get some sleep, she reasoned, *the pain might leave me alone*. The more the night wore on, the more the memories assaulted her from left and right. Her eyes welled up with tears, dried, then welled up again. In the end, she decided it must be the waiting: waiting for a call from her daughter, waiting for a call from Harlan, waiting for *anything* that might show the way to closure. Even a knock at the door by some police officer with bad news would at least give her something to grasp.

And then what? What if Harlan was dead and Jennifer was lost to the world forever, just like Justine? What if? Celine frowned at the thought then reminded herself that *"what ifs"* are simply made of sand, subject to the whim of the wind and the crashing of the waves. It was *"what is"* that was concrete, set to endure the pounding surf, the howling winds, the driving rain—all the elements nature and life could throw at it. *"What is"* was a stone that Celine didn't want to carry any longer.

Her mind turned back to the day when she walked into Justine's room and found her missing. The window was broken and revealed the red sky and the dust blowing from all directions. A sudden gasp from her chest and emptiness rushed in to take over her soul. It was a parent's worst nightmare, alive in her bedroom. She recalled looking at the shattered glass on the floor, the blinds torn from the rail lying in a tangled pile.

More tears fell and the ceiling fan seemed lower. She wanted all of this to end. The pain of losing one daughter was too much for anyone to handle, and now she was burdened with the pain of losing two daughters and a husband.

What next?

Celine stood and straightened her blouse. There was nothing more that staring at the fan could do for her. She had to escape, to get some sleep, to visit a far off land where problems were behind her and she could be happy — if only for a brief moment.

She walked to the kitchen and grabbed some sleeping pills from the medicine cabinet. They were about two years old, but who cared? If they still worked the way they said they would when she was prescribed them, soon she could escape into her subconscious and let the body rest.

Four pills and a cup of water later, Celine was asleep on the couch.

DESERT DUNES.

Except for the distant horizon, where jagged mountains stabbed into the sky, there was nothing but sand, sand, and more sand. Celine stood on the crest of a large dune. The wind softly kissed the top. It pulled a layer of sand off grain by grain and deposited it a few feet away. Above her — above the vast expanse of almost nothingness — the sky undulated dark gray, clouds mutating from shape to shape in slow motion. The air was cool — that much was a relief — but the sheer emptiness of her surroundings put Celine in an uncomfortable position. She thought she must be dreaming, but her lack of experience as to this particular dream worried her. There was virtually no reference point for her mind.

She looked around, past the dunes to the mountains in the distance. They beckoned to her, called her name in whispers on the wind and pleaded she go forward. She looked to her left. The sand dunes stretched on for miles and finally merged with the dismal sky on the horizon. To her right there was nothing but the same. There was no reference point, not even a blade of grass or a yucca plant to offer some change. A footprint would be something, even if it were her own. If this was how the next few hours of her dream world was going to be, she might as well have a seat and wait it out. She sighed, and sat in the sand.

At least it was escape.

Just as she stretched out her legs, a casual glance to the left revealed something she didn't see the first time. In a trough between two dunes, the drifting sand slowly uncovered a small object. Celine stood and walked down the side of the dune, slipping every now and again as the loose ground gave way to her weight. After falling twice, and sliding the rest of the way down the side, she looked over at a small, stuffed bear, half buried in the sand.

Carefully, she picked it up and turned it over. The fur was matted, mostly in the center. An ugly brown leopard pattern dotted the outside, the eyes two simple buttons. Her heart skipped a beat and a breath of air escaped her lungs as she held the bear—the very bear Justine always slept with—in her trembling hands.

"Justine! Baby, where are you?"

In the nineteen years since losing her, Celine had never dreamed of Justine so vividly. She had once seen her talking to a man, but the image lasted only a second before she woke up in a sweat, clutching her breast and breathing hard. This was different, though. The colors of the dream were so vivid, the sand so lifelike under her feet, the feel of the air so cool against her skin, and the simple memory of a simple bear was almost too much to take.

Celine ran up the side of the next dune, hoping to find something that might lead her to Justine. Her feet dug into the sand, but the effort needed to climb the dune at a trot was nothing to the surge of adrenaline rushing through her veins. She reached the top, still clutching the bear, and called out her name one more time. "Justine? Where are you? Mommy's here!"

The wind kissed Celine's legs as she turned around. Her eyes scanned every inch of her environment. She called out her name two more times then ran across the crest of the dune looking for a better view of the landscape.

There was nothing save the kiss of the wind, the expanse of the sand, and the dark, undulating sky above.

Celine stopped and looked down at the bear one more

time. She *had* to be there. No dream she could remember had ever been so full of detail and no memory could ever have reached the pinnacle of her mind like this one. The touch of the bear was too real. Justine just *had* to be there.

As quickly as it had come, the feeling of elation turned into the dread of losing yet another chance.

"Mommy?" The voice was soft, mixed with the wind. It wavered even with the sheer power of the word. It struck Celine like a brick, flooring her emotions and leaving her body in shock. She turned around slowly, not wanting to miss a thing, coveting every moment of what she had wished for over nineteen years.

Justine stood behind Celine still wearing the very pink nightgown Celine had dressed her in the night she disappeared.

Celine's eyes welled up with tears and a wide smile broke out across her face. Instinctively, she held her arms out and ran to Justine, picking her up and wrapping every last bit of love she had around the little girl. Celine cried and closed her eyes tightly, wishing the dream was real, but accepting that this was good enough for now. Celine held the embrace for what seemed an eternity. To let go meant recognizing the end that must inevitably come. She just couldn't allow herself to feel that way. Not now.

"Mommy?" Justine softly said, her head resting on Celine's shoulder. "Why didn't you come?"

The words, so simple from the mouth of a four-year-old, sliced through Celine like a knife. Ragged edges tore the flesh from her soul. She relaxed her grip a little and brought her daughter forward to see. The last memory Celine had, as Justine lay sleeping, played through her mind as she gazed into the little girl's green eyes. There was a love inside that was remarkably clear, almost adult, and sent warmth searing through Celine's body. "I tried to find you, baby. Honestly, I did. Mommy loves her little princess."

"Why didn't you come when I called?"

Celine looked deeper into Justine's eyes. *When I called?* She didn't remember ever hearing her daughter call her name.

There was only the sound of breaking glass.

"Mommy?" Justine looked past her mother toward the horizon.

"Yes, baby?"

"Can you make the Angry Man stop yelling at me?"

CELINE WOKE up in her house. She clutched her breast as her heart raced at what seemed like a thousand beats per second. She struggled for a moment to open her eyes against the lights she had left on, and then focused on the coffee table. Her hands trembled. Sweat beaded across her forehead. Her temples pounded, the flow of blood so strong that she tried not to scream at the pain. In her mouth a sickness brewed, the salty taste of bile gathering for the final ride out of the stomach. She raced to the bathroom and threw up.

She wiped her mouth with a towel and looked in the mirror, hating everything she saw. There was a woman just turned forty, bags black under her eyes, hair a tangled mess that resembled the snakes of Medusa.

The memory of the dream suddenly hit her hard.

Can you make the Angry Man stop yelling at me?

CHAPTER THIRTEEN

"Some Good Samaritan you are," David said. He hopped down from the windowsill and stood in front of Marie. "Don't even offer to take me home."

Marie dropped her keys and gasped for air. There was the Naked Man again, hairless skin stretched across his chest and stomach. His eyes were black, and the more Marie stared, the more they looked like deep, hollow sockets. He grinned and his teeth shone white in the dim glow of the living room lights. His cheeks were raised high against his bones. The hair was pulled back and tied, and his fingernails looked long and stretched out. "Have I lost a little weight since we last met?"

Marie had no answer. She simply stared at those eyes. Now those blue eyes were gone, and in their place were empty sockets that stared back. It was the same look he had on the road. She took a step back, recoiling at the hideous sight in front of her.

Jacob stepped into the house behind Marie, and seeing David across the room, he quickly jumped out in front of her. The room changed for an instant. The light of the Alaska sun turned red, bathing the occupants of the room in an evil glow. Jacob bared his teeth and took a defensive stance.

"Don't get in my way, Jacob!" David shouted. His brow curled downward over his eye sockets. "You know this isn't a game anymore."

Jacob turned back to Marie and whispered for her to take the keys and run. She backed up a step more, fearing not only the hideousness in front of her, but the anger that swelled inside Jacob like an ember set to kindling. Her mind swirled with thoughts, but not one of them could tell her what she should do.

"*Pick up the keys and go!*" Jacob's command hovered in the air around Marie's ears for a second, escalating the sudden, overwhelming feeling of dread. "I'll take care of him."

"Where are you going to go, Marie?" asked David, taking a step toward the two. "You can't leave the party yet. We have some issues to discuss."

"Leave her alone." Jacob held his hands out in front of him, the fingers poised to grab something.

"This isn't with you, Jacob. This is between the little hit-and-run girl and me. Now, please, get out of my way."

David leapt forward and flew through the air. He raised his arms out and hit Jacob in the chest, sending the two of them into Marie then over in a tangle on the floor. Marie fell back. She reached over, grabbed her keys and backed away from the two.

Jacob righted himself and stood. David, still lying on the floor, reached out and grabbed Jacob's foot, digging his nails into the flesh. Blood trickled down the side of Jacob's pants. He grabbed his ankle and grimaced.

David jumped up and ran at Marie. Screaming, she turned and ran toward the kitchen, hoping to get out of the house through the back door. She dodged the kitchen table as she leapt for the doorknob. David pulled her down onto the floor and wrapped his fingers around her neck.

"Don't be so feisty, Marie," said David, his voice coarse and decidedly different from before. "I know you don't understand what's going on, but believe me, it's much bigger than you think." David let loose one hand from around her neck and reached a fingernail under Marie's blouse, popping a button off.

Marie struggled to get free, pulling on David's hand. She closed her eyes and tried to gather as much strength as possible, shifting her weight back and forth, fruitlessly trying to wiggle out from underneath David.

David popped another button on her blouse. "You see, my

little Marie, you are one of the special people. Did Jacob get a chance to tell you that?" He popped another button, reached his hand inside her blouse and grabbed her right breast. "My, my, my. What a work I missed."

Marie increased her struggle to get free. "*What do you want?*" she cried. She moved her free hand from her neck and grabbed the hand that groped at her chest.

David squeezed her breast harder and smiled. "It's not what *I* want, Marie. That's about two and half feet south of where my hand is right now. It's a game we play to win, and not because we want to." He squeezed once more. A scream of pain erupted from Marie as his fingernails dug deeper.

Blood and flesh exploded onto Marie from above as David's chest was ripped open from behind. David reared his head back and screamed, the sound almost unbearable to Marie. Jacob stood over David, his arm almost extending through David's chest. Marie screamed again and tried to back away from underneath the dying beast on top of her. Kicking as quickly as she could, she broke loose and righted herself. David's limp body fell to the floor, his heart in Jacob's right hand.

Jacob looked up at Marie. His eyes had faded to black, much like David's, and blood covered his arms. He fell to the floor next to David's lifeless body and dropped the heart like a piece of trash.

Marie's chest heaved with her labored breath. One hand clutched her blouse together, while the other reached behind her for some support. A spot of bright red appeared above her wound. She looked down at David and watched a pool of blood grow larger and surround his body. In the center of the pool, Jacob sat, breathing heavily.

"I suppose you're wondering—"

"*What the hell was that?*" Marie pointed to David. "What the hell is going on here?"

"I can explain."

"You can take your explanation and shove it up your ass, Jacob. You just ripped out his heart. You said you were here to protect me, but I don't need to see *this*."

"You're going to see more, if you don't listen."

"No. No. No, I don't. I've been through *way* too much to listen to any more crap." Marie picked up her keys and ran for the door. "I'm leaving."

"Marie?" Jacob called out to her. "There's a little more to this than just a dead man in your kitchen."

Marie stopped at the door and turned around. A brief manic chuckle escaped her as she looked at Jacob sitting on the floor in a pool of blood. She wiped her face with the back of her hand and sniffed back another flood of tears.

"Really?" She ran out the door, got into her car and drove away.

THE SUN was setting when she hit the highway that led to the road where she found David. She rolled down the window and stared into the distance. The night air, though humid, was more refreshing than Marie could have imagined. She had been crying for some time. She didn't know what happened or where to go. The last two days were slowly trying to coalesce into some form of reason. She was frightened when she almost ran over David, but his eyes had calmed her. At first she perceived him as different, not evil. At least she *thought* he wasn't evil. Next, revelations at dinner. Revelations that her only real Alaskan friend had actually *guided* her to this place. Now it was apparent the two knew each other. How was all of this related to *her*?

Marie pulled the car to the right and onto the gravel road she had traveled a hundred times before. The headlights bounced up and down with every bump she took, but it wasn't long before she found the place where she'd nearly ran over David. She could remember the trees and the puddle, still there but not quite as big. She slowly drifted to the side of the road and parked. She didn't know why she was here, but she stepped out, anyway.

As she walked toward the puddle, Marie sensed something wasn't right about this place. At first, she couldn't tell what, but as she stopped at the edge of the water, she began to feel like something was missing, out of place. Sure, there were the trees, there was the gravel on the road, there was a big, vast openness around her. Everything looked like it had the night she'd meet David. But even then...

Marie looked down at the puddle of water and stopped herself from thinking of anything else. *This* was the problem. She bent down and looked closely for her reflection, fully expecting to see her haggard face.

There was nothing. No reflection, not even so much as a ripple. The puddle wasn't a puddle and it wasn't even a hole. The idea tugged at her curiosity. How was this even possible?

Holding her breath, she reached down toward the nothingness.

CHAPTER FOURTEEN

On a hillside north of Phoenix, Stephen Casey stood looking at the image of a woman with her head beaten into the ground and her heart ripped out of her chest with forceful vengeance. He had become more and more confused and realized that perhaps the best step was a step backward. In his hands he held a small file folder containing some photographs of the area, the woman and the rock used to crush her skull.

He held a photograph out at a distance and tried to place the exact location the woman had been found. The crew that cleaned up the mess had returned the scene to its original state, so intact that the identification would be more difficult than he wanted. Footprints appeared to have been dusted away, but he knew that wasn't right. More likely than not, the rain of the night prior erased any signs of the men who walked around, took pictures, collected evidence and stared in disgust.

Casey cocked his head to the right and thought he figured it out. He walked forward and stood about six feet from a tall saguaro, his body facing north. Looking down toward his feet, he could tell faintly that he stood where the woman spent her last moments alive. But aside from a few stones that appeared out of place, there was nothing Casey felt he could use in his investigation of the murder of the woman. He turned around a few times and took in all that was near him. He sighed and put the photograph back into the folder.

In the distance, clouds were forming once again along the ridges to the north and northeast. The sun wasn't near finished with its daily baking of the desert floor, and the temperature felt closer and closer to the century mark—a moment that marked the end of spring and the beginning of Hell. Casey wiped a bead of sweat from his forehead and walked to the east, closer to a ridge just tall enough to hide whatever was behind it. As he stood at the top of the ridge, he saw the expanse of the desert floor rush out in every direction, butting up against mountains not so far away. Speckled greens and mottled browns dotted the landscape, but here—to the north of one of the largest cities in America—Casey felt like he was the only living creature for miles. No other signs of life stood waiting to greet him as he gazed out over the landscape. There were no power lines that cut a swath through many desert areas. There were no roads, dirt or otherwise, to lead travelers into this barren stretch of land. He knew if he turned around these things could be seen, but for the sheer majesty of the unknown, Casey refused for a moment and let the serenity of nowhere sink deep inside.

Closer to where he stood, a barren wash snaked its way through the desert, revealing stones and, in a few spots, the signs of vegetation. It would take a great rain to fill this wash, and that just hadn't happened in some time. A few Palo Verde trees lined the side of the wash maybe a hundred feet downstream, and in the shadow of the spiny leaves, Casey saw one or two beer cans sticking out of the dirt.

Well, that ruins the moment, he thought. He sighed and walked down a small embankment and onto the wash, then followed a path to where he saw the cans. He wondered if, perhaps, the killer and victim consumed them before the night was over and she lay lifeless. But as he approached, he saw the rust, the chipped and aged edges and the markings he had once seen on cans in a grocery store when he was a teenager trying to buy a six pack of beer. Half buried in the dirt, the cans showed more than their age—they showed Casey a memory of a long time ago and a world so far removed from the one he toiled in daily.

Casey regarded the cans with a little jealousy and faint reflection, then walked past the Palo Verde trees and farther down the wash. A small bend to the left took him through more Palo Verde trees, more beer cans and a condom wrapper stuck up in the brush under one tree. As the wash continued farther still, the slope became greater and the bank rose up like new found canyon walls—at first only a few feet high, then towering more than fifteen feet in some places where the wash narrowed and sloped even farther down.

Casey stopped at one point and looked back from where he had come. He wondered for a moment just what possessed him to travel so far from the murder scene. Was it the beer cans of yesteryear? Was it the feeling of being a child again, exploring an unknown untouched by most? Or was it something completely incomprehensible that pushed Casey's legs farther into nowhere?

He shrugged and decided he just didn't care why. Instead, he continued on and constantly scanned the banks of the wash for some other clue or some other memory.

Another bend in the wash—now more a small canyon—brought Casey to a pool of standing water a few feet deep that ducked underneath a nearly vertical wall of eroded rock. Sudden surges of the wash over time had created a small hole that almost looked like a tiny cave dug into the side of the wall. It created a gloriously wet and shady resting place for the weary rabbit or gecko running from the predators of their environment. As such, it even looked inviting to a weary and confused man who traveled a path he wasn't sure of and wanted so much to step out of the sun for just a moment.

Casey walked across a few rocks and underneath the enclave, free from the sun. He found a spot of sand, took off his hat, sat and leaned against the side of the rock. He closed his eyes to rest them from the brightness that was all around. Decades had passed since he had been in such a place, and the memory of his teenage years flooded back to remind him of a time that was both carefree and reckless, both difficult and easy, both romantic and free.

Through the blackness behind his closed eyes, he saw his first love swimming the waters in front of him. Her blonde hair and blue swimsuit accented the beauty of the moment.

Friends long since forgotten swam with her and splashed about in fits of laughter, seeming to dance around the wonder of life that was his girlfriend—someone a teenage boy with testosterone to spare could say was his and his alone. Or so he had thought. Apparently teenage love was blind. Nevertheless, Casey sighed at the memory and let a small smile creep across his face.

"Pickin's ain't good, mister," a voice called out from across the stagnant pool. Casey opened his eyes to see an old man dressed in rags. He stood at the edge and looked at his reflection in the undisturbed mirror of water. "Nava-joes took it all."

Casey stood and fitted his hat back on his head. As he regarded the man—frail, almost fragile to the touch—he wondered for a moment if he was the same onlooker from the evening they had found the body. Something was familiar, at least. Casey watched the man look at himself in the pool—his back arched uncomfortably over, knees bent from years of holding up the weight of the body. White hair poked out from beneath a straw hat and his beard hung to his chest, knotted in places and stained with food or drink here and there.

Casey approached the man carefully. "Are you alright, sir?"

"What?" The man swung his body around more forcefully to look at Casey and let his neck rest. "Ain't I a looker?"

"That's not what I meant," Casey said, then realized how much he struggled for words at awkward times. "Are you lost? There's really no place around here for miles."

"Pickin's, I said. Didn't you catch that? They ain't no good 'round here." The old man pointed a finger at Casey and closed one of his eyes. "You see a Nava-joe walk by here, mister?"

"No. Why?"

"*He took my pickin's!*" The old man pointed to the pool. "Ain't a lick of pickin's in there anymore."

Casey forced back a small smile he found he was showing. "Anything I can do for you?"

The old man opened both eyes wide and pointed his

finger back at Casey. "You can help me find some pickin's! *Dammit!* Don't you people learn to listen in school anymore?"

"Sorry, I—"

The old man waved Casey off with his hand and a quick "Bah!" then turned around. "You can't help me. Pickin's just ain't good 'round here no more."

"Can I help you some other way?"

The old man walked away from the pool and waved his hand for Casey to follow. "Let me show you somethin', young man. Let me show you somethin'." The old man walked slowly down the wash, testing each step as if the next rock would cause a tumble.

Casey followed close behind, irritated at the old man's slow gait. However, there was something to the man that intrigued—perhaps he was an old hermit who lived in a cave guarding an old treasure chest full of gold stolen from a stagecoach years ago. Perhaps it was simply the nonsense he spoke. Curiosity might also have come from the dialect the man used, which, although poor in grammar and full of many common clichés, was interesting to hear nonetheless. Whatever the reason, Casey felt an urge to know more.

"I once knew a girl," the old man said as he paused at a rock and negotiated a pathway around it. "She was lovely. A true looker with hair of gold." He stopped completely and turned to face Casey. "You ever know a girl, mister?"

"With hair of gold," Casey reflected, the sudden memory of years ago failing to fade away into the recesses of his mind. "Yes."

"Wanted so much to belong to her. But we was young—hair just starting to grow in places the sun don't see too often." The old man looked down slightly, not so much at anything physical. He seemed to focus his vision on the past. "Was right here, mister. Was right here. Kissed her in the wash."

Casey tilted his head slightly and wondered what may have prompted this thread of conversation. Was it old age? Was it the wash? Was it a memory that wouldn't go away, like his own? To Casey, the memory of the girl with hair of gold was one that remained ever so present. It occasionally retreated for maybe a month or two, then came back each time a catalyst was noted by the brain: a television show they watched, a movie they went to, a road they drove on, even a restaurant they ate at once or twice. He smiled inwardly as more visions of the past floated up to greet him. "What was her name?"

The old man looked up at Casey and smiled, weakly, displaying three teeth in front of a gaping black hole of a decaying mouth. "What's it matter, mister? She's gone." He turned back around and analyzed the next footstep to get him closer to wherever it was he wanted to take Casey.

Casey watched the old man take three or four steps before taking one himself. He realized suddenly that he was absorbed by all the thoughts that flooded in, memories crashing upon the shore of his life. One of the pool of water in the wash, another of heated passion in the front seat of a car, another of a kiss in the rain by a lake while camping, and still another of the day they told each other goodbye. Inwardly, Casey whispered her name—*Christine*—then outwardly sighed. Seemed the first true love never went away.

The old man had quickened his gait, and Casey walked faster through the center of the wash, past the towering banks on either side that had been narrowing ever so slightly.

"Case you is wonderin', mister," the old man said, not looking back, "her name was Christine. Stole a kiss from her in the rain, once. Best lips I ever laid mine own on. Did you ever kiss a girl in the rain, mister? Water drippin' on your face. Hair getting all wet."

"Once." Casey narrowed his eyes and slowed down a little.

"The one with the hair of gold, eh? Somethin' about that color. Makes you do crazy things. Hopin' you don't mind me askin' you now, mister," the old man said as he walked across the wash to the wall of rock now thirty or forty feet high. "What is it 'bout first loves? Why do they stick to your ribs like pig fat? Ain't nothin' but you in heat, ain't it?"

"Has to be more than that."

The old man stopped at the wall and looked up. Above his

head about ten feet there was a large hole, about three feet across and three feet tall. From Casey's vantage point, he saw inside far enough to know that it was a lot more than a minor indent in the bank of the wash. A ladder made up of sticks and some old rope hung down along the side.

"Climb on up, mister," the old man said. "Curiosity's gotta be killin' you."

Without warning, the old man crumpled to the ground in a heap of dust and sand, his remains blending in with the floor of the wash. Casey stared at the spot where the man once stood. As the dust settled, his heart beat wildly in his chest.

PART II: THROUGH THE VOID

> With shuddring horror pale, and eyes agast
> View'd first thir lamentable lot, and found
> No rest: through many a dark and drearie Vaile
> They pass'd, and many a Region dolorous,
> O're many a Frozen, many a Fierie Alpe,
> Rocks, Caves, Lakes, Fens, Bogs, Dens, and shades of death,
> A Universe of death, which God by curse
> Created evil, for evil only good,
> Where all life dies, death lives, and nature breeds,
> Perverse, all monstrous, all prodigious things,
> Abominable, inutterable, and worse...
>
> —John Milton, *Paradise Lost*, 2.615-625

CHAPTER FIFTEEN

Nothing would be something.
Jennifer stood in the middle of an emptiness and felt the pit of her stomach flip over in protest. She wrapped her arms around herself and tried to find some sort of tangible object that might lend a clue about her new environment. There was only the void that surrounded her, enveloped her body, her mind and her soul. The freak that chased her—was he nearby? Would he appear out of this nothingness and kill her as well? Overcome with despair, Jennifer cried.

"Jennifer! Dinner's ready!" The voice was faint, like it had come from a mile away. To Jennifer, though, it was the most pleasant sound she ever heard. She stood and looked through the blackness toward the sound. Mother was there.

"Mother?" she called out, cupping her hands around her mouth. "Mother, where are you?"

The emptiness answered her with silence. Not even an echo responded to her voice. Maybe Mother didn't hear her.

"*Mother!*"

Silence. The word still vibrated in her throat and her breath grew faster with every second. She looked and looked, turned her eyes from left to right, then back left again. Jennifer stepped forward and called again. "*Mother, where are you?*"

"Jennifer! Dinner's ready! Are you coming or not?" The voice was much clearer and Jennifer's heartbeat quickened in response. She *was* there.

"Mother, I'm coming! I'm over here!" Jennifer waved to the blackness and jumped up and down. Even if she couldn't see, maybe her mother could. "Help me, mother! I can't see you!"

"Well if you're not going to answer me, I suppose you're not going to eat."

"*Mother! I'm... right... here!*" Tears exploded from her eyes. Her face grew red. The frustration was too much, and Jennifer fell to her knees.

Nothing made sense. From the man who killed Jonathan to the mysterious hole in the cabin, to the voice of her mother, Jennifer was a mess of emotions. She tried desperately to come up with answers. The obvious ones—this was a dream, this was nightmare—were strikingly wrong. She felt herself, felt the pain in her side from tripping over a fallen tree and landing sideways on a rock. She felt her breath, hot from her lungs as she ran from the maniac. She felt the cold space around her now that encased her inside of nothing. She felt fear more tangibly than she ever had before.

Jennifer closed her eyes and curled into a fetal position. She hadn't even had time to grieve for Jonathan. The image of his back exploding in front of her replayed itself, followed by an image of the assailant holding his heart. *What did he do to deserve that?* Jennifer thought. *What? What? What?*

"What are you doing?"

Jennifer jumped up. The voice was clear and right behind her. She spun around as a smile cracked across her face. She fully expected to see Jonathan.

Nothing.

Jennifer's smile faded briefly until she heard it again. "What are you doing, Jennifer?"

"Jonathan?" Her voice was weak, choked with tears. "Jonathan, where are you?"

"Why are you taking off your bra?"

All of a sudden, the thought of Jonathan rescuing her from her loneliness dissolved into the realization that this was a memory she had wanted to forget. Her smile fell from her face entirely as she listened.

"You're a little drunk, Jenn. Come on, and I'll take you home."

Jennifer closed her eyes, trying to shut out the memory. It wasn't working. There was the living room, a party, people watching her. She stood on a coffee table and spun around like an idiot.

"Come on down, Jennifer." She remembered him below her, holding his hand out. His face showed the embarrassment he must have felt. But she didn't listen to him. Her first taste of alcohol was about to turn sour. She remembered spinning, spinning, spinning. And then she fell, face first into a glass end table on the side of the couch. The glass shattered and cut her cheeks and forehead. Blood poured from the open wounds. She heard the others scream, rush to help her, rush to get her a towel, a Band-Aid. But she had been too drunk to realize the gravity of her ways. She laughed hard and rolled onto the floor, over more shards of glass. A few of them cut into her neck, her back, her arms. Finally, blackness came.

Jennifer opened her eyes. She hated that memory. Not only was it embarrassing, but she'd had to wear the scars of her stupidity on her body for the last few months. Every day, it seemed, someone had to remind her of what happened. But not Jonathan. He never said a word.

"What are you doing?"

Jennifer winced at the voice. The first time it was refreshing, but she finally realized it wasn't real. She fell to her knees again, crying.

"Jennifer! Dinner's ready!"

A drop of water struck her on the cheek. Instinctively, she wiped it off and looked up. To her amazement, she could barely see the outline of a tree in the distance, gray against a black background. Her cry gave way to shock as she stood and looked around. Everywhere it seemed, things appeared. At first the tree, now fully green and bright. Then another. Then another. A bush, a fern and the ground under her materialized into a blanket of deep brown dirt.

"You're a little drunk, Jenn. Come on, and I'll take you home." The voice of Jonathan was softer, but still clear. Jennifer let the sound of his voice drift past her ears and disappear.

The sky unfolded. Deep gray clouds rolled through the distance. Out in front of her, what was nothing became substance, a place to explore and find answers. What was nothing was now a forest that covered hills and mountains as far as the eye saw. Just as the endless expanse of emptiness had engulfed her, Jennifer found herself basking in the ethereal light of something new.

"I suppose you're not going to eat!" Her mother's voice carried through the trees and bushes and right past Jennifer's ears.

Ignore it, she thought. *Move on.*

JENNIFER HAD come into nothing out of wayward chance, misplaced bad luck or fate. Whatever the reason, none of them relinquished the feeling of dread that her circumstances were real and overwhelming. For a seventeen-year-old rebellious teenager, life was supposed to be about choices—smoke that cigarette, sleep with that guy, which acne medicine worked best. Life was supposed to be posing the questions, and Jennifer was supposed to be sorting them out one by one. She shouldn't have to be faced with what was, by all rational thought, irrational situations forced upon her by choices she *didn't* make. Nevertheless, she found herself immersed into giving her soul to the man she was to marry, and then struggled to come to grips with his death, the man who was out to kill her, and the nothingness she had thrown herself into the minute she decided to hide in a closet in a cabin far from civilized life.

The blackness that had surrounded her in the beginning was, at least for the time being, a distant fading memory. The voices she heard—memories of past choices—were still present, but at least soft in their presentation. She stood on a hill, a dew soaked fern at her feet, and gazed upon a forest like she had never seen before. The trees, immense in their composition, were heavy with mosses, vines and life. The wind softly brushed by her hair, picked up a few loose strands then set them down again. It gently pushed at the weaker leaves and plants then moved on down the side of the hill.

She looked past a few trees, into the distance, and tried to surmise what lay ahead, and even if that was a direction she should go. In the irrational world that surrounded her, Jennifer couldn't decide if *any* place warranted the curiosity necessary to say it was a place she should go. She had to go somewhere, however, learn something, and try to sort out exactly what it was which encompassed her being at that moment in time. With a sigh and a resolve to place a rational explanation in her mind, she set out toward the distant horizon beyond the trees in front of her.

After walking no more than a few feet, Jennifer saw a little rise that almost looked inviting—moss covered boulders at the top highlighted in the dim sunlight that tried to shine through the gray sky above. She quickened her pace toward the rocks, then sat for a moment and peered over a small precipice. A creek meandered through the forest floor far below and the sound of a distant waterfall hung faintly in the air.

The moss was wet, more so than she anticipated, and almost felt like a sponge. She peered out at the horizon again and tried to judge the distance to the next outcropping of rock. For Jennifer, who was fond of camping in remote places, beauty was a mountain, a sunset and a green blanket of life. The beauty that surrounded her was striking. The color green, in various shades and hues, wrapped the hillside like a blanket. In places, a few purples shone through, along with a few reds, and yellows—the elements of flowers that couldn't be found in the local flower shop. Even the gray of the rock she sat on took on a green quality, not so much because of the moss, but because of the environment the rock was a part.

"Nice view, I say."

The voice came suddenly from somewhere below Jennifer. At first, she reasoned it was nothing more than a memory coming to haunt her, like the others that just wouldn't go away. The distinct clarity of the voice, however, made her think twice and wait quietly for it to say something else.

"How the colors bleed into the night," it said, this time a little louder and harsher. Jennifer cocked her head to the side and wondered for a moment how a line from one of her own poems—scribbled in a fit of fear a few months ago on a notebook meant for economics class—was being recited by someone she couldn't even recognize. Her heart quickened a beat as an uncomfortable feeling rushed in to replace the calm she had achieved by focusing on the beauty surrounding her.

"Now, let's see if I can remember the rest of it," the voice called out. "'He takes to killing like a demon out of Hell. He's bent on revenge for a life I cannot give to him. The colors bleed, from green to red, and he feels nothing more than the lust. The lust. The color of red. The color of night that seeps into my pores and tries to overcome my morality.'"

Jennifer stood and looked around, trying to find the owner of the voice that had just recited a poem no one read. As she frantically searched her memory for who might have seen the poem without her permission, she distinctively remembered ripping out the page from the notebook and tearing it into pieces shortly after it was written.

Jennifer's pulse raced and she felt the blood rush through her neck, beat by beat. She turned around and scanned the trees, scanned the hillside, then took a few steps forward and leaned over the precipice.

Standing far below in the creek that trickled aimlessly, a man stood looking up at her.

"At least that's how I remember it," the man called up to her. "You know, you could help me out by telling me the rest of the poem. I think it's beautiful in its simplistic way. A little bit of the teenage gothic angst, but you're only seventeen. I can forgive that."

The tone of the man was hard to gauge, masked by the use of force in his voice to raise the words to her level. She couldn't tell much about his composition either, other than he was far from being slender. His eyes, his hair, and the general features of his face were hidden by the distance. The fear she had felt transformed itself into curiosity, then a morbid sense of relief. At least there was someone who might be able to answer the thousand questions that ran through her mind.

"I hope you don't think me rude," the man called up. "I can't exactly find a way to come up to your level right now."

"No," Jennifer called down. "How did you know that poem?"

The man looked down at the creek for an instant then back up at Jennifer. "I can't exactly answer your questions, right now. I'm afraid they'll have to wait."

"Where am I?"

"Like I said, I'm afraid you'll have to wait for answers from me. But rest assured, they will come."

Jennifer frowned. "Can you at least tell me what I'm doing here?"

"Oh, isn't that like a teenager—questioning the why of life. If I had *that* answer for you, life would seem a little useless now, wouldn't it?"

"That's not what I meant."

"I know. Listen. Take the path you'll find over the rise to your right. There's an old adobe dwelling that I can meet you at. As it is, my feet are getting cold standing in this water and my throat is turning sore yelling up at you."

Jennifer looked to her right and found the rise the man had just mentioned. It wasn't much of a climb, and she reasoned that if it had a path, the travel would be a lot easier than it had been so far. She turned back to face the man below.

The trickle of the creek greeted her with quiet loneliness as the first man she met in this irrational place had disappeared from view.

CHAPTER SIXTEEN

It was a time of wanting. Not so much for the promise of love, or even the *thought* of the promise of love, but wanting for the pure need to be loved and consumed by another. Marie remembered the feeling well, and it was that feeling she carried with her on her journey through life. Through all the trials and tribulations—the day in a dirty clinic waiting for an answer she didn't want to hear, the day she married the man who was to fill the void, the day she gave birth to the very angel that was there to make her life complete—she carried the memory of Harlan. Sometimes it was a brief, hapless thought. Other times it was an hour of contemplation, of reflection, of wondering and wanting. None of this was a replacement for feeling his touch or smelling his sweet breath just a few inches away. These were not feelings that were foreign to her, and although she hadn't seen him in years, the memory was always as vivid as that which comes the morning after. Even the day she learned her family had been killed in an accident, there was the memory.

How would Harlan comfort me now?

Marie was alone with the memory. A chance look into a pool of what she thought was water, a pulling sense of curiosity, and she was wrapped up in a blanket of nothingness with no reference point for reality. She didn't stop to wonder how she got there. She did, however, question *where* exactly "there" was.

There were voices at first, and to Marie they seemed distant yet almost real. They spoke in rhymes of her history, the past unfolding in ways she never would have imagined. The voices—not loud, not crass—were the only indication that either she was asleep in a coma for some unknown reason, or she entered some world where the memories were as real as anything tangible.

The latter thought was not, in itself, inconceivable, given what she had witnessed maybe an hour ago inside the kitchen of her home. There was a man—no, a demon—who sat on her chest, ready to rape her physically while he spoke of her part in something greater, something more grand than she would ever realize. He was, at first, a curiosity—naked on a road miles from any civilized area. He tugged at her soul, and the next moment he wore an ugly expression that exuded hate more than anything else. Whatever happened in Marie's kitchen, she reasoned, was not natural.

So it was when she entered a place where nothing existed but the voices from her past, Marie was neither shocked nor amazed. There had to be a reason, and that reason waited to be found. Marie sat on whatever surface she felt herself standing on. The voices had faded, though they were never very loud or traumatic. She studied the blankness in front of her, checked nothing to her left, looked at an empty space to her right and finally laid down to rest. Meaning would come, but not right away. She closed her eyes and wondered if Harlan thought about her, about them, about anything in the novel they had written together using life as a blank page.

"Are you sure you want to do that?" The voice was clear, more so than the rest. Marie opened her eyes to see if maybe someone was really there, talking to her right now. The voice echoed inside her head as she stared at nothing. Finally, she closed her eyes again, the memory of the voice fresh in her mind. It seemed as if she was back in the café, drinking coffee, learning to play a simple game of chess. It was a wonderful memory, and if that's what this emptiness wanted to bring her, so be it.

"You have a gift, Marie." Harlan's voice, unmistakable, drifted past her ears. "Why don't you use it?"

Marie thought back to that day, so long ago. She had come

to the café with friends, not knowing what else to do on a rainy Friday night. As she walked through the front door, she saw him sitting on a couch, reading a book by the light of a small banker's lamp. It was a weird feeling at first—the teacher, the student, there together in a hang-out for poets, artists, and trend-setting nerds—but after the initial shock, she mustered up the courage and sat next to him, peeking at the book he was reading.

"Look at the board, Marie. There are so many moves available. You don't have to sacrifice anything right now."

The chess game. It started after a brief conversation about this and that and nothing in particular. It was a part of the night Marie could never remember clearly. Harlan offered to teach her how to play chess, and as the two sat at a small table, she could tell there was more feeling in him than he let on. He was not simply the teacher who was a target of affection from a student. He was a man who could move mountains for her, and was willing to do it no matter the cost.

Marie always wondered about that first meeting. Was it fate that called the two of them to the café, or was it a chance encounter written somewhere in the stars? Was he returning the affection simply because he was thrilled to have someone beautiful look at him lustfully? Whatever the answer to these questions, it was clear the fire was alive in both of them, and any amount of passion they would share in the future would be forbidden. He was the teacher and he was married.

"Do you want to know the answer?"

A woman's voice this time. Marie opened her eyes again and wondered what happened to Harlan's voice. She had been enjoying the memory—reliving the day they realized passion was inevitable—and now she was pulled away from that into something else. She hoped she saw something this time. Maybe even a faint outline of a tree, or a chair, or a bush, or a mountain.

Something would be nice.

The woman's voice came again, this time from an opposite direction. "Looks like you're pregnant."

Marie's stomach churned once then rumbled with anger.

It was a memory she wished she could do without. The sinking feeling in her stomach grew stronger as images of the café melted away inside her mind to reveal images of a stuffy woman's clinic on the other side of Phoenix from where she lived.

She closed her eyes again and tried to change the scene back to the café, back to Harlan, back to the happiness she'd felt.

"That's a choice you'll have to make on your own," the woman said in response to the memory of the question Marie just asked. She recalled staring at her feet, remembering the passion with Harlan and then... what was she going to do now?

"You want us to leave you alone, dear?" Another voice from the past, screaming past her ears like a bullet. "I'll take Susan out for pizza so you can study."

Marie sat up and cupped her hands around her ears. Of all the pain she might have felt in life, this was the *one* memory that *needed* to go away. It was her fault, after all.

If she hadn't yelled at Susan trying to show off her drawing...

If she hadn't been fed up with a simple request for a glass of water...

If she hadn't been so focused on studying for a stupid test...

If she hadn't...

A tear fell from her face, the first since she stepped into the nothingness that surrounded her. Suddenly, the air felt cold, more so than before, and she wanted nothing more than to be held and comforted by Harlan.

"Mommy?" Susan's little voice resounded all around. Marie pulled her legs up close to her body and buried her head in her hands. The tears flowed continuously, one falling off the eyelid quickly chased by another.

"Mommy? Are you alright?"

"Yes," Marie whispered to the emptiness that surrounded her. "Yes, I'm alright." She couldn't take any more than that. Where was the memory of Harlan, the vision of the café? Hell, the woman's clinic was better than this. What was happening? Why did she have to succumb to *this* torture all of a sudden?

Marie cried, softly at first—her gentle whimper lost to the void around her.

"Mommy? Don't you want pizza, too?"

"*Stop!*" Marie screamed. She couldn't take any more of this. She buried her face in her hands and lost herself in the rush of emotions that threatened to topple her already unstable notion of sanity.

"Mommy?" This time the voice wasn't her daughter's, and it sounded much farther away than the others.

Marie looked up, expecting to see the emptiness around her. Instead, she sat on a sand dune. A desert stretched out to the horizon then finally blended in with distant mountains. She stood quickly and reached to wipe the tears from her face. A few grains of sand scraped across her cheek as she brought her hand across it, and the gritty sensation it left felt like it was more than just another dream. This was real, and she had to fight hard within herself to believe it.

"Mommy?" The voice came again, from the right.

It was the most beautiful sound in the world simply because it was *real*. She looked over the dunes and tried to find the source.

Up on the second dune over, clear as crystal, sat a little girl in a pink nightgown.

IT IS a fallacy of human thought that one can ever truly be alone. There will always be the ghosts that follow, the ghosts that stand in front or whisper in the ear of the past, or the present, or the future one dreams of but can never attain. For some, these ghosts are faint images that hover briefly in view as painful reminders of failure or sweet reflections of success. For some, these ghosts are whispers, caught in the wind or dancing among the raindrops that fall on a summer's eve. They speak of the past, of the present and then show the way to the future. For some, however, these ghosts are loud, obnoxious beings that manifest themselves more as demons than as memories. They coax and prod and poke at the person's insides and try ever so hard to remind them of failure or rejection. The fallacy is that the human mind can set aside these ghosts and exist purely in the *now*, oblivious to the synaptic explosions encased inside the fleshy, convoluted cortexes of the gray matter.

To a child, loneliness can only come when the monsters leave and the imagination stops running rampant. To a child, the ghosts speak more of the present or the future, relating only to the past with faint images of traumatic events. To a child who is physically alone, the ghosts come in droves. They hover about the undeveloped mind and swirl in chaotic patterns that lead to fear and the longing for companionship in the form of an adult. The need for a parent, the cries in the night, even the cries that come from a newborn who has very few memories—these are raging rebuttals to the ghosts that swarm from all directions.

Justine had heard the ghosts for what seemed like forever, although time was a concept she never quite grasped. Memories of windows blowing open, strange feelings of flight, the choking dust and sand all spent time as companions to the little girl who now sat on a sand dune. She cried a thousand times for Mommy to come and take her back, to show her the ghosts were not real, the demons and the Angry Man were only figments of her imagination brought on by the isolation she experienced. And Mommy *had* finally come, not long ago. She came and held Justine tight against her warm body and filled every ounce of her soul with love and understanding and comfort and all the good things mommies have to give their children. But just as sudden as she had come—after a forever of calling her name—she vanished and left the little girl to seek solace inside herself once again, to try to fight off the ghosts that inevitably came back. Her only companion was a tattered bear she clutched to her chest each time she felt the fear come on stronger.

She was resolved, however. Calling out her name had worked once, and although it took such a long time, there was the possibility of Mommy's return. Justine called out again, louder than before. She screamed at the top of her lungs and forced more air out than she ever thought possible.

"*Mommy!*"

The ghosts responded with screams of their own and flashed images and memories across her eyes. Justine fought back and called again, louder and louder.

"*Mommy!*"

The ghosts answered back.

Isolation tried to seep in one more time.

"*Mommy!*"

An image of fire, followed by the sound of the Angry Man shot forward in front of her, and another tear fell from her face. Slowly she became more and more aware that no one was going to answer her.

"Are you okay little girl?" A woman's voice called from behind. Justine spun, hoping to see her Mommy, but happy that *anyone* was there. A woman stood down the side of the dune and looked up with a smile. She was shorter than Mommy, and her hair was much longer, but Justine could care less about the appearance. A savior is a savior, regardless of looks. The little girl wiped her cheek with the back of her hand and stood.

"Are you lost?" the woman asked.

Justine ran down the side of the dune, slipping on the sand under her feet. She came to stop and reached out and grabbed the woman's legs, hugging them as hard as her little body could.

This strange woman wasn't Mommy, but she would do. If this adult didn't disappear, there might yet be respite from the ghosts.

MARIE FELT odd, but fulfillment rushed in like the water behind a dam when the gates were opened. She placed her hand on the little girl's head and let her fingers run through her hair, gently caressing a being who was definitely more upset at the isolation than she was. The voices of the past still hovered around her ears in whispers, but with a little focus, the words had become a jumble of nonsense—except for her daughter standing at the dinner table asking "*Are you alright?*"

over and over again. She looked down and remarked inwardly at the sight of such a beautiful little girl trapped in the insane world around them. She reminded her so much of her own daughter—the same long blonde hair, the same small frame, even the same mannerisms in the way she held onto Marie's legs.

The girl relaxed her grip slightly and looked up at Marie, her cheeks wet with tears. "Are you a mommy?" she asked, her voice melodic, yet simple.

Marie offered a weak smile and bent down to meet the child's green eyes with her own. She wiped away a tear from the little girl's cheek and—out of instinct more than anything else—she kissed her forehead.

"I am a mommy," she finally whispered. "Are you okay?"

"Better now, thank you." She smiled and wrapped her arms around Marie's neck just as tightly as she had around her legs. "I need a mommy. My mommy won't come back."

Shivers ran down Marie's back and she wondered just what had happened to this innocent child. Sure, Marie could at least rationalize where she was, and knew exactly how she ended up there, but could a little girl with very few life experiences? How could a child find herself pulled into a nightmare such as this? And what would she think about? What were the voices *she* heard?

Curiosity flashed across Marie's mind as she looked into the face of the little girl. "Was your mommy here?"

She nodded. "I thought she was going to take me home, but she went away again."

Marie wished she could relate more to the child and tell her everything would be alright. She wanted to tell her that Mommy would be right back, but she didn't believe that herself. The promises of an adult to a child seem so innocent at times, but in reality, they are often attempts to cover up the reality of them never coming true. Marie could remember a thousand promises she had made to Susan, and she recalled all of them the day she died. She would never have the Barbie doll she wanted, never have the dress that looked so pretty. She would never wear the tiara she saw in a toy store and pleaded to Marie to get for her.

Next time, Susie. I promise.

Marie pushed back the feelings of loss and tried to focus on the needs of the child in front of her. What were the promises *she* had been told? What were the desires of *her* heart? Did this little girl want the tiara or the doll or another stuffed animal that looked as ragged as the one she held in her little hands?

The girl wiped another tear from her cheek. "Are you going to go away, too?"

"No. I'll stay right here with you."

"Promise?"

"I promise." Marie smiled again to show the little girl the conviction she felt. There was another promise, but this time Marie felt she could keep it, no matter the personal cost. "What's your name?"

"Justine."

"Nice to meet you, Justine." Marie held out her hand and shook Justine's. "My name is Marie. Do you want to get out of here?"

Justine nodded. A spark of light rushed into her eyes as they opened wider. "Do you know how?"

Marie shrugged and stood. She looked around at the dunes and the desolation. "A little girl your age once told me that if I just tried and tried again I could make it up any hill."

"I know that story," Justine said. "But which hill are we going to try to go up?"

Marie scanned the horizon, looking for some direction to take, some sign that there was reason behind the two of them being there together. Off in one direction, mountains loomed ominously above the horizon, dark and foreboding. She looked again in the other directions, but saw nothing save the expanse of the desert dunes. If there was a reason, she thought, there was a direction. If there was a direction, there was a goal. If there was a goal, there had to be an attempt—and a first step toward it.

Marie grabbed Justine's hand and pointed toward the mountains in the distance. "Looks like we go over that hill first. Are you ready?"

"Ready."

"Then we're off like a dirty shirt."

Justine looked up a Marie. "You're weird. But I like you."

"Thank you, Justine." Marie smiled as her heart filled up with something she never thought she'd feel again. "I like you, too."

Two lonely figures took a first step together and set out to find a reason for the isolation they had been thrust into. Two lonely figures set out in a direction that only seemed natural, but left a sinking feeling of fear inside each of their stomachs. To Marie, it was a feeling of uncertainty—was this the right way to go? To Justine, it was a feeling of fear—was the Angry Man out there, too?

At least they were together, and the ghosts could finally go away.

CHAPTER SEVENTEEN

There was the beauty of the moment, the passion of forever coupled with the sweet taste of forbidden passion. Then there was the emptiness of loss, the pain of letting go, and the agony of a faded marriage that twisted and turned upon the heart until hate sat side by side with love. There was the voice in the distance, the whisper of love in his ear, and the cries of unbridled desire. Then came the voice of anger, the hate carried on the wind, and the screams of the lost souls that tried to cling onto each other for the purity of two children. There was cold, heat, comfortable warmth, and then a bone-chilling cold snap. Finally there was emptiness, blackness, figments of imagination and a mirage of meaningless design.

Harlan wrapped his body around his knees and curled his feet into his thighs, holding on to the only vestige of substance—himself. A walk to a deserted cabin had turned surreal as a thick fog rolled in around him. Within moments, the world of trees and rocks, broken branches and moist ferns had disappeared. The void that formed around him became mystic and finally dark. What had seemed curious hours before had become a frightening journey into a land where nothing was the only proven element of the environment. To the schoolteacher, father and lost husband, the place he was in was a sick and twisted manifestation of his latest feelings. But he had heard voices that came suddenly and, in fact, were the catalyst to pulling him.

"Checkmate," she had said, as he stared into the fog. "Smile. You look like you've seen a ghost."

At first, the voice was like a crystal goblet that echoed through the disappearing forest. Harlan's mind suddenly raced to fire the synapses that, combined together, formed a dance and a memory. That memory, in turn, cascaded throughout his body and set nerve endings on fire. It pushed his heart two, three, four beats faster per minute until he felt it in his throat. His stomach—tied in knots from the original fear of losing his daughter—relaxed. Involuntary muscles in the hands clenched but not in anger. The brow furrowed, the neck tightened and a smile grew across his face.

He must have been drawn into the void inside the fog by the sheer power of the voice. When he turned around to see if the deputy was still with him, there was absolutely nothing— not even the tree he had just passed.

The voice came again and beckoned him ever closer to the full realization of the memory.

"Mr. Reese," she said, looking at him. "Do you want to get out of here?"

His heart had fluttered then, and there, in the nothingness, his heart fluttered still. It responded with the words he had uttered at the very moment he realized the dreams of a faithful marriage were about to be shattered for the chance to lay with a woman who was not simply a student, but a soul that he needed to consume. Harlan closed his eyes in the void and let the vivid memory carry him to that faraway place inside his own heart—a place of sand and fire, of passion and the promise of a future, of forbidden love and the night it all began.

"CALL ME Harlan." His hands gently touched the top of Marie's. The chess game had finished, with she the victor and he the man who had let her win. The café was filled with students—luckily none of his own—but they were all familiar faces in the crowd who walked the same halls that he did and made the same mistakes he made. Oblivious at first to their presence, Harlan focused his attention on the paragon of beauty in front of him. There was so much he wanted to say then and there, but the realization that he could easily be seen struck him. He let go of her hand and leaned over the table, not only to whisper to her but to get closer so he could breathe in her fragrance and let the pheromones quicken his pulse. "Where were you thinking?"

"Someplace special where we can talk. I found a secluded spot not too far from here that my friends and I used to visit whenever we didn't want to be disturbed by passing cars." Marie stood and adjusted her blouse. Harlan wondered if it was more a seductive move than a needed one. "Meet me outside in the back parking lot. I'm going to tell my friends I'm going for a little walk to clear my head."

Harlan nodded in agreement and watched her walk away into the crowd of faces. Her body moved sinuously down two steps, a black skirt tight against her thighs highlighting the curve of her buttocks. She was shorter than the others — maybe only a few inches over five feet — but she easily stood out from the crowd.

He shook his head, smiled to himself and looked back at the chessboard. White had won, a checkmate from the corner of the board across two spaces and the king was trapped between a knight, a bishop and a pawn of all things. He could have easily won the game about seven moves ago, but she was just learning. He supposed it was all an attempt to build up her confidence.

He chuckled softly. *I need confidence.*

The room was dark and allowed Harlan an unnoticed escape out the back of the café to the parking lot. The night air, cool but wet with the recent rain, greeted him with the promise of exploration, adventure and new ideas all wrapped up in an environment bred for the moment. A thought crossed his mind — if only for a second — of running off, jumping in his car and speeding home to his wife. He could have very easily saved himself from the sin he was bound to commit. He pushed that thought back, however, the minute he spotted Marie by a beat-up red sedan in the corner of the lot, a street lamp directly overhead highlighting her hair. She had unbuttoned the top of her blouse, and Harlan took that small gesture as an invitation to come and teach her something else besides Shakespeare and chess. He imagined she wanted to learn about love and passion and wanted to be taken to the brink of insanity then slowly carried back... if only to do it all one more time.

Quickly, Harlan stepped into her car and just as quickly, Marie sped away into the night toward the special place she had promised to take him. The trip there was quiet, but not silent. Harlan had adjusted himself in the passenger seat, riding up Marie's skirt with his hands. He knew that if this was to be forbidden, it might as well be the most ravenous, bestial sex he could imagine.

It wasn't long before they turned onto a dirt road. Marie smiled as she pulled up next to a sign in the middle of the road and turned the car off. Harlan looked out the windshield at a sign—yellow with rusted paint, two bullet holes and the single word "END" written in bold, black letters across the middle. He chuckled softly to himself as he placed the sign with the dirt road they were on, miles from any civilization. His moment of wonder, however, soon gave way to the moment of pleasure that awaited him.

Marie stepped out of the car and walked toward the front, leaning up against the hood. The clouds had separated and the stars were out. Far from the city lights they shone brighter. If it wasn't the stars, then the moon softly illuminated her hair and gave her eyes a sparkle that matched the passion burning in Harlan's heart. Harlan stepped out and joined her, leaning up against the hood of the car and looking out past the signpost and into the desert beyond.

"I found this sign a few months ago," Marie whispered. Harlan wondered if she was taking things a little calmer for fear of ruining the moment, or if maybe she was as nervous as he. "I was just learning that driving meant going out and finding something new every day."

"I like it." Harlan turned to face Marie. In the night air, she was even more beautiful than in the full light of a classroom or even the smoky light of the café. He wanted to kiss her, to hold her, to tell her that he would be there for her night and day if that was what she wanted. The words, however, which had formed in his heart, couldn't leave his throat. Inside, there was only the animal instinct to lie with her and be inside of her.

"WHAT THE hell were you thinking?"

The voice pulled—no—*ripped* Harlan from the memory of the first night with Marie. The blackness that surrounded him felt more like a crushing rock than a comforting quilt of memory.

"You think this is normal?"

It sounded like Celine screaming, and was so loud that Harlan felt the hair on the back of his neck stand on end. The shivers of a cold, desperate air flooded in from all directions. Harlan saw her—if only the memory—standing at a kitchen counter of an apartment they once lived in. The memory seemed so vivid. Another rush of adrenaline shot through his body, this time aimed toward the pit of his stomach as he relived the moment Celine found out about Marie. He wasn't about to relive the whole memory, though—not the stab with a kitchen knife, not the tossing of a spice rack, not the pure hatred that filled a small apartment with the very air of Hell.

He closed his eyes again and tried to think of Marie, whispering her name in the emptiness around him. He tried to grasp the memory of that night—*any* night—once again, but the voice came again, this time from another direction though equally as strong.

"You sleep with a student, and you think it's normal?"

"Stop," Harlan whispered. His voice was lost in the breath of air in front of him. "Think of Marie, not this."

"You worthless sack of spineless jelly!" Another voice, another time. Harlan opened his eyes and looked around. "You reason that in this man's Army you can think? If I wanted you to think, I would have had you sign for brains! Private Reese, do you understand me?"

Harlan pushed the heels of his hands into his eyes. Why was a voice so dear to him, yet so removed from his life, screaming again? He remembered a drill instructor, the green Smokey Bear hat tilted on his head, green shirt stacked with ribbons and other shiny trinkets of an excellent military life.

This was the man who had given him discipline, trained him to love the military and let him know what his place in the world was. There were times that scared Harlan in Boot Camp, but in retrospect, the drill instructor who had yelled at him repeatedly was the cornerstone of his life.

"*Do. You. Understand. Me?*" The drill instructor yelled again, sounding out the words as if each were a sentence unto itself.

"*You think this is normal?*" Celine cried out. Harlan cringed at the voice then stood. There had to be a reason for this nonsense. He looked around at the blackness, and tried to focus on shapes that weren't there, or were simply cast out from his memory.

"You want to get out of here?" Marie's voice, mixed in with the others, was a relief. If only she could stay. If only she would appear next to him and offer her comforting words as a physical being instead of a memory trapped in nothing.

"*You think this is normal?*"

Harlan shook his head and took a few steps forward, intent on finding a way out of the blackness. He reached his hands out, like a man in a dark room looking for the light switch. Nerves twitched, and the fear of running into something kept haunting Harlan's every move.

"*If I wanted you to think, I would have had you sign for brains!*"

Harlan's steps become more pronounced, not the cautious baby steps instituted with the fear of not knowing where the edge was. He reached out farther and waved his arms back and forth, trying to ignore the voices around him. Even Marie's voice was becoming annoying, if only because he knew it wasn't real.

"Meet me outside..."

The voices slowly became weaker, perhaps because he focused on something tangible, or perhaps because they were fading memories not meant to stick around, like mirages that disappear the closer or farther you get from them. Perhaps they were meant as an introduction to this place, Harlan reasoned, whatever this place was. It certainly wasn't a dense fog like it appeared initially, and it certainly wasn't any place that would make the television news.

His hand brushed against something sharp. Harlan stopped. He looked at his finger—amazed he saw it at all without light—and watched a small spot of blood form, grow and then drip down the side in a random, chaotic pattern.

Reality *was* attainable. Harlan just wished he could see it. He looked up above his head, hoping to see more than nothing, then down at his feet, praying that whatever surface he walked on would magically appear.

A small stone appeared next to his foot, and the needle broken off a cholla cactus lay beside it. In front of him, shaded by the light of a sun buried in clouds, Marie stood looking out over a vast desert.

CHAPTER EIGHTEEN

Celine tossed and turned in her bed until the sheets became a tangled mess that covered maybe a knee and her hip. She had tried to fall back asleep after the dream she had about Justine a few hours ago, but no amount of persistence was going to allow that to happen. The sleeping pills she had taken were obviously bad, and probably contributed to the fever she felt now and the all too frequent trips she made to the bathroom. She wished for nothing more than a moment's peace—solace in Never-Never Land—but the turn it had taken once before subconsciously prevented her body from sleeping.

Celine was tired. She had seen only a few hours of sleep in the past few days, and the waiting drove her to near madness. Tommy understood, but only to a point. He was still a small boy who had needs, and every poor attempt at a sandwich or pathetic test of her ability to boil pasta wore even more at her already frail body. There were moments she simply wanted the pain to go away, to drift off into the undiscovered country and leave it all far behind. The nagging knowledge that Jennifer was out there, however, kept her resolve in life alive, if only for the time being. Harlan was looking for their daughter, and she knew somehow the end of this nightmare would soon come.

What of sleep? When was that to come? When could her body finally relax and recover from the degradation it experienced? Celine turned again to her right and stared at the window on the far side of her bedroom. A light from a street lamp filtered in and cast a shadow of a cross through the lace curtains onto the floor. The simple pattern threw her mind into a spin, and she saw the window from another point of view — the same window that shattered so many years ago inside Justine's bedroom. That memory sparked another attempt to understand the nightmare she had earlier, standing on a dune seeing her child for the first time in years. The very realism of the dream sent chills down her spine, and Celine silently wondered if the dream was a sign, a premonition, a gift from God. Maybe she *was* going to see her daughter again, and the pain of loss would finally go away after so many years.

What of Jennifer? Should the revelation Justine was still alive and well really fill the void, when Jennifer's whereabouts were still a mystery? How could this happen *again*, twice in a lifetime? Celine choked back the sensation to cry and forced herself not to go that far into a depression again. No sleep aside, she felt she needed to be stronger than the first time. She didn't need to upset Tommy any more than he already was, and should she be called upon to help out in the search for Jennifer, she needed to be... needed to be...

Celine rolled over to her left and closed her eyes again, trying to force sleep upon herself. *Free the mind*, she thought, *and the body will follow.* Celine tried to focus on the myopic lights inside the blackness of her eyelids, a trick she learned long ago, when insomnia was a nightly event that lasted for weeks and even months. She had read that trying to focus on the little, yellow pinpricks of light would, in turn, free the mind and relax her senses. Sometimes the lights would make patterns, zipping about back and forth, coalescing into weird shapes or fantastic images. Other times, the lights would simply exist and hold still in one place so her eyes could try a little harder to focus and make out what they really were. It wasn't a guaranteed method of falling asleep, but it had worked in the past. Celine felt anything would be worth the attempt.

The lights flickered for a moment, and she thought she saw one of them disappear. Another pinprick of light zigzagged in from the right and swirled around in a circle. She focused on the light and let it draw a pattern for her or dance inside the blackness for a while before it too disappeared. Another light—she focused again, as it drew more of a square than a circle. Two of them, coming together, followed by a third and fourth. They met in the middle of the blackness then flared slightly before rising out of sight.

It didn't seem to be working, but Celine's body was so tired she began to feel a tingling sensation, like all of the nerves had given up at once and let go of any remaining electric impulse. She shuddered then opened her eyes to try something else.

She couldn't move. The tingling sensation in her body grew stronger and left a faint ringing in her ears. Her eyes were open, and she saw everything around her—from the dresser to the closet door to the panties on the floor—but every attempt she made at movement was met with a stronger tingling than before. Celine wondered if this was yet another dream or if she was really awake and paralyzed in her bed. The thought of the latter scared her, and she fought within herself to move a leg, an arm, *something* that would let her know she wasn't really incapacitated.

Nothing worked. The more she fought, the louder the ringing in her ears and the stronger the tingling rushed throughout her body. It felt almost as if she was grounded to an electrical socket and the pulse of a thousand volts filled every pore. She tried to call out, to cry for help, but her mouth refused to open. Only her eyes could move and they darted back and forth from the right to the left, from the ceiling to the floor.

She saw him, standing in the corner of the room like a sentry, his hands clasped together in front. He was tall and hidden in the shadows. The few hairs she saw fell lazily to the side, but she couldn't see his face.

Internally, Celine let out a scream, but her body refused to respond. She tried again to move but soon realized there was nothing she could do but stare at a man in the corner of her bedroom who wasn't moving, wasn't speaking, and wanted to hide within the shadows. The only sound was breathing—from Celine, fast and laborious, and from the stranger in the corner, soft and quiet.

The breathing continued for too long. Finally, Celine mustered up enough strength within herself to ask a question. She knew her lips couldn't move enough to make the sounds, but she prayed the stranger heard her thoughts. *What do you want?*

The man in the corner of the bedroom stood silent and unmoving.

What do you want from me? Celine asked again, wishing there was an easy answer to that question.

Still the man stood silent, unmoving.

Are you here to kill me or help me? She didn't know what else to ask. Fear ran rampant inside her body between the paralysis and the stranger, but she couldn't think of anything else to say.

The man stood silent.

Was her idea of telepathic thought even working? Could he even *read* her thoughts? Could he understand them, or had she forced herself to believe the supernatural was taking place in her bedroom?

"I can hear you," the man finally said. His voice was soft, deep, and sank into Celine's ears like a lead weight.

What do you want? she asked again.

"Go to the mountains and look for your daughter. You will find her."

Celine felt her heart beat faster in time to the quickening of her breath. *How do you know this?*

"You're a part of something greater than anything you've known and more horrific than anything you will ever experience."

I don't understand.

"You won't."

The tingling suddenly stopped, and Celine sat up in her bed, breathing hard. She moved her arm and found she could bring it to her breast to feel the pounding of her heart.

In the corner of the bedroom, the stranger was gone, but his voice was still heavy in her ears.

Be afraid.

—

Tommy didn't know what to expect when his mother burst into his room. He had just fallen asleep, all the while clinging to the hope that his family would come back together and these strange events would end. He opened his eyes to see his mother rush to the dresser and pull out clothes—two pairs of shorts, a shirt, a sock with no match and underwear. She went to his closet, threw open the door, and fumbled around for something. She emerged with his backpack. Quickly, she crammed the clothes into the pack and zipped it up.

"What are you doing, Mom?" Tommy said through a yawn. "Are we going somewhere?"

"Get up and get your shoes on." Celine opened another drawer and pulled out a sweater. "You're going to your grandmother's house."

Tommy sat up in bed. "Why? What's going on? Did you find Jennifer?"

"*No!* Now get up!"

The tension in his mother's voice was too thick to try to cut through with any more questions. Whatever was happening was going to happen no matter what he felt about it. He pulled on his slippers and walked downstairs, leaving his mother rummaging through his drawers.

"Get in the car, Tommy," Celine called down the stairs. "And grab an apple on the way out the door. I'm hungry."

A moment ago he was asleep, dreaming of whatever his mind had conjured up. He had done enough crying for the family earlier, and he was too tired to stay awake any longer. Tommy did as he was told and grabbed an apple from the kitchen before stepping out of the house. He opened the car door and sat. He feared something horrible was about to happen, but afraid to mention it or ask any more questions.

Celine came out of the house, leaving the lights on and forgetting to lock the front door. She was still dressed in the sweats she had worn for days. She threw Tommy's backpack in the back seat and started the car. The lights on, the transmission in reverse, she stepped on the gas a little too hard, crashing past the garbage dumpster on the street and squealing the tires on the pavement.

Tommy stared outside the window and watched the other houses pass by in a blur. He still shook from the shock of everything and felt tears well up inside. He turned to his mother and watched her eyes—wide open, scanning the streets for the next turn or the next stop sign. She didn't say anything, and that made it all seem more traumatic than perhaps it was. Her eyes—they glowed with something Tommy had never seen before and could never describe fully.

Tommy mustered up enough courage to finally speak. "Is everything alright, Mom? You're scaring me."

"Don't be scared." Celine slammed on the brakes in response to a stop sign, looked both ways, and then stepped on the gas again. "Do you have that apple?"

Tommy reached down and picked the apple up from the floor of the car. "Right here."

"Thank you." Celine took the apple and bit into it with a ravenous zest, as if she hadn't eaten in days. "You're just going to your grandmother's for a while."

"Why?"

"Don't ask questions, Tommy. Just do what you're told."

His mother's tone stabbed Tommy in the chest a little too hard. Tears fell from his face. He turned away from his mother and looked out the window at the passing houses and storefronts with their lights out. He had tried to be strong and not cry, but everything was going too fast. There was nothing else a little boy could do.

Celine turned another corner sharply, squealing the tires again. They were almost at their destination and had made it there in what must have been record time. The stoplights had been good to them, and there must not have been enough cops on the road to notice her reckless driving and obvious neglect for the posted speed limits. Another turn and finally Tommy's grandmother's house was in view, the lights off. Had his mother not called in advance?

The car came to a stop and Celine reached behind her seat to grab the backpack. She looked up at Tommy, who watched her through his tears.

Celine sighed and set the backpack down on the front seat.

"I'm sorry, Tommy. I haven't been a good mother the past few days."

Tommy choked back the cry he wanted to let loose and let his mother wipe away the tears from his cheeks. "Are you going to look for Jennifer, like Dad?" he asked.

"Yeah, I am. And I'm going to find her. I just need you to be brave and wait for me here."

Tommy reached across the seat and hugged his mother. The fears of a child about to go it alone were alive inside him, but he refused to show it—he knew she wanted him to be brave. No matter what, he would do his best.

He closed his eyes and whispered in her ears, "I love you, Mom. Come back soon."

CHAPTER NINETEEN

Harlan took a tentative step forward and collapsed on the dirt below his feet. The moments before he realized Marie wasn't in front of him were wrought with more pain than he ever thought imaginable. He stopped questioning where he was or why he was there the second he looked out over the desert and saw Marie standing with her back to him.

He'd searched for his daughter and found the past waiting for him. At the moment of discovery, his heart had skipped a beat, sweat formed on his forehead and a fistful of butterflies fluttered in his stomach. Could it be that all the wishes he'd cast in all the fountains he could find had finally come true?

Marie's body disappeared the moment he called out her name. Her voice lingered in the air, sour and indifferent. *"Do you want to get out of here?"*

Harlan stood and surveyed the world around him. The desert stretched for miles, rising in a few places, falling in others. In the distance, darkened and ominous, jagged mountains stabbed heavenward. He'd been here before, at least once in his dreams, and if those dreams were an oracle to the future, then he should see a lake bed not too far away.

The air was decidedly cooler than he expected, and certainly cooler than the environment he'd just left. He turned to look for a puddle or cave, a doorway or portal — something that would lead him back to the forest, back to the deputy who was probably running to tell the others there had been another disappearance. Would that mean more people would find themselves wrapped up in a fog and end up here? If Jennifer did the same thing, where was she?

"Jennifer?" Harlan called out. He scanned the horizon looking for some sign of life. "Jennifer? Are you here?"

The wind picked up around Harlan, and for a moment, he thought it was in response to his voice. The land seemed a little too unwelcoming, a little too out of sorts. Still, what if he'd just found a gateway between two places on earth—a wormhole, or whatever it was those rocket scientist people called it? What if he was only in a desert somewhere in Arizona or New Mexico and help was just a shout away?

The mountains in the distance seemed to oppose his thought process. They were too surreal, and coupled with the feeling of being in this same spot at least once before in a fitful dream, the idea that he was still in Arizona faded quickly.

"Jennifer?"

Harlan took a few steps and stopped. In front of him, weaving through the desert brush like a snake, lay a well-worn footpath leading into the distance. He followed it with his eyes to his right and over a small hill. Could Jennifer have taken this path?

The path was easy to follow, but oddly designed. He saw it climb up the hill in front of him, but then wound to the left and right more than seemed necessary. He followed it quickly, taking note of all the plant life around him, and every once in a while, looking at the surreal landscape to his left, far away. He refused to believe he was being called in any one direction, but there was still a nagging sense of purpose tugging at his reason.

Harlan reached the top of the hill in less time than he had anticipated and looked out at what lay ahead. The hill angled sharply down toward a wash then over a cliff into a small canyon. The clouds above prevented little light from reaching the lower canyon walls, and its depth and character were difficult to make out. If Jennifer followed this footpath into that canyon, she would certainly be lost.

He sighed and began the trek down the opposite side of the hill, toward the canyon.

Marie's voice floated to him on the breeze. "You never

finish anything you start, do you?"

He stopped at the bottom of the hill and looked around. The voice was clearer than it had been since coming out of the void. He'd all but put the voices out of his head, focusing more on where he was and how he was going to find his daughter than trying to relive his past. Apparently, the past wanted some attention.

"You lied to me," Marie said, her voice tinted with sadness.

Harlan searched his memory for something that would match Marie's words. He closed his eyes.

"You lied to me. You said you would be there."

He tried harder to put the words into some past event in his life so he could relate better to what she'd said. It hurt more not knowing the context of the speech. Without a memory, it all seemed too real.

"I died that day, and you weren't there to comfort me." Marie's voice faded from sad to bitter. "I can't forgive you for that."

Harlan opened his eyes. Marie stood with her back to him, her arms crossed in front. The wind lifted her hair, and the air turned bitterly cold. "Marie?"

"I killed our child, and you disappeared."

"Child?" Harlan squinted. "*Our* child? What are you talking about?"

Marie lowered her head. It seemed to Harlan like she was crying, but without seeing her face, he couldn't be sure. His stomach rumbled nervously, much as it had when he first came out of the darkness and saw what he thought was Marie. This time, though, the nervousness was tainted with the hint of secrets kept from him.

"I never told you," Marie said, still not turning around. "You weren't there for me, Harlan."

"I— I didn't know." What else was he to say? He stepped forward and reached out to touch her on the shoulder.

The wind picked up suddenly and Marie's body faded from view. He stepped back, not sure he understood what just happened, but certainly repelled by the realization that this world was a little too close to him than he liked. Dreams aren't *this* real.

He looked past where Marie had stood and saw the jagged mountains in the distance. Increasingly, everything seemed like the premonitions he'd been given.

Everything, except the realization Marie had ever been pregnant with his child.

HARLAN REACHED the side of the canyon and looked down. The closer he'd come to it, the more it seemed less like something eroded and more like a crack in the face of the earth with steep walls created violently. If Jennifer had come into this world at the same point he had and followed the same footpath, she certainly wouldn't have tried to go into that place.

"Jennifer?" Harlan could barely see the bottom, if it was the bottom at all. The light didn't penetrate far enough. His call to his daughter echoed off the walls and mocked his attempt to find her.

He sighed. She wouldn't have gone down there, but without any real reference points in this world, he wasn't sure where she would have gone. He looked up at the distant mountains and once again felt their pull.

A thought crossed his mind that he was more dead than alive. The trip through the forest, into the darkness, and finally here in this desert was likely a journey a dead person would take. He scornfully chuckled at the thought, while at the same time not sure he was ready to discount the possibility. He didn't feel dead, and nothing in the forest would have put him out. Still...

No. Harlan sighed. He was just lost and Jennifer was just out there. Somewhere.

"She's not where you think she is."

Harlan turned toward the voice. At the edge of the canyon, Marie stood looking down in to the void. He could barely make out the features of her face.

"You know you can't go back," she said.

Harlan noticed his hands clench. "Who are you?"

"It's a one way trip. From here to there or there to here, but never back again."

"Marie?"

The image faded again, this time without the wind. Harlan's hands relaxed, but he stood transfixed to the spot, pretending he could still see her like a ghost on the television when the power goes out.

"Do you want to get out of here?"

Harlan spun around, but saw nothing. Marie's voice was disembodied this time and not as clear. His memory flashed back to a night of passion and her words that hung in the air as an invite to visit the wonders of her world.

"Meet me outside..."

The air was cold, the clouds darker than they had ever been. In the distance, the mountains pleaded for attention. Harlan looked down at the canyon one last time, and took a step toward the great unknown. If Jennifer was here, she needed help. If his memories were becoming all too real, what were hers becoming?

"You weren't there for me, Harlan."

New memories mixed with old, and Harlan found himself accepting the pain.

THE WIND wrapped around Harlan, pushing at his clothes and forcing the cold air inside his body. He stood at the edge of the desert looking out at a lake bed with his arms around his body. The horizon disappeared inside the dust that had been kicked up. He *had* been here before, and the lake bed was the proof, but now it was less friendly.

The voices were more persistent, caked with the past, and not a past Harlan wanted to relive. Celine was the most vocal. She berated him, spat words of hate and then took them back. She ranted about missed turns, Marie, and not getting the laundry done on time. For every drop of venom she spewed out of her ethereal mouth, however, there were drops of love. For the first time Harlan could remember, he felt that love like he'd never felt before. It was painful.

If he was dead, then this must be Hell. The realization that he'd lived a lie for so long pushed at him emotionally, mimicking the wind that pushed at him physically. The longer he stood at the edge of the lake bed, the colder everything became. The only recourse was to try to force Marie's voice back into his head, but even that seemed to fail. Every time her voice appeared, it brought with it failures and the knowledge that whatever he had done in the past was responsible for the pain he felt now.

The screams came next. They mixed in with the voices to create a cacophony of failure, hatred and fear. There was no memory here. He realized during the first few moments that the screams were something this world brought with it; he didn't bring it to this world like he had the voices. Within seconds, it seemed, the screams had overpowered the past and increased in volume. Like a well-tuned equalizer, the increase in volume increased the wind, and Harlan had to force himself to stand upright.

Ahead of him, the mountains loomed like saviors, calling to him in ways he'd never felt before. If he could get to them—if he could get anywhere but out in the open—he might find relief. Even the past was less painful.

The first physical blow came from the right and pushed Harlan to the ground. Against the onslaught of blowing dust, he turned to see who had brought him down. Through squinted eyes, wincing in pain from the blow to his side, he thought a shape moved.

His other side exploded in pain, like a knife had been jammed into his ribs and twisted. Hot pain shot through his body and Harlan screamed.

The voices screamed back, louder, pushing the wind even harder. Dust enveloped Harlan's body as he lay on the ground, the tiny bits of sand and dirt biting into his exposed flesh. Maybe if he'd found a way into the canyon, this wouldn't have happened.

Another strike on the back of the head pushed his face into the dirt. Something was there, and it was pissed off enough to keep him down on the ground. Red flashed across his eyes as another strike hit him in ear and then the neck.

Harlan turned his head as much as he could toward the direction of the last hit and opened his eyes. A few feet away, a disfigured face stared back, eyes wide open.

The sight of what lay before him stopped Harlan's heart for a moment as the will to run rushed in to replace the resignation he'd begun to feel. There was a demon in his midst and it didn't like him very much.

The wind suddenly stopped.

The screams died, too, but left a ringing in Harlan's ears. Even the voices from his past were no longer audible.

Harlan lay on the ground, curled into a fetal position, listening to his ragged breath. He tasted dirt and blood in his mouth, and still felt the hot pain shoot through his body. Whatever attacked him — at least for the moment — had left him alone.

"What do you want from this?"

He looked up to see Marie standing over him. Her hands were clenched into fists and her breath came in spurts.

"What do you expect to find here?" she asked. She knelt down in front of Harlan.

Harlan spit some dirt out of his mouth and realized he couldn't move much without exacerbating the pain in his side. Was he bleeding? "Who... are... you?"

Marie smiled, her face contorted in the shadowy light. She lay down on the ground next to Harlan, her face less than a foot from his. "You're not seeing the big picture, are you?"

"What's to see? I'm lost."

"No, you're not. You were lost before you came here. Now you've been found."

Harlan closed his eyes and did something he never thought he'd do: wished Marie would go away. "What are you?"

"What do expect to find here? That's the question."

"My daughter."

"What about *our* child? The one I had to give up in a nasty clinic because I knew you wouldn't be there for me. Why don't you look for our child? Surely the souls of children live on, don't they?"

Harlan winced at the pain in his side as he tried to move his legs. "I didn't know you were pregnant."

"But you knew I disappeared from your life."

"Yes."

"Did you question why?"

"Yes." Blood dripped from a wound over his eyes and trickled down his cheek. He reached a hand up and wiped it off. In the shadows, Marie's face seemed to change to the face he'd seen while being attacked.

He blinked. "You're not Marie."

The wind picked up again and Harlan closed his eyes expecting the worst. The voices from his past reappeared — Marie mixed with Celine mixed with Brian mixed with Jennifer. Voices replayed his memories over and over. The screams, however, did not come back.

Harlan opened his eyes, expecting to see Marie — or the thing that wasn't Marie — staring back at him with evil eyes. Instead, he saw nothing but the dust picked up by the wind. Harlan slowly pulled himself to his feet, holding his side.

He had to find Jennifer and get out of this world as quickly as possible.

THE PAIN in Harlan's side was dull — apparent, but not overwhelming. The clouds still covered the barren landscape, and the more he looked up, the less real it seemed. The light never changed; the sun never moved. He'd been walking for what seemed like hours, half fearing the darkness that was bound to come with the night. It was slowly becoming obvious, however, that night wasn't on schedule.

Since the last incident, the voices had become more violent in their tone. He struggled to hear the sweet words of his past love; however, more negative histories were written on the wind. It was as if the world around him evoked the deepest of his pain and spread it around like crumbs to feed on. He could stop and pick out a single moment, chew on the negative aspects of his life, or he could step around it all and try to find meaning in the meaningless environment he'd been thrust into.

And thrust into it he was. There was no urge to visit the cabin, just a hunch based on a need to help find his daughter. If she had come through the same fog he'd gone through, he could only pray she was safe from the same type of pain.

His side throbbed again. Emotionally, this place was draining. Even uglier, however, was the physical pain mixed with it.

Harlan stopped and looked behind him. He'd traveled quite a distance, and the hillside he'd left was shrouded in haze. To his right was the bank of the lake bed, as desolate as the desert he'd walked into. He'd kept as straight a course as possible: toward the mountains free of any obstacles.

He turned back to the goal and willed himself forward. His legs were tired, but surprisingly, he didn't seem thirsty or hungry. He was, for the most part, annoyed at the voices but determined to find his daughter.

She's a whore, Harlan.

Celine's voice lifted above the others, like oil separating from water. He felt comforted by it, if only for the familiarity.

She sees power in you, but that's about it.

"More than you ever saw in me." Harlan sighed. He'd found himself talking back to the voices on more than one occasion. It kept a sense of sanity wrapped around him, like the voices were cerebral psychologists and he could sort out his own problems.

"No, I saw a lot more in you than you give me credit for."

Harlan stopped and looked to his left. Celine stood against a backdrop of the lake bed and painted clouds. Her clothes were torn from the pages of his memories: a sun dress she hadn't worn in years. This had to be another trick, more simulacra of a life that wanted to be revisited.

"You're not real," Harlan said, and took another step.

"Maybe not as real as you'd like me to be."

Harlan kept walking. "Back there, you kicked me when I was down, and you looked like Marie. Why the costume change?"

"To prove a point."

"What point is that?"

"You're an open book out here, Harlan. You're inviting us inside."

Harlan turned to the thing that masqueraded as Celine. "Us?"

The figure vanished as soon as his words had trailed away in the wind. It had been another trick, but at least he hadn't been attacked.

The wind picked up like a vortex around Harlan, pushing his body from right to left and back and forth. Dust pelted his skin. He closed his eyes and put an arm up to cover his face. Inside the wind, voices screamed at him, throwing words that stuck to his ears like mud, blocking out all other sounds. Harlan tried to focus on the words, to hear what they had to say, but nothing was clear. It didn't even sound like a language he understood.

Harlan peeked out from under his arm and looked for escape. The edge of the lake bed was only a few hundred yards away. He ran toward it, hoping there was a safer place to be than out in the open.

The wind followed him and made his steps, at best, erratic. The screams increased in pitch the closer he came to the edge, but the words still made no sense.

As his feet left the cracked ground and landed on the desert floor, the wind stopped.

Celine stood in front of Harlan, her arms crossed. "You just don't get it, do you?"

Harlan leaned forward, trying to catch his breath. "Get... what?"

"You're a victim of yourself."

He looked up and watched as Celine vanished. Whatever wanted to toy with his emotions—rip out his thoughts and play them on a stage in front of him—didn't like to stay around very long. It was almost as if they were afraid of something, or maybe his life was simply too boring to act out.

He let his heart settle down before moving. The desert wasn't easier to walk on than the lake bed, but it felt safer. Vegetation spotted the ground and what looked like a well-worn path followed the edge. Harlan kept his face down, arms wrapped around him, and tried to tune out his past as it was replayed over and over on some sick and twisted ethereal speakers.

The path turned away from the lake bed and rose up a little hill. The distant mountains were visible, their dark, craggy faces a vibrant contrast to the beige desert. Harlan cleared a yucca plant and stopped at the crest.

A few buildings, made of either rotting wood or adobe, stood silent about a mile away. Their construction left much to be desired, but it might as well have been a lean-to made of twine weaved together. It was shelter and as he looked down on the little group of buildings, his stomach twisted with something he thought was hope. Was there life out here that wasn't dependent on his past?

The path down the hill was rockier than it had been coming up. More and more vegetation sprouted up—cholla and yucca plants, a few barrel cacti, sagebrush in all directions. As he came to the bottom of the decline, it all opened up, like a road made for four-wheel drive cars or—he smiled at the thought—stagecoaches ripped from the Westerns he'd watched as a kid.

The road cut through the buildings, making it look more like a town. Under the dull glow of the sun still buried in clouds, diffuse shadows covered everything. Harlan took a few more steps forward and stopped.

If the world behind him was so violently opposed to him being there, then what waited for him inside the buildings? He shuddered at the thought of another one of those creatures that had masqueraded as Marie. It was unpleasant at best, and offered him the physical pain he could do without.

Harlan took a few tentative steps forward. His stomach, so twisted by the idea of finding hope, twisted again and filled with acid.

"Hello?" The sound of his voice mixed in with all the other voices and seemed to be absorbed. He called louder. "Hello?"

He took a few more steps toward the buildings then stopped and waited.

Nothing moved.

Confidence didn't quite swell inside of Harlan, but fear took a step back. He slowly walked up to the first building and stepped onto a makeshift porch. There was no glass in the window, just a hole next to a door. He took a deep breath and peered inside.

"Hello? Is anyone here?"

A crack of wood—perhaps someone moving on the floor—made Harlan take a step away from the window. Maybe this was a bad idea.

He waited as his eyes passed from what he saw inside the building to his left and right.

Nothing moved.

Harlan took another breath and stepped toward the door. There was no handle—just a piece of rope tied in a loop. He pulled and the door opened with a creak.

"If anyone is here, I need some help."

He took a step inside the building and looked around. Dust covered everything, from a fireplace to chairs to a bed of grass in the corner. A table—nothing more than a board over two large rocks—sat up against one wall. He couldn't be sure, but Harlan thought he could make out a bowl and spoon along with a plate of bones, the meat long since eaten or rotted away.

Just under a window to his right, a hand moved.

Harlan jumped back. An older man, probably in his sixties, sat with his back against the wall. He stared toward the opposite wall. His lips quivered.

Harlan let his heart slow down. "Hello? I need some help."

The man stared at the far wall.

"Are you alright?"

With what seemed like great effort, the old man turned his head to the left and looked up at Harlan, looming above him. His lips quivered more as his hand slowly came up off the floor.

"I asked if you're alright." Harlan didn't feel well. All of the hope he thought he might have felt when he first laid eyes on the buildings had turned itself into fear first and now disappointment. The man on the floor was a vegetable.

Harlan knelt down next to the old man and took his hand. His skin was clammy and cold.

The man opened his eyes a little more, looked down at his hand, then turned back to face the wall he'd been so intently looking at before.

"Seems a shame to lose someone like that," he finally said. His voice cracked, probably dry.

"Lose who?" Harlan asked.

"No, honey. We don't have the money."

Harlan furled his eyebrows. Was there someone else here? He looked around the room, but it was as empty as he originally thought.

The man closed his eyes. "I needed to go to his funeral. I needed to see it for myself."

Harlan let go of the man's hand and stood. Did the old man hear voices as well? He remembered talking back to his own past as he walked across the lake bed. Maybe this old man was doing the same thing.

"Is there anyone else here?" Harlan looked out the door at another building across the dirt road. "I need help."

"I should have gone, Carol. You were right."

Harlan sighed and stepped out of the building. There were at least four other buildings, four more chances to find someone who was coherent enough to talk to. If he was able to find one old man in a building—despite the fact that he was rambling to himself—there was still the chance he could find others.

HARLAN STOOD at the end of the road past the last building. He had found only one other person: a woman in her fifties who rocked back and forth on the floor. She didn't even notice Harlan talking or kneeling down in front of her. She did nothing but sing a lullaby and cry.

He let out a sigh as resignation of his loneliness. There were people here—those who must have come before, trapped like rabbits in cages long forgotten. The two he'd met both seemed transfixed by what he could only guess was their past, thrown at them the way he'd had it thrown at him. If they had succumbed to the difficult mirror of their lives, would he do the same? Was there no one in this world that could help?

Harlan turned to follow the road farther on. The distant mountains—now closer but still far away—stood high over the horizon. The road narrowed to its previous incarnation as a footpath as it wound through the desert and over another hill. Perhaps there was another town, another chance at finding someone who wasn't a victim of themselves.

"You weren't there for me, Harlan." Marie's voice seemed to be the only constant through the last few moments. It was unnerving, to say the least. The last time her voice overpowered the others, Harlan had found himself curled on the lake bed floor while some... thing had beat the crap out of him.

It wasn't possible. Harlan searched his past with Marie and tried to find some inkling of her pregnancy that was only visible upon reflection. Yes, they'd made love—several times—but at each coupling there was protection. She even mentioned once that she'd started taking birth control pills. There was no way she could have been pregnant.

He had another child, of course. Tommy, the ever-inquisitive seven-year-old. He was the answer to a prayer, an attempt to keep his marriage on track. It's not that he wasn't wanted in life—Harlan relished his moments with Tommy—but he wasn't exactly planned. Before Tommy was born, there were moments when his thoughts would stray back to Marie, and those thoughts would lead to communication of innocent origin. But in the back of Harlan's mind, that communication was an attempt to seek out the way back to her side. It was only when Tommy was born that the search for a reunion ended.

There were still moments of relapse, however. Harlan couldn't deny his love for Marie, and he imagined she couldn't deny hers. Even if there was no chance—no visible alternative to the lives they now led—there was still that nagging need to be with one another, like a perfect puzzle that could only be completed with each other as the missing piece.

Another child? Harlan breathed in, hoping to squash the rush of emotion that coursed through his veins. If Marie had been pregnant, the child would have been... eight? Nine? He didn't want to put an age on him or her, though; that would itself be an admission that the thing portraying Marie told the truth. Besides, if she'd really been pregnant, the thing said she'd had an abortion. The thing said she hid this from him and lied to cover it up.

Anger brewed inside Harlan, an emotion he didn't feel he should have while thinking of Marie. Sure, he'd made mistakes, pushed her back as much as she'd pushed him back. There was so much pain trapped in that relationship, but anger had never been an emotion tied to it.

What was happening to him?

The path crested another hill and Harlan stopped dead in his tracks. Below him, a town of buildings no different from the five he'd left behind stood out in the haze. They butted up against the edge of the lake bed which stretched out for miles too his right.

Rather than the buildings, however, Harlan found himself more shocked by the hundreds of people standing at the bottom of the hill. They stared at him, their bodies pushed against each other like a curtain of flesh.

He wasn't sure, but he thought he recognized all of them, and no one looked happy.

CHAPTER TWENTY

"I'm four years old," Justine said with authority and conviction. "I can walk by myself."

Marie held back a smile at the words from such a frail little child as she watched the girl bounce up the side of another dune. They had been walking for hours, but to judge by the sun rising or setting proved to be impossible—it simply shone through the thick gray clouds and offered no indication of the time of day. Marie shrugged off the enigma of the solar cycle in this strange world she was in and took a few larger strides than normal to catch up with Justine.

"Look, miss," Justine called out. She pointed out past the dunes toward the mountains in the distance. "I can see for miles."

Marie reached the top of the dune and followed Justine's finger. "Looks like we're in for a walk."

"Is that where we're going?"

"I don't know, Justine, but I don't see any place else to go. You don't want to sit on these dunes anymore, do you?"

"No. The sand is making me itch."

Marie smiled and placed her hand affectionately on Justine's head. "Me, too."

"Are you ready?" Justine asked.

"Ready for what?"

"I'll race you to the next dune."

"I think we could walk this one, Justine." Marie frowned at the realization that there really was yet another sand dune to cross over. How many had they crossed in the last few hours? Ten? Twenty? *Too many to count*, she thought. "I'm a little older than I thought."

"Mommy used to say that to me, too." Justine's smile faded as her eyes dropped slowly to her feet. "I miss my mommy."

Marie still had no idea what to say to her. How do you tell a child that everything will be all right if you don't believe it yourself? The thoughts of her own daughter at this age kept assailing her at every turn. Is that how she would react? Marie couldn't help but notice how both Justine and Susan were similar in certain respects. She had spent the previous dune or two thinking about her own loss, but Marie knew her feelings were probably less than that of Justine's mother. To know your child has died brings with it a sense of closure. To know your child is missing, but not know the well-being of that child, must be a pain altogether different.

"Can I ask you a question?" Marie knelt down to face Justine. "How long have you been here?"

Justine closed her eyes, turned her head away from Marie, and pulled her stuffed bear close to her chest. "I don't know."

Silence fell on the two atop the dune. The wind picked up a few more loose grains of sand and blew them over the side to join the sand below, forever changing the landscape. Marie had feared Justine wouldn't know the answer to the question. Time was a concept children had trouble grasping.

"Justine?"

Suddenly, Justine opened her eyes and turned to Marie. Tears welled up at the bottom of her eyes. Her smile was gone and what had been a face of joy and elation at the sight of another person had turned into a face of sadness, fear, anger and the frustration of not knowing which emotion to show.

Marie pushed back Justine's hair from her forehead and tucked a few strands behind her ears. She bent down a little farther, brought Justine's chin up and looked directly into her eyes. "How did you get here?"

Justine pulled back. "*I don't know!*" Jerking away from Marie, she ran down the side of the dune.

Marie stood and watched her run, wondering just what it

was that she didn't know—or didn't want to say. She looked down. In her haste, Justine had left her bear at Marie's feet.

THE VOICES that had come so strong when she first entered the nothingness were still with Marie as she chased after Justine. The little girl was determined to get to the top of each successive dune and, at the same time, lengthen the gap between the two of them. Marie could have walked a little faster and easily caught up with her, but she decided to let Justine have a moment to let out her frustrations. Whatever it was that brought her here—regardless of whether or not she knew—was a touchy subject for the four-year-old.

Marie let the voices come in clearer. A little louder now, they spoke of banal memories and those that were as fresh as the sand dune she just left. There was a football game where she stood at the fence with her friends. Coupled with those voices, however, came the voice of Peter, telling her to how she needed to straighten up and get her life on track.

"Go to school, if you want," he had said, with a less-than-concerned look on his face. "We can get by without a second income for a while."

That was a sore subject, and Marie's stomach fell as she listened to his voice. Although she felt loved by him, and at times she knew he was the answer to all of her problems through life, she was never convinced that Peter ever really wanted what was best for her. He seemed more concerned with how it would benefit or disrupt his own life. The picture perfect life she thought she married into was actually falling to pieces from the inside, and Peter never wanted to talk about it. Their child was enough to keep them happy, but internally Marie wanted Peter to be more like Harlan who had tried to show her there was a reason for everything, and it only took a good look in the mirror to find it.

Marie watched as Justine disappeared down the far embankment of a large dune just ahead of her. She stood in the valley between the one she left and the next one over and stared up at the massive mountain of sand, small footprints made larger by the shifting sand trailing up the side. Marie had long ago grown tired of the walking, wondering just when the next dune was going to be the last. There was no particular destination in mind, but a flat field of grass that stretched on for miles would have been more preferable to her than mountain upon mountain of sand.

Marie sighed and climbed up the hill, following the footsteps of her little trail guide. She heard Justine say something, but the words were hard to make out between the barrier of the dune and the still-present voices that followed her. When she reached the top, Marie found Justine sitting down just on the other side staring out at a whole different landscape: a lake bed, cracked from years of no water and a constant beating of the elements, stretched out in front of them until it disappeared into a haze near the horizon just below the mountains.

Marie sat next to Justine and looked out over the vast expanse of an even more barren landscape than what they had just crossed. She began to miss the sand dunes, though she still sat on one. She feared that to cross the lake bed would be more laborious than anything before.

A direction meant a goal, however, and no matter how she dreaded the attempt, the only way to find out what the goal was, was to take that first step.

Marie handed Justine the spotted bear. "You dropped this. What's his name?"

Justine took the bear, looked at it briefly, and then pulled it to her chest. "His name is Bear."

Marie smiled and thought to herself of all the stuffed animals she had named in the past as a little girl. "Now that's original."

Justine sighed and looked up at Marie. "Do we have to cross that, now?"

"Looks like it, but it can't be all that bad." Marie doubted her own words as soon as she said them.

"I'm tired of walking."

"So am I." Marie looked down and brushed back Justine's hair once again. "But how do you climb a ladder?"

"One step at a time. Mommy used to say that, too."

"Your Mommy's a smart girl, Justine. You know that?"

Justine turned her gaze out toward the lake bed and let out an exaggerated sigh that made her sound a little more grown up. "Yeah. I know that. But Mommy's not here anymore."

THE DIRT was hard, not at all like the sand they had just been through. Occasionally, a small piece would break up as Marie put her weight on it, but the majority of the dirt between the cracks was hard as rock. Justine hopped over the cracks, trying not to step on them.

To Marie, the trek was a little more relaxing than she first thought it would be. The voices were still present, but she tried not to listen to them. She sang a song, hoping Justine would join her, but every song she sang it seemed the little girl didn't know the words. Instead, they jumped over cracks for a while until it became boring for both of them.

The sky was still cloudy and the light that shone through was no brighter or darker than it was in the desert behind them. Marie wondered if night ever came here, or if there was really only one moment trapped in time. No matter how long you spent here, the second hand never ticked away. At least it was cooler on the lake bed—not so much an Alaskan extreme, but cooler nonetheless. The wind felt a little stronger and Marie thought about finding a way to keep Justine warm.

"Are you sure you want to do that?" Harlan's voice filtered through the wind and struck Marie again. She smiled inwardly then tried to focus more on what was around her in the now, rather than the past. It was a wonderful memory, but she didn't come here to relive the past—although, in reality, she had no idea why she had come here. She told herself that if she could simply ignore the voices, they would eventually go away. In the time she had been here, however, none of the voices had really gone, nor had they changed. They spoke of the same things, like a scratched record turning around and around. There was Harlan, there was the clinic, there was Peter, Susan and her friends from years past. There was even a faint voice of Jacob, although she could never really make out

what the voice was saying. Nevertheless, all of it repeated rather than offered any new insight into the life she once had.

Justine had run up ahead of Marie and stood still waiting for her to catch up. Marie walked up next to Justine and placed her hand on the girl's head, then looked out ahead of them toward the horizon. "Do you see anything out there?"

"No," Justine sighed. "I think we're lost."

"Oh, I don't know about that," Marie lied. She tried to focus on the distant mountains then brought her eyes down to the edge of the horizon, where a haze blended in with the lake bed and left a fuzzy line across the scene. She couldn't be sure, but the longer she stared, the more it looked like the haze could take the shape of something. What it might take shape into wasn't clear.

"Are you cold, Justine?"

"What's that sound?" Justine asked, ignoring Marie's question. Marie straightened up and listened to the wind. Between the voices and the wind, Marie hadn't heard anything else for a while and had almost become comfortable with the situation. She closed her eyes as if that would open her ears up a little more, but all she heard were memories, whispers on the wind.

"I don't hear anything but the wind, Justine. What is it you hear?"

"Sounds like someone... someone yelling." Justine wrapped her arms around her body. "I don't like it when people yell."

Marie listened again, hopeful to hear the same thing as Justine. Was this a voice from the child's past she couldn't hear, or was it something tangible in the present both of them shared? "What does the voice say?"

Justine tried hard to listen again. She shook her head and looked up at Marie. "I don't know. It sounds like your name."

Marie perked up and turned around in circles, looking for the voice that called her name. Still, she couldn't hear. All the while, the voices from the past attacked her ears and became louder, making it difficult to separate what was real from what was imagined.

Suddenly, through the din of the voices, she thought she could make out another—distant and left of the direction they were headed. It rode in on the wind and pushed past the memories and whispers in her ears as much as the word "Marie" could from miles away.

Marie looked out over the barren lake bed toward the horizon. Her heart quickly jumped as she watched a figure emerge from the blur between the land and the sky. It was too far away to make out any distinct features, but it looked almost like the figure was running, and running straight at them.

Marie grabbed Justine and pulled her tight against her thigh, fearing whatever it was that called her name in this world. Her heart beat faster and a lump grew in her throat as a thousand scenarios struck her at once. Maybe it was a demon, bent on killing them both. Maybe David had survived the fight with Jacob in her kitchen and was out for revenge. Maybe Jacob was after her now and sought to do her harm in this strange world. Maybe...

Maybe she was just making things worse than they really were. As the figure grew closer, she heard the voice a little clearer. She continued to watch the figure, slowing from a run to a trot. Its face was still masked by the distance, but the body of a man was coming more into focus. He was taller, but not so tall that he would be noticed in a crowd of people. His clothes wrapped around his body in such a fashion that she couldn't tell if he was a muscular man or a fat man able to hide the folds of his skin with flannel and denim. As her heart quickened with the anxiety of the looming moment, she began to feel that the shape was almost familiar.

Justine tightened her grip on Marie's thigh and tried to hide a little more behind her. "I'm scared," she whispered.

Marie reached back her hand and rubbed the little girl's head. "Don't be, honey. Everything will be alright."

The figure slowed to a walk about a hundred yards from where Marie and Justine stood huddled together on a dry lake bed in the middle of God-knows-where. He raised his hand, waving it back and forth, and Marie swore she saw a smile break across the man's face.

"Checkmate," he finally called out.

Marie's stomach sank and her heart stopped for a moment as the face of the figure walking toward them resolved itself into Harlan.

As quickly as it had appeared, though, the figure vanished in a gust of wind. Marie dropped the smile she was about to wear and stared into the emptiness in front of her. Justine tugged at her pant leg.

"Is that someone you know?"

Marie nodded her head. Were the memories now so vibrant they took a life of their own? "Yeah," she said finally. "He was a good friend."

"Why did he go away?"

Marie fought back the urge to answer the little girl with something a little more analytical to her life. *He went away*, she thought, *because I pushed too hard and wanted too much.* "I don't know, Justine." She sighed and turned back toward the mountains without giving it another thought.

THERE ARE moments that define a person's life—moments that force a person to question the self or to question God or to question the empty air in front. To some, they are moments born of anger, lashing out without care as to what's in front of them. To others, they are moments born of fear or frustration, crying out for something to come along that might erase the problem or situation. There are times in a person's life when they wish to become something they are not, or to say something they cannot, or to do something they're simply physically or emotionally incapable of doing. There are times when the whole world is pushing down, and all they can think of is why God would put them in this situation.

Marie had lived through many of these moments in her life, and the longer she spent in the strange world she had stumbled across, the more she was forced to relive these moments. She had crossed the lake bed, thinking to herself, even as the voices cascaded around her, that there was a *reason*. No matter what was about to happen—even if nothing *was* going to happen—there was a *reason*. There was a reason for David to appear before her and Jacob's violent reaction. There was a reason for reaching down into a puddle of nothingness when the urge to explore was so strong. There was a reason for the journey she was on toward the mountains in the distance. There was a reason for there to be a child at her side.

Finally, to get to this point, there had to be a reason. Harlan had left—or, more truthfully, she had left him. She'd tried to divorce herself from his memory by making that choice in the woman's clinic, as if she could somehow start over. But journeys don't start over, she heard. Journeys take different directions, but you're always a step beyond where you were. With that light, she could never get beyond Harlan or the memory of what she could have had with him. To get from Harlan to some semblance of family, she had to take into her life another man, someone who would paint over the past on the canvas of her life. Peter was that painter, and with another child, she could pretend that life was new again.

Marie looked down at Justine, quietly walking beside her. The child was so much like Susan, both in age and mannerisms. Rather than feel the pain of loss even more, however, Marie found herself resuming the role of the protector—a role a child needs to see played on their tiny stage of life.

Justine looked up at Marie. "Are you sad?" she asked. Her face was dirty, and Marie mechanically wiped at a smudge on her chin.

"I am. Why do you ask?"

"Because I can hear you crying."

Marie stopped and knelt down. "I wasn't crying, Justine."

"Not here," she said, pointing to Marie's face. "Here." Justine pushed her little finger into Marie's forehead. "Where you think."

Marie smiled.

"Well, why would I be crying?"

Justine looked down and pushed a small rock around with her foot. "Because he's mad at you, but you like him."

"Who?"

"The ghost man."

"Mad at me?" Marie furled her eyebrows and stood. She scanned the horizon for a sign of this "ghost man" before accepting that any appearance of Harlan—for real—was a foolish thought.

"Miss?" Justine tapped Marie on the leg. "What's that?"

Marie turned and followed Justine's finger into the distance, to the edge of the lake bed. Barely, she could make out something less natural than the world around her. A building?

"I don't know. Maybe we finally found ourselves."

Justine let out a cheer and ran ahead. The idea of a protector might have filled her with more security than she had, or perhaps it was just the adult in her wanting to push forward and make her face her fears rather than live with them any longer. Marie watched Justine and felt the child was finally free of the loneliness she must have felt for so long, and now in the comfort of someone she had just met, she was excited. She hopped over another crack and smiled.

A sudden gust of wind, cold and strong, knocked Justine down as one foot came out from underneath her. Marie ran forward. As she reached her side, another gust of wind hit her square in the face. The chill sent needles throughout her cheeks that dug deep inside and filled Marie with a cold she never knew could exist.

She braced herself against the wind and the cold and fought to stand. The wind screamed, a thousand voices merged together in a cacophony of pain. No sound in life could have prepared Marie for the agony that filled her from inside. She covered her ears with her hands, but there was no way to block the screams.

Out of the corner of Marie's eye, she saw Harlan standing in relative calm. With the power of the wind assaulting her body and the screams attacking her sanity, she was shocked to see that not even his shirt moved.

Harlan took a step forward and smiled.

Was this all in her mind?

As suddenly as it had come, the wind stopped and silence fell.

Marie cautiously took her hands off her ears and sat next to Justine. Her chest heaved and matched the pounding of her heart with every gasp of air. To her right, Justine shook and held Bear tightly against her. Her face was buried in its cloth fur. Marie looked at her and pulled her little body tight against hers, fearful she heard the same as she did. Praying it was only in *her* mind.

"Are you alright?" Marie finally asked.

Justine let out a soft cry then closed her eyes. Marie looked up to see if Harlan—or whatever the thing was that took on his shape—still stood, observing them.

The emptiness of the lake bed seemed all too oppressive.

"What was that?" Marie touched Justine's chin and brought her face up. "What just happened?"

Justine looked past Marie and out toward the mountains. "I don't like your ghost man."

CHAPTER TWENTY-ONE

There is freedom on a highway in a desert at 2 a.m. The freedom to roll down your window and yell, to roll up your window and sing, to swerve from the right lane to the left lane, to turn off the lights, to turn them on again, and the undeniable freedom to think. The vibrations of the tires rolling across asphalt fill the body, rush in from the ground up to the head and envelop the lonely driver as his or her hands grip the wheel. The yellow lines, sometimes broken, sometimes solid, streak toward the car and fly into the diffuse lights then off to the driver's left. A solid white line — ever visible on the right — shows a few tire treads, a few dirty spots, and a few ghostly reminders every now and again of those who have gone before but failed to keep the course.

In the middle of these two lines — the yellow to the left and the white to the right — Celine gripped the wheel of her car and felt the vibrations of the road, the rumble of the engine and the wind rush in through the open window. It pushed and pulled strands of her hair up and around. The air was warm, wet and filled with the scent of the recent rain that must have just passed the lonely highway to the north of Phoenix. Her mind was elsewhere, however, bouncing between the thoughts of a man standing in the shadows of her bedroom telling her to look for Jennifer in the mountains, the thoughts of Harlan's failure to fill her life with the love he promised at the altar so many years ago and the thoughts of Justine alone in a desert, clutching the bear she had made for her while still carrying the child in her womb.

The speedometer in Celine's car read just over ninety miles per hour, but she wasn't concerned about the speed limit or the dangers of driving so fast on wet asphalt. Her mind was as focused as it had been in days, and although the focus was on three separate things, all three were an integral part of her life. All three merged together to form a cross she would have to bear—alone. There was no support base any longer, and whatever she felt she could tell Harlan in the past, he wasn't around to listen. She had borne the pain of losing Justine for years now, and she had hidden that pain deep inside hoping that a new family and a new start would fill the emptiness of her life.

Miles ahead of the car, lightning raced across the sky to strike the Earth with fearsome vengeance. The sudden flash illuminated much of the desert, and for a second, Celine saw the mountains rise above the desert floor. They were still miles away, though. The storm seemed closer, and she began to wonder if all of this was a mistake. She hated to drive in the rain, and the thought of anything that might slow her progress down irritated her.

She didn't even know where to look once she got there.

She sighed and turned her focus from the mountains back to the road and her life in general. She was a mess, and after forty years there was little anything could be done to correct it all. With a failed marriage, two missing daughters and the sudden guilt of abandoning Tommy hanging over her, she wondered if life wasn't trying to show her a different way altogether. Maybe it was trying to tell her something about her past, that although she couldn't change it, she could still accomplish *something*. In those four decades, Celine was convinced the only accomplishments of her life were three children—and she had failed with all three. If life was trying to show her something, what the hell was it?

Lightning flashed in front of the car once again, and large drops of rain began to pelt the windshield. Celine frowned, rolled up the window and turned on the windshield wipers. The drops were spaced apart but large, and struck the glass like tiny bombs, exploding upwards as the car moved forward into the storm. She let her foot off the accelerator just a little, afraid to drive so fast in the rain. With all the horror stories of cars trapped in washes that only fill when the rain comes, she wanted to have the time to react if she saw the road covered with water up ahead.

A tire burst. Celine's eyes opened wide as she fought to control the crippled vehicle and pull off onto the side of the road. The rear of the car spun around to the right while she fought with the steering wheel. With the squeal of brakes, the car finally came to a rest sideways on the opposite side of the road, in the dirt up against a sharp rise into the desert beyond.

With Celine's heart pounding in her chest, her shaking hands let go of the steering wheel. She sat back to let the adrenaline taper off as the wiper blades whipped back and forth.

SHE MUST have sat silent in the car for some time. The clock had changed to 2:49, its alien green light illuminating the front seat. The rain still pummeled the car, streaking down the front windshield then disappearing as the wiper blades came back. Celine turned off the wipers and then the car. The sudden silence of the mechanical escalated the volume of nature as the rain hit the roof and hood. Each drop pounded out the rhythm of life and the fury of the thunderstorm over her head. Through the sheets of rain, she saw the deserted road and realized just how alone she really was. She sat in a crippled car, miles from help and trapped by the rain outside.

Celine beat the steering wheel with the palms of her hands and simultaneously let loose a scream of anger and frustration. No matter what life wanted to hand her, at every turn she took, somehow it mocked her.

The Lord had no mercy.

"*No!*" she cried and beat the steering wheel again. She looked out at the rain and bit her lip. To accomplish her goal of finding Jennifer and understanding the dream she had earlier, she would have to get out and change the tire. The storm didn't look like it was going to let up, and the longer she waited in the solitary confinement of the car, the more the memories would creep up and try to kill her.

Celine pulled her cell phone from the dash. "No Signal" flashed across the front. Of course there would be no signal; there was no life out here.

With a grunt, she unlatched the trunk of the car from inside and opened the door. The outside air, thick with warmth and moisture, flooded in around her and wrapped her body in a sticky sheet that made her feel suddenly dirty. The sound of the rain accosted her as it beat the desert floor and filled puddles around her car.

At least I'm not in a ditch.

With a burst of energy, she stepped out of the car and ran to the trunk. The rain was cold and the drops so large, by the time she reached the truck of the car, her hair was wet and clothes soaked. Lightning flashed in the sky above, and the thunder that came with it was loud enough to force a short cry out of her.

In the rain behind her, just over the rise, someone screamed in response.

Celine's heart skipped a beat then raced faster than it had ever before. Her breath came in short spurts as she turned around slowly. How the hell was she going to protect herself?

The worst of scenarios flooded her mind at once. She saw a madman—half coyote, half human with four-inch claws. A split second later, she imagined an escaped convict screaming in pain from a gunshot wound, his eyes filled with rage and in his mouth the taste of blood.

Whatever it was, it existed, and in a storm in the middle of the night in a vast desert, Celine had no defense save the God she had cursed for years.

She looked through the rain as she inched her way back to the car door. If she could get inside and lock the door, maybe she could stay safe until a passerby came and rescued her. If she could drive for just a few miles on a blown tire, she might be safer. Maybe there was a small gas station up ahead where she could wake up the attendant and get to a phone to call for help. If she could just make it back inside the car.

"Help... me." The voice was weak, so much different than

the scream she heard. It wafted in through the rain and snaked its way into Celine's ears, filling her with more fright and quickening her pulse even more. At the same time, however, the simple soft words made her stop.

Help... me. There was a man in trouble, and she was the only one around to help. Her mind filled up again with more scenarios. Perhaps it was a driver beaten by gangs and left to die in the desert night, or maybe it was an old man, deserted by his family and left to walk alone up the highway looking for help or a little handout from someone.

Help... me.

As the rain continued to fall and soak her body, Celine began to reason in different tones.

"Please, help me," the voice called out again, this time a little stronger. Celine thought she sensed hurt and loneliness in the voice—something she was acutely aware of recently. She could be the Good Samaritan or she could just get back in the car, lock the door, and try to hide.

Damn it.

She looked out through the rain and tried to pinpoint just where the voice was coming from.

"Please."

The man lay in a puddle, curled in a fetal position, completely naked and covered in blood. He turned his head toward Celine as she walked slowly to him and squinted against the onslaught of the rain. His breath seemed labored, and with each rise and fall of his chest he grimaced in pain.

Celine stood at a distance as fear pulsed though every vein, every artery, every nerve in her body. She watched him closely and pushed aside her wet hair to get a better look. His arms looked like they were carved of stone and his legs the same. Curly brown hair was pressed against his forehead, and even in the darkness she saw he was injured. Blood poured from a wound above his hairline and mixed with the rain and mud. There must have been other wounds for there to be that much blood covering the rest of his body, and even with the rain, it was ever present.

He looked at her and raised his head up slowly, then laid

it back down again as if the effort caused too much pain to continue.

"Help me," he said once again. He closed his eyes and grimaced. He arched his back and let out a scream through clenched teeth, then relaxed once more and tried to sit up.

Celine took another step forward and held a hand out as if to say, "Stay there." She watched his movements, still not convinced she was safe. She felt she needed to be ready to run at any moment.

"Are you okay?" Considering the circumstances, her question seemed rather stupid. If she were naked in the desert in a thunderstorm and grimacing in pain, would she be okay?

The man looked at her again and laid his head down in the mud. "I'll be alright."

"What happened to you?" Celine took another step forward, but still kept her distance.

"I fell."

Celine internally questioned his answer, but her mind reasoned the man must be in so much pain he didn't realize what he said. Would she?

The man screamed again, arching his back and turning completely over. Celine jumped back, her throat involuntarily swallowing her breath. She watched him as he arched more and more, screaming as if he had just lost an arm or leg with no anesthetic. Finally, he let loose a loud breath and fell back to the ground.

Celine watched for a moment, expecting him to maybe scream again, or writhe around in pain, but the longer she watched, the less he appeared alive. His chest had stopped moving altogether.

The rain began to let up a little and came down more as a creek than a river. The bloody naked man lay face up in the puddle, his arms and legs outstretched and eyes closed.

Five minutes passed, maybe ten, maybe one. Time was inconsequential to the moment, and Celine was as wet as she was ever going to be. The rain had covered her entire body as if she were naked herself and standing at the bottom of a pool. Water dripped from her hair, her nose, her ears, her lips—so much of it she had stopped trying to wipe her face with her hand.

Celine kept an eye on the man while she tried to think of what to do. All the problems she had faced in the past few days faded fast, eclipsed by the strangeness of events at this moment. Had her tire not blown in the exact spot it did, she would not be staring at a bloody naked man who now looked dead. If she hadn't dreamed of someone in the corner of her bedroom telling her to look for Jennifer in the mountains, she would never have left her house, and Tommy would still be asleep. Life was showing her something, but she couldn't imagine what it might be.

She sighed, more out of exasperation than anything else. In the puddle, the naked man was obviously dead. Celine looked at him one more time then turned around to go back to her car, fix her flat, and be on her way.

"Why do you leave me?"

Celine stopped and turned around. Her breath caught somewhere between her lungs and her mouth. The naked man stood in the same puddle she had just declared him dead in, his body no longer covered with blood. He was tall, very muscular as she had previously thought, and as he raised his hand up to wipe his face, she could faintly see a small pinky ring.

"You're just going to leave me for dead? What kind of a Good Samaritan are you?" The naked man took a step toward Celine.

"I'm... I'm..." Celine took a step back and found she was at a loss for words. The fear she thought had faded rushed back in from all directions, stronger than ever. "I'm sorry."

"You were going to leave me for dead in this... this..." The naked man looked around him quickly then back at Celine. "Where am I?"

Celine took another step back and tried to judge the distance between her and the car. If she could make it to the door, she could jump inside and drive to safety. Forget that the tire was flat; a ruined rim was better than a dead woman.

"Now I remember." The man pointed to Celine. "You're Celine, right?"

Celine's eyes opened wide and her breath stopped altogether. The naked man who knew her name took another step toward her.

How is this possible? Her mind screamed a litany of thoughts. *Then again, how is any of this possible? The man in the corner of my bedroom. The flat tire. Now this. How? How?*

"I bet you're wondering just how all of this is possible, aren't you?"

Celine nodded and took another step back. She glanced behind her to make sure she had a clear path to her car.

"Well, well, well. Let's see." The naked man crossed his arms and tapped his foot on the ground. "I know. Here's a good answer for you. Ready?"

Celine nodded once again and forced herself to get up enough energy to run. Just a few steps back, down a little hill then off to safety. She could make it.

"You're the mother of a little girl. What was her name? Justine?"

Celine stopped thinking about the car and the run to safety.

Justine. Did he just say that name? Did he know where she was? Is this what life was trying to show her? Her mind switched gears completely from thoughts of fear and death to curious thoughts about a naked man in a thunderstorm who knew her daughter.

She took a bold step toward the man. "You know where she is?"

"Maybe." The naked man looked down at the ground and moved around a little mud with his toe. "What are you going to do about it?"

Celine stepped even closer and raised her voice. "Where is she? Please. For the love of God, if you know—"

The naked man raised his eyebrows and smiled. "'For the love of God.' How often people say that in the wrong situations."

"Where is she?"

"Don't scream at me! You were going to leave me for dead!"

The rain let up more as the thunderstorm moved off. In

the darkness, Celine saw something altogether new: hope. She felt that hope well up inside. Maybe, just *maybe*, this angry, formerly bloody naked man she was somehow put into contact with held the answer to the deepest of her secrets.

"I'm sorry," she said softly. "If she's alive, I just want to know where she is."

The naked man looked again at the ground and pushed more mud around. "I can take you to her."

Hope. It filled more and more of Celine in the darkness. *I can take you to her.* The words hung inside her ears and caressed her soul like nothing in the nineteen years since her daughter disappeared ever could. That *must* be the reason for all of this, then. Somehow, someone pulled all the right strings in the cosmos, and now she was at the verge of discovering her daughter. All of her pain could go away and all the mistakes of the past could be erased forever.

"Tell me how," she asked. A tear fell softly from her eye and mixed with the rain that fell only in spurts now.

"I'll have to kill you first."

The naked man jumped up in the air and landed directly behind Celine on the edge of the rise between her and the car. She screamed as all the hope that had just been given to her was knocked away by sheer terror. He reached out and grabbed Celine by the waist with one arm and pulled her hair back with the other. She screamed as her head fell back. With a burst of adrenaline, she pulled away from him, leaving a chunk of hair still in his hands.

She ran away from the car, wishing she had done it earlier. In the darkness, the desert was difficult to navigate, but she found the will to look ahead and dodge any cactus or shrub or rock that got in her way. She kept running, faster than she had ever run before, determined to get away and find safety. He *knew*. He knew where Justine was, which could only mean one thing: Justine was alive. She was now more determined than ever to find her *and* to find Jennifer. Life was giving her a chance and she was going to go for it.

The ground gave way beneath her and Celine tumbled down the side of a steep embankment, face first into a raging wash. The deluge from the thunderstorm earlier had filled the tiny canyon. It was alive and pulled her under the muddy water and threw her about raging rapids. She reached out for anything she could find to grab, but at every glimpse of a branch or a rock, she was pulled under. Gasping for air each time she surfaced, her eyes darted around looking for the bank, trying to swim against the torrent and find safety.

Please. Please let it be on the other side of the bank from that man, she prayed.

Just as she was pulled under once again, her arm wrapped around a thick root. She held on with all of her strength and pulled herself against the flow to whatever it was the root was grounded in. Her strength about to give out, she reached one last time and dragged herself into a small cave just above the water. Her chest heaved as she crawled on her hands and knees farther away from the entrance of the cave, safe from the water and safer than she could ever hope for from the naked man who knew where Justine was.

Celine rolled over on her back and raised her head up just in time to see the entrance to the cave collapse and bury her in the desert just north of Phoenix.

In the darkness, Celine faced a fear worse than death, worse than being killed by the naked man who held the answer to the greatest mystery—and worse pain—she ever had. The musty smell of dirt weighed heavy and filled her nostrils, making her breathe softer, but faster. The ground under her body was riddled with tiny rocks and sticks that poked at her skin. Her clothes, soaked from the rain and her getaway in the raging wash, made the cave a muddy mess.

Life, which had taken so much from her and left her with hopelessness, was really starting to piss her off.

Celine laid her head back down, her mind rapidly running through ways to get out of the cave and find help. She had no idea if the naked man had seen where she ran or even if he waited outside the cave to kill her, but she needed to do something.

A sharp pain shot through her thigh. She reached down to find the cause then realized she must have cut herself during the escape. As if in direct response to that realization, her arms, the left knee, and her shin responded with sharp pains of their own.

Great, she thought. *I'm buried and now bleeding. What's next? Spiders?*

Celine clenched her hands and tensed her muscles. She hadn't considered that most animals escape the rain by going inside the earth, and now that she was in the dark she had no way of knowing what else was buried with her. She needed a light. She needed to know what was lurking in the darkness before her mind came up with answers of its own. Celine reached into the pocket of her wet jeans, searching for her lighter. Windproof and probably waterproof, she was at least comforted with the knowledge that she would soon be able to see what was crawling around her and—soon—crawling all over her.

"No," she whispered. The lighter was in the car.

That was it. There was no alternative but to dig her way out and pray the naked man wasn't waiting for her.

Celine raised her head up one more time, followed by her hand. How low was the roof of the cave anyway? In the darkness, she had no idea if the cave was just a borough dug out for protection, or if it was a much larger space. Carefully, she reached up with her hand, expecting to feel the dirt above her rain down with the slightest touch.

Nothing. Her arm was fully outstretched, and not even her fingertips felt the ceiling or even a root that might be sticking down. Celine sighed and sat up in the darkness, still unable to see anything, but now at least a little more comfortable with the situation. She had room to move and air to breathe.

As hope rushed back through her body that there might possibly be an end to this nightmare, her nerves began to relax. Celine brought her knees up to her chest and held them tight against her body with her arms. There was hope out there. She had always known that, sometimes even seen it. Nevertheless, it seemed that when hope was given to her, life took it away minutes or hours later and pulled her back to the realization that she was a failure. Two daughters missing, an abandoned son, and two husbands who were never responsive to her needs. Although Harlan wasn't as abusive as her first mistake, he still couldn't fill the emptiness that threatened to engulf her every day. Nothing, it seemed, could ever do that. No person, and definitely no man, could ever complete the puzzle.

Celine ran her fingers through her hair and felt the tangled wet mess full of dirt. "I must look like hell," she thought out loud. "Who'd want me now, anyway?"

"Oh, you *are* in there!" The naked man's voice filtered in from outside the cave, muffled by the dirt blocking the entrance. "And I was just about to give up."

Celine stopped breathing, her heart now the only sound she heard, thumping wildly inside her ears. *How did he find me? How?*

She slowly backed up in the cave, her butt moving across the ground an inch at a time. Not only was she buried alive inside a cave, now she was trapped between whatever the hell was behind her and the naked man she heard digging her out. Again, she prayed there was more than just the back wall of the cave.

"I know you want me to take you to Justine," the naked man called out. "I just know you're *dying* to see her again."

Celine inched back a little more, still not feeling the back of the cave.

A few pebbles fell. "Don't you want to know?" the naked man called out again. His voice seemed to sing an evil tune. "Don't you want to know? Don't you want to know where she is?"

A few more inches.

Still room for more.

Celine quickened her pace as the sound of more pebbles falling grazed her ears.

"There once was a little girl..."

Inches now feet. She pushed herself faster with her arms.

"...born to save the world..."

Celine pushed again. Her back hit the wall of the cave.

"...some people thought it bad..."

"*No!*" Celine cried out as a dim light broke into the cave.

"...and left her mommy sad."

"*What do you want from me?*"

The naked man's hands reached in and pulled the last of the dirt from the entrance of the cave. "Just the last moments of your life."

"*No!*" Celine pushed back against the wall of the cave. Her eyes focused in the faint light on the naked man quickly crawling toward her. Anticipating the worst, she closed her eyes, turned her head and pushed one more time, just as the naked man reared back and lunged at her.

DEATH WAS a solace to her as she floated free in a darkness that was warm and comforting. The pain was absent. Life had finally given her something it couldn't take away.

Celine raised her arms up, stretched out then spun to her right. A smile broke across her face as she righted herself and imagined she was flying, high above whatever existed inside Death's domain. She was free, and life couldn't have been kinder. If the naked man told the truth and she had to die to see Justine again, then so be it. Death was a blanket she could wrap herself in and feel—for once—what it was like to be warmed up by something from the inside out.

She smiled again. A feeling of sheer joy rocketed itself throughout her body and touched the farthest corners of her mind. It reached in as if to wipe clean all the pain, all the failures, all the wrongs that were commonplace when she was alive. Joy the like she had never felt before slowed her heartbeat and made the smile on her face grow just a little bit wider.

Celine turned again, suddenly wondering if she could flip over and over like a diver going for a perfect score. She threw her arms down and pulled her head to her chest before letting the momentum carry her body around. Once. Twice. Three times, then her arms reached out above her head like she was about to enter the water.

She laughed. She laughed again, and spun again and flew again, all the while letting the joy consume her body and fill the empty spaces. Her body itself dissolved into a non-existing vessel for her soul. She brought her hands up to her face and wondered if she even had flesh left over. In the darkness, however, she couldn't tell, but it really didn't matter if the flesh was still there.

Death was such a wonderful feeling!

The voices came next. From all directions, they began to barrage her with memories of a past life she once had. The bastard, cheating husband followed by the empty words of a man she loved but couldn't love her back. Celine shook off the first few voices as nothing more than her imagination, but the faster and louder they became, the more she realized death was not the comfort she first experienced. They spoke of pain and loss and failure and all of the wrongs she just couldn't put out of her mind. They spoke in tears and spoke in screams and spoke with voices so angry the very words ripped and tore at her insides and shredded the feeling of joy she was given a glimpse of. The voices came at her with lightning speed, occasionally sorting themselves out to tell a story, then jumbling together in a cacophony that hurt her ears. She screamed for them to stop, screamed at the voices carried in the blackness around her until her throat screamed back with the raw fire of yelling too much.

Finally giving in to the pain, Celine wrapped herself into a fetal position and let Death have its way with her. Was she really bound for Hell and this was just an introduction to eternity? Could Hell be worse than life was, if all life ever handed her was pain after pain after false hope and then more pain?

The warm blanket she had wrapped around herself became colder and colder, and Celine prayed for an end to come quickly.

CHAPTER TWENTY-TWO

Images painted by the mind's eye coupled with voices from Casey's past. They floated by like a river in the nothingness and whispered to him as he stood in a place he once thought was a cave. Led there by an old, intriguing man, he had climbed a ladder and stepped inside to quench his sudden thirst for knowledge. Curiosity drove him inside even farther. At first, the darkness caressed his nerves with a tingling sensation as the copper taste of fear flooded his mouth. The dirt floor beneath his feet disappeared and he felt like he was floating in midair, engulfed in a black satin blanket.

The voices had come suddenly. Casey thought they might be present with him, maybe people lured inside by the old man. As he listened, however, his mind translated the words into forms he recognized: deep and hidden secrets, pleasant memories and pain.

"You're eight years old, Stephen."

Casey pictured his third grade teacher hunched over her metal desk piled high with papers and notebooks and pencil holders and knickknacks brought from home.

"Why don't you play outside with the other boys?"

He smiled at the thought of how he would shuffle his feet and look down when asked anything by an adult. "They pick on me," he said. "I want to be better than them."

"So you're going to stay in here and study at recess? Is that how you become better?"

"I guess so."

"Stephen, life is right now. If you focus on the future,

you're going to miss the present. Go play. Have fun. Be a boy."

Was there a reason for recalling this small event in his life? Did it hold some sort of clue as to who he had become, or was it just synapses firing in random patterns that dug up this old woman and her Zen attitude?

Another voice erupted like thunder, pushing away the teacher.

"It was just a little kiss. It didn't mean a thing."

Christine. Casey closed his eyes and wished the memory gone. He knew there had to be something more than testosterone that drove at the core of a first love. Of all the moments of his life he had remembered, the greatest were always of her. The minutes they spent together—whether it was locked in heated passion or arguing on a street corner— were minutes to be cherished. Three years wrapped up in a woman that was older and more mature. Three years at a time when his environment and the people that surrounded him defined the man. Three years when life began and Casey blindly filled in the empty spaces with everything she had to offer.

"It was nothing more and nothing less."

Nothing less. The words kicked Casey in the side. *Nothing less.*

Sitting in her car at the end of a dead end street, Christine told him about Michael. For a few days they had been seeing each other secretly, and one night he kissed her. The thought of that kiss had twisted his stomach into a tight knot that never fully recovered even after twenty or so years. It wasn't the jealousy so much as it was the realization that the half of him she had become was walking away with his best friend.

"I'm sorry," she whispered. Casey watched the scene replay itself on the inside of his eyelids. She turned away from him and looked out the driver's side window. "It just happened, and I didn't know what to do."

Casey remembered the silence. She kept her gaze away from him as he sat in the passenger seat looking out through the windshield. The rain fell from a gray winter sky and where there used to be a window that fogged up in the heat of their passion, there was now only patterns drawn with water that mocked his agony. What could he have done to have never let this happen? It was a question that persisted for years and even resurfaced as he sat under the overhang in the wash he had just left. If he could have relived any moment of his life, he would have never said what came out of his mouth as the rain continued to draw patterns in front of him.

"I guess that's it, then," Casey whispered back. "It's over."

The nothing that surrounded Casey had never felt colder. It was the physical manifestation of what his life became the moment he uttered those words. There were times he had tried to take them back, to say "I forgive you," and "can't we try again." He had prayed to God to turn back the seconds and let him live it over again.

Nothing worked. She was half of Casey, and who he was now was directly related to that relationship. So how on Earth could he ever truly come to forget and forgive himself for letting her go?

The worst of his life swept by relentlessly after that. A tear formed, threatening to fall as a woman screamed at him through the darkness.

"My baby! Get my baby!"

Her voice painted a scene he never wanted to revisit. A woman in a car screamed at him, crushed between the dashboard and the passenger side seat under a flipped over semi-truck. He witnessed the last few seconds of the accident and had run up to help in any way he could. The smell of spilled gasoline on the hot asphalt wafted by him as adrenaline rushed through his veins. The woman, no older than Casey at the time, looked at him with eyes bulging. Blood spilled like tears as he tried to open the door.

"Get my baby out, please!" she cried, forcing the wind out of punctured lungs. She wheezed and gurgled blood then cried out again. "My baby! My baby!"

Casey winced in the darkness and wiped his cheek. *Not this memory. Anything but this.*

The world around him was relentless, however. It forced the image of an empty infant carrier, barely visible under the crushed roof. He turned back to the woman to calm her down when he saw the child in her lap. The majority of the blood covering the woman's body didn't belong to her.

Casey fell to his knees in the darkness and shook his head. He felt the salty taste of bile rise from his stomach as he forced his tears back. In all his professional life, first as a street cop then a detective, he had never witnessed something as horrid—nor as negligent—as that accident. Had the woman placed the infant in the carrier where he belonged, the child might have lived. Anger swelled in him at that moment in his life as he stood next to death under the baking Arizona sun.

He felt sorrow, fear and a hatred he thought he'd never have.

"Is my baby okay?" The voice of the woman in the darkness was soft and raspy, but to Casey, she was whispering in his ear.

Casey wanted to yell, to scream at the woman and make her understand. Instead, he looked into her eyes that day and saw her resignation. She let out a soft cry, closed her eyes and turned from the window. Death would be her only comfort now.

Casey wanted her to die, *wished* she would die.

There were events he had put out of his life for a reason and those he had relegated to the deepest corners of his mind. In the lonely place he had stumbled into, however, it seemed these memories were the only ones that would surface. He couldn't think of anything positive, and the harder he tried, the more the memories flooded in: failed loves, his wife as she left him, a partner he lost to a crack dealer.

The voices spoke to him, and Casey had no other recourse but to listen. He curled his knees up to his chest, his eyes wide open, and prayed for the end.

THE TIME passed. The voices were still unavoidable, but Casey felt better about them, as if they were slowly becoming background static to his present life. That's what they should have been, he reasoned, and if he had perhaps tried to learn from them rather than hide them, the voices might not have been so hard to deal with. Casey stood and looked around in the blackness for some sort of life, or even some sort of inanimate object he could register as reality.

The longer he stared, the lighter the emptiness became. There was still nothing to register, but at least it wasn't black anymore. He was wrapped up in a gray blanket that was becoming less oppressive. He looked up, and began to see shades above him, like clouds forming an overcast sky with no signs of transition. Casey looked back down and noticed other shades around him, not one solid gray anymore. There were areas that looked like white sand dunes viewed through a thick haze.

He took a cautious step forward and heard a light crunch under his feet. He looked and thought he could make out a footprint where he once stood. The ground was much lighter, more a white than a gray.

He stood in snow.

The light came finally, and the gray dunes as viewed through haze took on the shape of massive snowdrifts with hills and valleys everywhere. He stood on a snowfield, the air suddenly cold and bitter with a gentle breeze that dropped the temperature. Casey wrapped his arms around his body as the cold dug deep into him, and he shivered.

ALONE ON a snowfield in a world Casey knew nothing about, failures were all he could focus on. Although the initial shock of the rush of voices that accosted him earlier wore off, the pain of losing a thousand personal battles was pervasive. There was his wife and son, partners transferred and partners killed. There were friendships lost to distance or anger and cases that had to be closed with no answers. There were victims pleading for life, and victims pleading for death. And for each one of these, there was cause that pleaded for reason.

Lastly, there was Christine.

Casey stood in the snow and looked out over the horizon, scanning the distance for a sign of life or a meaningful direction of travel. The cold bit at his exposed arms, nibbled at his face and gnawed his ears. If he was to survive this ordeal, he needed to find warmth. In the distance, mountains loomed like giant fists, stabbing at the gray sky as if in defiance of something not seen or known. Riddled with jagged edges and cracks, they seemed somehow evil. He could find no other feature, however, that might lend him a clue as to where warmth might hide.

Casey took a cautious step forward, not knowing if the snow would hold his weight. The crunch under his foot didn't last long, and he felt better about the ground he stood on. He took another step and another cautious look around, before deciding the vast snowfield was safe. With a sigh to expulse the doubt, Casey walked toward the mountains and maybe a reason.

He tried to sort out the events of the past few days, categorizing them and struggling to make sense of each one individually. There were no answers so obvious, no writings on the wall or even simple notes that said "The woman was killed because of..." Casey had always wished this was the case: find a dead body, examine the evidence collected, read the fine print hidden in one or two clues, and—*bang!*—corner the suspect, arrest him, try him and convict him. Rarely did this happen, although many criminals tended to stick to patterns that made solving puzzles easier. Casey frowned at the thought of never coming to a conclusion, but quickly passed off the despair and refocused his mental faculties. Failure was not going to be so easy.

First there was a dead woman, Casey thought, sticking out a finger as he walked in the snow. He kept his chin against his chest and his arms wrapped around his body. *Head crushed, heart removed. That's a mystery in itself. On autopsy there were no signs of sexual abuse. Fingernail in chest.*

Casey looked up for a moment, his mind wrapped around his last thought. "What kind of a person," he said out loud, "could punch through the breastbone and take out this woman's heart?"

"You're too hard on yourself, sometimes." Christine's voice filtered in from nowhere and stopped Casey in his tracks. The clarity of the voice was too real and less like the static he'd relegated his memories to. It kissed his cheeks and warmed him up from the outside. "Why don't you just lighten up?"

He took a look around, a faint hope sparked inside of him. What if she was here? Stranger things had just happened.

The snow reflected nothing, but stretched on for miles in every direction. Quietly, a soft wind picked up a few flakes and set them down again.

"Take a look at yourself, Stephen." It sounded like she was behind him.

Twenty some years ago, Casey had been in a snowfield not unlike this one. He had come skiing with a group of friends—fifteen altogether—and was slowly trying to fit into the lifestyle Christine wanted for him. For the most part, he never took his teacher's advice and focused more on study than building social skills or participating in the experiments of age. Casey was basically a lone man, content at times with being isolated, but still yearning for the companionship others had.

As Casey stood alone in a place he was a stranger to now, he was absorbed with Christine's voice and let his memory take him back to the moment those words were spoken.

"They don't like me," Casey said to the ghostly voice that had pulled the memory back to the forefront of his mind. "They never talk to me."

"No," Christine's voice came back. "You don't talk to them. They're people just like you. Why can't you give them a chance?"

"I don't know."

"Stupid answer. What are you afraid of?"

"I don't know."

The solitude of the snowfield melted around him as Casey closed his eyes and watched the scene unfold. Every last detail painted itself all over again: a field of snow, friends playing football in front of a ski lodge. He sat on a bench outside the entrance and watched the game with Christine. For a moment, he swore he felt Christine's hand on his back, rubbing the worry he had away—a ghost ripped from his mind.

She removed her hand and stood as the scene became more and more real. In the snow a few yards away, all of her friends huddled together.

"You need to be a little more outgoing," Christine said. "Look at them. They're one short of two matched teams. Why don't you go and play?"

"I want to stay here with you."

"I don't *want* you to stay here. We see each other every day, and sometimes I just want to be alone. Did you ever think of that?"

Casey leaned forward and placed his elbows on his knees. He looked at the ground. "It's all about Michael isn't it?"

Christine let out a short, quick laugh. "You're impossible. Michael is your friend and there never has been—never *will* be—anything between us. Why can't you see that?"

"He asked you out."

"*One* freaking date. *One* time. We've been through this before. He asked me out, and I said yes because I was pissed off at you. Nothing happened. Dinner, a movie, and he took me home. What more do you want me to say?"

"Tell me the truth."

"*I just did!*" Christine threw her hands in the air.

Every bone in Casey's body rang out with fear. Michael hadn't talked to him in days, and at every opportunity he was seen talking with Christine out of earshot. If Casey came over, the two stopped talking and pretended their conversation was over. In reality, Casey figured, they were being interrupted.

After a silence that lasted a little too long, Casey looked up. "Did he kiss you?"

Christine folded her arms and looked out toward the football field. Michael was in that crowd of "friends" and Casey wondered if that was her focus. After a second that answered Casey's question before she even said a word, Christine looked back. "No."

"You're lying."

"What the hell do you want me to say? Do you want the truth or do you want to hear whatever your mind has been thinking about for the last few days?"

"I just want the truth."

"Fine. I kissed him. He didn't kiss me. And what's more, he's good in bed. You're such a loser, Stephen. Someone tells you the truth and you're not satisfied until you're proven right. For the last time: *nothing happened.*"

Christine turned and ran into the lodge, leaving Casey alone on the bench outside. He had pushed the issue—pushed Christine to tell him what he believed happened, when in reality, she *had* told the truth.

All of it was a figment of Casey's mind.

A week passed before Christine finally told the real truth in a car on a rainy winter's night.

Casey opened his eyes. The scene sat in front of him like he'd stared at the sun too long. At least it wasn't real, and for that Casey was glad. There was no reason to relive these events of the past, these failures that had haunted him throughout his life. There really was no reason for the Hell he stood in.

With a sigh, Casey moved forward while he tried even harder to push the memories back and focus on the reality. There were two dead people, not related except by the method of death. There was a missing girl, a distraught father. There was a dream about a little girl that seemed all too real, and a stranger at his door with strange words. Throw all of that together in a bowl and mix it up. Then add an old man who had peered into Casey's soul and a cave that was more of a threshold to this place...

...and all Casey could come up with was an unappetizing recipe for certain failure.

Ma abad rab.

The visitor in Casey's apartment had muttered those words. Nothing else he said made sense, but those three words mocked him.

"What does that mean?" Casey asked out loud.

"Whatever your mind tells you it means." Christine stood a few feet in front him, the wind picking up the strands of blonde hair that stuck out from under a wool hat. "You make up everything else, why don't you make up the meaning of that?"

Casey swallowed. She stood in front of him, no longer an aural manifestation, but a physical memory to face. "Christine?"

"Who do you think it is?" She folded her arms and looked at him. "You never were one to believe what's right in front of you."

"How did you get here?"

Christine smiled and, within seconds, Casey's nerves put him on the edge of a breakdown. Something wasn't right.

"Why do care how I got here? Isn't it just as well that I am? You wished me here, didn't you?"

He did, and now he regretted it. There was nothing sane in this world—from the void he walked into to the emptiness of a snowfield he stood in when he'd just been walking through a wash in a sweltering desert.

Casey closed his eyes for a moment and tried to wish Christine away. For every moment she stood in front him, he felt more and more uneasy.

"You're not answering me, Stephen. Why do you care how I got here?"

"You're not real." Casey opened his eyes.

She was gone.

He wrapped his arms around himself tighter and took another step. The wind had picked up, and the temperature dropped. The snow gave in too much, and with each new step, Casey sank farther. He had walked maybe a mile or two, cognizant of the cold and the snow, but oblivious to a destination. What made the trek worse was the feeling that he was climbing a shallow hill, and there didn't seem to be any crest in sight. Nevertheless, he needed to find warmth.

He needed to find respite from the past that hated him so much.

Casey looked up at the sky and prayed for a break in the clouds to give the sun a chance. The longer he looked, however, the thicker the clouds appeared.

As his eyes returned to the journey, they landed on Christine once again.

"Have you ever thought of reaching out to me?"

Casey sighed and took another step. "Every day."

"Don't you care?"

Before Casey could answer, the ground gave way. As his legs buckled, he saw Christine smile and turn away. A small cry erupted from his chest, and he slipped, hitting his head on the side of a large sheet of ice that rushed up to greet him with a punch. The ice held Casey for only a second—enough time for him to look up at the entrance to the crack he'd just fallen in—and then he slid down the side of a large fracture in some glacier, headed for whatever lay in the darkness below. Ice broke off and pelted him, beating at his side and legs and hands and head. He held out his arms to try to slow his descent, but each time he reached out for something, another piece of ice crashed into him.

After what seemed like an eternity of plummeting down into oblivion while ice demons punched and kicked and tore at his skin, Casey hit solid ground. He landed on his hip with a force that shot yet another pain faster and more hideous than all the others through his body. Casey let out a scream.

With frigid ice clawing at his bare skin and pain in his hip tearing at his insides, the world turned black.

HE SHOULD have died. By all counts, Stephen Casey *was* a dead man, buried in ice and alone. His scream had echoed off the walls of the crevasse then dissipated into the unknown. Failure had once again taken hold of him and pulled him from the verge of discovery into a pool wrought with unknowns.

In the battles of everyday life there are saviors, some small, some tall, some known, some invisible. For ages, people have prayed to their gods for just one of these saviors to come and aid them in their time of dire need. For ages, people have learned to accept that their god didn't listen, and their time of dire need was a lesson to be learned. Some become despondent and wary of their belief, until one day—perhaps while shopping at a store—they lose their keys or their wallet. They frantically search for the missing item and retrace their steps, looking over their shoulders for any sign of it. Life would be upended if they couldn't find it. Credit cards cancelled, new driver's licenses issued, new photos taken, new keys made and new locks re-keyed. Finally, in despair and utter disbelief that this could ever happen to them, they sit, head in hands, and start to wonder what to do next.

Then a child walks up—a savior encased in a little body—tapping the despondent on the shoulder and saying in a still, small voice "Did you lose these, mister?"

There are other saviors, like the one sitting next to the choking man in a crowded restaurant who remembered just enough of high school health class to make a difference. There is the man with the pocketful of change standing in line at the checkout counter behind the boy who didn't bring enough money for a gift he wanted to buy his mother. There are saviors who stumble across a woman and her dog, trapped in a truck in the middle of a rising river, and there are saviors who pass by, unknown, and leave bags of groceries for the destitute.

Some would arguably call them guardian angels, as if their whole purpose in life was to protect that one person from harm.

Some would arguably call them chance encounters, as if the planets had aligned just right and two people who didn't know each other found themselves tangled up in each other's life for just a second.

Some would arguably call them people, sticking to their firm belief that there was no God and there was no Hell and whatever anyone said or did wouldn't sway them. These people were just being nice.

To Stephen Casey, passed out and freezing to death on the floor of an ice crevasse, there was no way to call out to God or to utter a simple prayer to the entities of Heaven. He was dying, broken into pieces and failing fast.

The light from outside was almost too far away and too dark to do any good, but the faint illumination that did make it to the bottom of the crevasse was enough to shroud Casey in an ethereal glow. The light, however, did not catch the eye of an old man a few yards away.

The man walked up to Casey, dressed in rags and dirty

from head to toe as if he had never once bathed, showered or even stood in the rain to wash away the filth. As he knelt over the body curled in a fetal position on the floor of ice, bones cracked with each new movement, coming alive and expressing their dismay. He placed a hand on the side of Casey, curious as to how anyone could have survived the fall he'd heard from the depths of his home.

"Humphf," he muttered. "Alone for years and the first person to ever come and visit me is out cold."

CHAPTER TWENTY-THREE

The voices battered Jennifer as she climbed the hill. They were louder than ever and all mixed together. There were people laughing. There was Jonathan. There was her father. There was her mother, her brother and a stranger who had accosted her in a park years ago. The stranger yelled at her, just as he had done the day she ran away, fearful of what might happen. Jennifer tried hard to fight off the feeling to shout out and make the voices stop, but every step she took she felt weaker and closer to madness. She wanted to stop climbing, stop the burning in her chest, stop the beating of her heart, stop the sweat, stop the pounding of her head. She wanted nothing more than to curl up, close her eyes and make everything go away.

The grade of the hill grew steeper, and Jennifer was forced to use her hands at times to navigate over fallen trees and rock outcroppings in her way. The stream she had been following was smaller, but rushing faster down the hill. She stepped on a ledge, pulled herself over the next and noticed for the first time the blood dried to her hands. She looked up. It was more of a cliff than a hill, and she found it increasingly difficult to find a way to navigate upstream.

The gray sky overhead darkened, and Jennifer wondered if the sun was going down or if the color meant the first sign of rain. The thought of climbing the hill in darkness or rain made her want to quicken her pace. Unfortunately, as the grade became steeper there didn't seem to be any sign of relief. Even in despair, Jennifer knew there had to be a source of this stream and from what she could tell, she had climbed to nearly the top. God forbid if there was another hill to climb.

Jennifer sighed and grabbed another rock above her, pulling herself even higher. As she righted herself and looked for the next step, a drop of rain struck her on the hand. The pit of her stomach sank. Time was running out. Another outcropping, and another rock later, she was no closer to where she wanted to be. She followed the stream a little farther with her eyes where it disappeared maybe a hundred feet above. Wondering if it was the top of the hill or an easier slope, Jennifer pushed on to find the answer.

Another raindrop struck her cheek then an arm. Another drop and finally the deluge came, quick and cold.

She cried out loud as she fought to pull herself over the next obstacle, looking for shelter more than anything else. The stream rose, rushing down the hill louder and louder as the rain pummeled her body. The dried blood broke apart, loosening on her hands. What soil was exposed between the rocks fast turned to mud. Her foot slipped, and she quickly fought to get back on the rock and pull herself over the next outcropping.

She rolled over and found herself lying face up to the elements.

A man stood in the middle of the stream, his face covered in mud. "Come here!" he cried. "Don't you think of running away from me."

Jennifer pushed herself back. As she righted herself to face the man in the stream—a man whose face she had tried to erase—her heart beat rapidly and pushed blood so fast she felt the flow of it through her neck and around her temples. He was a nightmare—the man who tried to rape her in a park months ago. It was a memory she didn't want to carry anymore, and she certainly didn't want to see it come to life.

The man held his hands out toward her as if he was asking for a hug or some other sort of sick ruse to get to her. He cocked his head to the side and let his tangled, black hair, drenched with rain, stick to his cheek and cover an eye.

"Don't you want to play, little girl?" he quietly asked.

"That's what you're dressed for, isn't it?"

Jennifer's chest heaved with the pressure of her racing heart and quick breaths. The voice had become a vision, she reasoned, nothing more.

"You didn't answer me, pretty thing." The man smiled, revealing stained teeth. "Do you want to play?"

Was she supposed to answer? This was a memory. He wasn't real and certainly wouldn't be standing in this strange world taunting her. Would he?

Jennifer stood and brushed herself off. Her breath slowed as she began to believe the man was nothing more than a projection of her mind and could do her no harm. Without saying a word, Jennifer turned to climb the hill again, trying hard not to look at the man in the stream. She felt him follow her movements as she came closer. She moved to the left to avoid being within reach, fighting hard against the urge to look one more time.

The man screamed, an unnatural piercing that shattered the sound of the rain pelting the forest floor. Jennifer scrambled away as quickly as possible as her eyes drew to look. Something above his hairline split wide open. A crack quickly ran down his face, his neck, and his body, shattering the skin like a glass sculpture. Flesh and blood exploded in all directions, raining pieces of the man onto Jennifer, onto nearby trees and into the stream. She lost her balance again as she tried to back away from what was left of the man. As she fell, she saw the water in the stream turn bright red where he once stood. It flowed both up and down the hill turning the entire stream into a river of blood.

Jennifer wiped the blood from her face and felt a chunk of flesh slip between her fingers.

She screamed.

She had to get out of this place. Everything seemed to be against her, and now her memories were coming alive and exploding before her, as if their constant presence—which had previously been nothing more than an aural attack on her conscious—wasn't enough. Whatever she was to learn up the hill, she needed to do it soon. Jennifer stood, fighting the urge to vomit as her eyes caught a glimpse of more flesh stuck to her shirt.

She wiped the rain from her eyes and tried to look up the hill. The rain kept falling, making it harder to see her destination, but she knew that was the only way she was going to find safety. Had she stayed there, the stream would become a river, and the water that flowed would be joined by her blood as her body was bashed up against the rocks below and carried to the creek where she began this journey. She was determined not to die here, at least not without answers.

With a grunt, she climbed again.

The next few steps were arduous at best. She slipped and caught herself. The old blood washed away, replaced by new blood that flowed from cuts and gashes she received with every new step. The rain fell harder. At times it nearly pushed her down with the force of the drops. The stream edged precariously close to where she was, and Jennifer feared she would run out of time and be pulled into the torrent next to her if she didn't keep moving.

She pulled herself over one last rock. Through the driving rain, she saw what appeared to be a wall of adobe. She stood as a smile broke across her face at the sight of shelter. A doorway had been built into the wall, timbers holding the adobe apart.

She wiped her face and walked in through the doorway, out of the deluge of rain. She heard the once tranquil stream crash outside, and as she turned away, the outcropping she had stood on just a second ago broke loose and fell into the raging torrent of water.

In the darkness of the room, Jennifer saw little. *At least it's dry*, she thought. She walked over to a corner of the little room and sat, her clothes soaked. In the freedom from the rain outside, she shivered.

JENNIFER EMERGED from the shadows. The rain tapered off more and more, and the stream showed signs of receding back to its original size. If this man was supposed to meet her here, where was he? She didn't climb that hill and face her demons for nothing, and she wasn't going to leave again without knowing why she was here and how she was going to get home.

"You look tired."

Jennifer looked up. In the doorway, a stranger stood in shadows.

"You scared me," she said, then smiled weakly. "I'm sorry."

"Sorry for what?"

"I guess I don't know what to expect anymore."

The stranger pointed inside the dwelling. "Can I come in, or should I stand out here in the rain and catch my death?"

Jennifer nodded and watched the stranger enter the dwelling and walk to the far side. She was quick to notice his full build and imposing height, muscles cut from stone. He sat on the dirt floor and leaned his head against the wall, his face hidden in the shadows.

Silence descended on the two, the rain outside the only constant. Jennifer studied the stranger, captivated by his looks. The stranger, in turn, seemed tired, lost in his own thoughts, as he stared blankly at the far wall.

"So," Jennifer said, attempting to break the uncomfortable silence. "Why am I here?"

"That's a loaded question, don't you think?"

"Not really. I'm assuming I'm here for a reason."

The stranger picked up a small stick and drew indecipherable shapes in the dirt by his feet. Finally, he broke the stick in half and sighed.

"Let me tell you a little secret," he said.

THE AIR was cool and wafted in from the outside on a gentle breeze. The rain was gone, and the only sound outside the adobe dwelling was the trickle of a stream that had recently been a raging torrent of bloody water. Light had come inside, too, not so much from the sun, but from a gray sky less dark than before. Jennifer sat on the floor, her back against the wall staring at the stranger who rambled on and on about something called the *ma abad rab*.

"This all sounds like crap." Jennifer sighed. "You expect me to believe this?"

The stranger sat in silence for a moment then pointed outside to the stream. "Has anything that just happened to you made sense? Did the man in forest make sense? Did the death of Jonathan make sense? Did nothing at all convince you there was, perhaps, something more to your philosophy than sex and music?"

Jennifer frowned at the last comment. She never felt her philosophy was as empty as that.

"Did the forest not astound you with its grandeur? I bet you never saw or even heard another living creature from the moment you started your journey up the hill. Take what you want from this, Jennifer, but what I tell you is truth, and that's what you were looking for all along."

Jennifer had been mostly silent, her legs brought up to her chest and her chin at rest on her kneecaps. She had tried not to look directly at him, but morbid curiosity and an odd sense of attraction forced her to take a quick look every now and again. Aside from the azure blue of his eyes, there was something powerful in him, something that captivated and transfixed her.

"So why haven't you killed me?" Jennifer realized the question probably sounded more absurd than she wanted it to, but if a bacon-cooking madman was out to get her, why wasn't this man, too?

The stranger stifled a laugh. "There are some people in this world who were born for no other reason than to ensure the well-being of others. We all have gifts—a butler has the gift of service, a teacher has the gift of speech, even a good psychologist has the ability to listen better than most."

"So you're here to help me?"

"In a way, yes."

"And how did you know about that poem I wrote and destroyed before anyone could read it?"

"Tools of the trade." The stranger smiled and warmth filled the small shelter, wrapping Jennifer.

She leaned her head against the wall and sighed again. "Tell me why *I'm* here. You've told me all of this stuff about angels and resentment then stuck in a few words in some language I've never heard before. But why am *I* here?"

"You don't believe, do you?"

Jennifer shrugged her shoulders. "I've had my share of religious nonsense fed to me over the years. I stopped believing in God a long time ago. With no God, there is no Hell, but *nothing* that's happened to me since I left my house has anything to do with this great rift in the fabric of humanity you've been talking about."

"So, where are you?"

Jennifer closed her eyes. "I don't know."

"Sometimes the question is more important than the answer."

"What does that mean?"

The stranger shuffled his feet on the floor, and Jennifer wondered if he was gathering his thoughts or ignoring the question. "Of all these religions you despise—"

"I don't despise them," Jennifer interrupted. "I just don't buy into them like other people."

"And that's fine. But what if every religion in every corner of the world contained *some* truth—a passage from the Qur'an, a chapter of the Bible, an ancient ritual written on the wall of a cave thousands of years ago? Do you really think everyone is an idiot and blind to the truth? Or do you think it more probable that everyone *feels* something and sees a *part* of the truth?"

"I don't know what the truth is."

"Not very many people do. It's a puzzle, and one that you're a very large part of."

Jennifer looked up at the stranger, lost in thought. She couldn't be a part of anything this large. Small people don't matter in the grand scheme of things. Do they?

The man stood and walked to the doorway. On his face, Jennifer thought she saw exasperation. "*You* have a gift—something I can't possibly have, but one that I'm not jealous of, either. With it, you can unite a country or even a world. That's not a bad thing. You haven't realized that gift yet, but you will."

Jennifer let a small chuckle escape from her throat. What kind of gift could she possibly have? If anything, she felt like what she was: a scared teenager, lost, wanting nothing more than to reverse the clock and listen to her father. She wished she had never met Jonathan.

The stranger turned from Jennifer. He stepped out of the doorway and looked up toward the top of the hill. "There's one more thing."

Jennifer stood. "What more could you tell me?"

The stranger smiled weakly. "A child was born years ago, with the same gift as you. She is one of many, but together all of you can do amazing things. In an attempt to ensure her part in the *ma abad rab* was never accomplished, she was sucked into this place you don't think exists, even though you're standing in it. She has been in limbo ever since. You were meant to replace her."

Jennifer swallowed a lump she felt grow in her throat.

"Find her, get her safely back, and the stack will favor humanity more than it does now."

The stranger turned to look at Jennifer. "Jonathan was killed because of his relationship to you, nothing more. There's no doubt you were next. You're lucky to still have a heart."

Jennifer put her hand on her chest. Images of her boyfriend's limp body screamed across her mind. Although her mouth was dry, she swallowed. "Who is this girl?"

"Your sister."

CHAPTER TWENTY-FOUR

Marie stood at the edge of the town and looked on with wonder. The buildings were held together poorly—some with nails, some with rope, some with nothing more than the weight of four walls leaning against each other. There were adobe huts, wooden shacks and woven tents numbering in the hundreds stretched out on the shore of the dry lake bed for miles. The streets, dusty and well worn, snaked through the buildings with no particular pattern, cutting right, then left, then right again. Plants accustomed to the lack of water grew sparingly down the middle of the street, in gutters, or poking through cheaply constructed front porches.

The silence of the town was overbearing. Marie found herself uncomfortable with the ghostly image of the buildings. Justine stood quietly holding Marie's hand.

"What the hell?" Marie whispered. "What happened here?"

She scanned the empty streets and peered into a few open doorways and windows, looking for signs of life.

Marie took a few cautious steps forward, her heart echoing her fear of the unknown. If this world had shown her anything remotely normal, she must have missed it. Life didn't exist here, or at the very least, it didn't seem to exist in any form she could recognize.

She walked up to the first building on her left—a wooden shack, its roof caved in. She peered through the window and saw that dust covered everything, from the fireplace to the chairs to a bed of blankets in the corner.

"What is it?" Justine called out.

"A whole lot of nothing," Marie said, still peering through the window. "It looks like whoever lived here didn't have much at all. Either that or they took everything with them."

Marie walked away from the building and over to another. Inside, she found much of the same: a few table settings, beds made of nothing more than blankets, and the remnants of a few meals. There didn't seem to be any artifact that might lend a clue as to the people who lived here. Every building she went to was different. The tents smelled the worst, the wooden shacks stood precipitously on their weak foundations and the adobe huts were all missing roofs. Whatever happened to the people of this town, it wasn't catastrophic, but it was sure enough weird.

Marie and Justine looked around a bit more, walking in and out of the dwellings, around the outside, the inside and peering through windows. Justine, for her age, was exceptionally curious and brave, rushing into buildings that looked close to falling over altogether. Marie held her back from running inside more than one building that looked like its roof was on the verge of collapse.

Marie stopped in the middle of the street, confusion evident on her face. She couldn't mask the fact that she felt, in a way, let down. There was hope when they originally spotted the town— the hope that maybe someone would be able to tell them what had happened or answer a thousand questions. What about the thousand new questions they formed after being in the town for only a short time? Who was going to help them now?

"I don't like this place," Justine said, pulling on Marie's blouse. "I want to go."

Marie bent down. "We can't go right now, honey. We need to see if anyone lives here who can help us."

"Why do we need help? Can't we just keep walking?"

Marie smiled. She wished she could just keep walking, but there was something that needed to be learned here, even though she had no idea what it was.

"No, Justine," she said. "We've been walking for a while. Don't you want to rest?"

Justine looked down. "I guess so, but this place is dirty."

THE NEXT building they entered seemed sturdier than the rest. It resembled more of a house than any other, and despite the lack of glass in the windows or doorknobs on the door, the effect was comforting. Marie walked inside, found a corner, and sat with Justine curled in her lap. There was time to rest.

The past that tried to overwhelm Marie on so many occasions had—at least for the moment—eased up a bit. There were still faint whispers on the wind, ghosts of the past that wanted so desperately to bring her down from wherever she was into a pit of despair she could never escape. It was a pit, Marie knew, both dark and lonely, and she didn't want to find herself there again.

Within moments, Justine snored quietly, her head pushed up against Marie's stomach. There was innocence in the girl, but also something powerful—a feeling or a sense their companionship was to mean something in the grand scheme of life. How long had she been here?

A whisper of penance rose from the din of other voices. Marie tried to put everything else behind her and listen to what it had to say, listen for who even said it. At first, it sounded like her father—dead so many years ago—but the more she listened, the more it sounded like Harlan.

"I should have asked you," the voice whispered. "You didn't tell me."

Marie tried to place the voice in a memory, a time when she was maybe pushing Harlan away. The harder she tried, however, the less familiar the words became.

"You didn't tell me you were pregnant. You didn't tell me."

Marie's stomach sank. No, she didn't tell Harlan she was pregnant. In fact, there was no way he could have even known that. She hid it from him well.

She lifted Justine's head up and put her gently down on a pile of grass next to them.

Someone else was in the room.

"Tell me about my child, Marie. Tell me what I want to hear."

Marie looked at the shadows in the corners, trying to pinpoint the location of the voice. She slowly stood and brushed herself off.

"Hello?" she whispered. "Is anyone here?"

"You could have let me know."

"Hello?" Marie scanned the shadows again. "I can hear you, but I can't see you."

"You didn't tell me. You didn't tell me. You didn't tell me."

In the far corner of the room, Marie saw a figure rock back and forth. It was too dark to make out any features, but it was definitely the source of the voice.

"You didn't tell me."

Marie decided to play his game. "I didn't want to ruin your life."

The figure stopped rocking. Marie took a step back, her hand over her rapidly beating heart.

"You're not real," the voice said. "Why don't you stop this masquerade and let me see who you really are?"

"Harlan?"

The figure pushed itself to his feet and stepped out of the shadows. Marie swallowed as an image from her past—his clothes torn, face beaten, blood trickling down his arms—emerged.

"*You're not real!*" He narrowed his eyes into slits.

Marie took a tentative step forward. She pictured the rush of wind on the lake bed and the image of Harlan walking toward her. If he *was* a mirage—or something far worse —then she was sure to have to find a way out.

"Harlan, I never told you I was pregnant."

Silence descended while Justine stirred in her sleep. After a moment, Harlan took another step forward and reached out his hand to touch Marie's cheek. "Marie?"

HOURS PASSED, full of conversation, and eventually Harlan and Marie found themselves lying down much like Justine. The journey this far had taken its toll, though not necessarily for the physical distances they just crossed. The mystery pulled at their minds, tugged at their sanity, and poked through in discussion. Nothing lent itself to an explanation—or, at the very least, one that had any merit. With the unknown still as fresh as it was when they each encountered it, Harlan and Marie fell asleep.

The sun outside had never set. Indeed, it remained in the same place behind the gray clouds that stretched out over the town like a blanket. Between the buildings, the dust moved softly, rising with a gentle breeze before settling back down again. A woman, old and wrinkled, shuffled through the dust, keeping her head down and humming softly to herself. She tapped the ground in front of her with a long, crooked walking stick then stopped.

There were footprints in the dust, something she hadn't seen in years. Her breath quickened as she looked around. Someone else was here.

She followed the footsteps as best she could, quickening her pace, her guard up. With each tap of the walking stick, she looked back up then to the right and left. She took another step, another tap, another look around. No one was there. After some time, she came upon the end of the footsteps and followed them up and into a small shelter. Whoever made the prints was probably inside, maybe waiting for her or maybe just lost. She couldn't imagine why anyone would come to her town, but then again, she never understood why she stayed herself when so many others had moved on.

The woman stood at the doorway and looked inside. Three figures were laid out peacefully on a makeshift mattress. She smacked her toothless mouth and stepped inside. They didn't seem like they were out to harm her, but that didn't curb her fear. They were strangers, and if they were anything like the last stranger to come into her town, there was bound to be trouble.

HARLAN WAS the first to notice the old woman. He opened his eyes as the woman laid her walking stick down on the table and picked up a Bible. As she thumbed through a few pages, Harlan slowly sat up, shaking Marie slightly.

"What is it?" Marie asked, her voice cracking but soft.

The woman heard the voice and dropped the Bible. She picked up her walking stick and started jabbing it in the air.

"*Get back!*" she shouted. "Get back!"

"Whoa!" Harlan raised his hands. "Calm down. We're sorry we invaded your house."

"Not my house," the woman said. She pointed the stick at Harlan. "Who are you? What do you want?"

"We just wanted to rest," Marie answered. "We've been walking for some time."

"Come off the desert or the swamp?"

"The desert." Marie looked over at Harlan and shrugged her shoulders. "Didn't even know about a swamp."

"We don't mean you any harm." Harlan stood. "My name is Harlan Reese."

The woman grunted then stood silent for a moment as she appeared to look them over. Finally, she put the walking stick down. "Names aren't important."

Harlan motioned for Marie to stand. "Where are we?"

"You don't know? Humphf. This is my town."

"We really don't know much of anything," Marie said. "We sort of came here by accident."

"Didn't we all?" The old woman motioned toward Justine. "Who's the girl?"

"We found her out in the desert. Does she belong here?"

"There aren't any girls here. Nobody lives here anymore, except me. That's why I'm wondering what you're doing."

"We were headed toward the mountains," Harlan said.

The old woman opened her eyes a little wider. "I think you should just turn right back around and get out of here."

Harlan looked over at Marie. They finally found someone to bounce their questions off of, but neither of them knew exactly where to begin.

"What's so bad in the mountains?" Marie asked. "I don't know if we're headed in the wrong direction or the right. I still haven't even figured out where we are."

"Sit down," the old woman said. "Make an old woman's heart jump around when you stand up like that."

Harlan and Marie found themselves doing exactly what the old woman suggested. They watched her shuffle to the middle of the shelter and slowly sit, grunting several times along the way. Her demeanor was odd, a little caustic at times, but nevertheless, both Harlan and Marie were elated to have found someone that might help them out.

Justine stirred in her sleep and finally opened her eyes. Groggy, she sat up and leaned against Marie, then closed her eyes once more.

"Beautiful child," the old woman finally said.

Marie wrapped her arm around Justine. "She is. Afraid we don't know where her family is, though."

"She probably doesn't have a family. Not here, anyway."

"How do you know that?"

"I take it that you haven't the foggiest clue where you are. That's a normal reaction to the situation, but I always wonder about the people who come through here sometimes."

"There are other people? So far we've met a total of one—you."

"People come and go. Most, I assume, just fade away. This isn't a Mecca waiting for a population of soul-searchers."

Harlan furrowed his brow. "Exactly where are we? This town—this world, frankly—is out of my experience."

"I don't think it's out of your experience. Actually, it *is* your experience. That's what makes it Hell."

"So this is Hell?"

"No."

Harlan furled his eyebrows, relieved to know he wasn't in Hell, but confused nonetheless.

"What about you? How did you come to live here?"

"We just came." The old woman turned her eyes to the ground. "We just came."

"Look," Harlan said, "I don't mean to be rude and insensitive, but you haven't really told us where we are. We are tired. We are lost. I've been attacked numerous times, I'm missing my daughter, and I'm not happy. So tell me, where are we?"

The old woman grabbed her walking stick and drew a

large circle on the floor of the shelter. At first, Harlan and Marie both wondered if she might be drawing a map, a clue, or a symbol of some sort, but after about a minute of watching, it looked more like a doodle and nothing more.

She stopped and looked up. A tear fell from her eyelid and struck her wrinkled cheek. "I don't know where you are. I have learned little from being here myself, and sometimes I simply wish my age would get the better of me and I would die. But I don't, and don't imagine I ever will. I simply walk around this town because that is what I know.

"There were about three hundred of us. Lonely, destitute people who wanted to be part of something greater. A man by the name of Eli Jonas promised us that if we followed him, we would all become part of something wonderful, something far beyond what mere religious belief taught us. I don't know why I jumped on the opportunity to uproot my family from my simple life, but I did it. I followed him. In the end, we just came here."

The name "Eli Jonas" sat in Marie's mind. She'd heard it someplace before, but couldn't for the life of her remember where. Was it in a book? On the news? Or was it simply a name that sounded familiar and misled her now jumbled sense of memory?

"Eli Jonas," Marie repeated the name in a whisper. "Where have I...?"

She stopped and looked at the old woman sitting silently across from her. More tears had fallen and the woman's cheeks were wet with a sadness that was real, painful, and—much like Marie's pain—had never quite faded away. Marie didn't know how she could understand that pain. She *did* know that name, however, and now she was even more confused.

"You were part of the Circle of Light, weren't you?" Marie finally asked.

The woman nodded once. "Yes, child. I was."

"The Circle of Light was a suicide cult," Harlan added. "I didn't know there were any survivors."

The old woman looked up at Harlan and smiled weakly. There was nothing ironic in her eyes. "There were no survivors."

JUSTINE HAD opened her eyes and listened to the old woman talk for some time. However, the lofty words took their toll on her; there just didn't seem to be anything intelligent to listen to for a four-year-old, so she let the fatigue of the recent walk overtake her small body once more. What adults talked about was really beyond her, and she could care less about whatever "suicide" meant.

Harlan and Marie listened intently, however, learning more about the mystery of the Circle of Light than they ever expected. Even if the Circle had been criticized for its radical views and otherworldly expectations of life, there was something grand buried beneath what the press had told the world. Eli Jonas had promised them too much, and what he delivered was a trap. He took the destitute, the depressed, the young and the old who had lost hope, and lifted them to heights they never dreamed possible. There was magic in his voice and power in his sermons. In the end, there was the answer each of them sought.

The woman told the story as if detached from it, like the pain she had lived through was something she read in a magazine and not lived. But every now and again, she would stop, wipe a tear from her eye and move on. She was a disillusioned innocent, trapped in the words of Eli Jonas and eventually brain washed into killing herself and—most painfully—her two children.

"But the *ma abad rab* called to us and had to be finished," she said. "Or at least our small part in it."

"What does that mean? *Ma abad rab*?" Harlan had fidgeted throughout the story, bothered by her description of the night they all agreed to commit suicide. He had yet to come to the realization that the old woman was, in fact, dead; the prospect that he would be in an equal state was something he didn't want to question.

"In the simplest terms, it means 'great work'. There are other words for it, but Eli was a linguist and felt that *ma abad rab* described this 'great work' so much better than any others."

"So what was it?"

"It's not a 'was'," the old woman answered. "The Great Work *is*. It's all around you. It's the all-encompassing battle of good versus evil, whatever you want that battle to be. If you want to believe it's God versus Satan, then do so. If you want to believe it's Vishnu versus whatever it is Vishnu would be against, then do so. You're a part of it. Always have been, and you always will be."

"What about now?" Marie asked. "You said you killed yourself to finish your part in this Great Work. So what is this? Your afterlife? Your punishment?"

"I don't know," the old woman sighed. "Eli told us this would be it. We would be transformed and live among God in Heaven. If you ask me, I don't consider this much of a heaven."

"A little barren, to say the least."

"We all wandered the desert you came from for some time. A few people went crazy when they heard the voices. They ran, and most of those who couldn't handle the pain of their life really just vanished."

The woman sighed and looked out the doorway. "The rest of us grouped together among the ruins of this town we stumbled across."

Harlan perked up. "You didn't build these shelters? You mean there's someone else here?"

"There are others." The woman sighed. "I haven't seen them in a long time, though."

"And after you found this place?"

"We forced ourselves to ignore the voices and focus on the reason for us being here. In the end, they fell. One by one. Some ran off into the swamp. Some disappeared into the desert again."

Marie watched the woman wipe a tear from her eye and stare out at the other buildings. She wondered how this frail old woman made it through the pain of her own memories, but as the woman said, there had to be a reason for everything.

"What did you do?"

"I stayed here alone." The woman turned back to look at

Marie. "Even my lover left me. He couldn't handle the pain."

"What happened to Eli?" Harlan asked.

"The bastard left us immediately and ran to the swamp. I never thought he would abandon us like that, but he did. He never came back."

Harlan looked at Justine, still sleeping on Marie's lap. Was she one of the people Eli Jonas had led astray? Was she killed by her parents?

The woman must have sensed Harlan's thoughts. She stood and brushed the dirt off of her ragged dress. "The girl is something different."

"How so?"

The woman took a step toward Justine then stopped. Her eyes seemed to look beyond the little girl.

"When we came here, there was a man who wandered through the town. He was unusual and we all sensed it. He said he came looking for a small child, about four years old. He didn't say much about her, except that she was an unrealized empath—could sense the needs of others and react accordingly. She was of use on Earth, but missing.

"Of course, none of this sat well with us, especially since we still thought this *was* Earth. He briefly explained what he called the *Maskiyl el Hanephesh*—a race of humans created to meet the needs of a troubled world. However, he said, not one had been allowed to realize their potential. Someone has been hunting them down, taking them from power, preventing their ability to assimilate into the human world."

"That's Hebrew, isn't it?" Harlan said, a little amazed at himself that he recognized the language. "I remember *nephesh*."

The woman smiled and looked at Harlan. "Yes, Hebrew. It means 'one who understands the soul.' In the end, a few of the smart men in this town decided he must be evil—a hurdle to cross on the way to realizing the *ma abad rab*. They grouped together, and in their infinite wisdom, cut out the heart of the stranger."

The old woman closed her eyes for a moment then pointed her walking stick at the little girl. "That girl—Justine, that's her name, right? — is most likely part of the Maskiyl he spoke about."

Harlan didn't like any of this, but the eccentric words of a dead woman coupled with the strangeness of this world pulled at his senses and let the metaphysical seep in. "She's just a small child, probably lost in the same way we came here. What could she possibly do?"

The old woman smiled. "She will grow, son. She will grow." She walked to the doorway then turned around one more time.

"But not here. Here, we cannot grow old, and we cannot die. You need to take her past the swamp. If you look hard enough, you will find the City of Sha'ar. It lies at the doorway to Hell. There is a gate there that will take you home. I only wish I could go with you, but there's no possible way for me to make it through that swamp. Demons live inside the bog, or something so hideous I hear their screams in the wind. I'm sure they took Eli. They will try to take you."

THEY FOLLOWED the directions the old woman gave them and soon found themselves outside of the town in a grassy field. Off in the distance, the mountains still loomed, but they were much closer now. The jagged spikes and treacherous cliffs warned the three of them that what they were about to face was more challenging than anything in their life. Justine, well rested and full of energy, ran around in the grass laughing, occasionally doing a somersault, and every once in a while asking Harlan and Marie if they were there yet. Neither adult could answer that question, since they had no idea where *there* actually was. It was closer, but that meant nothing.

The field rose gently, giving the impression that, perhaps, there was more and more lush landscape over the ridge. As they walked, Harlan and Marie found conversation light, even with the realization they were no longer with the living of Earth, but the dead of the Earth's past.

"Are we dead?" Marie asked.

"I don't think so," Harlan said. "At least, I don't feel dead."

"Do you know what dead feels like?"

"Not really."

"I came here after looking at a puddle of water that wasn't really a puddle. You came here after walking into a fog. Somehow, I don't think either situation lends itself to death."

"How did she come here?" Harlan pointed to Justine. "Do you think she may have died like the old woman?"

"No. I can't tell you why I don't think that. I just don't." Marie watched Justine do another somersault then turn to the adults for approval.

"Very nice, Justine," Marie called out. "Try not to get too far ahead, okay?"

Justine said nothing and continued to perform more gymnastic stunts.

"Something's after her," Marie said. "When we were on the lake bed, the wind screamed at us, told us to go away. I can only assume that was the Angry Man she keeps talking about."

"So if she's one of these Maskiyl, how did she end up here? Do you think she was kidnapped?"

Marie looked at Harlan. "The woman did say that someone was looking for her. It's a possibility, that's for sure."

Harlan sighed. One mystery after another kept rearing its ugly head, and the sole reason for his even being with Marie was a mystery that seemed like it was being eclipsed by everything else. "Do you think I'll ever find Jennifer?"

"I found you. If she's here, she can't be that far away."

"What if she never disappeared in that forest? What if she's back in Phoenix with Celine and Tommy, and now they have no idea where I am?"

Marie smiled. "You know, Harlan, someone told me a few years ago that 'what ifs' are made of sand and get blown away with the slightest of ease. What is, is rock solid."

"What idiot fed you that line of crap?"

"You did."

CHAPTER TWENTY-FIVE

Casey opened his eyes. There was little light wherever he was, but what existed flared like the sun. He blinked, rubbed his head then blinked again. As his eyes adjusted to the light, he saw white: white walls, a white ceiling and a white floor, all tinted with a faint blue. He couldn't be sure, but it looked like a cave, with stalactites made of ice and smooth striations in the patterns that became clearer on the walls.

To his left, an old man sat staring at him.

"Feeling better?" the man said.

Casey turned to face him, but as he rotated, a pain greater than he'd ever felt shot through his hip. Wincing, he grabbed his hip and lay back down. "*No!*"

The man stood and walked over to Casey. Bushy eyebrows spilt over the edge of his eyes like Niagara Falls in gray. "You about died with that fall, mister."

"I think I broke something."

"I *know* you broke something. Heard a crack when you fell. Alright though, I think I fixed you."

Casey rubbed across something slimy. "I'm bleeding."

"No, you ain't. Fixed that, too. Sorry I don't got one of those washing machines. You'll have to do with wet jeans."

"Thanks." Casey laid his head back on the floor of the ice cave and closed his eyes. "Where am I?"

"You're about a lifetime from where you should be, but that probably doesn't help you much."

"No." Casey opened his eyes again and tried to sit up. Surprisingly, despite the pain in his hip, he managed to prop himself against a wall. The old man still squatted on the floor and stared at where Casey had been.

"Well, mister, it ain't easy to explain, so I won't. But to make it simple—you ain't in Hell and you ain't in Heaven and thanks to a little magic I picked up along the way, it looks like you ain't dead."

"Thanks, again." Casey rubbed his hip. "I really should get going, though."

The man looked up at Casey. "I don't think that's a good idea. You ain't got enough strength to get no place, and I'd bet you don't even know where you're headed."

The man was right. Casey assumed he'd walk in the general direction of the distant mountains, but he really couldn't say why. The dreams he'd had? He couldn't even find a reason for why he was walking at all. A chance encounter with a strange old man in a wash, and an even stranger pull toward a cave, but other than that there was no reason for being where he was. Was he supposed to be looking for something? Or was he supposed to be looking for some way back to his desk?

"I have no idea why I'm here," Casey said. "You think you can help me out with that?"

"No, but I'd bet my eyes there's a reason."

"You're blind."

The old man chuckled. "How'd you figure that one out?"

"You didn't look at me when I moved and I'm not wearing jeans."

"Good brain on your shoulders, mister. You're right—I looked the wrong way one day and this is what I have to show for it." The old man stood and walked closer to Casey. "Name's Eli, by the way. Eli Jonas."

Casey took Eli's hand with his own. "Stephen Casey, but I think I've been stuck with Casey for most of my life."

"Pleased to meet you. I don't get many visitors these days."

Casey took a quick look around the cave Eli called home. "I wonder why? What brought you here?"

"It's a long story, mister, and I know we got time. Frankly, though, I don't feel like retelling it right now."

"Understood." Casey tried to stand, careful with how much weight he put on his legs. His hip still throbbed, but with a grunt and the help of the ice wall, he managed to make it to his feet.

"I really need to get out of here," Casey said as he looked past the old man toward a small tunnel where the light filtered in. "I take it that's the exit."

"There ain't no exit for me, mister. I never go very far." Eli wiped the gray stubble on his chin and walked over to the other side of the cave. "If you must go, though, I can't stop you." With a grunt, he sat back down.

"Look, I don't know where I am or what I'm doing here. All I remember is being lured into this place by an old man in a wash. Suddenly, I'm walking through a snowfield and end up down here."

Casey let out a sigh and hung his head. "Now, I'm not much for astral traveling or religious mumbo, but I do know that whatever is going on with my life must have some meaning. I didn't meet a ghost for nothing."

Eli smacked his lips. "Nope. Don't suspect you did. If you're looking for a why, I can't tell you. If you're looking for something a little more tangible, that I might be able to help you with. You got to promise me something, though."

"What's that?"

"You take me with you."

"Done." Casey hobbled over to Eli and sat next to him. On a pile of blankets that looked like a makeshift bed, Casey noticed a small, weathered journal. "If you're blind, how do you read that?"

"It's nothing, really. I spent many years with that book. Even though I can't see the words anymore and don't have a pen to jot stuff down, I know what's inside. You might call it my crutch."

Casey rubbed his head and looked out toward the exit tunnel. The light that poured in really wasn't all that bright, but his eyes were quickly becoming used to his dim surroundings. For a home—if indeed that's what it was—Eli had little.

"Where am I?" Casey asked, knowing the answer couldn't be anything more specific than he'd already been told. So, it wasn't Hell and wasn't Heaven. Whatever that left, Casey knew he'd have a hard time buying off on the idea.

"You ever read Milton or Dante?"

"Milton in high school. I think I bought the Cliff's Notes and scored a 'C' on the test. Why?"

"I have a theory—something I've been thinking about for some time. Lucifer had to cross what Milton called a great Gulf before he reached the Garden of Eden. Basically, it was an area between Heaven and Hell that held the Earth."

"It was empty."

"Exactly. It was void of substance. I think that's where we are."

"So what's with all the mountains and the snow? If I'm in a void, why am I sitting in an ice cave talking to you?"

Eli chuckled. "I have no idea. Like I said, it was just a theory. I think I've poked a million holes in it since I've been here, but I can't seem to make this place fit any other description."

"So how did you get here?"

Eli sat quietly for a moment, as if he was ignoring the question. Casey watched the old man purse his lips then wrinkle his forehead and look down. Was it something horrible? Was it something traumatic that he just didn't want to bring up, or did Eli Jonas come to this place under conditions more frightening than Casey had?

"Have you ever heard of *ma abad rab*?" Eli asked.

Casey's stomach sank. *Ma abad rab*. They were the same words used by the visitor to his apartment, and the same words he'd thought about for the last few days.

Casey nodded, a lump growing in his throat. "What does that mean?"

"The Great Work. It's actually Aramaic. I used to stand behind a pulpit, spouting off all I knew of the *ma abad rab*, only to find out what I thought I knew was only a small part of a much larger puzzle."

"I don't understand."

Eli pursed his lips. "When you were a child, did you ever go to church?"

"Occasionally. Usually on holidays and the like. My parents weren't very religious."

"And you learned what?"

"Bits and pieces of the Bible. Bits and pieces and nothing more. I'm more of an atheist, I guess."

"Bah." Eli swatted away Casey's last statement like an annoying fly. "Atheism is a religion no more or less concrete than any other out there."

"How—"

"Look, an atheist believes in not believing, and these days most atheists spend their time proselytizing to the masses, trying to disprove someone else's faith. Faith is what? Believing what can't be proved. Too many atheists spend their energy trying to convert or put down anyone who has a belief in something other than nothing. Believing in nothing is, therefore, belief, and some of these atheists are as bad as a hellfire and brimstone Baptist preacher on a hot Alabama Sunday afternoon."

Casey said nothing, his thoughts still on Milton's Gulf—the void he could now believe in.

"Anyway," Eli continued, "back to those bits and pieces. Imagine studying that book your whole life and suddenly realizing that it, too, is just bits and pieces. Imagine studying *every* religion—buy yourself the Qur'an, dive into the Jewish Kabbalah, immerse yourself in the rituals of Native Americans, the incantations of druids. Sit on a mountaintop in Nepal and chat with a monk. See Vishnu as something more than a golden statue. What do you think you'd learn then?"

"Bits and pieces."

"Exactly, and that's what I preached about. That's what I tried so hard to get across to my followers. It's all just bits and pieces, and it all adds up to the *ma abad rab*—The Great Work."

"Sounds like an impossible puzzle to put together."

Eli chuckled and leaned his head against the ice wall. "More impossible than you'll ever realize. And there I was, a conceited bastard who thought he could piece it all together and lead my people into the Promised Land." Eli's smile faded as he stared through blind eyes. "I didn't know enough."

Casey let the words of Eli merge with what he thought he knew. It made sense, and it was something he'd wondered about often. If there were so many different religions and so many different *sects* of those religions, who was right and who was wrong? What if none of them were right, or maybe just right about *one* thing? He considered the pain Eli must have gone through, thinking he had the answer only to find out that he didn't know the question.

"So where does that leave me?" Casey finally asked. "A bit or a piece?"

"Let's just say that I think you're here to do your part."

"My part? And what part would that be?"

"How the hell should I know, mister? I don't even know what *my* part is, and I'm here because I thought I was finished with it."

"Sorry." Casey looked up at Eli with his head back against the ice wall, his eyes trained in front of him.

"What do you think?" Eli asked.

Casey turned his head toward the exit. "I think you might be right, but I have no idea what my 'Great Work' is supposed to be. Until I find that out, I guess I won't know why I'm here. Isn't that about it?"

Eli smiled. "Bingo."

"Where should I be headed?"

"Wherever your heart leads you, mister. Just take me with you. Take that journal, too. You just might learn something new."

Although Casey really didn't want to be saddled with a blind old man, his mind reasoned there was no alternative. What Casey needed was a reason—a reason to be here, a reason to continue walking, and a reason to his very existence. If he was part of the *ma abad rab* like Eli said he was then he needed to find out how big or small that part was. What Casey really needed was some guidance and, fortunately, it sat in front of him.

—

THE AIR outside the cave greeted Casey and Eli with a cold blast and much less of a stale, stagnant smell than what existed inside Eli's home. In front of the two, the snow lay virgin down a slight hill toward a valley of nothing. The mountains held the same mysterious quality that initially pulled Casey toward them. There was a reason for feeling this way, and whatever it took, they had to cross the valley in front of them to get there.

Casey led the way, watching his step a little more than before and feeling enough pain in his hip to force a small limp and a grimace. Eli trudged along behind him, keeping only an arm's reach back. The snow wasn't as deep as Casey originally encountered and it soon gave way to small patches on a hill of grass. The temperature rose quickly, and even with the simple exertion, Casey sweat. With a zeal he had never felt before, Casey raced as fast as an injured man and a blind follower could, down the rest of the hill to enter the valley below.

Grass soon gave way to rocks interspersed with sparse vegetation. The gray blanket of clouds kept the shadows to a minimum and Casey saw the journey become easier. The voices that seemed constant when he first arrived on the field of snow were now whispers he barely recognized or simply ignored altogether. He stopped for a moment and looked around, feeling an unease he couldn't quite place. It wasn't the voices or the sudden change in landscape. No matter how hard he tried, Casey couldn't decide what it was.

He turned to Eli. "Is there any life here?"

"I can't say for sure," Eli replied. He smiled and looked blankly at Casey. "Can't say I've seen anything, either."

"You haven't been held up in that cave the whole time, have you?"

"No. I've traveled. I didn't lose my sight for a while."

"How did it happen? You said you looked the wrong way."

Eli sighed. "Another time, son."

Another time. That comment sat swirling inside of Casey's mind. He had trouble digesting the idea that this place was a void between Heaven and Hell, but the longer he stayed and the more he learned, the more plausible that idea became. *Another time.* He'd have to pry the story from Eli eventually, but it was apparent now wasn't that time.

The air around Casey and Eli was decidedly warmer than it had been. A musty smell of humidity hung in the air, reminding Casey of time spent in the Southeastern United States. The air was thicker and almost pasted itself to Casey's skin, leaving a clammy feel to his hands. Soon, if he kept walking in the direction he was headed, he felt the heat might become unbearable—a stark contrast to the field of snow they'd just left. So not only was this place weird and barren of life, it changed climatic zones within miles.

"Where to?" Casey looked out in front of him toward the mountains. The valley stretched out, bumping up against a dark forest. To the left of the forest there lay little more than a difficult path, rife with tall, monolithic rocks and barren of grass. To the right, Casey saw a sight that answered the deepest wish of his heart at this moment—was there life in this place? He saw buildings, and more appeared to be hidden behind gently rolling hills. Wooden shacks and makeshift shelters of canvas or grass dotted the landscape at the edge of a large dry lake bed. From his vantage point above everything, the lake bed stretched on for miles, finally losing itself in distant sand dunes and haze.

"What do you see?" Eli asked.

Casey smiled. "Hope, I think. It looks like a town at the edge of a lake bed up ahead a few more miles."

Eli placed his hand on Casey's sleeve. "You found Hope, alright. If it's what I think it is, that's the name of the town, anyway."

"You know of it?"

"Know of it?" Eli laughed. "Shoot, mister. I guess I really didn't tell you anything. I used to live there."

AT HOPE, there was desolation. Casey had a hard time describing the scene to Eli, but there was a shared feeling of loneliness. The buildings, shacks and shelters were all empty save a few miscellaneous items of little value. Only the voices

Casey carried with him since first entering this world spoke on the wind. There were ghosts at Hope, but the ghosts belonged to Casey.

Casey stood in the middle of the street—if that's what it could be called. "What happened here?"

"Death." Eli didn't ask how everything looked, if the buildings still stood or if there was anyone around. He must have known. "We came here to live a new life, one that we shouldn't have had in the first place."

"I don't understand."

Eli sighed. "I knew God called us to some higher purpose, that if we followed Him into the next life our lives would have purpose, meaning, the final explanation of the *ma abad rab*. In truth, we found nothing—except the past attacking our sanity."

"You said you led the Circle of Light. Did you really think what you taught them was real?"

Eli let a small chuckle escape from his throat. "I *know* what God told me was real. There is a Great Work we're all a part of. How we lead our lives determines our place in the Work. Will we be leaders, followers, or will we blaze our own trail? Will we aid the angels or inhibit them? Will we let God guide us, or will we simply exist as a nuisance to those who know of the truth and fight every day?"

"And you still don't know what your part is, do you?"

"No. I'm guessing I still haven't finished it, and the people I brought here with me didn't have much of a part to begin with, I suppose." Eli turned his head down, as if looking forlornly at the ground despite his missing eyesight. "I brought them here, and this place brought them confusion and pain."

Eli grabbed Casey's hand. "You don't believe in anything, do you, son?"

"I have my feelings, but that's all they are—feelings. Like I said, I'm probably more atheistic than anything else. I can't say for sure if I believe in a higher power, or in a world that was created and left to its own devices. I've seen too much evil in the world to think there might be another purpose behind it all. If we were all meant to take part in some grand scheme, why are we left to figure out what that part is on our own? Why don't we all climb a mountain and let God inscribe in us some purpose?"

"Would be nice wouldn't it?"

Casey spotted a wooden hut, held together with crude twine. He walked forward a little bit and looked inside. There was nothing—as he suspected—but in the doorway, he saw what might have been footprints, gently disturbed by the wind but still visible.

Eli stood still.

"You coming?" Casey asked.

"Not until you lead me. I've been lost before, and wandering this world alone in the dark is more painful than you could ever imagine."

"Fair enough."

"Tell me something, Casey. When you entered this world, what did you see?"

Casey turned from the hut. "Nothing. There wasn't anything at all, just voices from the past that seemed real, like whatever event they were replaying was happening all over again."

Eli smiled. "And you believed at that point that the world you knew wasn't the world you stepped into, right?"

"I suppose. I knew *something* was different."

"Different or just new, like your eyes had been opened and the meaning of your life was somewhere out there, just within reach?"

Casey thought about what Eli said for a moment. "I suppose it's all new. But I don't see the meaning."

Eli smiled. "All in good time."

Casey pursed his lips in thought then shrugged off Eli's comment. He walked up to another small building with a poorly built porch and sat. The gray clouds and dusty streets did little to take away from the desolation or the feeling of watching the prospect of finding answers dashed apart in the ruins of Hope.

"I thought for sure we'd found something." Casey looked

at Eli. "You don't have any ideas as to where they all went, do you?"

"Once I left, they had no leader and no direction. They were left on their own. The voices you hear, Casey, are as individual as the person. To some, they're too much. I know most of them wandered off, crazy. A few..." Eli let his words trail off.

"A few what?"

Eli sighed. "A few tried to kill themselves... again. The problem is you can't die here. Pain is just a cross to bear."

Casey sat in silence for a moment. To kill yourself was bad enough. To kill yourself at the behest of a leader, was even worse. *To do it twice, though,* Casey thought. *Well, I can't even picture that.*

"Now what?" Casey picked up a small stone and threw it toward a building on the other side of the street. The stone struck a plank then fell calmly to the dirt below. "You think we should give up and find a place to sit this out?"

"Sit what out? There ain't nothing of your life left, mister. You came here, you're stuck here. Can't offer you more than that."

"I thought you said my part in the Great Work was still unknown."

Eli chuckled. "Your part might just be to die, though."

"First off, you just said you can't die here, and second, you're depressing."

"And he's right." An old woman appeared from around the corner of the building. She walked slowly toward Casey and Eli, pushing a knotted walking stick before her. "You can't die here, but it might as well be death."

Eli looked in the direction of the voice as a smile widened across his face. "Well, I'll be. If it don't sound like Miss Congeniality."

"Hello, Eli." The old woman snorted some phlegm from her nose and spit it on the ground next the porch. "Thought you'd be dead, by now."

"Ain't finished yet."

"Finished with what?" The woman laughed. "Are you still

believing that crap about the Great Work, old man? You should know better than that."

"It ain't crap, Jessie."

"You lied to us, Eli," Jessie said, poking her walking stick down at the feet of Eli.

"I didn't lie, Jessie. I just didn't know."

"Same difference. I suppose the swamp didn't eat you alive like I thought."

"No."

"So what happened to you?"

"I met God."

Jessie laughed and leaned forward on her walking stick. "You met God many times when we were on Earth. Usually, He appeared in the form of an LSD tab or mushroom."

"That's not funny."

"Neither is this." Jessie's smile faded. "I trusted you and so did everyone else. Now what do you have to say for yourself?"

"I have nothing to say, except that you and I aren't finished."

"You don't get it, do you Eli?"

Casey spoke up. "Excuse me. I don't mean to interrupt your little reu—"

"I don't?" Eli said, ignoring Casey's interjection. "I told every last one of you that our realization of the *ma abad rab* was complete and we could go home. I led you here, and so far the only thing I've been wrong about is exactly *how much* we had left to realize. I didn't know we weren't finished, but as God is my witness, I *will* finish it."

"Excuse me," Casey said again, this time a little more forcefully.

"You led us here, alright." Jessie spat again. "You abandoned us in our confusion and let us figure things out on our own. Do you know where your children are, Eli? Do you know what happened to your wife? Do you have any idea what pain is?"

"*Excuse me!*" Casey shouted, stepping between Eli and Jessie. "Look, I have yet to find an answer I can accept and still can't figure out why I want to go toward those mountains. You two aren't helping me. There must be someone else here that can help."

Jessie looked at Casey then back to Eli. "I just sent three of them into the swamp."

Casey blinked.

"You did what?" Eli asked, his voice full of irritation. "Are you crazy? Who were they?"

"I don't know. A man and woman and a child."

Eli took a step back.

"*Maskiyl el Hanephesh*, Eli. You were right about that much."

"And you sent them into the swamp?"

"I told them to go to the City of Sha'ar. How else are they going to get there?"

"How did you know about the city?" Eli voice resonated with surprise.

The woman cocked her head to the left, as if she knew something Eli didn't—finally. "There have been visitors since you left."

Casey's eyes were wide with anticipation. "There's a city here?"

"Yes and no," Eli replied. "I mean, yes there's a city, but I don't think we'll make it."

"Why not? Don't you have anything positive to say?"

"The voices, Casey. You remember them?"

"I still hear them."

"They become something the closer you get to Sha'ar. I can't say what exactly, because I ran away before I went over the edge."

"They can't become anything worse than I've already seen." Casey walked out into the street and pointed toward the mountains. "Is it there?"

"Yes."

"Buried in the mountains?"

"I'm afraid so."

The answer was finally becoming clearer, if not yet fully understood. If he was here to fulfill his part in the Great Work, then it only came to reason he was also led more by fate than anything else. Fate drove him to the wash and whisked him away into this void. Fate pulled him toward the mountains, and it was fate that led to his discovery of both Eli and Hope. There was a reason to the pattern, and Casey began to feel that maybe—just maybe—he would come to see the light soon enough.

Closer and even more unpleasant looking, the mountains loomed large.

CHAPTER TWENTY-SIX

Jennifer stood atop the last rise and looked over a valley that seemed endless. On the horizon, jagged mountains were awash in haze, and below her a dry lake bed silently beckoned her forward. She didn't know where to go, but now that she knew about her sister and a brief understanding of her purpose in life, at the very least, she had direction. Justine was out there. So was Hell, and she knew it.

The voices she heard upon first opening her eyes after entering the closet, were all but washed out. It seemed if she didn't think of the past, the past wouldn't talk to her. But it was difficult. Images of Jonathan constantly assailed her, and the rift she had with her father—the reason, she surmised, she was there in the first place—wasn't sitting well with her. On top of that, she prayed the man would never reappear.

Every rock and every branch and every small tuft of grass became an obstacle for Jennifer. At first, she bounded down the side of the mountain, letting gravity accelerate her descent. It wasn't easy, however, and she soon realized she had to pay more attention to her surroundings. She didn't know where she was; there might be a cave full of demons for all she knew. The stranger she met seemed odd, almost out of place, as if there was nothing indigenous about this land. All of its inhabitants were unwelcome guests or unknowing souls trapped in a world that defied explanation. If Jonathan was killed because of something she did or was a part of or because of who she was, did that mean the bacon-cooking madman still hunted her? The stranger left more questions than answers. Sure, a man in a forest killing people out of the blue wasn't unheard of, but a man in a forest killing out of the blue people *she* knew and then targeting *her*, definitely was.

The path ahead of Jennifer thinned out. Gone were the trees. Boulders were farther apart and even the grass was shorter, the dirt starting to take over. The lake bed lay only a mile or so away, and Jennifer stopped to take in the view. She had climbed more and walked more than ever before. Oddly enough, though, she wasn't tired. Or hungry. Or thirsty. It was almost as if the world around nourished her body, kept it alive, kept it fit and ready for whatever it decided to throw at her next.

Jennifer sat on the last of the large boulders and looked out toward the horizon. The lake bed didn't seem that large, at least not as large as it had from above. Beyond its edges, she could faintly make out trees and beyond that, the mountains that pulled her forward. She was certain she would find Justine there, although she didn't know why or what possessed her to think that.

And what of Justine? Should she be angry with her mother for not telling her, or should she be elated someone else in her family existed besides Tommy? There was certain uneasiness in knowing the truth, almost as if the proverbial cat had been let out of the bag and her mother had carried that bag around with her for years. Jennifer knew nothing of her parents' history, except for small glimpses into past lives that didn't seem at all unlike her own. She knew of another woman in her father's life, but only enough to understand why her mother was upset if the subject ever came up. Did her father know of Justine? Was he kept in the dark as well, or was this something he was forced to carry as well?

Questions continued to mount as she stood and began the final leg of her trip down the side of the mountain toward the dry lake bed and eventually—at least she hoped—answers.

THE DRIED mud cracked under her feet and Jennifer found herself stepping lightly. The clouds were gray and ominous, almost like they were pregnant with rain but weren't due for weeks. A calm breeze touched her face, providing slight relief from the exertion she put forth getting down the mountain. She slowed several times, stopped once even and looked around wondering if her chosen direction—dictated more by feeling than anything concrete—was even correct. What if she was walking farther from where Justine was? How much more did she have to go through?

The ground crumbled beneath her, her right foot sinking into the lake bed up to her shin. She stumbled forward and caught herself with her hands, the weight of her body crushing more dirt in front of her. A quick squeal escaped her lips and she realized just how much silence had encompassed her. There were no other sounds—just the cracking of mud, her breath, and the occasional wisp of wind by her ears. The voices were entirely still.

Jennifer righted herself and stood. If this was the extent of how much the lake bed was going to crack, then she shouldn't have a problem walking a little faster. She had been timid at first, afraid of collapsing into a netherworld of nothing. This world surprised her more than once, and there was no reason why the lake bed should be predictable when nothing else was.

A gust of wind slapped her in the face, cold and biting, like a million needles of ice on a stale washcloth. Jennifer looked up at the horizon, startled by the wind, and suddenly more fearful of the unknown than she had been. She walked faster, more afraid of the change in weather than the possible collapse of the lake bed.

The ground continued to disintegrate under her weight, making travel more difficult. The wind picked up again as suddenly as the first time, pushing her body back. She leaned forward against the onslaught, not expecting it to shift to the other direction and push her down. The wind blew harder and ripped the air around her, filling her ears with screams. It didn't seem like the simple screams of nature; this was evil, like a thousand voices filling her conscious at once, all of them in agony. She wrapped her arms around her chest and pushed her head down, praying the wind would pass.

It grew stronger instead, and the voices no longer filled her ears; they erupted from inside her. Jennifer cupped her hands over her ears as tight as she could, wincing in pain at the horrifically loud noise. The more she pushed on her ears, the louder the screams became until her entire body vibrated violently at the cacophony of Hell.

She screamed, half hoping someone would hear her, half expecting her own noise to drown out everything else. Instead, the wind began to swirl, beating her from every direction, lifting at her clothes, pulling her hair upwards, pushing back then pulling forward any exposed skin. The screams coalesced, from a sickening din of unimaginable pain, into a singular voice that echoed both inside and outside.

Come with us!

The words were unmistakable, the voice deep, hoarse and sinister. Jennifer screamed again, prayed she would wake up and find it all a dream, or at the very least, the wind would stop. The exposed parts of her skin burned, adding to the pain she felt from the sounds of Hell.

Come with us!

With a final scream, Jennifer pushed herself up on her feet and thrashed about wildly at the wind, completely unaware of what she might be trying to hit. She willed herself forward, then again, keeping her direction in mind but her eyes closed. Tears of pain formed and fell against her cheeks, turning quickly into ice that scratched and pulled at her already frozen skin.

The wind stopped.

Jennifer fell onto the lake bed one more time. The dirt crumbled beneath her and erupted in a fine dust.

The screaming stopped with the wind, but silence didn't replace it. Once more, she heard the voices she first encountered—aural images of the past erupting all around. Jonathan, her father, her mother, the stranger, and a hundred more from different times in her life all spoke at once.

At least these voices were known, and whatever is known can be comfortable. She looked up at the horizon once again. The trees on the edge of the lake bed were much closer than they had ever been. She pulled herself back to her feet and headed for the other side, looking for Justine, her father or just an idea of what was happening to her and why.

PART III: OUT OF THE VOID

And they took and brought me to a place in which those who were there were like flaming fire, and, when they wished, they appeared as men. And they brought me to the place of darkness, and to a mountain the point of whose summit reached to heaven.
And I came to a river of fire in which the fire flows like water and discharges itself into the great sea towards the west.

— *The Book of Enoch*, XVII:1-2,5

CHAPTER TWENTY-SEVEN

Marie stepped on something squishy. The ground became softer and softer the farther into the swamp they walked, and the light of day was allowed only through a few small spaces in the ever-increasing canopy above them. Harlan reached back, grabbed Marie's hand and pulled her up while Justine held tight atop his shoulders.

"Sheesh." Harlan wiped his forehead and turned to walk again. "You'd think a place like this would have a few roads built to walk on."

"What are they going to do with a road?" Marie asked. "I didn't get the feeling these people brought stuff with them, much less cars."

"True."

A large cypress tree stood in the path Harlan had taken. The only route around it looked to be to the right through a puddle of stagnant water. Since they entered the swamp, both Harlan and Marie heard the voices louder and more distinct. It was as if they were being warned of something impending, but the only words were memories of the past.

Justine tightened her grip around Harlan's shoulders. "I don't like this place."

"Neither do we, honey," Harlan said, placing his foot carefully into the pool of water. "I don't think it'll last much longer."

The water was cold, and Harlan hoped it wasn't too deep or the bottom of the pool wasn't loose where he'd lose his balance and drop Justine. She had taken to Harlan immediately after entering the swamp, refusing to walk for herself and get her feet wet. Harlan consented to allow her to ride on his shoulders, but he warned her that if there was any horseplay, she'd have to dismount.

There was no horseplay. Justine was as scared as she could be, and the change in lighting made matters worse.

"What's that noise?" Marie called out from near the tree.

Harlan stopped and listened. The voices were too loud to make out anything discernible and he had to concentrate to hear whatever didn't sound familiar to him. A low rush followed by a growl filtered in through Celine yelling at him and Marie talking about running away.

"Sounds like a growl," Harlan whispered. "I didn't think there were any animals here."

Justine buried her head in Harlan's shoulder. "I'm scared."

"Don't be. I think we'll get through this just fine. And when we do, do you know what's on the other side?"

"What?"

"I don't know." Harlan sighed. "I was hoping you did."

IT SEEMED like hours they trudged through the swamp, stepping in pools of water, sinking into soft mud and walking around trees that were just getting larger. Marie was in the lead and had taken Justine off of Harlan's shoulders. She walked around another tree and stopped.

"How bad can this get?" She exhaled a labored breath. The ground gave way in front of her to a weed infested bog that looked like it stretched for miles. Only a few trees grew in the bog, letting a little more light in, but all it really did was illuminate a much more difficult path.

Harlan stood next to Marie and looked out at the vast expanse of water in front of him. Wisps of steam rose from the surface like so many tiny snakes trying to breathe. "You want to go back?"

"No. What is this? You want to give up?"

"No, I don't," Harlan lied. "I was just mentioning it."

The growl came again, loud enough to be heard above the

voices. It rose in pitch and volume then slowly subsided again.
"Something's out there," Marie whispered.

THE BOG couldn't have been worse, and Marie was buried to her waist at times in the water and mud. Justine held on tight and cried. There didn't seem to be any hope of them ever reaching the other side, and the longer the three of them were in the swamp, the more agitated they became.

"Tell me again why I'm here?" Marie looked at the other side of the bog and silently wished for a boat.

"Adventure. We all need it."

"Not this kind."

Marie took another step and lost her balance. Justine screamed as she flipped over Marie's head and landed in the water.

"Harlan!" Marie yelled out.

Harlan turned around in time to see Marie jump to her feet and frantically slap the water in front of her.

"I can't see her!"

The growl came once again, so loud this time it froze Harlan and Marie in their tracks.

"Quick!" Harlan yelled out. "Get her out of there!"

Marie ran forward and reached into the water with her arms.

A small hand reached up out of the bog in front of Harlan.

"Over here!" He reached in with a grunt and grabbed hold of Justine's dress, pulling as hard as he could. Something had her leg.

The growl drew closer and seemed to slither behind Harlan. The shock of the sound made him lose his grip.

"No! I lost her!"

Another hand reached out of the water in front of Marie, ghostly white and covered with mud and moss. Its open palm grasped the air then sank below the surface. Marie screamed and fell backwards. As her arms flailed, she hit Justine's side and instinctively turned around to pull her out.

Harlan ran toward Marie to help. As he took another step, something caught his leg and tripped him up.

"Got her!" Marie cried. She turned and ran as fast as she could toward the far end of the bog.

Harlan righted himself in the rank water and stood, looking around for Marie and Justine. Ahead of him, he saw them both burst out of the weeds and moss and onto solid ground next to a tree.

Something else caught his leg again. He screamed as he felt a sharp pain rip through his flesh then fell backward. The water rushed around him as Harlan was pulled under. He opened his eyes.

A face stared back. Its nose was distorted, almost bent to the side. Harlan stopped thrashing for a moment and saw for the first time the evil around him—something he sensed but had yet to lay eyes on. In the face in front of him, the eyes blinked. For a second, Harlan thought he'd caught of glimpse of something he'd seen before.

Harlan couldn't even imagine what it was, though. Was this one of the demons the woman from the town mentioned? How many more were there? Five? Ten? A thousand?

He pulled again at his leg as missiles of feeling shot through his body, exploding under his flesh. Whatever had a hold of him gripped tighter. His arms thrashed about, fruitlessly trying to push his body farther from the face and at the same time pull himself up out of the water.

A sudden rush of adrenaline gave him the strength to break free. He burst to the surface with a gasp and immediately heard screams from Marie and Justine. He swam as fast as he could, praying the ground would rise up to meet him and he could run. With a scream of pain coupled with exertion, Harlan finally pulled himself out of the bog next to Marie and Justine and rolled over on his back.

Harlan screamed, and sat straight up, grabbing his leg and arching his back.

Justine gripped Marie as tight as she could, tears running down her face and mixing in with the mud and grass.

"Mommy," she whispered through tears.

In the bog, the water splashed where they had been, and the growl came one last time.

Harlan looked out at the water and pushed himself a little farther from the edge. "What was *that*?"

THE REST of the swamp wasn't any easier, and Harlan had a difficult time walking with the pain in his leg. He stopped next to a tree to rest and look at his wound. Blood still poured from a gash a few inches long just below his right knee, and the water from the bog mixed in to make the pain much worse. He needed to get it cleaned off, but he knew that—at least in the swamp—clean water wasn't in abundance.

"I saw its face, Marie." Harlan shivered at the thought. "It's like the thing was... empty."

Marie stopped and sat. Her body ached, and with every step they took it seemed they weren't getting anywhere. "Empty how?"

Harlan sat next to Marie with Justine between them. He sighed and looked out through the trees where they'd just walked. His gaze shifted past the ferns, past the wisps of ground fog and into the darkness. He thought he saw something, but he knew it was probably nothing more than the images left over from the trauma of the journey or the pain of a lifetime. Still, they floated on the air like so many ghosts, and to the tune of the voices from his past, they danced.

For the first time, Harlan noticed the voices themselves had merged, each word becoming a syllable recognizable only to Harlan's soul. Celine's anger and frustration, Marie's love and admiration, Jennifer's angst, his drill instructor's stern warnings on life and structure—they were all one. They finally spoke to him, as if he'd opened his ears for the first time and was able to understand the message that was imprinted on the folds of his memory.

"Do you remember going out to the shelter when you were in high school and helping out with the food line?"

"Yes." Marie smiled. "You were with me. I remember a lot of things that day."

"Before *that*." Harlan looked at Marie and thought he saw the same spark she had before, visible in the darkest of places and the darkest of times.

"What about it?"

"There was an old man sitting against the side of the building."

"The one staring into space. I thought he was high or something."

"So did I, but when you went inside I sat next to him. I don't know what I thought I could do—offer a dollar or two? He just sat there, empty." Harlan focused on the distance behind them. "His eyes looked the same as whatever I saw out there in the bog."

Harlan grabbed his leg again. The pain was worse and began to eclipse his thoughts. If he didn't at least wash out the wound soon, he wasn't going to make it very far.

"Are you alright?" Marie reached over and pulled back the shredded material around the gash. The bleeding was continuous, and covered the lower half of Harlan's jeans with a dark red color. "You need something for that."

Harlan winced and grunted as Marie pulled out a piece of grass from the gash. "You want to head on down to the corner store for me?" he asked. "I think they might have some peroxide."

"Very funny. Take off your shirt."

"What?" Harlan looked over at Marie and briefly wondered about her intentions. "Oh, for the bandage."

"It'll have to do. You need to stop the bleeding somehow. Didn't life in the military teach you that?"

"No," Harlan said as he unbuttoned his shirt. "I can stop a sucking chest wound, stick a tampon in a gunshot, and mend a paper cut, but I don't remember anything about tending demon-caused flesh wounds."

Marie smiled and watched him take off his shirt. "So what did you say to this guy?"

"Nothing. I just followed his gaze to the other side of the street to see what he saw."

"And?" Marie folded the shirt and tied it around Harlan's leg. He winced and grunted again as she tightened the knot as much as she could.

"Needs to be tight," she said. "Sorry for the pain."

"And," Harlan said through clenched teeth, "he finally spoke. 'I'm waiting,' he said."

Marie furled her eyebrows and leaned back against the tree. "Waiting for what? A paycheck? A job?"

Harlan smiled weakly and closed his eyes. He thought he saw the old man, propped up against a wall, gray whiskers stained with the grime of the city. He was waiting.

Justine looked up at Harlan and tapped his arm, dragging him back from the depths of his memory and the pain in his leg.

"*Ma'arab*," she whispered. "They lie in wait."

Marie and Harlan both looked at each other and then down at Justine. She let loose a giggle and smiled.

"They're waiting for something."

"What are they waiting for?" Marie asked.

"Someone to talk to."

AFTER A few more hours, the three weary travelers saw the last tree ahead of them. The rise and closeness of the mountains just beyond made the moment seem a little less exciting than it should have been. As they entered a clearing, they saw in front of them the true nature of the mountains they had been pulled toward for so long—pure rock, rising at odd angles and speckled with small stones and massive boulders. It was daunting, to say the least, and hope was soon dwindling that they would ever reach Sha'ar and the gateway home.

Marie set Justine down on a small patch of grass as Harlan collapsed on the ground. He was exhausted, more so than he'd ever felt. Every last bit of energy he had must have been consumed by the journey through the swamp, and the only thing he wanted was a little pillow, a little blanket, a little mattress and a long nap.

Marie walked closer to the mountains and sighed. "Well, no one said this was going to be easy, but how are we going to cross that?"

Harlan slowly stood and joined Marie at the edge of a chasm a few hundred feet wide. The mountains on the other side undulated orange and red with what looked like lava flowing hundreds of feet below them.

"Can it get any worse?" Harlan asked. He turned around and looked at the swamp. "I thought *that* sucked."

"It did." Marie turned around to join Justine. Obviously tired of walking, she had curled herself into a fetal position with her eyes closed. "There has to be a way across."

"Ever the optimist, aren't you?"

"Ever the pessimist, aren't you? Where there's a will, there's a way and right now I have a pretty strong will to take a shower and curl up with a cup of cappuccino."

Harlan limped over by Marie and sat. "I thought you liked hot chocolate."

"I do." Marie smiled. "I just feel like having a cappuccino."

Their eyes caught each other in an unguarded moment and Harlan soon found himself caressing Marie's neck softly. There was meaning behind the moment, the closeness Harlan needed to feel. With a timid effort, he placed a kiss on her lips. But whatever smile he might have felt emerging from this moment was quickly dowsed by a feeling he couldn't grasp. Slowly, he pulled away.

Marie caught the look on his face. "What is it?"

"I've been thinking about what that... that thing who beat me up in the desert said." Harlan shifted his gaze away from Marie looked back into the darkness of the swamp. "She—it—said I was an open book here, but I didn't know you were pregnant. How did *it* know if I didn't?"

"Maybe we're all open books."

Harlan turned back to look at Marie. Her expression matched his own, and in her eyes he saw the fear he'd been feeling since he first stepped into the fog back in the forest looking for Jennifer.

"I came into this place the same time you did," Marie said. "I'm probably just as open as you, like our past is reflected on a giant mirror and everyone else can see it." She shifted nervously. "Maybe the thing that told you I was pregnant had found it out from me."

"Why didn't you tell me?"

Marie looked down. "I don't want to talk about it right

now, Harlan." Her voice was tinged with irritation and pain. "It's enough to find ourselves in this place, and I'd like to think there's a good reason for it."

"A good reason?" Harlan stifled an ironic chuckle. "For this hell we're in? I just can't see it."

Justine stirred in her sleep, restless. Marie nodded in her direction. "There's a motherless child there," she said as a tear which must have formed earlier slid down her cheek. "And I'm a childless mother. Reason? Why is that so hard to see?"

Harlan didn't say anything. What could he say? There *was* a reason for everything that had happened so far, but he couldn't make sense of it.

"We've both made mistakes," Marie said. Her voice was soft, pensive. "Having an affair made us sinners, and pretty bold sinners at that. You can be a total atheist, but you still can't deny the wrongness in it all, even if you don't call it sin. There's nothing good in what we did, and a lot of people outside of us were hurt in ways we don't even know."

Harlan felt his stomach sink at the sting of Marie's words—a sting that was laced with truth. He'd always known they were in the wrong, but he didn't like to hear it.

"But I believe in what happened to me," Marie continued. "I believe in what happened to you, and I can believe that I'm sitting next to a river of lava in a world that reflects our past. If all of that belief is there, why can't I believe that we can be forgiven for things we've done in the past, that we don't have to live a lie or have it thrown back in our face every day?"

Harlan watched Marie wipe her cheek. She looked down at the ground between them and fidgeted with a blade of grass.

"Forgive and forget?" Harlan said, not sure he could have said anything else at that moment.

Marie's lips turned up in a tiny smile. "I don't think this place will let you forget."

She opened her mouth as if to say more but remained silent. In the silence, Justine's sleeping breath was loud, and Harlan turned to her curled form.

"Reason," he whispered. "I guess I just have to believe there's a reason."

Harlan and Marie had been through so much both in this world and in the years they were apart. And even while apart, there was unity neither could deny nor imagine life without. Harlan and Marie were somehow one, their souls interwoven in a pattern of love and respect, of pain and tribulation, all born from a moment of sin. Still, it was there, and what happened to one, the other felt.

Marie touched Harlan's hand with trembling fingers. "We all have to believe in something. Why not believe we can be forgiven, too? Or that we can start over?"

CHAPTER TWENTY-EIGHT

Casey stood by a cypress tree and looked into the darkness in front of him. The ground had become something soft and unforgiving in the last few miles, and with each step, the path ahead of them became more difficult. They'd made good time at first, bounding through the undergrowth as fast as Casey could lead Eli. It didn't take long for solid ground to lead to mud, however, and the small trees that let through some light turned into monsters whose canopies were unforgiving.

Moss grew against the trunks of each tree like a pestilent shawl that covered all it could find. It glowed a vibrant green, bathing the darkened path in front of them in a surrealistic light. It wasn't enough to actually illuminate the way, but it was enough to make Casey feel uneasy about his surroundings. Since walking into the swamp, Casey had wondered if indeed there was life in this void. He hadn't seen anything that might have given him that impression save two souls that were as lost as he.

There was Eli, the blind leader of a cult he'd read about in the papers but knew nothing about. If what he said was truth, then it was no wonder hundreds of people followed him to their deaths. But did they die? No. They simply vanished from the physical Earth, a place Casey could only remember as a haven for the distraught and those depressed. Still, he wanted to go home, to be with his beer and partake of its goodness. He didn't care if his bed was made or if there was a stack of papers waiting on his desk for him to sign and file. Home would be home and it was a lot better than this place.

"How much worse can this get?" Casey looked into the darkness.

Eli stood next to Casey, as he had through the whole journey. "Oh, it's not so bad. I can almost see the end over there."

"Very funny." Casey sighed and took a few more steps, navigating around a fallen branch. He noticed quickly that the branch was devoid of moss, as if the tree fed on the slime and kept it alive. If a branch broke free from the trunk, the moss — the life that fed on it — would die.

"I knew this would happen," Eli said. "I followed this path once, thinking I could make it on my own. There's something out there that draws on memories and pulls you deeper into it."

As if in response to Eli's statement, Christine's voice floated around the trees and pasted itself to Casey's ears. "It was just a little kiss. It didn't mean a thing."

Casey stopped and closed his eyes. There were other memories in his life. Why did this place seem to take all that was bad — all those moments that defined his life — and repeatedly beat him with the message he should have learned years ago. He tried to shrug it off one more time.

"Who's controlling all of this?" Casey didn't know if he wanted to hear the answer or just know that an answer existed.

"From what I can tell, you control it. This place feeds on you and you alone, just as much as it feeds on me. For each one of us, this world is a different experience, but the experience is nothing more than your life. There really isn't much to it."

"But it's all so depressing. Tell me something, Eli. How much of this world have you seen?" Casey winced at his poorly chosen words. "I mean, when you..."

"...could see?" Eli smiled. "You know, being blind isn't as bad as you think. You may not be able to see the path ahead of you, but you also have no idea what you're stepping in."

Casey looked down, if only to satisfy his curiosity.

"It's endless," Eli said. "What you've seen—a snowfield, a lake bed and swamp, those mountains—they're just a small sample of what's really out there. I've seen mountains full of lush trees and running creeks, beaches on the shore of a vast green sea, cliffs overlooking valleys as far as the horizon. If Milton was right—and I'm pretty sure he knew just bits and pieces like everyone else—then the distance from here is farther than you think."

The distance from here. Casey had heard that phrase before, and he found it frightening in a way to think that twice now, Eli had spoken words he'd first heard from the visitor in his apartment. There were too many coincidences to shrug it off.

"Why am I here?"

"That's a loaded question, don't you think?" Eli laughed and sat on a rock. "I mean, why are *any* of us here?"

"That's not what I meant. I could easily have been sitting at my desk right now, filling out reports or at home, watching television and drinking a beer. But I was so curious about this girl in the desert."

"Someone you knew?"

"No. Someone that was murdered. Her heart was ripped out of her chest, and from what I can gather from the medical examiner's office, it was ripped out by hand. There was a fingernail broken off inside her chest."

Eli swallowed audibly. "Sounds lovely."

"That wasn't all. Her head was crushed beyond recognition. I mean, to kill someone is one thing, but then to attempt to erase her identity is something totally different."

Casey let the images of the murder scene play over in his mind. He saw the sunset, the thunderstorm brewing in the distance, the cactus next to the girl. He saw the photographer capture death with snap after snap of his camera, Byron standing next to him with his smug expression, and...

Casey frowned. There was a medallion around the woman's chest. Something he'd seen only once again in a dream.

"Do you think she was a part of the Great Work you've been going on about?"

"I told you we're all a part of it."

"No, in a larger way. Jessie mentioned the Mass... Mass..."

"*Maskiyl el Hanephesh?*"

"Yeah. That's it. What does that mean?"

"It means 'one who has understanding of the soul.' It's a legend, really. One of those bits and pieces I uncovered through my journeys."

A low growl resounded through the trees. The two travelers listened, trying to gauge its distance. As they feared, it was in the direction they were headed.

Casey swallowed. "That doesn't sound good."

"Probably isn't. I didn't like this place the first time I was here, and even though I can't see it, I still don't like it."

Casey sighed. There was so much he didn't understand, so many different "bits and pieces" that made no sense even when put together. "How could you know that a legend you read someplace was a truth? I've read quite a few legends and I wouldn't have a clue."

Eli stretched and rested his head on his hands. "There's so much more to it, my friend. So much depends on what you feel in your heart."

"Then it's the same as all religions; it boils down to faith."

"Not exactly. Faith is believing in something even if you can't see it. The Maskiyl I've seen, and I know they exist."

"And this girl that's traveling with the other two? She's a part of the Maskiyl?"

Eli nodded. "As much as you are a part of the Great Work. Someone is hunting them down, trying to rid the world of their very existence."

"Why?"

"They resent us."

THE DARK canopy opened up, and for the first time in what must have been hours, they saw light. Before them lay a daunting task, however—a bog, full of weeds, steam rising from the waters. They had traveled for miles, and now it looked like the only way out was by the most difficult of paths.

They sat at the edge of the bog, resting. The sky above

them undulated red and orange then back to the gray they had known for so long. Even though he couldn't see them, Casey knew the mountains were much closer. He felt the pull even stronger than before. What Eli feared—more a result of his experience with it—Casey anticipated and looked forward to. If he was to find answers and solve these little problems, he knew it had to be in either the mountains or on the streets of Sha'ar.

There was no going back.

"We're going to go across *that*?" Casey stared in disbelief at their luck. So many obstacles already crossed, and now they were faced with walking through something that was foreign, watery and no doubt cold.

Eli sighed. "If you're looking at a bog, this is the only way. I walked for a day in either direction trying to find another route. This is it."

A deep growl emanated from the bog, the vibrations shattering Casey's nerves. He stood at the edge of the water and swallowed. He could easily turn around and go back, but to do so would mean failure. That failure was something he was all too familiar with, and for once in his life, he knew he couldn't go down that path.

"Well," Casey said as he stepped into the water, "it looks like we have no choice."

Without warning, a hand reached up and grabbed Casey's knee. He screamed as his body was pulled into the water. Eli fell forward with him.

Casey emerged and took a deep breath. He stood and then reached in and pulled Eli up as well. The two of them stood together and looked around. The water was only knee deep, but their worst fear was now realized: something lived in it.

"If we're going to cross, we have to do it now and do it fast." Casey turned and looked toward the other side. "Come on. There isn't any time to lose."

Fear swelled inside of Casey, pushing him a step back. He didn't see what pulled him in, but he had been listening to the growl for a while. Each time it filled his mind with more dread. What were these creatures, and what did they want?

Then again, he hadn't walked through Hell to be eaten by zombies.

Casey held his breath and took another step. It was cold, and the chill crept through his skin and enveloped his body. There was something in the water, and he knew—without any doubt—they had to get across as fast as possible.

Casey and Eli trudged farther ahead, each step they took both purposeful and cautious.

CHAPTER TWENTY-NINE

She didn't like this place. There was nothing in Jennifer's experience to prepare her for what lay ahead. This was something she knew, and that knowledge fed her fear that much more. The lake bed was hours behind her, and the screaming wind — if it could even be called a wind — was now a distant memory, but still a solid building block of frustration. Someone wanted her dead, and it wasn't shy about telling her.

Jennifer slid down the side of a large tree and cried. The environment around her had changed from a dusty lake bed to a grassy field to a mossy swamp that engulfed what dim light existed in the first place. She had traveled for hours and hoped against hope she might meet up with someone who could guide her, lead her in the direction she needed to go. Since leaving the adobe shelter so long ago, there hadn't even been the hint of life outside of that which wanted her dead.

It wasn't a good day.

Despite the words of the stranger, Jennifer couldn't understand anything that happened to her or threatened to happen to her. A few days ago, she argued with her father about camping. She knew her lies were probably transparent, but it really didn't matter what her parents thought. She was going, and the times she planned to spend with Jonathan were memories she wanted to take with her for the rest of her life. It was too perfect — a weekend living in the ruins of nature and satisfying each other's desire to grow up, lust and learn what it meant to love unconditionally. If she had really thought about it though, the sexual innuendos and talk of marriage were something she wasn't ready for.

Jennifer let a chuckle escape her trembling lips. Tears had fallen from her eyes, down her cheeks and lightly touched her lips. She licked them off. "Why didn't I listen to you, Dad?"

Despite the relentlessness of the voices in the air around her, her father couldn't answer back. Perhaps he wouldn't have even cared if she begged for forgiveness. But what was there to forgive—the notion that she was a teenager and wanted to explore her body, her life, her sexuality? Her father wasn't exactly the most moral person in the world. He had cheated on her mother and, in essence, cheated on the whole family. What he did—and everyone knew—was as morally irresponsible as you could get.

Or was it? Jennifer always knew her father was deeper than he let most people believe. There was more to a man than just what people saw on the surface. Was this Marie—a student of his, no less—someone that meant more to him than just a romp in the woods? Then again, did Jonathan really mean any more than a romp in the woods?

She shuddered at the thought of Jonathan's back exploding against the window of his car. The image of the Bacon Man's hand reaching through his flesh and holding her lover's heart was one she knew she wouldn't forget. She closed her eyes and tried to imagine him at a different time, even one that wasn't such a pleasant memory.

It didn't work. His voice had taken a backseat to other voices from Jennifer's past, and it seemed the farther she walked into the swamp, the louder the voices became. At first, there were pleasantries, followed by her parents, then her father, and finally the man who accosted her in a park, rape an obvious sparkle in his eye.

"How ya doing little girl?"

Jennifer opened her eyes and looked up. The voice—that man, each word laced with evil—was too close, too loud, too *real* to be just another memory. She looked around through the trees in front of her into the dense forest beyond. If the voices were to become something more than background static that could be regulated with little effort, then the road ahead wasn't going to be as easy as she prayed it would be. She prayed the man wasn't back to haunt her. Didn't he explode in the stream?

"What's wrong? Don't I look good to you?"

Jennifer swallowed what little saliva was in her mouth. She didn't want to breathe anymore. Slowly she stood, the tree against her back. The trees ahead couldn't be easy to navigate in this light, but she knew if she needed to run—again, like so long ago—there was no alternative.

"Got a prize for you in my pants, if you want it." The voice was louder and for a moment Jennifer thought she felt his hot breath on her neck. All of the fear she had in the park, all of the fear that she kept inside of her for months afterward, all of the fear that could possibly leak through her thin emotional barrier, now brimmed at the edge of her mind. Her heart raced. Her breath came short and uneven. Sweat replaced the tears on her cheeks.

"Think I'm not man enough for you?"

Jennifer slowly turned her head in the direction of the voice, praying what sights entered her eyes was not the evil she feared.

He stood against the next tree over, picking at his fingernails with a knife. His eyes were the same as she remembered: black, soulless and empty. And his face.... She could curse herself for remembering that face, seeing it every day as she tried to sleep, looking for it in the newspaper or in the mall or on the streets. He was so tall, lanky, each appendage so frail.

A coy smile crept across his face as he looked down at his fingers. He held his hand out and checked his nails, like a perfectionist admiring his work. The knife in his other hand—the same knife Jennifer remembered as much as she remembered his face—looked polished and caught what little light there was. He brought the knife up and tapped the tip on his chin.

Jennifer's body was frozen in place. Her mind screamed instructions at her nerves to kick her legs into motion and get out of there. But other parts of her brain, catapulted into confusion over recent experiences, told her that nothing in this world was real. The voices weren't real. The very idea that this man of Hell stood a few feet from her was a contradiction to reality. He surely would have been caught if he'd kept to the park looking for teenage girls. His voice—the very words he spoke—were dragged from her memory, not the abysmal depths of a flesh and blood rapist. She'd faced him not too long ago, and *that was just a memory.*

"Whatcha got for me, sugar?"

It's not real! Jennifer's thoughts screamed against her will to run. *It's not real!*

"Bet you're thinking this isn't real." The man pushed his back off the tree and stood straight. He held the knife out a little from his chest.

Those weren't words from her memory. Jennifer silenced the doubters of her mind and finally let all the fear she had built up inside transform into just enough energy to get her legs moving. She leapt from her spot next to the tree and ran as fast as she could into the dense woods.

"Watch your step, Jennifer!"

He knows my name? Jennifer pushed her legs faster and jumped over a fallen log. The ground came up to meet her as she tripped and fell face first into a puddle of mud. She righted herself, pushed up on her hands and knees and took off again. She'd run away once, and even if she knew then the way home, at least she could get some distance in the swamp.

Why is he here? Jennifer wondered how this place could pull memories from the depths of her mind and transform them into living, breathing monsters. At that point they became more, and that little extra was enough to create new memories, new experiences in fear and failure and all the rotten things that life throws down on the road to death. She didn't think any of this was possible a few days ago. Who would?

The next tree loomed ahead of her and she bolted around its trunk. She didn't care if it was a mile or a thousand miles to safety—she wasn't going to stop.

She stopped.

The man stood at the next tree and smiled, tapping his

knife against his chest. "Oh, come on now. You're making this harder than it has to be."

How the — ? Jennifer looked to her right then ran in the direction of the next tree. Her arm brushed against the bark, the rough wood shredding part of her flesh. She winced at the pain but kept running. She considered her next move and wondered if going back would be a better idea. At least on the lake bed—even on the hill where she'd entered this world— there was more room to move, more light to see, more of at least the *illusion* of safety. If she could find him again, maybe that stranger she'd met would help her out.

"You look hot." The man stood in front of her again. He slid the tip of the knife over his bare arm. A fine line of blood oozed out of the cut then over his skin. "Take your clothes off and relax."

Jennifer turned to the left and ran faster. The Bacon Man had done the same thing—make her think the path was clear then show up where she'd thought she could find a place to hide or at least rest. She shuddered as she considered the possibility that this man *was* the Bacon Man.

The trees ahead were closer together. Jennifer quickly gauged the distance between them and opted to leap through the tiny opening. Bark scraped across her open wound and she winced again. Any more of that and she'd bleed to death before her pursuer had the chance to cut her open.

The ground on the other side of the trees was little more than a deep mud puddle. Her right leg sunk to her shin and toppled her over. As she looked up, she saw in the distance a little more light than where she was now and much more than she'd seen in a while.

The man's foot came down inches in front of her face. The leather of his boot—cracked with age and spotted with mud and moss—smelled of garbage. Jennifer looked up farther, past the man's jeans, the knife in his hand, the blood on his arm and the smile on his face.

"Nice that you're finally on the ground," he said. "Mind if I take off my pants now?"

Jennifer screamed and pushed herself out of the mud

puddle, letting the motion of her body and all the weight she had slam into the legs of the man. He tumbled backward, dropping the knife.

She pushed back again and stood. To her right, a large branch leaned against one of the trees. Without considering reason or safety, she picked up the branch and let the knotted end of it crash down on the man's head. He screamed as she pulled the branch back and hit him again.

"*Leave me alone!*" she cried. The branch swung down again. All the fear Jennifer had brewed morphed into adrenaline and hatred.

"*I hated you then –* " The branch fell again against the man's face. "*And I hate you now!*" One more time, Jennifer pulled back and swung, every ounce of energy she had left transferred into the wood.

Splinters merged with blood and flesh as the man's body exploded. Screams the like Jennifer had never heard before erupted into the air around her while the force of the fleshy blast pushed her back against the tree. The wind picked up and swirled around the spot where her attacker had just been. It picked up pieces of flesh and bone, trapping them in a violent whirlwind that churned around Jennifer, pushing her hair up and around, pushing her own flesh back and forth. The screams escalated in the wind until they were so loud it felt more like they were ripping her from the inside. Her body convulsed against the side of the tree as she tried to hide her face from the hellish scene around her.

The wind stopped. Larger pieces of flesh dropped to the ground with a splat while smaller pieces rained down. She leaned against the tree, breathing fast. Her body was covered in blood, dirt and moss, and tears streamed down her face. In the spot where she'd beat her attacker with a branch, the knife lay motionless, its metal reflecting a bit more light than it had before.

Jennifer wiped her face and walked forward, fearful of anything else that might happen, but knowing the knife might come in handy. This world had shown her too much and tried to kill her twice. If she was ever going to find her sister and make it back home, she needed all the help she could get.

JENNIFER WAS tired. All the walking, all the running, all the exhausting effort to simply exist wore on her already frail body. Her mind, as well, was filled with so many conflicting emotions and theories and voices from her past that it seemed there wasn't the smallest portion of her that didn't want to cry or just lie down and sleep. The mysteries became more complex, the answers became harder to see, and the light at the end of the tunnel looked more and more like a faint glow in front of a brick wall.

She wiped a tear from her cheek and looked ahead of her at the light between a few trees. If she kept walking, she assumed the swamp would open up again and let her out of this stinky, watery, depressing prison she'd been in for far too long.

The memory of the man exploding in front of her stuck to her clothes and to her mind. The screaming was something else, something she'd never expected was possible, but it also reminded her too much of whatever attacked her on the lake bed. Were they the same person, if in fact, it was people after her? Was the man in the swamp the physical manifestation of the wind that wanted her dead? Was this the same person from the stream?

"Daddy, where are you?" Jennifer whispered to the nothing around her. It wasn't exactly the same nothing she had jumped into through a closet in a cabin, but it was still nothing. Nothing made sense, and because her environment was as illogical as everything else she'd experienced, she was in the middle of it all.

"Your daddy's not here, but you can call me that if you want."

Jennifer caught a scream in her throat and turned around. The man who was supposed to be in bits and pieces on the floor of the swamp stood a few feet from her against another tree. He was bathed in shadows, his face completely hidden by hanging moss. She must have walked right past him without seeing his grisly shape.

She ran again, suddenly realizing that no matter what she did, there was no way to escape. This place wanted her dead, and it was going to use all her worst memories to make her death that much more painful.

The swamp suddenly opened in front of her, revealing a little more light from the sky above and a bog in front of her. She heard the footsteps of the man behind her, his boots beating the damp ground with a sickening slurp. She looked to the left and right and realized the only way out was through the water in front of her. It reeked. The stench penetrated through all of the other smells and pierced her nostrils like tiny needles.

"Looks like you're trapped." He was too close to run in another direction.

Jennifer looked across the bog, past the two or three cypress trees that stuck up from the water. The bank seemed miles away, but if she swam fast enough, she just might get there in time.

"Daddy's got something for you."

Jennifer looked at the knife in her hand and let the smallest notion of stabbing the guy intrigue her weary mind. But if he had survived being beaten by a branch and exploding into a million pieces, what was a knife going to do?

A low growl rumbled through the swamp. Vibrations settled on Jennifer's body. She shook.

"Oh, that's too bad. There's something out there and it probably won't let you across. I guess that leaves you no choice now, does it?" Jennifer smelled the breath of the man even through the horrific stench of the bog. "Might as well go down having fun."

Jennifer screamed in frustration and anger and fear all at once. She spun around and pushed the blade of the knife as far as she could into the ragged, misshapen body of her father.

She stepped back, her mouth wide open. The handle of the knife stuck out of his chest, covered with blood. The figure of her father looked down and laughed. "Sucks not knowing who's out to get you, doesn't it?"

Jennifer's body shook wildly, her sense of failure wanting so much to surface and push her to the ground, crying and alone. She fought back that sense and stepped into the bog.

"I'm telling you, girl," the man said as he pulled at the knife handle, "there's something out there and it might be worse than me."

"*Go to Hell!*" Jennifer turned and dove into the water. The stagnant bog accepted her fully and pulled her under. She opened her eyes quickly to gauge her direction, then pushed with her arms and legs as hard as she could to get across. The longer she held her breath and stayed under the water, the farther she should get.

A face appeared in the water in front of her, the silt she stirred up drifting around its features. She pushed back. She needed to scream but feared letting out the air and having to resurface.

The face stared back, its eyes sunken deep in its face. The skin was pale and tightly pulled back around its bones. It wrinkled its misshapen nose and reached out a hand, one finger pointing at Jennifer. She felt a rush of sensation that emanated from her innermost being. At first, impulses fired from her midsection, sending tingles down her arms and legs as if she were a conduit for some magical electrical storm. Her eyes narrowed as she stared back at the face. To Jennifer, its features faded in and out, but always present and as bright as the noon sun. A light was dimly visible in its eyes.

Jennifer watched the light grow brighter until a tendril of energy shot forth from the center. From Jennifer, an equally matched tendril erupted from her fingers.

The two touched, mind to mind, emotion to emotion.

Jennifer's eyes closed. The light she saw in the face under the water expanded in her mind's eye, pulling her closer until she was engulfed in its glow. Within seconds, she was flying over the swamp, across the lake bed she'd just crossed, and then over a limitless expanse of sand dunes. Her body slowed and she set down on the highest of dunes.

The water was gone, the bog a distant memory. She opened her mouth and took a deep breath.

The face belonged to an older woman, the years unkind to her features. She smiled at Jennifer and pointed toward a sand dune in the distance.

Across the sand, Jennifer saw her sister, Justine. She stood alone—pink nightgown tattered—and clutched a ragged bear in her arms. A woman approached, her face hidden by distance. The woman called out "Justine!" and spun around in circles, lost like the child she sought.

"Mom?" Jennifer's lips barely parted, and had anyone else been nearby, the word would have been difficult to hear. To the old woman and Jennifer, however, they were as loud as ever and reverberated through their bodies as if they stood next to the bells of Notre Dame.

Justine held her bear closer to her, calling out to her mother, calling out for someone to hear anything at all. Jennifer sensed fear, longing, hopelessness that shouldn't exist in the emotions of a child. All of that fear and longing and hopelessness merged with her own emotions, creating a powerful single desire to reach out and offer all the comfort she could.

"Where am I?" Jennifer turned to the old woman next to her.

"A place of waiting."

The sand dunes disappeared and Jennifer found herself in the same nothing she originally entered. The voices were gone, however, and the sudden silence weighed heavy on her. The old woman smiled.

"What are you waiting for?" Jennifer asked, her question echoing through the emptiness.

"For you."

Trees and rocks and hills and clouds and life exploded around the two. Jennifer looked on with wonder as all around them more and more appeared. It wasn't just a single place—it was as if they sat in a moving theatre and screens larger than life showed a million film clips of a million things all at once. She couldn't keep track of any one particular scene; a mountain shot forth out of the sea, a tree in a forest fell, caribou stampeded across a wilderness. The sun rose and set and followed the moon around in a circle. The night came then disappeared. Constellations she thought she recognized transformed themselves into ones that she didn't know. Birds flew overhead while fish swam in oceans and rivers and lakes on the edges of valleys and deserts and swamps.

"Who am I?" Jennifer asked but her lips never moved. She spoke with her heart and felt the very essence of Creation brewing within her. "Am I dead?"

"No. You cannot die here." The woman touched Jennifer's hand. "But you can die at home."

"Why are people trying to kill me?"

"They resent you, hate you for what your part is in the Great Work you see before you."

The scenes on the screens around them changed again, from nature to man-made objects, buildings made of stone and adobe huts with grass roofs. Warriors swarmed through the cities and villages, pulling the hearts out of frightened people. Great cities fell, their buildings burned to the ground; bodies littered the streets. The screams were magnified by the grandeur of the screens in front of Jennifer, and combined, she felt they were the same screams she'd heard on the lake bed and in the swamp by the same being that hunted her down.

Jennifer watched as the scene changed again, from the death of millions to a much larger picture of a woman in a desert. A man stood next to her. He was naked save for a small ring on his right hand. His eyes, black and hollow, showed Jennifer an anger and resentment she'd never thought could come from any person.

"*Naphalyn*. The fallen ones." The old woman's voice floated through Jennifer's body, words transforming themselves into meaning and meaning into emotion.

The naphalyn punched through the chest of the woman. Jennifer jumped back then felt a screaming pain in her chest like the scene played something from her life. It was the same thing that happened to Jonathan, the same punch, the same explosive spray of flesh and blood through the back. The naphalyn pulled his hand out of the woman's chest, her heart clenched in his fist. The woman's body fell forward.

Jennifer put her hand over her heart and felt the beating she prayed she'd never lose to a creature with such strength. The scene in front of her changed again. A suburban street, much like her own, was bathed in the fading light of day. Through a window, she saw a little girl, her mother tucking her in for the night. The mother bent over the bedside and kissed the girl on the forehead then walked over to the window to close it. Jennifer watched with amazement at the sight of *her* mother—not much older than she was at the time.

"My sister," Jennifer whispered. "What does she have to do with all of this?"

"Gifts, and you're experiencing yours for the first time."

Jennifer looked over at the woman. "Who are you, then?"

"We are naphalyn, but we realized the error of our ways. Hell will not have us, and Heaven cannot take us back."

Jennifer furled her eyebrows and looked back at the scene in front of her. "So you're angels."

"We are children of God, as much as you are children."

The scene played itself out as Jennifer wondered about everything that she'd been shown and told. On the screen, the window shook. Jennifer's mother looked outside as the color of the sky changed and a dust storm began to pelt the side of the house with thousands of particles of dust and sand. The palm trees on the corner of the street bent in homage to the strength of the wind. Trash that had been lying in gutters and other people's yards floated about in swirls, danced on the wind and waltzed across the street. Celine closed the blinds and turned to her daughter. Justine's eyelids had lost the battle against sleep and shut the world out.

Jennifer watched as Celine touched her daughter's soft cheek, kissed her good night then tucked her stuffed bear under the blanket as well. As her mother closed the door, Jennifer saw something on the side of the house, forming out of the dust. Its body shifted back and forth in the wind, but she could sense that evil was present in its form. It might be, itself, evil incarnate. She'd seen that twice now.

The figure slowly crawled up the side of the house and looked in through the window. Justine turned over in her bed. Jennifer wanted to scream out, to warn her sister somehow, but she also knew this was nothing more than the world's memory of what had happened, of how her sister came to be on a sand dune, lost forever.

The window shattered and Justine screamed.

The giant screens flickered once then turned black. Jennifer and the old woman were thrust back into the nothingness.

"Why didn't they kill her?" Jennifer tried to piece things together as much as she could. It was obvious that she shared this gift with Justine, but while she was hunted down in a forest north of Phoenix, Justine was taken from the world and dropped here, the place of waiting.

"A child's heart is clear. It cannot die in the way that yours or that of Jonathan can die. She was kidnapped, and in the end, left here to wait."

"And they can't kill her here. You said that you couldn't die in this world."

Jennifer blinked and found herself once again on the sand dune overlooking the scene of Justine and her mother. Celine held Justine in her arms then disappeared.

Justine was alone once again.

"No, not here. But take her back, and she will grow. Surely as she grows, she can be killed." The old woman turned to Jennifer. "We wish we could help, but we are damned in this place to wait."

Jennifer looked deep into the woman's eyes. A sense of sorrow — one so powerful she'd never felt before — overwhelmed her body. There was anger and resentment in the man in the desert. There was evil in the creature that took Justine. There was loneliness in Justine. And in the woman — in the naphalyn that recanted — there was sorrow and remorse. Deep behind that, however, in the depths of the emotional battleground that all children of God share as one, there was hope.

CHAPTER THIRTY

Harlan slowly opened his eyes and squinted. The clouds above him swirled in patterns he'd never seen before, reds and yellows and oranges cast up from the ground mixed with the gray blanket he'd come to know and despise. If only he could see the sun one more time.

He lifted his head off the ground and looked around. Marie was asleep next to him, her arms and legs curled around Justine. The two had come to bond so well — Justine more likely than not holding high expectations of the mother-figure Marie was, and Marie drawn to a child much like her own who had been taken from her too early.

Harlan reached down and winced as he untied his shirt from around his leg. The wound was deep and still bleeding. The pain had escalated during his sleep and now his thigh throbbed in response to his curiosity. Whatever had cut into him — and he held on to the notion that it was a *whatever* — had put yet one more obstacle in his way between where he was and where he wanted to go.

He tied the shirt back and looked past the trees deep into the swamp they'd just left. At least they had conquered that much, despite the warning the old woman had given them. He didn't doubt for a second that Eli had disappeared inside, nor did he doubt that many others had succumbed to the evil that lived in the bog.

What of the other side? Had anyone made it this far and traveled to Sha'ar to find their way home? The woman had known about the city, but she never explained how she knew or who had told her about it. Was it an oral legend passed down to give hope to an otherwise hopeless situation, or was there some credence to the notion of a gateway home? If it was an oral legend, who passed it down?

"*You weren't there for me, Harlan.*"

He turned and watched Marie sleep. Her voice was right: he wasn't there for her. Even though he didn't know anything about her pregnancy, he should have pursued the reasons she disappeared in the first place. It pained him—more than he was willing to admit—to know she suffered so much without him by her side. Maybe he couldn't have made things better. Maybe he couldn't have dried the tears. Maybe he couldn't reverse time and set them on a path of love when he had the chance. At least he could have tried.

Marie stirred and opened her eyes. She turned to Harlan and smiled then sat straight up. "What was that?"

Harlan hadn't heard anything save the voices from his past. His heartbeat quickened as he stood, fearing he'd overlooked something in the trees while looking for answers in his mind.

"I didn't hear anything." He looked up and down the line of trees and tried to filter out his memories.

In the distance, between the voice of Celine and Marie, he heard someone talking. He listened to the words, trying to match the voice with someone from his past. One of them sounded familiar, but the other was unknown—at least unknown on the surface. The way his mind played tricks on him in this world, it might very well be just another memory.

Marie pulled Justine tighter to her body. The tiny figure stirred and rolled over, burying her head in Marie's stomach.

"Did you hear *that*?" Marie whispered.

Harlan nodded and furled his eyebrows. "It sounds like someone I know." Harlan searched through his mind trying to put the first voice with a face.

"Someone we know together? Because if this is just another memory, then it's the first time we're both hearing the same thing, and I really don't want to meet all those people who attacked you."

Branches moved in the darkness of the swamp, and Steven Casey stepped out into the clearing. He stopped and looked up. An older man stumbled behind Casey and fell over.

A smile crept across Harlan's face. "Well, I'll be."

Casey reached down to help the older man up. "And I thought what happened back *there* was weird."

The old man stood and put his hand on Casey's shoulder. "What's wrong? Are we out of the stupid swamp yet?"

"I think so."

Marie looked at Harlan, both concern and relief painted across her face. "You know these two?"

"One of them, anyway." Harlan limped forward, suddenly aware of just how intense the pain in his leg really was. "Marie, this is Stephen Casey. He's the detective who's actually responsible for where I am."

Marie smiled and gave a curt wave. "Hi."

Justine opened her eyes and wrapped her arms around Marie.

MARIE STARED at Eli. The idea that she sat near the leader of a cult that had graced the front page of newspapers was something she still couldn't get over. It may have been years ago, but what happened to the Circle of Light—to the men, women and children who had followed Eli Jonas to the end—still remained in the back of people's minds as a reminder of how fragile life is at any moment. These weren't hippies or people who had disavowed the modern things of life. They weren't a group of radicals who were easily swept away by the words of a madman. Sure, they were the destitute and the lonely, the lost and the baggage of society, but they shared their vision with businessmen, housewives, normal citizens of their community who had simply found a message that spoke to them with words of comfort and hope.

They were the same words she'd heard from Jacob during long conversations over coffee, the same words she'd felt in her heart during moments where she dived into her soul and searched for answers. If she'd listened to those words, she might have ended up here like Eli with a better understanding of her role in the *ma abad rab*.

Marie looked at Justine. "Is this girl a part of the Great Work? We think she might have been kidnapped and trapped here."

Eli shifted his blank stare to the direction of Marie. "What makes you think that?"

"She keeps talking about this 'Angry Man' and, unfortunately, we've already come into contact with him once." Marie looked down at Harlan's leg. "Maybe twice."

"We all have our bit part in the *ma abad rab*."

"We've heard that before," Harlan said. "From the woman in the town."

Eli nodded. "Jessie. She was one of my people."

"I thought you didn't make it through the swamp."

"Bah!" Eli waved the comment off. "Jessie must've fed you that line of crap."

Marie looked toward the mountains. "Well, yes she did. She also told us about the city."

Eli smacked his lips and turned his face down. "Don't think you'll make it."

"Why do say that?" Harlan asked.

"The voices—the memories that have been following you around—become something else on the way to Sha'ar. You've probably already seen them materialize in front of you."

"A few."

"It doesn't get any better. I tried to make the trip a long time ago, back when I could see. I didn't get very far."

"Wonderful." Casey sighed and stood.

Harlan looked out over the chasm to the mountains on the other side. "Have you seen my daughter?"

Casey shook his head. "I'm sorry, but no. Aside from Eli and Jessie, I haven't seen anyone."

Marie looked up at Harlan. His expression seemed hollow, like he'd seen the light at the end of the tunnel but realized it was nothing more than a dying match. She had considered the pain Justine's mother must have gone through—to never find that closure to tragedy—but she hadn't thought of Harlan's own pain. She inwardly cursed herself for being so blind to the pain she knew she could ease.

Harlan caught Marie's stare. She smiled weakly and put her hand on top of his much like he had done when they first played a game of chess so many years ago.

He stood and limped over to the edge. There were no clues about which way to go. The ground rose gently in both directions and the edge of the swamp followed along the whole length. "Well, I see one problem."

"What's that?" Marie asked.

"How are we going to get over there?"

Eli stood with a grunt. "Didn't I just say I tried to make the trip once already? I don't know which direction it is, but there's a bridge across this thing."

Harlan turned and looked both ways again. He sighed and pointed. "I guess we should head that way. It's fifty-fifty."

"Not the best of odds," Casey said, "but I'll take it."

THE WALK along the edge of the chasm was easier than any of them had dreamed possible. With the edge of the swamp to the left and the orange undulating glow of whatever flowed through the chasm to their right, the path seemed more like a road than anything else. In small areas, there were worn-down patches of grass as if someone had crossed this way before.

Above them, the gray overcast was darker than it had been before and looked ripe for a rainstorm. None of them had actually considered the possibility of being trapped in the open if the rain ever came, but the clouds looked heavier and in the back of their minds they wondered what might happen.

Justine walked hand-in-hand with Marie. Marie couldn't get over the simple word that Justine had spoken to her after their ordeal in the swamp. *Mommy.* She hadn't heard that word in months, and the sensation she felt was like nothing in her experience. She *was* a mother, and even though her child was gone, there was a sudden glimmer of hope that maybe, just maybe, a new life could begin.

—

HARLAN LOOKED over the edge of the chasm at regular intervals, lost in his own thoughts. The idea of never returning to his house had begun to cut away at his nerves, and he wondered if he'd ever find Jennifer. What he'd come here for, he couldn't find, but what he found was something greater than he'd ever imagined. Or was it? Was he just kidding himself, thinking Marie was the answer to all his problems, or was she just a plug for a dam that would eventually break no matter what? The latter confused him, and Harlan fought to keep that idea out of his head. He loved Marie—in that, there was no doubt. Equally, he knew she loved him, and through all of the pain they once shared and the pain they faced in their lives on their own, they were always together, even if the physical aspect was lost.

Harlan smiled. It wasn't worth thinking about right now. There were too many other issues at hand that required his attention. He didn't need to be thinking about Marie. Still, he couldn't help it.

Marie shot a quick glance coupled with a smile in his direction. The unspoken drifted through the air and both of them felt at ease.

Justine looked up. "Where are we going?"

"To find a way across that thing," Marie said, pointing to the chasm.

"What's over there? All I see is rocks."

"Actually, we're hoping to find a way home. You want that?"

"I don't care. My mommy's dead."

Marie frowned and looked down at Justine. "What makes you say that?"

"I just know."

Harlan heard the conversation and stepped up next to Justine. "Did you ever see your mommy since you've been here?"

"Once, but she went away."

"Do you know where your home is?" Marie asked.

"I know the street, but not numbers. We're not going back there, are we?"

"Someday."

"I don't want to." Justine looked down.

"Why not?"

"The Angry Man lives there too."

HARLAN STOOD at the edge of the chasm and looked across. A long bridge made of thin rope and too few boards hung from one side to the other. It swayed in a gentle breeze high above the undulating orange glow deep in the canyon.

"You have *got* to be kidding me." Harlan turned around and walked away from the edge.

"You see," Eli said holding onto Casey's sleeve. "It ain't going to be easy."

"There's no other bridge?" Marie stared out at the daunting path ahead and sighed. "I mean, a concrete enclosed walkway would be nice."

"Well," Casey said, "it looks like we have no other choice."

Harlan sat. "Sure we do. We can look up and down this place until we find another crossing."

"I don't think we're going to find one."

"We haven't even tried yet."

Justine pulled on Marie's shirt. "Are we going there?" she asked, pointing toward the other side.

"We have to, hon. You want to go home, don't you?"

"No. I like it here."

"*We* want to go home, Justine—all of us—and if this is the only way across then we have to try."

Justine walked up to the edge of the chasm and looked across the bridge. To her, the distance seemed like miles, but she knew to the rest of them it wasn't that bad. Trust was inherent, and if they said it was okay, then it must be okay. She looked back at Marie and smiled.

"Race you!" Justine was off, stepping on the first board with a crack. The bridge swayed violently to the left and she instinctively grabbed the ropes on the side.

"Justine!" Marie cried out. "*Wait!*"

Marie ran toward her and reached out for Justine as she

took another step across a gap almost as wide as she was tall.

"See?" Justine called out. "It's not that bad."

Marie took the first step and felt the bridge move under her own weight, nearly knocking Justine off balance. She was only a few feet away now, but it seemed like miles. Another step and the bridge rocked even more. Justine grabbed one side of the bridge with both hands and held on tight.

Harlan jumped up and followed the two onto the bridge. He hated heights but forced himself not to look down. To do so would jeopardize his life and the lives of both Marie and Justine.

The bridge swayed again as Marie took another step toward Justine. She quickly grabbed the girl and held on tight as Harlan came up behind her.

"Are you alright?" Harlan asked.

Justine looked over Marie's shoulder, her eyes wide with fear. She wasn't alright. Why did she do that? What was she thinking?

"Get her across," Harlan said to Marie. "This bridge isn't going to hold out much longer."

Marie nodded and took another tentative step. The next board cracked louder than any of the others and sent a chill down her spine. *Don't look down*, her mind screamed. *Whatever you do, don't look...*

Marie looked down. Through the haze of the chasm, a deep orange, lava-like substance flowed swiftly hundreds of feet below her. It rose and fell in bubbles and twisted itself around rocks that jutted up in the middle. She swayed to the left and almost let go of Justine.

"*Don't look down!*" Harlan screamed behind her. "Get your head up!"

Marie did as she was ordered. She took a deep breath and stepped again, feeling the board shift under her feet.

Behind them, Casey led Eli across the bridge slowly, careful the blind man placed his foot squarely on each board.

"You know," Eli said, stepping across another board, "I don't remember this bridge being wooden."

Harlan stopped and looked back. "What do you mean?"

"I think it was a log thrown over the chasm." Eli thought for a moment. "Yes. Now I'm sure of it. This isn't the bridge."

Harlan and Marie looked at each other then back to their destination. They were now in the middle of the bridge, with the same distance to cross either way. If they turned back now, the old man might not be able to find the other bridge, and if they continued on, no one knew where to go from there.

Casey took another step and helped Eli. "We made it this far. Let's finish it."

A cold gust of wind rushed up from the bottom of the chasm. It hit Marie with brute force, flipping her hair up and knocking her off balance. She screamed as the board she was on cracked loudly.

Harlan reached out and grabbed Marie by the arms. He pulled her back from the weakened board and the sure fall into oblivion. Justine screamed.

"*What was that?*" Marie yelled.

"*No, no, no, no, no, no!*" Justine repeated over and over. Her body shook.

"We have to get across *now*!" Eli cried. "That wind will be back."

Marie stood with Justine determined to get across the bridge. There was nothing that was going to stop her now. She had been through a desert, walked forever on a dry lake bed, and wallowed through a swamp with something that tried to kill her. She was *not* going to be bested by a gust of wind.

The wind came back. It pushed Marie from the front and forced her to hold onto the ropes as hard as she could. She winced against the onslaught on her face and grimaced in pain as the chill dug deep into her flesh. A thousand voices screamed at once, and all of them were calling Justine's name.

Marie scowled and took another step into the wind. The board cracked again and snapped in two. Her foot fell through as she screamed, her hand still holding tight to the rope.

"*Get Justine!*" she cried out.

Harlan reached out and grabbed the little girl. She clung tightly to Harlan's shoulders as he reached out to help Marie. The wind blew harder, making it nearly impossible for Harlan to reach out far enough to grab Marie's free hand. It tore into his flesh, instantly reminding him of the same wind he encountered on the lake bed. It was after her, and there was no stopping it.

Casey grabbed Justine from Harlan, freeing him to fight to get Marie onto a solid board. The wind forced his eyes closed as the little girl dug her hands into his back, crying.

"*Don't let him get me!*" she screamed out through the wind and the tears. "*I don't want to go!*"

Casey wrapped his arms around Justine and turned his head down to shield his face. Eli grabbed the rope and took another step.

The board cracked, sending Casey off balance. His foot slipped and Justine flew backwards. She hit the side of the rope and flipped over the side. Using nothing more than instinct, Eli jumped, his hand outstretched. He caught Justine's arm just before she fell into the chasm. Fighting both the wind and the wild kicking of Justine, he pulled with all of his strength.

"*You're not going to get her!*" Eli cried out. "*I won't let you!*"

Casey pulled his leg up and reached out to help Eli, grabbing Justine by the arm and pulling her over. He picked her up once again and wrapped his arms even tighter than before, closing his eyes.

The wind shifted coming from the bottom instead of the side. The thousand screaming voices became louder as the speed picked up. The bridge swayed violently, rocking everyone on it between the ropes.

Casey opened his eyes and saw Eli trying to hold onto the ropes. The wind shifted once more, pulling the old man's body over the side. He screamed, holding the rope with one hand as tight as he could. Just as Casey was about to reach out one more time, Eli's hand let go and Casey watched in horror as his body flipped over and over until it finally disappeared into the lava below.

As suddenly as the wind had come, it stopped.

Casey turned away from where his traveling companion had been pulled over and looked at Harlan and Marie. "We have to go."

—

THEY RESTED on the other side of the chasm, each one thankful for reaching their destination but feeling the weight of Eli's death. None of them could say they knew him well enough to grieve, but he was a savior to Casey and Justine both. They owed him their lives.

"Something bothers me," Harlan finally said. They sat on a boulder and looked down into the chasm. "Jessie told us that you couldn't die here."

Casey nodded. "That's what Eli said, as well."

"If that's the case, what happened to him?"

They each looked down at the undulated orange river of lava. Eli was in there, but unless he was swept against some faraway shore, he was eternally damned to burn.

Marie sighed and pulled Justine close to her. "So that's what he gets for finishing his part? Pain?"

Silence descended on the travelers as they each answered her question quietly. Maybe — just maybe — Eli's part wasn't finished.

CHAPTER THIRTY-ONE

Marie reached the summit of the hill ahead of Casey and Harlan, so focused she was on getting Justine home. This land was inhospitable, unforgiving, and pissed her off by the minute. As she reached the crest, she saw a valley stretched out in front of her for miles with nothing but rocks in the way. The sky was a dark gray, almost black as if the sun were finally setting on this world and the night was about to come.

She tucked a wind-blown strand of hair behind her ear. They had reached a milestone, if not the final destination, and she finally felt at ease about the rest of the journey. Whatever Eli had seen while walking through the mountains, it wasn't bothering them. As she thought of the poor blind man pulled from the bridge, she realized she hadn't heard any voices at all since they crossed over to this side. They had become so much a part of the environment at one point, Marie pushed them to the background, like static on a poorly tuned television during an interesting show — it was annoying, but easy to ignore.

Justine yawned. Marie guessed this journey was nothing more than treacherous for her and climbing over rocks, though exciting at first, took its toll. "Are we there yet?"

Marie smiled. How often had she heard that before? "Not yet. We'll just wait here for Harlan and Casey."

"Do you like Harlan?" Justine looked up with a keen interest.

"Um, yes. Why do you ask?"

"No reason. I just saw you two kissing." Justine giggled at the word.

Marie smiled again.

"YOU SHOULDN'T have left me," Christine whispered. She stood in front of Casey, her blue eyes focused on his. Casey smelled the sweetness of her breath and wondered how a memory could be this clear.

"I didn't want to." From the moment he left her that night so long ago, he always wished he'd said something different, something that would remedy the small break in their love. Life would have been different.

Maybe.

Christine echoed his thoughts. "Life would have been different, Casey. Do you know what you did to me?"

"I let you go."

"You killed me."

"You didn't want me."

"I didn't know what I wanted. I don't even know why I wasted my time with Michael."

Casey took a step away from Christine. The memory had turned real, not only in the form of flesh and blood but it lived in the present. It was almost like the last time he saw her on the snowfield. He hadn't expected any of this and now wanted to get away.

"Where are you going?" Christine asked, a hurt look wiping across her face. "Do you want to leave me again?"

No, Casey thought. *I want to hold you in my arms forever.* "You don't exist."

"I don't? Look at me, Stephen. Is your life too difficult a mirror to hold up?"

"Why are you here?"

"You brought me."

The words sank heavy onto the heart of Casey. Did he bring her here? Was this the final confrontation with his past all men were bound to face? What if she was real, maybe even passed on from Earth to this world and her place in the Great Work was to finally meet up with him?

"I brought your memory with me, not you."

Christine stepped closer to Casey and took his hand in hers. Casey's heart beat faster as he touched the skin of a woman he failed to keep, a woman who created the man that he was, and a woman who knew more about him than anyone ever could.

"Come with me," she whispered, laying her head on his chest. "We can make it work all over again."

Casey felt himself well up with tears. He wanted to cry, to scream out and let his true feelings show. He wanted to release himself from the prison of failure he had put himself in for years and finally change the tired, lonely man he had become. Casey sighed and put his hand on Christine's head, looking out at the journey he had just undertaken. He had come so far to finally be able to fill his void.

"Where are we going?" Casey asked, as Christine turned to walk across the mountainside. "I should at least tell the others where I'm headed."

"No," Christine said. "There's no time for that. You let them worry about themselves, and you and I will worry about the here and now."

Casey caught a quick smile and returned one of his own. He had never felt so free before, so complete and alive. Christine was back in his life, and now his failures of the past could finally be reversed.

Still, Casey thought, *something doesn't feel right.*

CELINE CRIED.

"What do you want me to say?" Harlan was exhausted, more with the conversation than the journey.

"Tell me something. Tell me you love me still and you're going to come back. Tell me you're not going to run off with that whore."

"She's not a whore."

Celine coughed out a cruel laugh through her tears. "What is she then? Your true love?"

Harlan frowned and wished nothing more than to run away and hide. "She is," he sighed.

Celine turned from him, like she was unable to face his words. Harlan suddenly wanted to take them back. *Maybe Celine is right*, he thought. *Maybe this is just a matter of lust.*

"Then that's it." Celine took a deep breath to wash away her tears. "Go ahead, leave us. Forget about Jennifer. Forget about Tommy. You've already forgotten about me."

Harlan sighed. He had looked at his family as something he needed to keep Celine around for, but she wasn't going to live like that. Although he knew he would be a part of their life no matter what, the realization of losing contact with Jennifer and Tommy sank deep. It was something he didn't want, and that made him more afraid.

"I'm sorry," he said, more out of habit than out of honesty. "I didn't mean to hurt you."

"I won't forgive you this time, Harlan. It's obvious we're not meant for each other."

"No we're not."

"You lied to me. You told me you wouldn't see her again."

"Why should you care?" he asked. "You left me."

"No, Harlan. I stayed with you to the end. Do you know how many conversations I overheard between you and that whore? Do you know how many e-mails I read? Do you know what it's like to be married to a man who left the house years ago?"

Celine took a step forward and came within a few feet of Harlan. "Don't you think you've hurt me enough?"

"You're not real."

"You've forgotten your lesson, haven't you? You think that since you overcame your brush with failure, you passed through that swamp and you crossed over to this side, that you're more powerful for it."

Harlan swallowed. No, he wasn't any more powerful than before. This world had shown him nothing but pain, both emotionally and physically. How much more did he have to take?

"Why are you here? To find your daughter or get back together with your girlfriend?"

"You know why I'm here."

Celine smiled and took another step toward him. "So go find her. Bring her back to me." She wiped a tear from her cheek, and for a moment stood silent, as if deciding for herself what it was she really wanted.

"Come with me. I want to show you something."

MARIE SAT on a rock at the crest of the hill and waited for Harlan and Casey to catch up. She was surprised it took them so long. Worry crept up on her, and she wondered if they came across something that made them turn around.

"Where are they?" Justine asked. Marie had noticed the strong little girl had grown more and more restless. At times, she kicked her feet out into the air and occasionally stood to spin around in circles.

"I want to go."

"I don't know where they are." Marie sighed. "But I wish they'd get here."

"Maybe we should go get them. Boys are so slow sometimes."

Marie frowned and looked down the hill. "Maybe you're right."

Marie and Justine walked more than a few steps down the mountainside and suddenly wished they had stayed put. They had to walk back *up* the mountain soon enough.

Marie scanned the distance, looking for any sign of Harlan or Casey. Surely they couldn't be that far behind.

"There they are!" Justine pointed to Marie's right.

She watched as Harlan walked over a few boulders off in the distance. She was about to call out his name when she noticed something hover in the air next to him. She squinted, trying to get a better look, but they were too far away.

Marie hopped down a few more boulders, keeping Harlan in her view. She motioned for Justine to stay. Something didn't feel right, although she couldn't figure out what it was.

She climbed down and crouched behind another boulder. Harlan was talking, but she couldn't hear the words. Apparently, whatever it was, it was directed at the thing hovering next to him. She looked longer, trying to make out details.

She slowly walked closer and hid behind yet another boulder. The thing hovering next to Harlan came more into focus. She wasn't sure, however, but she thought she saw two scaly legs that bent backwards.

This wasn't looking good.

Another boulder closer and Marie was able to see plainly that Harlan was next to and chatting with a hideous creature. It snarled and laughed, reached out with long claws and pointed to this or that. With the other hand, it clutched that of Harlan.

Marie's heart pounded faster. Harlan was in trouble, but why was he so nonchalant about the matter? What is it that he's talking to? She remembered what Eli had said — memories *become* something. Was this the evil that made him turn around? Whatever it was, Harlan needed to get out of there.

"Harlan!" Marie called out. She stood and waved her arms in the air. "Over here!"

The thing next to Harlan turned and looked at Marie. She was spotted. It let go of Harlan's hand and leaped into the air, knocking Harlan onto the ground.

"Get out of there!" Marie yelled out once again. Harlan turned and ran up the side of the mountain.

The thing leaped again, clearing a few large boulders. A high-pitched scream erupted from its lungs as it came closer and closer. Marie, with eyes wide open, scrambled up the side of the mountain toward Justine.

"Harlan!"

Harlan quickly turned from his path and ran to help Marie.

"I'm coming!"

The wind picked up with ferocity, shrieking around Justine. Her hair flew wildly and she screamed. Marie quickened her pace, pushed herself over another boulder and grabbed the girl. A thousand voices screamed Justine's name, growing louder and louder.

Harlan hopped over one boulder and then another. He needed to reach the two of them before that thing that was once Celine got there first.

The thing screamed again, and thrust itself forward with lightning quick speed using its contorted legs and shape to its advantage. Marie looked over her shoulder, just in time to see the thing bound forward one last time, its arms outstretched and teeth bared.

"*No!*" The words escaped Marie's throat as she ducked her head and tried to cover Justine as much as she could.

The thing screamed again then exploded, raining flesh and bone all over the rocks around Marie. Marie waited for the last of the flesh to fall with a wet smack on the rocks before looking up into the wind once again. Casey, covered with blood and bits of flesh, stood holding a large rock.

Harlan leapt the last of the boulders and fell next to Marie just as the wind died down. For a moment, the only sound was the frantic breathing of Marie and the muffled cry of Justine.

"*What was that?*" Marie looked at Casey.

"Don't ask me," he said dropping the rock. "It was *his* memory."

Harlan looked at Marie. "My ex-wife. I think."

"I NEVER saw anything." Marie leaned against a boulder cradling Justine in her arms. They had quickly climbed to the top of the mountain and stopped to rest, feeling no safer than before. At least they felt comforted by the presence of each other.

"I wonder if all of the voices weren't real," Harlan said, musing at the possibility that both the thing that acted like Celine and the voices were actually an attempt to beat them all down. If it was an outside attempt, it made sense few people ever survived the journey to Sha'ar. Living with your memories is one thing; facing them is something entirely different.

"There's an idea—voices to drive us insane. I wondered the same thing when Christine asked to show me something."

"How did you figure it out?"

"I didn't. I think in my state of euphoria, she—it—decided that was a perfect time to attack me. I had to struggle, but when I picked up a rock and hit it over the head, the body exploded just the same."

Harlan frowned, embarrassed.

"Don't take it so hard," Marie said. "This place is a little more than we're meant to handle."

Harlan still didn't feel comfortable. "So what's after us, then?"

"Hell. Something we're not aware of. I don't know." Marie sighed and ran her fingers through Justine's hair. "Whatever it is, it's not us it wants."

Justine looked up at Marie and wiped a tear from her face. "Why won't the Angry Man leave me alone?"

"We won't let him get you." Harlan tried to force a smile he knew was sincere, but probably not comforting.

Silence echoed Harlan's promise as the wind shifted slightly, gently blowing cold air around them. A drop of rain hit Harlan's arm.

"Time to go," he said, looking up at the sky. "I was wondering when it would ever rain."

IT DIDN'T take long for them to figure out which way they were headed. A few hundred feet from the top of the mountain, down on the other side, the view in front of them changed. No longer was there a barren trek of nothing but rocks and more rocks to climb over, but a path had been dug. Boulders had been pushed aside and in a few places they could easily see footprints in the loose soil. Someone had been through here before.

The rain continued to fall, but gently enough they were hard pressed to notice it at all. They were tired, frustrated, and at the same time, looking forward to finally reaching Sha'ar and the gateway home. Harlan's thoughts bounced back and forth between the near death he had experienced and what life was going to be like once they reached their destination. Marie was a part of him, more so now than ever before. It was obvious to him they shared a love nothing could stop, and no matter what Celine wanted to say about it, he knew life was much shorter now than it had been. Why then should he waste it unhappy and continually empty?

Marie kept her eyes down on the path in front of her. She had been through so much in her life—from a chance encounter with the man who would steal her heart to the death of her family. Through it all, Harlan was there. He was a part of her, and she was coming to realize the only void they both felt was left by each other. In a world apart from that which was known, they were destined to fill it for each other.

But what about Justine? Marie thought. She had no family, no one to turn to, no one to raise her up, no one to call her own. She knew her mother was dead, but nothing of her father. She knew where she lived, but not where it was, and throughout the long trek since leaving the desert, Marie had come to think Justine had been trapped in this world for a very long time. Was there anything to return to?

Marie looked over at Justine. She held tightly to her teddy bear and watched every move Marie made. *There's something she can take back with her*, Marie thought. *I hope that's not all she has left.*

"Look!" Casey called out. Harlan, Marie and Justine stopped. They had been so lost in their own thoughts that none of them noticed the path bend to their left. They looked out over the valley in front of them and stood in awe.

A few buildings jutted up out of the barren landscape. It wasn't a massive city with spires stabbing defiant fists heavenward, but it was civilization and it welcomed the four of them home.

CHAPTER THIRTY-TWO

There were buildings made of brick, some of stone, some of grass and a few made from the ruins of others that had fallen. They stood on either side of the street, crushing the narrow path down to less than ten feet. There didn't seem to be any rhyme or reason to their placement—there were grass huts next to two-story brick dwellings with curtains in what looked like windows. A few papers floated across the street, dancing on a quiet wind. At least the buildings were evidence of life, but from what the four travelers observed, that's all the life there was. From the threshold of the city to the farthest their eyes could see, Sha'ar—if that's what this place really was—seemed more like a ghost town than a mystical gateway home.

Harlan took a few cautious steps ahead of the rest, scanning each building, hoping to find someone to help them. Between two mud houses, a tall brick building—maybe three or four stories high—stood like a sentinel, almost awkward in its place. Harlan slowly walked over to the door and knocked.

"Hello?" he called out to whatever lay behind the door. "Hello? Can someone help us?"

Across the street, an old woman poked her head out of a window and regarded the four strangers with interest. As quietly as she appeared, she slipped back into the darkness inside. Casey noticed the woman and walked over to the door.

"Hello? Ma'am?" He stood at the door patiently waiting for a response. Was this town full of life that simply didn't want to be seen, or was their presence frightening in some way? The journey here had been wrought with events that were undoubtedly confusing and odd, and it was highly likely that whatever they were to experience here on their way to finding home was going to be equally confusing.

"Hello?" Casey said again, knocking harder on the door. "We need help. Is anyone there?"

"I don't think this place is very visitor friendly," Marie said.

Casey stepped away from the door and walked farther down the street.

"So what exactly are we looking for?" Harlan suddenly realized that, although they were directed to this city, they had no idea what they were looking for or where it might be. Now it appeared there wouldn't be anyone to help them find it, either.

"Are we there yet?" Justine's voice weighed heavily on the three adults.

"Not yet, honey." Marie wished for once that she could give Justine a good piece of news. So far, this journey was filled with nothing but confusion and loss. At least the mind of a four-year-old wasn't apt to jump to conclusions like that of a woman in her late twenties.

Marie stopped and looked around for a moment. "I would think that if this gateway is so important then it would have street signs pointing to it. Or maybe a big monolithic-looking thing like that one." She pointed over Casey's head into the distance. The street ran on for about a mile or two until finally coming to what looked like a fork in the road. Off to the right of the fork, a tall building rose above the others, blending in with the haze around it.

Harlan sighed. "That seems too easy."

THE DOOR was open, more a sign of desertion than one of welcoming. Casey pushed it a little wider and stepped inside cautiously to look around. The room he entered was empty. Light filtered in from a hole or window twenty or thirty feet above. He stepped a little farther into the room, looking for maybe another door, a table, a book or even a piece of paper.

Nothing.

"Well, this doesn't look too promising," he said, motioning the others to come inside. "You travel through three or four different temperate zones, battle an evil you don't understand but knows who you are, enter a town that holds all this promise, only to find a room with nothing in it. Just our luck, I suppose."

"Was this the only entrance?" Marie stepped back outside, glancing around for another way in. It could have been more a dupe that anything else, a method of fooling would-be thieves into thinking the place was empty. Of course, why would there be thieves around here? What would they have to steal?

"Nothing," she said, coming back into the building. "This is the only thing I can see, and from the looks of it, this is the whole building."

Harlan put his hands up on the wall. "Do you think there might be some secret entrance in this place? A stone that moves or a hidden doorway that just looks like a wall?" He moved to the left, pushing on the stone wall in random places.

"This isn't *Scooby Doo*, Harlan." Marie sighed. "I don't think we're going to find anything else here. Maybe this isn't the place."

Casey stood in the middle of the room and looked up. The ceiling seemed cracked, bent in by an invisible weight above it. Each of the walls rose without feature, gray and gloomy. There was nothing hidden in the room, no matter where they looked. Casey mumbled something to himself, sighed and headed for the door. If there was a gateway home, this room wasn't it.

"Can I help you?" An old woman stood in the doorway. Casey thought he recognized her as the one in the window, but he couldn't be sure. She bent over a crooked cane and stared at Justine. The few strands of silver hair on her head fell to her shoulders, framing a face worn with more years than the four travelers combined. Her voice cracked. "Are you lost?"

Justine slid around the back of Marie and stared back at the woman with fear.

Harlan quit looking for secret entrances and ghostly walls and smiled at the woman. "Finally! Someone who wants to talk to us."

The woman turned her head slowly toward Harlan then back at Justine. "I don't want to talk to you, just the little girl."

Marie reached around to pull Justine forward, gripping tightly onto her shoulders. Instinctively, the two took a step back from the doorway.

Almost in tandem, the old woman took a step forward. "Are you lost, little one?"

Justine turned her face away and buried it in her hands.

"She's a little frightened," Marie said. "We've been through a lot."

The woman took another step forward.

"Can you tell us where we are?" Marie asked. Her grip on Justine became a little tighter. "We've been traveling for quite some time, and we just want to find our way home."

"Your way home?" The woman's voice cracked again as she raised a crooked finger to point at Justine. "Well, what about her? Does *she* want to find her way home?"

Justine turned her face a tiny bit toward the woman, fearful of whoever she was and all the wrinkles on her body.

"Where are we?" Harlan asked, a little sterner than the first time he spoke.

"You came here on your own. You should know."

"No, we came to a city we were told would take us home, get us out of this place."

"Why should you want to leave? You have everything you could ever want right here."

Casey let loose a frustrated chuckle. "Everything? How about a nice bed, a warm cup of tea or even a beer? Do you have that here? How about a job, a house, an income, a life that isn't besieged by angry voices all the time that suddenly take form and try to kill you? Do you have *that* here?"

The woman slowly turned to Casey and looked at him from head to toe. She took a step forward then looked him over once again. "Do you really want that?"

"Yes."

"Do you think it's fair you leave when others can't?"

"I don't think it's fair I was brought here in the first place."

"You weren't brought here."

The door slammed shut. Harlan and Casey jumped to a side wall while Justine let out a quiet shriek then buried her face as tight as she could. Marie pulled Justine back slowly toward the two men. In the dim light of the room, the woman's body was indiscernible, but to Marie, it looked like it was... melting.

Skin fell off in wet clumps, and massive amounts of blood poured onto the ground. They all watched as the tangled mass of blood and bone and flesh mixed together, then quickly reformed into something less recognizable than the old woman. It twisted and snapped and popped until it finally took shape.

Two legs — bent backwards — protruded from the main mass, pushing the body up. A sickening crack filled the room as a twisted spine formed on the back, growing vertebra by vertebra and finally ending in a bulbous skull. Eyes appeared from the bloody mass, followed by teeth cutting through what was beginning to look like a mouth. Finally, thin gray, leathery skin appeared, climbing up and around the exposed flesh.

"That hurts." The former old woman, now creature of Hell, coughed forcibly and spat out a green mass. Its voice echoed through the room several octaves lower than the voice it replaced. "Maybe it's time you learned the truth. Maybe it's time you found out what this is all about."

The room darkened even more, like curtains had been draped across the open windows. Justine screamed. High above them, something stirred in the ceiling, spinning around and around like a whirlpool upside down. Sparks of light erupted, quickly flared to life then died out while more and more appeared.

The room spun, and Casey stumbled back as he stared in disbelief at what he saw. What looked like a million welding torches flashed in the distance, each arc so brilliant it cast shadows of their own then faded.

"What is that?"

"That," the creature growled, "is an eye for you to see." Its voice surrounded the four, like listening to a movie in surround sound, the subwoofer turned on high. The ground rumbled as it spoke.

"The gateway you seek is here, in the City of Sha'ar. But there's far more than meets the eye. You have all lived lives oblivious to the wars that rage between good and evil, Heaven and Hell, id and ego. You're blinded by your mechanical religions, where going to church once a week is worth more than opening yourself to the words you want to know."

Harlan quickly spun around and looked for the door. The whirlpool of lights above cast an eerie glow on the walls and the floor, but the door they'd come through couldn't be seen.

There was no way out.

"Your gods are fast replacing your God, and the less you believe in and live with your mechanical religions, the more the gods take over. Each of you has come here because your God wanted you to, but each of you needs to understand that *here* is something intangible. It can't be felt with your fingers, but it can be felt with your hearts."

Marie couldn't keep her eyes off the whirlpool. The lights formed shapes that floated in and out of the swirl, coalescing into images of demons and angels, men and women, faces and bodies of people she thought she knew. "So this isn't real?" she finally asked. She feared the answer more than she realized at first.

"As real as the intangible God you seek, the intangible Hell you're afraid of, or the intangible faith you hide behind."

"I don't understand."

"And you won't. It's not possible for outsiders to see the truth they seek. Outsiders must believe it exists." The creature appeared in front of Marie, almost knocking her off balance. She pulled back at its hideous features and rank smell. "Are you a believer?"

"I believe in what I see and feel."

"So you believe the intangible building you entered is as real as the skin on your body?"

"If it's real..."

"Welcome to this side of Heaven and that side of Hell, Miss Evans. Welcome to the land where demons and angels tread, killing each other and fighting a war for the eternity of your soul."

Harlan pushed his way between Marie and the creature. "What does any of this have to do with us?"

The creature leaned forward, its face inches from Harlan's. Sharp, dingy teeth poked through a crooked smile. "Her."

Marie tightened her grip on Justine even more, unaware of the grimace on Justine's face. "What do you want with her?"

The creature sighed then stepped back. "You see, Heaven decided to cheat, and little baby doll there is one of a new breed, if you want to call her that. She can feel what you feel, know what you know, and guide you in directions only your heart knew it could go. She's an empath, and her kind—the Maskiyl—are running all over your world right now, screwing up the plans of Hell and making it just a little bit harder for us to do our work."

"What work?"

"To win." The creature looked up at the whirlpool, and Harlan's eyes followed. The lights grew brighter until the swirl was no longer apparent. In its place was something like a television set, or movie theater, the screen itself broadcasting images of hideous creatures fighting with angelic beings. Swords and lances, bows and maces, fists and fire all flew at each other.

"This was after the Fall." The creature's voice was fainter, but still powerful. "We were cast out into this place you've stumbled across to walk until we reached a home. We built cities on the shores of a lake of fire and licked our wounds. When we realized we couldn't make it back to Heaven—and our rightful place among the angels—we turned to the reason we were cast out in the first place."

The broadcast image flashed, showing a city street crowded with people. Casey wasn't sure, but he thought he recognized the buildings. "Humans," he whispered.

"Creatures of God who hold a higher esteem in the eyes of their Creator than the angels ever could. These insects were the reason we found ourselves struggling to survive and howling in pain. But we soon learned we could step right in, mold our bodies to look like them, walk around and act just like everyone else. With billions of people in the world, we knew we'd never be caught."

Harlan watched the image on the screen flash again. He saw himself, then Casey, Marie, and even Justine. Each scene that played starred someone else, and each time, the scenes repeated themselves.

Marie sat silent among friends and neighbors, dressed in black. In front of her, two caskets—one large, one small—silently said farewell. Casey sat motionless in a courtroom, while a verdict of "not-guilty" was returned for a rapist he'd seen in action. Justine slept in her bed, while her mom... her mom....

"Celine?" Harlan's mouth dropped open. Celine leaned over Justine and kissed her on the cheek. "Celine?"

"Oh?" The creature's voice shifted from all around to directly behind Harlan. "Something you didn't know? Something your wife forgot to tell you? Ah, yes. The mother of this child has a history she never wanted to share with you. She hid behind lies while you led your normal life pining after students."

Harlan couldn't believe what he heard. Celine? Justine's mother? All this time and she kept it a secret.

"Oh, but there's more."

The screen flashed again and Harlan's eyes opened even wider as he saw himself tangled together with Marie on a bed of hay. He turned his face for a moment, suddenly feeling the shame he never fully felt for every act of adultery he committed. His heart felt like it was being ripped apart, every act he didn't recognize as wrong turned into a knife with jagged edges, ripping and tearing at his insides.

Marie covered Justine's eyes then turned her face as well. She didn't need to see through some mystic eye to know her life was a lie and a poor one at that. As long as the thing doesn't show...

The screen flickered again. Marie sat in a waiting room, biting her nails. Harlan turned and looked up, unsure of what he was seeing. She fidgeted then stood as her name was called by some nurse. Hospital? But it didn't look so sterile.

"Do you want to know the answer?" The voice of a woman, out of view of the mystic eye, sounded stern, but caring at the same time. "Looks like you're pregnant."

Harlan turned to look at Marie as she wiped a tear from an eye. He suddenly realized this wasn't a memory of anything remotely innocent. She was pregnant with *his* child, and it was only by facing his past in this world that he found out. Marie wasn't going to tell him.

"Yes, so many truths are yours not to have, Mr. Reese." The creature chuckled, a raspy, disgusted laugh.

"Why are you showing us this?"

"The girl, Mr. Reese. Have you not been paying attention?"

"I heard you the first time. I still don't see what this has to do with us or this 'Great Work' people around here have been spouting off about."

"Ah, the *ma abad rab*. Let me tell you about the *ma abad rab*. You see, we the fallen—who were forced out of our home into a desolate wasteland—were doing just fine among the humans. We suggested things, made hearts feel heavy, caused little battles to rage inside of everyone so we could take what we wanted. Every soul up there deserves to be in our place, while we deserve to be back in Heaven. Things were going just dandy.

"And then along come the little ones. The Maskiyl el Hanephesh. The empathic little sons and daughters of not so much good, but of a seeping truth. They pushed and pulled at the minds of those we were trying to reach. They made it difficult for any of us to do our jobs and secure our future."

The creature moved from behind Harlan. Its shifts in the glow of the screen above were contorted, morose, evil. It slowly spun its body around until it stood inches from Marie and the trembling body of Justine.

"The Maskiyl are bad for business. They're a part of this Great Work as much as you and I are. We're all a part of it. It's a game of good and evil, but you have to look past the fairy tales of mechanical religion to see just what the good and evil really is. Was it good to cherish a race above your finest creation? Was it good to banish those who simply wanted respect? Was it good to burn our bodies and melt our features until even we are disgusted by our looks?"

The creature bent down and met Justine's eyes with its own. Marie pulled the little girl against her body and stepped back.

"Good and evil are relative. You've heard the old tale about how one can't live without the other. It's simple, really. The Maskiyl must die. They tip the scales."

Casey had enough. He couldn't bear to hear the voice of the creature any more than he could bear to watch the failing of his life broadcast on that screen above. He wanted to go home, get a beer, take off his shoes and relax.

He wanted out.

Casey swung around and kicked the side of the creature. Its body collapsed in the middle and flew backwards against a far wall.

"*Get out!*" Casey yelled to Harlan. "Find the door and get out of here!"

The creature righted itself and stood, fully extending its legs. Casey realized for the first time just how large it was as it took a step forward and towered above. "We can bleed, Mr. Casey, and let me tell you something else."

The creature took another step forward and stopped in front of Casey. "That hurt." It swiped the back of a massive hand against Casey's face. Casey felt the sting of a thousand cuts open up on his cheek. He fell back against the floor.

"We eat, we breathe, we expel gas, and we can most certainly die." The creature raised its voice. "*We* are creatures of God insomuch as you or that little imp are creatures of God. *We* are the keepers of this city, and *we* know its secrets. You can run all you want, but your journey across this land led you to *our* home."

Casey pushed himself back up and looked over at Harlan. "Find the door and *get out!*"

"It's not here anymore!" Harlan frantically felt up and down the wall while Marie held Justine as close to her as she could. There *had* to be a way out!

The creature swiped its hand again, connecting with the back of Casey's head. He felt an explosion of pain rip through his mind, complete with flashes of red and white light on the inside of his eyelids.

"All we want is what you took away from us. *We want peace!*"

Casey felt another blow to his side and fell against a wall.

"*We want justice!*"

The creature's foot slammed against Casey's stomach. For a moment, he swore he felt his intestines and stomach tear, gastric acid and blood mixing together.

"*We want to go home!*"

The creature lifted Casey up by the throat. His legs kicked in a feeble attempt to get away. He instinctively reached for his neck and tried to pry loose the grip he was in.

"We can't do that with your little imps running around making our jobs difficult. It's inconvenient!"

Casey fell limp. Harlan looked over as the creature slammed the body against the wall again and again.

Light erupted from a crack in the wall.

"Look!" Marie cried out. "The door!"

The crack grew wider and wider.

The creature spun around and dropped the wilted body of Casey. It bounded forward just in time to see Harlan, Marie and Justine jump outside and run.

CHAPTER THIRTY-THREE

They ran and they really didn't care where it was they were going. They retraced their steps, but found the city of Sha'ar more confusing with each turn. It wasn't long before they were back within sight of the monolithic building where Casey had been mutilated by that creature.

"This was a trap." Marie stopped at the side of an adobe building and looked down the road. It twisted to the right into an alleyway of poorly crafted shelters, their roofs tilted. "We were led here to die."

"You think?" Harlan leaned against the wall and breathed heavily. He hadn't been in shape for years, and the pace they kept was getting to him. Justine held out better. "You think the woman was lying?"

"I don't know, but we're not going to find that gateway here."

"It has to be here. There aren't too many cities or towns in this world we're in. I can't imagine this being a lie."

"No? Why aren't there other people around? Why was that thing trying to kill us?" Marie pushed back the hair from her face and looked down the road again. There had to be another way out, and even if it meant crossing that swamp again, at least the wilderness was more accommodating than Sha'ar.

"What do you want to do? You heard the truth—Justine is important and no matter what happens to us, she needs to get back."

Justine looked up at Harlan. "I want to go home."

Marie sighed and knelt down. She pushed back a few stray hairs from the girl's face and kissed her on the forehead. "We're going to get you back home. We just have to find a way."

Harlan knelt down as well, a strange thought racing through his mind. "Justine? Do you know what I'm feeling right now?"

"Harlan! This isn't the time to—"

"Please." Harlan held up his finger. "Justine, am I happy?"

Justine looked at Harlan then turned her eyes down. "No. You're sad."

"Do you know why I'm sad?"

"You can't find my sister."

Harlan blinked.

Her sister? He looked over at Marie and furled his eyebrows. "Your sister?"

"Jennifer. I've seen her."

Marie weakly smiled, more amused by the idea that Justine had seen something at all than about what she'd seen. Harlan, on the other hand, felt his heart pound and stomach sink.

"Where did you see her?" Harlan asked.

"In a house. On a street."

"What kind of house?"

Justine looked up and around at the buildings nearby. She was quiet for a moment as her little body turned around in a small circle. Finally, she stopped and pointed. "There. In a house like that."

Harlan and Marie followed Justine's finger and looked up at a building about a quarter of a mile down the street from where they'd just come. The walls looked like cheap brick, and there were holes cut out for windows. The door—if a broken piece of wood could be a door—stood slightly open.

Harlan stood and swallowed. It seemed impossible to him that after traveling for so long without a clue to Jennifer's whereabouts, he was now a few minutes' walk from where she just might be hiding. What did Justine see that would make her think Jennifer was in that building? And why did this little girl call Jennifer her sister? If the mysterious screen they'd recently been forced to watch was telling the truth, then, yes, Jennifer was Justine's sister. But...

"How did she know about Jennifer?" Marie took a step forward and picked up Justine.

Harlan quietly shrugged his shoulders and walked toward what may or may not be the finish line.

He pushed the door aside and looked into the building. In a corner untouched by the light outside, a figure stirred.

"Jennifer?" Harlan called out nervously. Marie and Justine stood right behind him, ready to run at the first sign of danger.

The figure stirred again and stood. "Daddy?"

A smile exploded across Harlan's face and he ran inside, embracing his daughter with all the might he could muster. He held her tight and felt all the emotions he'd experienced combine into one of pure elation.

"I thought I'd lost you forever." Harlan loosened his embrace and looked at Jennifer. He wiped a tear from her cheek and kissed her on the forehead. "How are you?"

"I want to go home," Jennifer whispered. She hugged her father tight then looked past at the two people standing by the door.

"Justine?" Jennifer left her father and walked toward her sister. She was just as she'd been shown, and for a moment, Jennifer thought she could make out her mother's features in her face. "I'm Jennifer."

"I know. You're my sister." Justine smiled and held out her hand. "Shake?"

Jennifer smiled back, amused by the innocence in front of her. She shook Justine's hand then looked up at Marie. Her smile faded.

"Hi, Jennifer. I'm Marie." Marie suddenly felt like an intruder, an unwelcome guest at a family reunion. She wanted to run outside and find a nice pub to drown her sorrows.

"Well," Jennifer said, without acknowledging Marie, "I'd say we get the hell out of here and go home."

Harlan smiled weakly. "That's what we planned to do, but so far we can't find this elusive gateway, if in fact, it even exists." He paused for a moment. "I thought you were dead."

"So did I." Jennifer looked out the door.

"What happened to you?"

"In some swamp I was pulled under by what I thought was a demon. It was weird, though. I felt like I could breathe underwater, and the more she pulled at me, the more I felt myself diving into her mind."

"Like they wanted to show you something?" Marie still didn't feel right saying anything. It was almost like Jennifer knew the past. What had happened between Marie and Harlan was history, but even though she tried to reassure herself, Marie couldn't get past the nagging guilt she suddenly faced.

Jennifer sat on the dirt floor and leaned against a wall. "They showed me stuff, alright." She paused and looked at Marie. "Stuff I didn't need to see."

Harlan followed suit, but sat across from her. As soon as his legs were stretched out, he realized just how much he'd needed to sit. "Like what?"

"Most of it was about some great work, fallen angels and what happened here so long ago. But there were times when I'd see someone I knew, or something I didn't know but should have." She stopped and looked up at Marie. "Like her."

Marie felt a lump in her throat. "Me?"

"I didn't know you felt so strongly about my father."

Harlan and Marie looked at each other, passing silent but not invisible fears between them.

"And you, Dad. I didn't know you felt so little for Mom."

Harlan struggled to find the right words. How do you tell your daughter that you love someone other than your mother, but stayed in a relationship that went nowhere just because you had kids? "I always loved your mother."

Jennifer looked between Marie and her father then let her eyes drift toward Justine. "I don't care. There's so much more and so much pain. Right now, I just want to go home."

Harlan felt a bit of relief that Jennifer wanted to drop the subject, but he knew deep down it would eventually rear its ugly head again. "Did you happen to be shown where this gateway is?"

Jennifer nodded. "I got an image of sorts. There's a shack, kind of like this one, but you'd never know from the outside. I've been moving from shack to shack trying to find out where it is, but I haven't had any luck at all. The only things I've seen so far are empty houses or despairing faces."

"Well we know it's not in that tower thing over there." Harlan waved his hand haphazardly in the direction from where they'd come. "We found that out."

"I could have told you that." Jennifer chuckled nervously, as if something that wasn't meant to be funny struck her as downright ironic. "I was told to stay clear of the place. There are demons here as well as angels, but you never know who you're talking to until it's too late."

Justine stepped away from Marie and sat on her knees in front of Jennifer. Between the two of them, sparks of emotion and knowledge passed, but nothing visible to either Harlan or Marie. Their eyes met, and Marie watched with interest as the two suddenly connected on levels she'd never seen before.

The sisters sat silent for what seemed like many minutes, but what may have only been a few. They closed their eyes together, reached out, and held hands. Justine's mouth parted as if she wanted to say something. Without sound, though, her lips began to move.

Harlan stood and walked closer to the two on the floor. He felt his heart pound in anticipation of something great, although he had no idea what was really going on. Everything he'd known in his life had been suddenly rendered useless knowledge, and the simple reality of good and evil was writing a new book of knowledge in his mind. His daughter was a part of something larger than anything he could have ever imagined. Next to her, and connected by an invisible web of energy, sat his ex-wife's first child, a child who'd been locked away behind a lie for years.

Marie looked over at Harlan, wondering how he could take all of this in and still remain calm. He'd been lied to—by his ex-wife and, most importantly, herself. She could hide behind her excuses for only so long, but this world had ripped away those masks and exposed a deep secret. Perhaps it was for the best. Perhaps there was hope in the knowledge that Harlan knew she'd been pregnant with his child once. But what would any of that matter? Once again, she had no one to call a family.

Jennifer opened her eyes. "It's not too far away. I say we get out of here as soon as we can."

Marie swallowed her sadness before it could overwhelm her. "What just happened between you two?"

Jennifer stood, helping Justine to her feet. "I don't know, but I think we just compared notes." She put her hand on Marie's shoulder and smiled. She leaned forward and whispered in her ear. "You have a family."

Marie smiled inwardly, if not so much on the outside. "Let's go home, then."

SHACK AFTER shack—whether adobe or straw or just boards leaning against each other—revealed what they all feared the most: nothing. Jennifer and Justine had a good idea what they were looking for, but neither of them had seen it. Those who had shown the way and revealed the mysteries of this world had left one secret hidden deep inside themselves. Maybe they didn't know either. If they did, why wouldn't they all have left by now?

Harlan wondered if there was something else that kept them here. Fear of the unknown, perhaps?

"This way," Jennifer said, as she quickened her pace and pulled Justine by her hand. Harlan and Marie followed closely behind, and let the two most knowledgeable of them all lead the way.

"Watch yourself," Harlan said then quickened his pace to match his daughter's. They'd been walking blindly through the city for what seemed like hours, but who could tell time in this place of a constant red glow that grew from the gray clouds above? He wasn't even sure of where they were inside of Sha'ar, and if they ever needed to get out in a hurry, they'd be out of luck.

"Right. It's here." Jennifer quickened her pace again then turned down an alleyway. Harlan and Marie nearly ran her over. She'd stopped suddenly, and pushed Justine behind her.

At the end of the alley, between two shacks of equal disrepair, Celine stood with a smile on her face.

Justine looked out from behind Jennifer. "*Mommy!*" she cried then ran for Celine.

"Justine, no!" Marie ran around Jennifer and grabbed the child right before Celine could get to her. She backed up with Justine kicking and screaming.

Celine smiled wider and cocked her head to the right. "What's wrong, Marie? Were you afraid we'd never see each other again?"

Marie stepped farther back, wanting to run as fast as she could, but she had a feeling that Jennifer had led them in the right direction. That would put the gateway in either of the two shacks, with only one obstacle to get through.

"My mother is dead." Jennifer took a step forward. "I watched her die in a hole in the desert."

Justine screamed louder and kicked Marie in the ribs. Marie wasn't about to let her go. "That's not Mommy," she said as quietly as she could through gritted teeth. "Listen to your sister."

Justine stopped screaming for a moment and turned to Jennifer. "I want my mommy."

Jennifer picked Justine off Marie. "So do I," she said. "This isn't our mom, though. Can you believe me?"

Justine turned to look at the woman standing at the end of the alleyway. She suddenly felt her body tingle and then a rush of emotions come over her. If she knew what half of the emotions were called, she would have cursed each one by name. Instead, she only picked up on one, an emotion so strong it reminded her of something—or someone—she'd feared since the day she was brought into this place.

She felt the Angry Man.

Harlan pushed past Marie and Jennifer and carefully stepped closer. He called back to Jennifer. "You said she died. How do you know this?"

"I was shown these things, among others. She was killed in the desert by another demon while trying to find us."

"And Tommy?"

"He's with Grandma. He doesn't know anything, but I can hear his cries constantly."

Harlan swallowed and fought back any feeling that might emerge which revolved around the death of Celine. He wanted to cry out, but at the same time he felt a sense of relief. The relief, however, was not that she was gone, rather it was tied to the fact she wasn't stuck here like they were. Harlan doubted if she would have made it half as far as they did.

"Jennifer's lying, Harlan." Celine took a step forward. "I'm right here in front of you. Don't you remember how much she hated you? Don't you think she would lie and cheat and steal just because she despised you so much?"

Jennifer gave Justine back to Marie and stood next to her father. "I don't hate him, and I never have. That's something my mother would have known."

"And you, Marie?" Celine called back. "Are you afraid because of who I am or afraid of what I know?"

Marie didn't answer. She pulled Justine closer to her and held on that much tighter. Harlan had seen Celine twice before while outside the city, and each time she'd mutated into a hideous creature that was focused on killing him. This couldn't be any different.

Harlan looked to his right and saw a board leaning up against a wall. He reached over and picked it up. "Why don't you show your true self?"

"Because my true self is something you'll never live to remember seeing. Even if you beat me down with that puny little stick, I won't rest until both of these girls are long dead."

Jennifer clenched her fists. "Try us. I want to go home, and I don't care who you are."

Harlan looked down at his daughter, suddenly realizing how much she must have grown since they'd last been together. When was that? A few days ago?

Jennifer looked up at her father, and in her eyes Harlan saw himself so much younger. "The gate is to the left of her, Dad. I really want to go home."

Harlan smiled and clutched the board tighter. "So do I."

They both took a step forward.

Celine's body suddenly seized like it was cast in stone. Cracks appeared rapidly across her skin, flying around her face and neck. Within seconds, her body was covered with a sickly pale leathery skin. What looked like plaster began to fall off in large chunks. Celine—or what looked like Celine—screamed from within the cocoon. The voice rose in pitch until it came from every direction. Harlan, Marie and Jennifer shook with the vibrations.

Justine screamed as loud as she could, knowing the Angry Man was coming to visit. *"Don't let him get me!"*

To the left, Marie thought to herself. If she could get in there, they would be home and none of what had happened here would matter anymore. But how was she going to get in there? And she couldn't very well leave Harlan and Jennifer behind.

Marie moved to the left wall and pushed Justine's face against her shoulder. She looked past Harlan and Jennifer, past the mutating body of Celine, and eyed the doorway to freedom. *Fifteen steps. Maybe sixteen.*

The body of Celine had completely disintegrated onto the ground, chunks still maintaining the shape of her face, her arms, her legs. Dust rose up and surrounded a writhing creature they'd never seen before.

It stood higher than the four of them. Its legs were twisted backwards and red, like the skin didn't exist and they were looking right at the muscle underneath. Its chest heaved with each breath and the expelled air filled the alleyway with a stench worse than bile and more pungent than ammonia.

Harlan turned his face and closed his nose. Although his eyes burned and his stomach turned circles, he also knew this was the only chance any of them would have. He looked up at Marie who caught his glance. If Justine and Jennifer were going to make it out alive, they needed a window of opportunity and one big distraction.

"And to think I shoved myself into that tiny woman's skin." The Angry Man's voice boomed through the alleyway, shaking loose dust from the highest buildings.

Harlan nodded once to Marie and prayed to God she understood exactly what he planned to do. If there was anything the two of them could share, it was an emotional connection that didn't care about distance, barriers or circumstances. They knew each other, and in that knowing, they felt each other's pain, triumphs and tears. They were one.

"Who's first?" The Angry Man shook his body like a wet dog, flinging the final pieces of Celine's body suit off him.

Jennifer felt her stomach tingle, like she had many times before in the recent past. She turned to her father and looked at him one last time. He was still looking at Marie, and although it pained Jennifer to know he loved someone other than her mother, there was nothing she could do about it. He loved *her*, too, and deep down inside, she knew that whatever he was going to do, he did it for them.

Jennifer closed her eyes and let the emotions that her father felt swell inside of her. They filled every crevice of her soul, and in their warmth, she understood what it meant to love someone unconditionally. She felt his pain, his sorrow and finally his love for his daughter, for Justine, for Marie, for Tommy, and even still, for Celine.

She opened her eyes and turned to Marie, praying she felt the same. Marie still held on to Justine as much as any mother would protect her daughter. In their brief encounter before, Justine had shown Jennifer just how protective and loving Marie was, and even if she wasn't their mother, she was no less loving and emotionally tied to all of them.

Marie turned her eyes from Harlan and caught Jennifer's gaze. The smallest yet most powerful of smiles crept across Marie's face. She nodded at Jennifer and knew she understood now what it was Harlan intended to do.

"Well?" The Angry Man knelt down in front of Harlan and Jennifer. His massive body was only feet away from them, and the stench of his breath was even more powerful than before.

Harlan winked at Marie and turned around. "It's no wonder God abandoned you and found favor with us humans. You stink."

The Angry Man furled his eyebrows and snarled. "You'll be the first to find out just how much God did the world a disservice."

The ground shook as the Angry Man took a step forward. Harlan ran and swung the board as hard as he could. It impacted the demon's leg and shattered in two. The Angry Man took another step past Marie and Jennifer and turned around.

"You know that hurt, right?"

Harlan looked down at the splintered board in his hand and finally up into the demon's face. "I hope it gets infected.

"*Now!*" Harlan screamed.

Marie bolted for the door with Jennifer right behind her. Justine looked up into the Angry Man's face and watched his attention turn from Harlan to them.

"*Faster!*" she cried, as the demon reared back and screamed.

Harlan waited until Marie and Jennifer were inside before he ran forward with his only defense. He felt his heart rip in two as life passed before him, but of all the failures he had to face—and then reface so recently—this was one that wasn't about to get the best of him.

"No, Harlan!" Marie cried out from the doorway. "We can make it together!"

Harlan let the words filter past his ear and into his brain, sounding like the first time she'd ever said "I love you." He smiled inwardly as the demon lunged toward the door.

The splintered board entered the demon's knee with a sickening precision. It plunged neatly through the muscle and bone as far as Harlan could drive it.

The Angry Man stopped and screamed. Buildings shook as if they were trapped in a high magnitude earthquake. Siding broke off. Poorly supported roofs collapsed. Even the ground shuddered at the voice of Hell in pure pain.

Harlan reeled back, seeing his moment to escape. Even if he couldn't kill the beast, at least he could slow him down. He stumbled back toward the door.

Marie reached out of the shelter and pulled on Harlan's

shirt just as the Angry Man finished his scream. "We can make it together. Come on!"

They both looked one more time as the Angry Man hobbled forward then stumbled back. He reached down and pulled at the board wedged in his knee. "Hell isn't through with you yet!"

Harlan and Marie quickly turned from the door and looked into the shelter, trying to find the gateway home, trying to find their last possible exit out of this mess.

There was nothing.

Jennifer had seen it first, and she stood in the middle of the room looking down at a puddle on the floor. "There's nothing here." Her voice was tainted with despair, with knowing they would never get home and would die at the doorway to Hell.

Marie looked around again then down at the puddle. Her memory flashed back through the mountains, the swamp, through the town and the dry lake. She saw herself finally standing on a sand dune and then...

"The puddle!" Marie set Justine down and pushed Jennifer toward it. "Jump in! Trust me."

"It's nothing but a puddle."

"No, it's not. It's what brought me here."

"*Hurry!*" Harlan yelled from the door. "There's a really mad demon outside and I don't think we have the time to argue."

Jennifer looked down at the puddle then up at Marie. "See you on the other side."

She jumped. The puddle accepted Jennifer's body without a splash or a noise. It just swallowed her whole.

Harlan looked at the puddle and prayed they'd found the right way home. He looked at Marie and Justine. "Go!"

"Don't dawdle." Marie picked up Justine and followed suit, jumping into the puddle without hesitation.

Harlan took one more look outside the door at the Angry Man. The board was gone and he screamed, his face twisted under a mask of pure hatred. Harlan quickly turned from the door and jumped toward the puddle, knowing there wasn't a second to lose.

The Angry Man reached the door, swung his fist through the wall, and grabbed Harlan around the waist.

"Welcome home," the demon hissed.

EPILOGUE

The headlights illuminated a sign in front of Marie's car. She smiled coyly, remembering all that it meant for her, for him, for the two of them when life was simpler. She turned off the car and looked behind her. In a booster seat, Justine was fast asleep; the excitement of the day had taken its toll and the gentle roll of wheels on asphalt had lulled her to a peaceful slumber. She prayed Justine's dreams would be sweet.

For once.

An indeterminate time had passed since Harlan and Marie traveled together in a world that was anything but hospitable, and in that time the world had changed considerably. What had felt like days to the travelers might have been years — even decades — to everyone else. The road less traveled was really, for all intents and purposes, the road never traveled. Still, they hadn't escaped together. As Marie, Justine and Jennifer stood in the middle of a forest in what turned out to be North Carolina, they all felt the combined weight of knowing Harlan wasn't coming out alive.

There was still hope, however. In her body, Marie knew the end wasn't really the end of the road. So much like the sign in front of her, the end was somewhere beyond the sign, in the undiscovered world between hither and yon. It called to her, and in the desert beyond — blanketed by the cold night — she would find Harlan again.

Marie stepped out of the car and watched a cloud of dust in the distance slowly gaining definition. If there was one thing she missed about the desert — not including the memories of

Harlan or the times they'd spent together—it was the relentless churning of Mother Nature that unfolded around her. From heat to wisps of moisture on the air, the atmosphere commanded attention, and Marie was subject to whatever was thrown at her.

The wind tossed her hair. She closed her eyes and imagined the ghosts of the past rising up out of the desert floor, caressing her cheeks and wrapping their ethereal bodies around her. She knew Harlan had to be there, in the wind, caught up with all the other ghosts the desert brought to life.

She could even hear him, words from their past kissing the folds of her ear. *"You have a gift, Marie. Why don't you use it?"*

She smiled and wrapped her arms around her body. The wind had picked up, and she smelled the familiar sweet scent of dust and rain. Soon the cloud of dust would be over her, and all the mystical powers of the desert would combine together to pull on her memory and show her the form of Harlan outlined by the billion dancing particles of sand.

The sign shook, and Marie opened her eyes. The notion that Harlan was hidden in the wind was probably nothing more than a dream, but she could accept that. As long as her dreams included Harlan then life could go on. Perhaps in those dreams, Harlan would come and kiss her goodnight one more time.

The voice of the old woman in the town filtered through the wind. Marie listened and let a smile creep across her face.

"Here, we cannot grow old, and we cannot die."

She needed to find Harlan, even if that meant going through Hell.

THE END

ACKNOWLEDGEMENTS

The transliteration of the Aramaic used in this work was done by my father, Dr. Dennis O. Wretlind, who once said he wanted more letters before and after his name than in it. (It's actually "The Reverend Dr. Dennis O. Wretlind, Col, USAF (Ret), Ph.D., M.Div, Th.M, B.A.", or something like that.)

I would also like to thank the editors and pre-readers who gave their time and consideration to this work, especially Bruce Blake and Michael K. Rose.

To my dog, Pepper: thanks for keeping my seat warm.

And to my wife Jesse: your love, support and encouragement is most appreciated.

BIOGRAPHY

Benjamin ran with scissors when he was five. He now writes, paints, uses sharp woodworking tools and plays with glue. Sometimes he does these things at the same time. He is the author of *Out of Due Season: The First Transit* and many other novels.

Benjamin lives with his wife Jesse in Colorado.

www.bxwretlind.com

Printed in Great Britain
by Amazon